Story Summary

Bounty hunter Bret Sterling kills Rufus Petty, thief and murderer, less than ten feet away from a frightened, half-starved woman. Rufus should have surrendered. The woman should have kin to help her. But Rufus went down shooting, and the woman has no one. Bret figures by the time he finds a safe place to leave Hassie Petty, he'll earn the five hundred dollar reward several times over.

Hassie doesn't mourn Rufus, but the loss of the ten dollars he promised her for supplies is a different matter. The bounty hunter gives her nothing, takes everything, ties the body on one horse, and orders her on another. Afraid if she defies him, he'll tie her down tighter than Rufus, Hassie mounts up and follows the icy-eyed killer.

Mismatched in every way, the sterling man and petty woman travel the West together, hunting thieves, deserters, and murderers. Wary traveling companions, friends and partners, lovers, Bret and Hassie must decide what they want, what they need, and the price they're willing to pay for love.

Also by Ellen O'Connell

Mystery
Rottweiler Rescue

Romance
Eyes of Silver, Eyes of Gold
Sing My Name
Rachel's Eyes, a short story
Dancing on Coals
Beautiful Bad Man (Sutton Family 1)
Into the Light (Sutton Family 2)

Without Words

Ellen O'Connell

This book is a work of fiction. Names, characters, and incidents are the product of the author's imagination. Any resemblance to actual events or persons is strictly coincidental. Some of the places mentioned may exist; however, descriptions may have been altered to better suit the story.

Copyright © 2014 by Ellen O'Connell
www.oconnellauthor.com

ISBN-13: 978-1502731241
ISBN-10: 150273124X

All rights reserved. No part of this book may be used or reproduced in any manner whatsoever without written permission, except in the case of brief quotations used in critical articles and reviews.

Without Words

1

Spring 1871
Central Missouri

Cassie fetched another stone and added it to the pile. Coyotes would be at the grave before a week passed unless she covered it with a heavy layer of stones.

The clang of the pick against frozen ground stopped. Rufus swore and switched to the shovel again, scraping up the few small clumps of dirt he'd loosened and throwing them alongside the grave.

He'd quit soon. The only surprise was he hadn't already. In the short time she'd known him, she'd learned Rufus wasn't much for hard work.

"I can't believe it," he said for at least the hundredth time. "I come home for the first time in years. Jube and Clete are gone, and the old man's dying." He pointed a long, boney finger at her. "Don't you expect me to be taking care of you. Ten dollars, I can spare you ten dollars, and after that you better find yourself another man."

Hassie's stomach clenched. Ten dollars' worth of supplies wouldn't last through the spring, even supposing she succeeded in getting to town and buying anything.

Rufus jumped out of the hole. "That's deep enough." His eyes widened, and he dropped the shovel. "Who the hell are you?"

Hassie whirled to see what Rufus saw. Only yards away a stranger sat his horse. With the late morning sun behind them, both man and beast were dark shadows with golden halos.

"I'm the man the army is going to pay five hundred dollars for dragging you back to Fort Leavenworth," the horseman said.

Rufus spit. "Bounty hunter."

Hassie saw it coming, saw Rufus tense and his mouth twist. His hand dove under his open coat and came out with a pistol.

Before he brought the gun to bear, a shot cracked through the cold air. Rufus fell like a puppet with strings cut, groaning and clutching his side, but he didn't drop the gun. His lips pulled back in a snarl. Eyes gleaming with malice, he tried to lift the gun again.

"Don't," the horseman said. "Don't be stupid."

Rufus didn't listen, found the strength to raise the pistol. Another shot rang out, and he fell back, twitched a few times, and lay unmoving.

The bounty hunter—for that's what he must be—dismounted, cursing in a low voice. He kicked Rufus's pistol away, leaned over, and touched his throat. "I suppose that was easier for you than hanging," he said, "but the army won't pay for your useless corpse."

He straightened, and his cold gray eyes swept Hassie from head to toe. Short, dark beard growth obscured his lower face, but she didn't have to see his jaw to know it would be strong. Light-headed with fear and shock, she stumbled back a few steps.

"Your husband?"

She pointed at the grave.

Hands on hips, the bounty hunter looked into the narrow hole. "That's sure not deep enough for two. Have you got other menfolk around to finish it?"

She shook her head.

"Family to help you out?"

Hassie started to shake her head again, clamped a hand over her mouth, and ran for the house. The sound of the door as he followed her inside turned her nausea to panic. She skittered around the kitchen table, grabbed for the iron skillet on the stove.

"Don't flatter yourself," he muttered, yanking open the flour bin.

After that he searched every cupboard, bin, and shelf in the kitchen. He pulled the cork on one of the jugs along the wall, sniffed, and smacked the cork back in place with the heel of his hand.

In spite of his words, Hassie kept the table between them. He was tall, taller than any of the men she had been around, as much as six feet maybe. Hat pulled down over dark hair, fine wool coat hanging almost to his knees, gloves, boots, everything but his hard face was hidden under winter clothing. Yet Hassie sensed quickness and strength that would make a mockery of her efforts to elude him if he took a notion.

Knowledge of what he was, what he had done and could do, stalked around the room with him.

"You can't be living on whiskey," he said when he finished his search, "and you sure won't live long on the food in this place."

His gaze roamed around the room, not missing one bare inch. His expression never changed, but contempt edged his voice. "So your husband starved to death?"

Indignation almost overrode her fear. Almost. She had spooned the best of anything available down Cyrus for months, done everything she knew how for him.

The bounty hunter disappeared deeper into the house, and Hassie sucked in a deep, relieved breath. Breathing was easier with him out of the room, even though the house rang with sounds of his presence. Drawers opened and slammed shut. The lid on the bedroom chest screeched as it opened and banged as it closed. He wasn't looking for food back there, so what was he doing?

Her knees trembled, and she leaned against the wall to stay on her feet in spite of another wave of nausea. She hadn't liked Rufus, but he had provided fresh meat for the table, and Cyrus had been so happy to see one of his sons.

She couldn't blame the bounty man for what he'd done. Rufus had left him no choice, but that didn't mean she wouldn't have nightmares about the way Rufus fell and died. It didn't make being alone with a killer any easier.

Did he look at everyone the way he looked at her, or did he only look down that strong, straight nose with disdain at women who lived on rundown farms? Or who had four jugs of home-brewed whiskey in their kitchen but only a few cups of weevily flour left in the bin and even less of beans and corn meal? Or women related to the likes of Rufus Petty?

The bounty hunter appeared again, empty handed. If he had taken anything, it must be small. He walked past her and out of the house without a glance. She moved to the window and peered out, watched him stride across the yard as if he owned it and go into the barn.

Right now, while he was out of sight, she should run outside and go through Rufus's pockets. He must have more than ten dollars to have promised her that much, and she should take the gun. It had to be worth something. Except there was all that blood, and the bounty hunter wasn't going to let her keep anything. He was already angry about not getting the reward.

At the thought of him touching her, taking away anything she found, Hassie turned from the window and sank into a chair. Five hundred dollars. What could Rufus have done that would make the army put such a high price on his head and that he would hang for?

He must have killed someone, and he must have stolen something, something the bounty hunter wanted. That Rufus would do such a thing didn't surprise her. That he'd gotten away with it, even for a little while, did.

As she waited for sounds of horses leaving the yard, Hassie toyed with thoughts of selling the whiskey the bounty man had mocked her about. Sooner or later one of Cyrus's old customers would come around, and she could sell him one of the jugs.

She tried to picture it. Failed. None of those men would pay her for the whiskey. They'd take it, and she didn't want to face any of them alone.

Hassie thought about the gun again. Thought about what might be in Rufus's pockets. She was halfway to her feet when sounds came from the yard, but not sounds of horses leaving.

BRET LEFT THE house disappointed. The money wasn't there, and neither was much else, although the place was surprisingly clean considering the rundown condition of everything outside. Weeds covered the fields. The fences were falling down. Like the woman, one of the horses in the corral was well on the way to starving.

The bay with the US brand on its left shoulder was still in good shape. If you didn't count robbery and murder—and Rufus probably didn't—keeping the horse had been his first mistake. Telling a stable boy he was headed home to the family farm was his second, the one that put Bret on Rufus Petty's trail.

Bret shoved his way through the sagging barn door, expecting to search the rundown building as thoroughly as the house—and as futilely. Rufus could have gambled away every penny he'd stolen by now and probably had.

So much light poured in through wide cracks between the boards of the siding Bret spotted the cavalry saddle easily.

The worn leather gleamed amid a dusty jumble of equipment heaped on the floor. The saddle didn't quite conceal bulging saddle bags underneath.

Bret's mood improved steadily as he counted the wads of bills stuffed in the bags. Hard to believe, but Rufus couldn't have spent much of it.

Even though he'd killed the paymaster in order to steal the Fort Leavenworth payroll, the army wouldn't pay for Rufus Petty dead. The poster on Rufus didn't mention a finder's fee for recovering the money either, but they'd pay one.

The bags held almost six thousand dollars. Bret decided to ask for ten percent, hold out for at least the five hundred they'd offered for Rufus.

Bret hauled all the U.S. Army equipment outside, shoved the saddlebags into one of the panniers on his packhorse, and contemplated the bodies. Tempting as it was to leave Petty where he'd fallen, packing the body to the nearest town would be wiser. With a choice, the army wouldn't care what became of the body. Without a choice, they'd probably get starchy about identification.

Hacking another grave out of this ground held no appeal anyway, and two in the shallow hole Rufus had dug would be coyote food with or without those rocks piled on top. Bret grimaced. Much as he didn't like it, tipping the woman's husband over the edge and filling in the grave wouldn't kill him.

He grabbed the body, planning to just roll it in the hole. No coffin here. A sheet for a shroud. The sheet rode up at one end, pulling a trouser leg up with it and exposing boney, blue-veined shins above black stockings. White hair stuck out at the other end.

Curious, Bret pulled the sheet down a little. Sickness aged a man prematurely, and men reduced to skeletons always looked ancient, but from the thin hair on his head and coarse hairs jutting from his nostrils, this one *was* ancient, or close to it.

In spite of the emaciation and yellow cast to his skin, the old man had a curiously well-groomed look, hair clean, face freshly shaved, shirt snowy white. Even so, not Rufus Petty's brother, but his father, grandfather even.

What was a young woman like Mrs. Petty doing married to an old man like this? Relatively young. She looked like she might be a year or two past his own thirty, but with a few good meals and enough sleep to erase the dark circles under her eyes, she could prove to be anywhere from twenty to thirty.

Maybe she'd been a catalog woman. If so, she'd made a bad mistake believing whatever the old man had written to lure her here.

Now that he thought about it, she had to be from somewhere outside this area. She didn't look anything like the people in these hills. They tended to be raw-boned, with narrow faces and close-set eyes that brought to mind cousins marrying cousins for too many generations.

The woman's chin was too wide for her face to be oval, not wide enough to make a square. Her purple eyes were anything but close set. The absurdity of that thought made Bret throw the next shovelful so hard the frozen clods bounced.

No one had purple eyes. Grayish blue, bluish gray. In decent light and without the shadows underneath, her eyes would be blue. Still, hair blacker than black, skin whiter than white, nose ever so slightly sloping and turned up at the end. During the war the camp followers and soldiers' wives with that look had been Irish. Maybe Old Man Petty had somehow gotten hold of the daughter of an Irish railroad worker.

Slapping handcuffs on a man in front of his womenfolk was bad enough. Bret had never had to kill a man in front of kin before. He glanced at the house, remembering the Colorado woman who stopped screaming at him, ran back to her house for a rifle, and shot at him as he rode away with her son in tow.

Even if Mrs. Petty were so inclined, the rusty musket in the house posed more danger to the shooter than the target. No, Mrs. Petty wasn't going to scream at him or shoot him, but if she was telling the truth about having no family to go to, she was a problem. He couldn't leave a woman alone in a place like this with no food and no prospects.

The army ought to pay him twenty percent of that six thousand. Or take her on itself. Since Mrs. Petty was now set to starve because of the army's reward, it should send a general to figure out what to do with her. Of course knowing the army, it would send a sergeant. Who would do a better job than the general.

Bret huffed out loud, his breath pluming white in the cold air. If anything resembling laughter hadn't dried up inside him and blown away years ago, he'd laugh. The army had no responsibility for Mrs. Petty. Breton J. Sterling, who had killed Rufus and left the woman without kith or kin, did.

Rufus's pistol would be worth a few dollars, but the saddle and the rifle hanging on the side belonged to the army just like the horse. The army would never know if he left her with a little of its money, but unless he wanted to leave more than a little, it would run out all too soon. All of it would only make her a target for someone like Rufus.

Bret scraped the last of the dirt over the grave, and there she was, straining as she lifted stones and placed them on top of the loose dirt. Out here she didn't seem so afraid of him, although she was still trying to stay as far away as possible and concentrating on the stones.

He stood back and let her do the work. She'd need to say some words over the husband too.

After that he'd pack up the few items worth anything, take them to town and sell them for her. And hard as he tried, he couldn't see any way around it. Leaving Mrs. Petty here alone to starve was not an option. He'd have to pack her along too.

HASSIE PLACED THE last stone, folded her hands, and recited the Lord's Prayer in her head. Cyrus had been kind to her in his way. She wished him peace, and anything had to be better than his terrible, drawn-out sickness.

She turned away, already tasting the bitter gall of having to beg the bounty hunter for at least whatever had been in Rufus's pockets. Somehow. The only paper in the house was between the covers of the Bible, and she wouldn't write in the margins of those pages even if she had a pen or pencil.

Surely the sun had softened the ground in some places enough by now that she could use a stick to scratch out her request. In spite of the bounty hunter's harsh words, finishing burying Cyrus like that had been decent. Maybe he would give her at least the ten dollars, leave her the gun.

Before she decided what to do, he said, "If you're through praying, get on inside and pack up anything you want from this place. I'm taking Rufus to Werver, and you're coming along."

Coming along to town! She needed to go to town, but she needed supplies, money for supplies, and why would a bounty hunter take her with him? Should she go with him? Did she dare? What if she refused?

He reacted as if he could hear her. "Don't even think about it. Shooting Rufus didn't bother me. Leaving you to starve might."

Might. If he didn't sound like he meant it, she could smile at that.

"Don't talk much, do you?"

Hassie made the all-too-familiar gestures, moving her fingers near her mouth as if speaking, shaking her head as she did it.

The grim line of his mouth tightened even more. "You can't talk."

She acknowledged the truth with the tiniest motion.

"At all."

Drawing in a deep breath, she said, "Not in a way anyone can understand." The humiliating sound of the hoarse whisper that bore no resemblance to speech grated over her nerves. Even Mama hadn't been able to understand except from the rhythm of simple, expected phrases. He'd change his mind now. Leave her here.

"Is that as loud as it gets?"

She nodded.

He blew out an impatient breath, reached for the pick and shovel. "Get your things. I'll saddle the horse."

Through the front window, she watched him for a moment. He tied the tools on the packhorse and went back to the barn.

If she did try to refuse to go, no doubt he'd tie her on a horse too, but she didn't want to refuse. She needed to get to town. Going with him would be better than going alone, and after that.... Well, after that, she could come back here if she had to.

Giving up watching for him, Hassie went back to the bedroom and pulled Mama's old carpetbag from under the bed. The embroidered tablecloth she had kept hidden away in the chest all these years was the first thing she packed. She stroked it reverently before placing it in the bottom of the bag, remembering how it had been, stitching one end of the cloth while Mama did the other.

Everything else went on top of the tablecloth. Another patched dress, a few under things, comb, hairbrush, and Bible.

In the time it had taken her to pack, the bounty hunter had added a few more tools to the load on his packhorse and saddled Brownie. He started to tie her bag behind the old saddle and cursed when the dried out saddle string broke. Her bag went behind the man's saddle instead.

A low growl stopped Hassie before she could mount the horse. Stiff-legged, with the dull hair along his prominent spine standing on end, Yellow Dog looked ready to launch at the bounty hunter, who already had his gun out, ready to shoot Yellow Dog as dead as Rufus.

Without thinking, Hassie pulled at the man's gun arm. He shook her off. "I'm not getting bitten by your mangy cur, and I'm not leaving it to finish starving. The thing needs to be put out of its misery."

Yellow Dog had returned home less and less often since there was no food for him. With Rufus providing meat for the table, Hassie had been able to set out bones and entrails almost every day, giving Yellow Dog at least a few meager meals.

No matter what the bounty man thought, Yellow Dog had foraged successfully through the winter. His ribs might be sticking out through his dull coat, but he was still alive and still ready to take on a stranger who didn't belong in his yard.

Hassie stepped between the man and the dog and walked toward Yellow Dog, humming a song for him in her throat. She touched his head, and he relaxed slightly; his tail gave a tentative wag.

"You're not doing him any favor." In spite of his words, the bounty man holstered his gun.

He was wrong. Today might be frigid, but spring was here. Yellow Dog's life would be easier when the weather warmed.

The bounty hunter said no more. He held Brownie's head while Hassie pulled herself into the saddle and arranged her skirt as best she could. He swung up on his horse and led the others out of the yard. Hassie followed, one hand over her cramping stomach.

2

The dog followed them. Of course a turtle—or a half-starved dog—could follow them at the pace of the woman's half-starved horse. Yesterday Bret had been certain getting a line on a substantial bounty only days after setting out this spring meant this would be his best hunting season yet. Today he heartily wished the stable boy he'd paid two bits for information had forgotten all about Rufus Petty and the cavalry horse Rufus hadn't had the sense to get rid of.

Rufus could have turned the horse loose and bought another. If only getting rid of Mrs. Petty proved that easy.

When Bret passed through Werver yesterday, stopping only long enough for a hot meal, no one had shown any interest in him. Today, as he led his ugly little parade into town, people stopped in the street and stared.

Bret reined up in front of the town marshal's office, surprised at the sight of a man with a badge on his coat sitting outside on a day barely warm enough to melt last night's ice from the horse troughs. A thin plume of steam rose from the cup in his gloved hand.

On second thought, the marshal had enough extra flesh for insulation against any temperature above freezing. His features looked small in his massive face, his eyes recessed dark beads. The short gray beard didn't hide his three chins so much as carpet them.

The big lawman stayed in his chair and hoisted his cup toward the body as if offering a toast. "What have you got there, or should I say who?"

"Rufus Petty."

"Rufus, eh? Haven't seen hide nor hair of him or his brothers since they took off before the war. Heard he rode with Bill Anderson."

"I wouldn't know about that," Bret said, "but I do know he stole the Fort Leavenworth payroll last month, killed the paymaster doing it."

The marshal whistled. "So the army sent you after him?"

"The army put a price on his head and waited for someone like me to find him."

The marshal's beady eyes glinted. "Bounty hunter, eh? Are you telling me the army is angry enough to pay for old Rufus dead or alive?"

"No, they only wanted him alive, and the damned fool not only pulled on me, he kept trying after taking the first bullet. If you direct me to your undertaker, I'll find out if the army wants a formal identification and if they care where he's planted."

"Never knew your kind to care about anything but the money."

Bret hid his reaction to that "your kind" reference. Like most lawmen, this one didn't like men who could make as much hauling one criminal to his jail as a town marshal would be paid for an entire year.

The Western Union operator would tell the marshal every word of any telegram to Fort Leavenworth, but Bret wasn't telling anyone his business himself.

He changed the subject. "I'd appreciate any information about Mrs. Petty's situation. As near as I can make out, her husband died yesterday or last night. She and Rufus were burying the old man when I rode up."

"So Cyrus is gone, is he? I suppose he finished pickling himself in his own whiskey. He made a pretty good living off that corn liquor for years, but after the boys left, he started drinking more and more and brewing less and less."

Considering the yellowish cast to the skin on the corpse, the marshal was probably right that the old man had pickled his liver, but Bret saw no reason to say so in front of the widow.

"So is Mrs. Petty right when she says she has no family? How about friends who can take her in?"

The marshal laughed, his belly shaking under his coat. "She says, does she? That would be quite a trick. So you brought her to town, did you? Didn't see her back there."

The marshal pushed up from the chair with a grunt, licking his lips as he stared at the woman. She sat on her horse stone-faced, the pale flesh of her legs exposed above her stockings because of the way her dress rode up in the saddle.

No wonder respectable women always rode sidesaddle. Bret had a sudden urge to yank the worn material of her dress down, hide that white skin from the marshal's avid gaze. Touching a spur to his horse, he reined it at an angle in front of hers, blocking the marshal's view.

"So you don't know about her family."

The chair groaned as the marshal settled back down. "Her ma died some years ago, came out here to marry Ned Grimes and dragged the dummy along. Pure class that one was and snooty with it. I always figured if she had anybody back East, she wouldn't have married Ned."

"This Grimes would be Mrs. Petty's stepfather then? How do I find him?"

"Ned never thought of himself as her step-anything. He had to put up with her to get the mother, so he did. You won't find him. GTT."

Gone to Texas. Bret scowled. Too many Missourians who came home from the war and found their homes in ruins picked up and left for Texas or other places. If a man had to start over, why not start over at home and build things back to what they had once been?

Bret considered asking more about the husband's family and gave it up as a waste of breath.

The marshal enjoyed telling him about it anyway. "The only Pettys left would be Cyrus's other two boys. Never came back from the war, so they're dead for all I know, and you wouldn't talk either one of them into taking on a woman, at least not permanent."

Bret gave up on finding family for Mrs. Petty. Maybe she had no voice, but she'd told him the truth in her way. "Have you got any church groups in town? A preacher who can help?"

"We have two churches and two preachers. One's off riding circuit, the other's sitting with a widow who lives an hour or so thataway," said the marshal, waving to the southeast. "If she dies quick enough, Reverend Lyons may be back tomorrow."

Maybe he could leave Mrs. Petty with the preacher's wife. Except on further inquiry, Bret learned the preachers of Werver were both unmarried. Resigned to waiting for Lyons to return, Bret got directions to the town's undertaker. At least he could get rid of the body. Getting rid of Mrs. Petty was going to be harder.

DISAPPOINTMENT FLOODED THROUGH Hassie at the news Reverend Lyons wasn't in town.

In the years since Mama died, since marrying Cyrus had been the only way to stay out of the position she was in right now, Hassie had been to town less and less often, and not at all for at least the last two years. She had no real friends here and no one to ask for help, but she remembered Reverend Lyons as kind.

The bounty hunter was determined to foist her off on someone, but what did he intend to do in the meantime? Uncertain, worried, Hassie followed him to the undertaker's.

Having learned her lesson the hard way, she drew her legs up under her skirts the minute her horse stopped and waited while the bounty hunter arranged for the undertaker to keep the body until the army had its say.

The next stop was the telegraph office. Cold gray eyes assessed her. "You better come inside with me," he said.

Hassie dismounted as fast as she could, relieved. She didn't want to be out in the street alone with everyone who passed staring.

The bounty hunter might look down his nose at her and treat her as an annoyance, but he didn't call her "dummy" in a voice dripping with scorn. He didn't have the respect not to curse in front of her or to apologize for doing it, but he didn't stare at her legs with undisguised lust as if she were a loose woman either. In the office with him had to be better than outside alone.

Pencils and paper lay scattered on the counter for customers to use to write their messages. The bounty man wrote. And wrote. Hassie picked up a pencil. No one paid any attention. She nudged a sheet of paper with a fingertip until it was in front of her.

"May I please have what was in Rufus's pockets to buy...."

"No." He was looking over her shoulder, reading her request before she finished it. He pulled the paper from under her hand, crumpled it, and threw it in the waste can with dozens of other discarded bits of paper. Having answered her question to his own satisfaction, he went back to his own message.

Hassie rolled the pencil back and forth in her fingers. She could use another piece of paper and argue. She put the pencil down. A man who said no in that tone wouldn't listen even if she could use honeyed words. Better to admit she didn't want to buy supplies, didn't want to go back to the empty farm by herself. Any argument could wait until after she saw Reverend Lyons.

The bounty hunter finished his message, handed it to the telegraph operator, and paid.

"I don't expect an answer until tomorrow, but if I'm wrong, I'll be at the hotel tonight."

Hassie followed him out to the horses, worrying. She had no money for a hotel. He didn't think she was staying with him, did he? But where could she stay?

Before the next hour passed, Hassie did have money. She had money the hardware man paid for the tools from the farm, money the gunsmith paid for Rufus's pistol. And according to the bounty man, she was going to have money from selling Brownie.

"You aren't going to get much for the horse," he said, "but no matter whether the preacher can take you in and find you a place, or how things work out, having a little cash is better than not. Since you can't exactly negotiate, I'll sell it for you."

Hassie stared at him, aware for the first time Brownie was hers. So was the farm, so was Cyrus's still. Not that she wanted it, but maybe someone would buy it. Or the whiskey.

As if he could read her mind, he said, "Too bad we couldn't have brought the jugs of 'shine along. They'd probably bring more than this nag."

Brownie was not a nag. She was too thin was all. Enough food....

Hassie really looked at the bounty hunter's horses for the first time. Not only were they in good flesh but they had small shapely ears, big eyes, and their heads didn't hang too large for their necks. They had good bone and feet, but not huge round bones and platter feet.

Like the man himself, his horses were everything fine. Like her, Brownie was just a problem for someone like him to solve.

Blinking against tears, Hassie nodded as if he had asked her opinion instead of telling her what he was going to do. He walked into the gloom of the stable and found the owner.

"Bret Sterling," he said. "And this is Mrs. Cyrus Petty. She's recently widowed and needs to sell her horse."

Sterling. Of course he had a name like that. Fine horses, fine man with a name that suited perfectly.

After all, her name suited too, didn't it? Petty. He was Sterling, and she was Petty. Hassie crossed her arms and pretended Mr. Bret Sterling was selling a pathetic horse of his own for next to nothing.

The stableman didn't want Brownie.

"You should pay me to take it," he said.

"A few weeks of decent feed, and she'll be fat and sassy," Mr. Bret Sterling countered.

"Fat and worthless. Look at her. There's more draft blood there than anything else, and it's mixed with bangtail."

"So sell her as one that can pull a cart and carry a saddle too."

"Anything can do that. The best use for this one would be dog food."

Hassie gasped and hugged Brownie around the neck. Mr. Bret Sterling gave her a disgusted look. "What if she came with four gallons of good whiskey?" he said.

"Does she?" the stableman asked suspiciously.

After that, negotiations progressed swiftly. Hassie hated sending Brownie to an unknown fate, but then that was what was happening to her too, wasn't it?

She shoved the money into her coat pocket and signed the bill of sale the stableman made out with her full name— Hassie Ahearne Petty.

Let the boun—no—let Bret see her real name, the name she had been born with. She could call him by his given name because he would never know she was doing it, and it served him right for cursing.

He left his horses at the stable too, pulled her carpetbag and a leather valise of his own out of the panniers, and shouldered his saddlebags, not the ones tied behind his saddle but ones from the packs. Before she could wonder about that, he said, "It looks like we're stuck with each other for a while longer, Mrs. Petty. I know this town has a decent restaurant. Let's go see what the hotel's like."

After one last regretful look back at Brownie, Hassie followed Bret down the street. At least Yellow Dog had turned back at the edge of town. He'd be better off out in the woods. People in town wouldn't be kind to a skinny stray.

By the time they reached the hotel, Hassie's heart thudded in her ears. She fingered the bills in her pocket. How much did a hotel room cost?

Bret Sterling didn't think she was going to share a room or a bed with him, did he? Because she wasn't. She'd buy supplies and carry them all the way back to the farm on her back first.

The big white hotel poked into the sky three stories high, higher than any other building in town. As they approached the front door, boots echoing on the boards of the verandah, Hassie tried to duck behind Bret, but he opened the hotel door and waited for her to enter first, gesturing when she didn't move right away.

Inside all was silent, hushed. Even her cracked old boots made no noise on the carpeted floor. The last time Hassie had seen anything as elegant as this hotel, she and Mama had still been in Philadelphia.

Striped paper in pretty blues covered the walls. Lamps with beautiful glass globes hung in sconces on the wall. Stuffed chairs. Polished tables with big ash trays. Live plants in pretty pots.

The people who owned this hotel were not going to rent a room to a woman in a patched coat and patched dress who didn't even own a proper hat.

Bret cupped a hand around her elbow and pushed her right to the gleaming desk straight ahead. He dropped their cases and smacked his hand down on a little silver dome. The ding of the bell sounded loud in the quiet lobby.

A gray haired, bespectacled man came through a door behind the desk, still buttoning his coat over his round belly. "Welcome to the Werver Hotel," he said, smiling. "Dennis Reston at your service. Do you need a room for you and your wife?"

A knot appeared at the hinge of Bret's jaw, prominent right through the beard. Of course he wouldn't like anyone thinking he was married to the likes of her. Hassie looked down, noticed a loose button on her coat, and switched to studying the crystal inkwell on the desktop.

"Two rooms," Bret said.

The man's smile changed to something Hassie didn't like. "Let me see what we have available in adjoining rooms."

"I don't care if they're a mile apart. I do care if they're clean," Bret said, his voice close to a growl.

Hassie let out a breath she hadn't realized she was holding. After Bret signed the register, he said, "We're going to get something to eat across the street. Can you have a bath ready when we get back? Two actually. First Mrs. Petty, then me."

Hassie only took in Mr. Reston's reply and mention of the cost with half an ear. A bath. She remembered bathing in a tub of hot water as a little girl, but after Papa died hot baths disappeared like so many other things. Here in Missouri the only submerged bathing was in summer in the creek.

Bret took possession of two keys to rooms that were side by side after all. He walked right into the room he said would be hers as if he had the right, which he did since he paid. Small, narrow bed, but a rag rug on the floor and curtains on the window. Hassie looked around uncritically, almost unable to believe the room was hers.

Not until Bret yanked back the bed clothes and lifted the pillow did she realize what he was doing—checking for bedbugs. She bit her lip to hold back a laugh. If Mr. Reston had climbed the stairs with them, he'd be properly insulted.

When Bret looked up from the bed, Hassie held out as much money as she knew the room and the bath cost.

He shook his head. "Keep it. It's not much, and you're going to need it. Figure it's part of my penance."

Hassie stared at the door after he closed it behind him. Penance? Did he feel guilt about Rufus? Nothing he had said or done indicated anything but aggravation over feeling obliged to deal with her, yet taking care of her, like burying Cyrus, was decent. More than most would do.

She was the one who should feel guilty. She had done her best for Cyrus but couldn't pretend to mourn. His death had only made her afraid for herself.

She didn't mourn Rufus either. At first his return had seemed like Providence—fresh meat, help with his father those last days when her back ached from caring for a man too sick to even turn over by himself, the promise of enough money for supplies until the weather warmed, help with burying—but what would Rufus have demanded in return?

The deaths and decisions of others had changed her life in an instant many times before, but never for the better. Maybe this time would be different. So far it was.

Rummaging through her bag for clean clothes, she shoved down fear of tomorrow, determined to enjoy a restaurant meal that wouldn't leave her hungry for more, a real bath, and a night alone in this pretty room.

Hassie answered a knock on the door, expecting to see Bret come to hurry her along. Instead a sullen young girl in a dark blue dress and white apron thrust a pitcher of water at her.

"Here. Mr. Reston said to bring you this."

The pitcher was cold enough to the touch the water inside had to be frigid. The girl muttered under her breath as she left. The only words Hassie caught were "not waiting on the likes of you." Hassie poured the cold water into the wash basin, not really minding.

The bath waiting for Hassie when she and Bret returned from the restaurant was barely lukewarm, but wonderful for all that. She was ready to climb in, grateful for the chance, but she didn't get a chance. Bret checked her bath water for temperature just as he had checked her room for bugs. The look on his face after he dipped his fingers in the tub must have cooled the water another ten degrees.

Mrs. Reston, a heavyset, red-faced woman, remedied the situation herself, complaining about "that girl" the whole time.

"You're Julia Grimes' daughter, aren't you? The one who came out here with her when she married Ned. Your father was some Irishman," Mrs. Reston said when she had finished with the bath.

Hassie nodded, eager to get into the tub before the water cooled again.

"The one who can't talk."

Since Mama had only brought one daughter to Missouri, that didn't seem to require an answer. Hassie sat on the chair next to the tub and removed her boots, hoping Mrs. Reston would take the hint and leave.

"You married Cyrus Petty when Ned lit out for Texas, but now you're here with this Sterling fellow."

Hassie rubbed the base of the finger of her left hand where women fortunate enough to have a wedding ring wore one, then pointed up. Of course since they were indoors that meant pointing at the ceiling not the heavens.

Mrs. Reston rolled her eyes toward the ceiling, frowned, and finally said, "Dead?"

Hassie nodded again, her fingers on the buttons at the high neck of her dress that she wasn't really going to undo until the woman left. After a final assessing look at the tub and at Hassie, Mrs. Reston took her leave.

The water was beautifully, decadently hot. Hassie sank down to her chin with a small moan of pleasure.

She wanted to stay in that tub until her fingers and toes wrinkled and the water didn't have one degree of warmth left, but after a few minutes of self-indulgence, she scrubbed, washed her hair, rinsed, and regretfully dried off and dressed. She didn't want to make Mr. Bret Sterling wait for his bath when he was paying for both of them.

Unsure if she should drain the tub herself, Hassie cracked the door and peeked out. The sullen maid shoved the door open so hard Hassie barely avoided a black eye.

"It's about time," the girl said as she pushed past into the room.

That answered the question about whether to drain the tub, wipe it clean, or try to help in any other way. Hassie started down the hall, her steps faltering as she rounded the corner and Bret straightened from where he leaned against the wall.

She had no reason to fear him. He wasn't going to shoot her. He hadn't even repeated his threat to shoot Yellow Dog when the dog followed them to town.

Without Mr. Bret Sterling, bounty hunter, she would still be at the farm, hoping Rufus would leave soon and really give her ten dollars, worrying what would happen if he didn't. Without Bret Sterling, her stomach would not be pleasantly full of good food, her skin would not be flushed and warm from time in a hot bath, and she would not be about to spend the night in a room with curtains on the window, a rug on the floor, and pale green paper on the walls.

"I'll walk you to your room," he said.

She smiled at him hesitantly, not surprised he didn't smile back. Did he ever smile? He'd be less frightening if he did, but she couldn't even imagine a smile lifting the hard, grim lines of his face or changing the rough look of him to something gentler. There was something closed down and joyless about him as if anger simmered under the surface.

He walked beside her across the hotel lobby. In coat and hat his height made her feel small. Now that he wore neither, his height was less threatening. Tipping her head back a little, she could meet his eyes, although she didn't want to meet those cold eyes, or study his features—like his mouth, a nice mouth really, just wide enough between strong jaws, firm lips. Lips set in an unyielding straight line of course.

The men she was used to were thin, all bone and tendon held together with knobby joints. Bret Sterling carried no extra bulk, but he wasn't skinny. Broad shoulders tapered to narrow hips and long legs.

Something about the way he had looked leaning against the wall, the way he straightened when he saw her, told her she'd been right to think she couldn't dodge around the kitchen table fast enough to stop him catching her.

By the time they reached her room, her heart was hopping around in her chest. The doorknob wouldn't turn.

"Here." He unlocked the door, held out the key. "Be sure you lock it."

She took the proffered key, being careful not to touch him or look at him.

Inside, she locked the door, tested it, and threw herself on the bed. Surely Reverend Lyons would be back tomorrow. Surely he would have ideas about what she could do. After Papa died and before Mama married Ned Grimes, Mama had found employment.

Hassie pushed away the thought that Mama had come to Missouri and married Ned Grimes because no job ever paid enough to support the two of them. After all, Hassie didn't have children to support. One of the effects of marriage to a sick old man, who liked his whiskey more than his wife, was no children.

Tomorrow Reverend Lyons would help her find a way to get by, and she and the tall bounty hunter with icy gray eyes would go their separate ways.

3

The next morning Hassie lay awake in bed, luxuriating in feeling clean and rested. She couldn't remember the last time she had slept through the night, not catnapped, listening for Cyrus's labored breathing or cries of pain.

A thump sounded outside the door, and she rose, hoping the sound heralded delivery of a pitcher of water. Before she put the key in the lock, thinking to peek out and see, she heard voices.

"Family is one thing, business is another," Mrs. Reston said. "If you had seen the look on Mr. Sterling's face when he felt that cold bath water yesterday, you'd know what I mean. We're going to lose business with her behaving like that. I can't do everything myself, and I shouldn't have to."

"We're the only hotel in town."

"And the next town and the next hotel are only a few hours away."

"I'll talk to her."

The second, male voice had to be Mr. Reston. If they were worried about business, shouldn't they be having this discussion somewhere else?

"You've talked to her every other day since she's been here. Now I'm talking to you, telling you, I want her on the stage back to your sister tomorrow. She's making work, not doing work."

"If you insist...." Mr. Reston's voice faded as the two of them moved off down the hall.

Hassie opened the door and brought the water pitcher inside. Warm. Nothing sat in front of Bret's door. Had he taken his water in already right under the quarreling couple's noses?

The words she'd overhead ran through Hassie's mind over and over as she washed, put up her hair, and dressed. The sullen maid was Mr. Reston's niece, and he had just agreed to send her away. Mrs. Reston didn't want to do the work herself. Didn't that mean they needed someone who was willing to do the work who would be polite?

A sharp knock sounded on the door, and Hassie threw it open, the solution to the Restons' problem and her own taking form in her mind.

"I figured if you were still asleep, those two woke you up," Bret said. "Ready for breakfast?"

The sight of him distracted Hassie from thoughts of employment. He had shaved. The rough look had disappeared with the beard, even if his expression was as stony as ever. The strong jaw and flat planes of his cheeks emphasized the breadth of his cheekbones. His tan was too even for shaving to be an unusual thing. Without the contrast with his even darker beard, his hair looked close to black. Mama would have called that sable.

"Barber," he said.

He had done that yesterday too, read her mind. What if she tried to tell him her idea?

She pulled her handkerchief from her pocket and put it on her head like a maid's cap, pulled the covers up on the bed and tucked them in, pretended she had a feather duster, and moved around whisking imaginary dust from the bureau and washstand.

Pausing to see if he understood, she could tell he did, and she caught a flicker of something more. Amusement? If so, not enough to last more than a second or raise a smile.

"All right, we'll talk to them after breakfast. If they have any sense, they'll agree, and they may put you to work on the spot."

Her stomach did more flips. This time in a good way, but she barely managed to eat a little breakfast. Fear of the future had changed to eager anticipation of a safe place to stay, enough to eat, work she knew how to do. She could buy a new dress with the money already in her pocket, a hat, shoes.

Hassie expected the Restons to worry about a maid who could not talk to their guests. She half-expected Bret to offer them a bribe to take her, although he no longer had four gallons of corn whiskey up his sleeve.

Instead the Restons all but fell on her with enthusiasm, but Bret—Bret's behavior reminded her of the way he had checked her room to be sure the bed had clean sheets and no bugs.

Not only did he want to know how much she would earn, he wanted to know whether she would have to pay for her own meals out of that. When the Restons assured him Hassie could eat with them, he barely grunted approval before insisting on seeing the small room on the top floor that would be hers.

"How hot does this get in summer? For that matter how cold does it get in winter?"

Was he trying to ruin everything? He wanted rid of her, didn't he? Mr. Reston started talking about windows and breezes that would cool the room if she left the door open and heat rising from the floors below in winter.

The frown on Bret's face didn't bode well, and Hassie toyed with the notion of shocking him by telling him to stop, except that would shock the Restons too. Better if they thought she couldn't make so much as a squeak than to have them hear the kind of sounds she could make.

The arrival of a boy with a telegram for Bret saved her. His scowl disappeared as he read it and so did his critical, time-consuming attitude toward her new job. He folded the paper and tucked it in a pocket.

"The Army doesn't care about getting Rufus identified, so I'll tell the undertaker to go ahead and bury him," he said to Hassie before turning back to the Restons. "If Mrs. Petty doesn't work out, you can't just dismiss her like a woman with kin to go to or who can speak up on her own behalf. I need your word on that. We were going to speak to this preacher, Lyons, before we realized you might have a position."

"We understand the particular, ah, difficulties," Mrs. Reston said. "My husband can address any other concerns you have. Hassie and I have work to do."

So a demotion from Mrs. Petty to her given name also came with the job. So be it. Hassie followed Mrs. Reston up the stairs eagerly. Name changes had come with life changes before, and Hassie liked her given name better than Petty.

BRET HAD OFFERED the Army the money, the horse, and the equipment Rufus Petty stole for ten percent of what he found in the saddlebags. Their counteroffer sat in his pocket. Five hundred, do what he liked with the horse, saddle, and other tack.

He wired an acceptance and calculated. Fort Leavenworth was a good five days' ride away, but it wasn't far off the path he had planned to take anyway, and delivering the money would save fees to Western Union or a bank for handling a transfer. He'd take the money to Leavenworth in person, bring the horse along, and get a decent bill of sale for it or talk them into paying for it.

A short talk with a land agent convinced Bret the chances of selling the Petty place were poor. Too many farmers with small holdings had pulled up stakes after the war and left their land for squatters. And most of those places were in far better shape than the Petty farm.

The fellow did agree to keep an eye out, let Mrs. Petty know if there was an offer, but he held out no false hope. Bret decided against even mentioning it to Mrs. Petty. She probably knew better than anyone else the place was worthless except for the still, and whoever found that and stole it wouldn't be coming around to pay her.

Back at the hotel, he packed to leave and went looking for Mrs. Petty—Hassie the maid—and something about that didn't sit right. She was in a room on the second floor, pulling sheets off the bed with vigor. For a long moment, he leaned against the frame of the open door, watching. A soft sound vibrated through the air—humming. She was humming.

Strange how different women—people—could be. Like horses, he supposed. Some were bred for racing and needed coddling to survive. Some were bred for plainer things like the cavalry horse tied outside. The women in his family mourned everything the war had cost them. The bitter lines beside his mother's mouth were so deep they'd never disappear.

Unlike Hassie Petty, Hassie Ahearne Petty, his mother, sisters, and Mary were gentlewomen. No Sterling woman would ever take a position as a maid and hum as she worked. What would Mrs. Petty look like after a month of decent food and few worries? She already looked years younger.

If following rumors of one outlaw or another with a price on his head brought him anywhere close to here again, maybe he'd stop back by and see. Then again maybe it was better to leave her alone, happy in a plain life that had her humming as she worked.

Arms full of linens, she caught sight of him. The humming stopped. She hesitated a moment before moving a few steps closer and mouthing, "Thank you."

Her eyes looked purple again in this light. They weren't, of course. Bluish gray. He'd decided that in the restaurant yesterday. "I'm glad it worked out. You'll be running this place in a year."

She smiled a little, not believing it any more than he did.

"I'm packed and pulling out," he said. "You be careful, Mrs. Petty."

She nodded but didn't come closer. Grateful maybe. Still leery definitely.

Bret slapped his hat in place, tipped it, and left her there.

4

Cassie went back to her work, disturbed at how her heart had quickened at the sight of Bret and her stomach had plummeted as he left. To be free of him was what she wanted. If there was ever going to be another man in her life, he wasn't going to have icy eyes and a hard face and kill people for a living.

That wasn't fair. He hadn't wanted to kill Rufus, very much the opposite, but still.... He was like everyone else, even Mama a little bit, acting as if having no voice meant having no opinions, no mind.

The way he had interrogated the Restons as if he was giving them charge of a child had been embarrassing. Except he hadn't talked down to her really, and those times he'd understood without words—no one ever did that before.

Strange in a way, right up till the end she was afraid of him, at least a little. If he came back right now, she'd still feel that way. Yet there was something about the way he moved his horse between her and the marshal when the fat man stared at her with hot eyes and wet lips that had gladdened her heart. Bret Sterling made her feel safe—from everyone but him.

If only a man would come along like Bret in some ways but different in others. A man who smiled often and was full of laughter. He'd have lighter hair. No, still sable. Blue eyes. No, still gray, but warm and alive with good humor.

Hassie flicked the feather duster around and chided herself for fanciful thoughts. One like that would have every woman who met him giving chase, tempting him with honeyed tones and fascinating conversation.

Bret's wife would have a beautiful voice. He could already have a wife like that somewhere for all Hassie knew. Blonde, blue-eyed, elegant, and haughty in the nicest possible way.

Finished with the room, Hassie carried the dirty linens out and shut the door behind her.

Mrs. Reston's head appeared on the stairs. "Hassie, dear, come downstairs a moment. Mr. Reston and I need to talk to you."

Hassie gestured toward the next room on her list. "Oh, don't worry about that. After all Clarissa is still here, and she can do some work before she leaves. Come on now."

The bannister slid smoothly under Hassie's hand as she followed Mrs. Reston downstairs, ready for new instructions. Polishing the beautiful dark wood would be a pleasure. All the way across the lobby and into the Restons' living quarters where she would take her meals, Hassie speculated what she would be doing next. Maybe heating water for someone's bath or doing laundry.

The first sign something was wrong was the presence of a stranger in the Restons' parlor. His beefy body blocked the door to the hotel lobby as soon as she walked through. Mr. Reston stood in front of the windows with almost the same posture, but he only looked determined. The stranger had a knowing, amused expression that started Hassie's stomach churning again.

Mrs. Reston dropped into an upholstered chair and folded her hands in her lap. "Mr. Reston and I have reconsidered our offer of employment. There really is no way we can have a mute woman interacting with our guests. However, we did promise your Mr. Sterling we would find you other, more suitable employment, and we have. Mr. Zachary works for a woman named Sally Nichols, and you're going to go work for her too."

Without knowing what they were talking about, Hassie knew she wanted no part of it. "No." The sound might be hoarse and ugly, but the word was one of the few she could say that everyone always understood.

"No," she repeated, backing in the only direction left to her away from both men.

"You're going to have to teach her not to make those kind of noises around customers," Mrs. Reston said to Zachary.

"We'll see. Some will probably like it, and some will want a real dummy."

Hassie fought. Reston was so ineffective he got in the others' way more than not, but Mrs. Reston was strong and Zachary was stronger. In the end he captured both Hassie's wrists and twisted her arms up behind her back until the pain left her hanging helpless, humiliating whimpers escaping with every breath.

"Don't bruise her face," Mrs. Reston panted.

"I'm not bruising anything. It's not like this is the first one I ever corralled and dragged to Sally's, you know. If her arms don't work so good tonight, the marshal ought to pay extra."

"Speaking of paying, I'm not sure a hundred is enough. We didn't expect to have to put up with the inquisition Sterling put us through, not to mention helping you subdue her."

"Did I ask for your help?"

"You needed my help."

"Talk to Sal if you think you can squeeze more out of her. Good luck."

"Well, at least we get this. That's the deal with Sally. We get to keep anything she brought with her." As she spoke, Mrs. Reston undid the chain of the locket Hassie wore around her neck, the one she kept Mama's wedding ring on. The woman pulled it away roughly and held it up to the light.

"If those are really gold, you're making out like bandits," Zachary said. "If you want me to keep quiet about them, you'd better fork over some of that hundred."

"Ten dollars," Mrs. Reston said, "and only if they're really gold."

"Done." Zachary shoved Hassie out of the hotel through the back door, his hold so unrelenting she almost passed out from pain on the steps. One block, two. She lost count. The world turned so blurry she hallucinated and saw a shadow stalking behind fences and hedges they passed.

Zachary pushed Hassie through the back door and into the kitchen of what appeared to be an ordinary house and finally let her arms down, although he kept a hard hold on her. Three women sat around a table in various states of undress, their faces bright with paint. Any hope that she had misinterpreted the Restons' intentions died.

"Here she is," Zachary said. "I don't think explaining things to her is going to be enough. She's going to take some breaking in."

Two of the women left the room in a hurry after giving Hassie no more than quick, furtive looks. The third woman was older, her hair orange with henna, the layers of pale powder on her face contrasting with blood red rouge on her cheeks and lips.

She grabbed Hassie by the chin. "Look at those eyes. Eyes like that could take a girl to San Francisco."

"This one don't want to go. Let me take her upstairs for a couple of hours and teach her a thing or two."

"I promised the marshal he could be first. He's paying through the nose for the privilege."

"You'll have to tie her down or he'll fall over dead before he gets the job done. She ain't ready to cooperate."

The woman stroked Hassie's cheek and laughed when Hassie tried to bite. "Don't be silly. The marshal's going to have a lovely time and so are the rest of her customers.

You're not some starry-eyed virgin, are you, honey? Working here is a lot better than emptying chamberpots at the hotel and taking orders from Lula."

Her voice fell to a husky whisper as if she were sharing some delightful secret with Hassie. "She may be fooling some of the people in this town, but *we* know she was one of us once, don't we?" Sally patted Hassie's cheek again. "Now you're going to be a smart girl and cooperate while we get you ready for your debut, aren't you?"

Hassie slumped and nodded, hoping she looked defeated, even as her mind darted from one idea to another, trying to devise a way out of this horror. The mention of tying her down had done what seemed impossible and ratcheted up her fear.

Fighting these people wasn't going to work. She had to escape, and to escape she had to be free to run.

For the second time in two days, Hassie bathed in a tub. This time under "Miss" Sally Nichols' assessing gaze and this time with no pleasure whatsoever.

"You're way too thin," said Miss Sally, who carried enough spare flesh to make two of Hassie. "Some men like it but most prefer a soft ride, so you make sure you eat plenty of potatoes with meals and pie and cake after."

Considering the way Hassie's stomach was behaving, never eating again was more likely. At least Zachary was outside in the hall for the moment. When Miss Sally finished pouring clear water reeking of some flowery scent through her hair, Hassie stepped out of the tub and wrapped up in towels.

"Now I told the girls to find every lavender, violet, and purple dress in the house and bring them all here. We'll find something that will show off those eyes, and that's going to be your name. Violet. For God's sake, Hassie sounds like a cow."

For once Hassie was grateful for her lack of speech. Frightened as she was of making anyone angry enough to tie her up, she might be unable to resist telling this gross woman who was really like a cow. An ugly, mean cow.

The other women arrived with one ghastly dress after another. They yanked the towels off, made crude remarks about Hassie's body, and stared at the scar across her throat with curiosity.

"She's gonna need a scarf or something to cover that up," one said.

"No, she isn't," Sally said knowledgeably. "She has no figure to speak of. Her appeal is all to men who like something different. That scar is going to get the peckers up on some men better than a French job."

These awful women could be speaking French for all Hassie understood, but it didn't matter. She tried on each of the dresses in turn, letting the women dress and undress her as if she were a doll, all the while thinking about escape. Getting away would be hard, staying away harder.

If the town marshal and the hotel owners thought forcing a woman into a place like this was just fine, who was going to help her? The only one she could think of was Reverend Lyons—if he had returned to town.

Even so, she couldn't wait. After tonight.... She shivered. She had to find a way out, take any chance, run for the church. The preacher had to be there. He just had to be.

BRET WAS MORE than five miles from town when he heard the first click. The sound was distinct and recognizable, but he didn't want to believe his ears and ignored it for another mile until the clicking came too regularly to ignore. He dismounted, checked, and found the loose shoe on his horse's right front foot.

The left hind was missing a nail. The left fore had all the nails, but one had broken off at the clinch and would be gone in short order. The packhorse had one shoe already missing two nails. On closer inspection, Bret saw where the clinches had been filed partway through on every nail.

Both horses had been fitted with new shoes the day before Bret left home less than two weeks ago. The last time he had checked, which was the day before he'd found Rufus Petty, he hadn't noticed a problem.

His brother Will's fine hand was all over this one. Bret closed his eyes, fighting anger. Did Will only have to suggest sabotage or had he bribed the blacksmith with money Bret spent months away from home earning?

Only good fortune had the shoes starting to come loose here where it was a mere inconvenience, not life-threatening trouble. Bret told himself Will hadn't thought that far ahead. Maybe he hadn't.

Leaning against Jasper a moment, Bret considered. The loose shoe would hang on until the next town. Or he could go back to Werver. Maybe it wouldn't hurt to check on Mrs. Petty while he waited on the horses.

Leaving her there bothered him. It shouldn't. The Restons' answers to his questions had been good enough. Her married life must have been far worse than her life working in that hotel would be. She'd be eating three decent meals a day, free of the burden of caring for a sick and dying old man. Still.

The way those fellows at the livery had stopped talking and exchanged knowing grins when he'd picked up the horses didn't sit right. A lot of people held bounty hunters in contempt, but there was something knowing and sly in the looks they'd exchanged. He didn't like it.

After swinging back into the saddle, Bret hesitated before reining the horses around and starting them back the way he had come. It would cost at least double to get a blacksmith to put aside work for regular customers and reset shoes on two horses for a stranger, but if that's what it took, he'd pay it. After all, he wasn't short on cash right now.

If no one could work on the horses today, he'd spend another night in Werver. One way or the other, he'd see how Mrs. Petty was doing.

5

The farmer who directed Bret to a smithy on the outskirts of town spoke well of the man. The problem was Bret had no one to speak for him.

The smith eyed the US brand on the cavalry horse suspiciously but didn't say anything. He did have something to say after examining the shoes on Jasper and Packie. "Someone must be pretty angry at you to do this. You have a problem paying for work done maybe?"

Bret handed the man twenty dollars, gold not scrip. "No. You keep what you think is fair out of that."

The man bounced the coin in his hand a moment, staring at the patient draft horse tied near his forge. "I'll do yours as soon as I finish old Bob there. He needs to get back into harness, and I promised to shoe him first thing this afternoon."

Bret couldn't asked for more. Resetting the shoes on his horses would be much less work than forging new, but even so, finding someone to do it yet today was good fortune.

SALLY SETTLED ON a purple dress that was too low on the top, too high on the bottom, and too big everywhere else. The bodice had been designed for someone much bigger in the bosom and gaped so far out from Hassie's chest she could look down and see her bare breasts, because there was nothing under the purple monstrosity.

Black stockings, lace garters. After everything else that was too big, Sally insisted Hassie cram her feet into shoes with heels that would have made her wobble even if they weren't so tight she could hardly walk downstairs. It made sense in a way. No one would have to tie her up if she was wearing shoes that crippled her.

"She's shivering, poor dear," Sally said. "Let's go down to the kitchen and finish this. Then we'll get her out of the dress, and she can eat while we take a tuck or two in the bodice." She laughed and patted Hassie's cheek again. "Just a little tuck, mind you. After all, you're going to grow into this dress."

The kitchen was warmer, but Hassie still shivered. The face paint was cold. And greasy. The women moved from her face to her still-damp hair, chattering away, talking about styles, debating whether to cut her hair as they worked with combs, brushes, and curling tongs.

The scent of her hair scorching, the too-sweet perfumes, and a trace of body odor—someone else's body odor in the purple dress—combined until Hassie worried about passing out. Losing any chance to get away by fainting for the first time in her life would be a disaster.

She distracted herself by working on getting the tight shoes off under the table. First the heel on one, then the other, and the shoes hung loose on her feet.

Zachary stood blocking the back door, arms crossed over his chest, looking bored. The only way out would be back past the stairs, through the parlor and to the front door. The door would be open. It had to be open. In a place like this they wouldn't want to lock customers out.

She hadn't run for months, not since the weather turned cold and Cyrus became too sick to leave. Even so, with a head start gained by surprise, and desperation for incentive, she could outrun Zachary for as long as she needed. He wasn't long-limbed, and he was heavyset.

The women argued about whether to stiffen her hair with sugar water. Zachary leaned back against the door, looking half asleep. Hassie pushed the shoes all the way off, knocked over the chair as she jumped up, and took off running. Shouts sounded behind her, a crash and curse as Zachary stumbled over the chair.

The door opened easily. Hassie barely noticed the gravel on the front walk biting into the soles of her feet. She ran, ran as if the hounds of hell pursued her, but the only hound who appeared was Yellow Dog, no longer a lurking shadow, but flesh and bone, frolicking along as if they were racing for fun, not for her life.

She had misjudged Zachary. His boots pounded on the road behind her, close and getting closer. Yellow Dog disappeared from her side. Furious cursing sounded, and she risked a look back.

Zachary sprawled on the ground, kicking as Yellow Dog worried at his legs. He pulled a small pistol and shot at Yellow Dog, missing the darting dog but driving it to the side of the street. As the brothel man lurched back to his feet, Hassie stumbled over a rut in the road.

Only the road ahead mattered. She had to ignore everything behind her. Still, if she had strength to waste on lifting facial muscles, Hassie would have smiled.

Without Yellow Dog's help, Zachary would have caught her already. She concentrated on the road and her footing, ignored people, horses, wagons, and buggies except to veer around them.

The sounds of Zachary's pursuit rose louder than her own gasping breaths. He was close again, gaining. Pain stabbed through her side. Her lungs burned. Her eyes streamed.

She leaned forward, pumped her aching arms, and ran faster.

AFTER STRIPPING THE packs and saddles off his horses, Bret shouldered Rufus Petty's saddle bags. "I'm going to walk into town," he told the smith. "I'll be back before you get far with mine. Neither one gives trouble."

The man didn't look up from the huge hoof in his lap. "Don't hurry. I don't need supervising."

The smith back home would probably say the same, Bret thought cynically. Maybe he'd have a cup of coffee and a piece of pie at the restaurant and then check on Mrs. Petty at the hotel. Or maybe check on her first.

Bret was still a block from the restaurant when he saw a flash of purple and heard barking. At first he didn't recognize the woman, only the dog darting between her and the pursuing man.

Ahead of him, two men stopped and stared, pointed and laughed. With more time, Bret would have grabbed the pair of them by the ears and slammed their heads together.

There was no time. Before she fled past, he stepped into the street, ignored her attempt to dodge around him, and hooked one arm around her waist.

She struggled and fought, breath coming in harsh gasps, face smeared with tears and paint. "Settle down." He lifted her so her feet, all but bare through what was left of black silk stockings, didn't touch the ground, and she had no purchase.

Recognition flooded across her face, chased by relief, then her eyes dropped, and under the paint her color rose. Shame. Something hot and ugly ran up the back of Bret's neck and settled behind his eyes.

The man who had been chasing her stopped a few feet away, catching his breath with his hands on his thighs. "Thanks, mister," he gasped. "Stop by Sally's tonight, and your drinks will be on the house."

The dog had stopped too. He stood between the pursuer and Mrs. Petty, a ridge of hair raised along his boney spine, growling and panting at the same time.

The man straightened and focused on the dog with single-minded fury. His eyes narrowed and his mouth twisted into something cruel as he pulled a derringer from under his vest and extended it toward the dog with a hand still shaking from the exertion of the run.

Intent on his target, Zachary didn't notice Bret pull his own revolver and aim it not at the dog but at the man.

"Pull that trigger, and you're a dead man," Bret said, his full-sized Smith & Wesson .44 American steady in his hand.

AT THE SIGHT of the derringer, Hassie struggled again. Futilely. The steel band of Bret's arm around her waist didn't yield a fraction of an inch.

"Pull that trigger, and you're a dead man."

At Bret's words, Hassie froze, unlike Zachary, whose gun still wavered in the direction of Yellow Dog's head.

"That cur tripped me, or I'd have caught her myself. It ripped my trousers biting at me."

Hassie looked up at Bret. Had he looked like that when he killed Rufus?

His face was like tan granite set with two ice shards. His voice had frightened her yesterday, but this had to be worse. The harshness rasped in her ears over the roar of her breathing and vibrated through the arm that held her and the chest the arm held her against.

Pride and knowledge of his own danger warred on Zachary's face. He lowered the gun and put it away.

"Fine. Marshal Dauber shoots any strays he finds pretty regular anyway. He can get this one. I'll just take the woman off your hands."

"You aren't taking anyone. If she wants to go with you, she can."

Bret's hold on her finally loosened. Without his support Hassie staggered and grabbed his forearm, shaking her head back and forth violently the whole time.

"She's new. She just needs a day or two to get used to things. Night or two." Zachary showed yellow teeth in a poor imitation of a smile.

Bret extended his arm straight out at shoulder height. The muzzle of the big revolver was less than a foot from Zachary's forehead. "Get back where you came from while you still can."

Bret's finger slowly tightened on the trigger. How much slack could there be? Zachary didn't wait to find out. He wheeled and started back up the street.

Hassie wiped her wet eyes and runny nose on the sleeve of the purple dress, unwilling to look at Bret again. She let go of his arm and tried to put some space between them. Tried. His hand clamped around her upper arm like a vise.

"Let's go."

Too afraid to resist, she let him propel her out of the street, up on the walk, past groups of curious bystanders. The pain in her side had subsided. Her throat and chest still burned, although her heart and lungs had slowed. Fear and humiliation burned worst of all, fear of what he was going to do, fear of what he thought. Humiliation over her situation, her failure.

The sight of the hotel changed her mind about resisting. She jerked and pulled against Bret's hold, desperate not to set foot in the hotel again. He ignored her, all but lifting her off her feet by the arm. Unable to bring herself to fight him the way she had fought the Restons and Zachary, she gave in.

He threw the door open so violently it crashed into the wall, cracking the etched glass panel that had graced the top half. Across the silent lobby, up to the shining mahogany desk.

Bret smashed the silver bell with the butt of his pistol so hard the bell fell apart with a sad little ting. Undeterred, he used the gun like a hammer on the polished surface of the desk. Hassie flinched at the sounds as one deep gouge after another marred the wood.

Mr. Reston emerged through the door to the owners' private rooms, his usual smile fading fast when he saw who stood at the desk. He reached for the door behind him as if to flee back through.

"Not unless you want to lose a hand," Bret said. "Get out here, and get your wife."

Pasty-faced and trembling, Reston called his wife and moved behind the desk when ordered.

At the sight of Bret, Mrs. Reston's face hardened, but she smiled. "Good afternoon, Mr. Sterling, we thought you left town."

"I bet you did. You round up everything Mrs. Petty brought to this place and get it out here. Now."

Defiance and anger flashed across the woman's face. "I understand you're upset, but we did exactly what we promised. Hassie did not work out here. Guests were already complaining about dealing with a du—mute. Sally Nichols offered to take her, and a job with Sally would be much more suitable."

"How much did you sell her for?"

"Don't be ridiculous. We didn't sell...."

"One hundred dollars," Hassie said, knowing no one would understand the words, but hoping like her mother, Bret could understand the rhythm of an expected phrase.

"Hear that," Mrs. Reston said self-righteously. "No one could understand that. She sounds like an animal. If we'd heard that before we hired her, we wouldn't have done it. You left. We did the best we could."

"I understood. You sold her for a lousy hundred dollars. Now you get her things."

"We don't have anything of hers. She didn't have anything worth a nickel. Go talk to Sally."

The glass globe of the lamp on the wall to the right of the desk exploded. The sound of the gunshot hurt Hassie's ears so much she covered them, even though it was too late. Glass showered down over Mrs. Reston. Mr. Reston squealed and disappeared behind the desk.

Mrs. Reston twisted around to look at the ruined lamp, the scratches on her cheek disappearing amid the bright red that suffused her face. "Do you have any idea how much those lamps cost? We had them shipped from New York City."

The lamp to the left of the desk exploded. Another squeal sounded from under the desk.

"Run to the brothel if you have to. If you don't get her things and get them fast, you're going to need a whole new hotel shipped from New York City."

Still angry but a lot less defiant, Mrs. Reston crunched across the broken glass back to their rooms.

Bret banged the pistol on the desk again. "Get up here, Reston."

Mr. Reston's hands appeared first, gripping the edge of the desk, then the top of his head, then his wide eyes. One eye had a bruise developing underneath, a nice complement to the scratches on his wife. The sight gave Hassie considerable satisfaction.

"Please," Reston whispered. "Please, I didn't want...."

"I don't give a damn what you want. Mrs. Petty had almost forty dollars this morning. We'll round it off and call it forty. I want it back. Now."

Reston stood all the way up and turned as if to follow his wife back to their rooms.

"No," Bret said. "You get it out of that drawer right there in the desk."

"I don't have forty there."

"Find it."

Mr. Reston fumbled with his keys, opened the drawer, and counted out thirty dollars. He dug in his pockets and added a ten dollar gold coin. Bret finally let go of Hassie's arm, scooped the money up, and shoved it in a pocket.

Mrs. Reston returned with Hassie's carpetbag and thumped it down on the ruined desktop. "There. That's all we have. I tore some of her clothes for rags and threw the rest in the burn barrel. I'm sure Sally did the same."

Bret pulled the bag toward Hassie. "Check and see if anything else is missing."

Hassie opened the bag. Her Bible, hairbrush, and comb didn't even cover the bottom. She looked up, tempted to tell

Bret everything was there just to calm him down and get him to leave. Except the things missing were Mama's things, the ones Hassie most treasured, and Mrs. Reston had a smug look on her face as if she knew a dummy wouldn't, couldn't complain.

Stretching to reach, Hassie grabbed the register from the other side of the desk and the pen from the inkwell tray. She uncapped the ink, dipped the pen, and wrote.

Bret read aloud. "Embroidered tablecloth, gold locket on chain, gold ring."

Mrs. Reston disappeared before he finished the last word and reappeared seconds later with the cloth in one hand. She raised the clenched fist of the other hand.

"Don't," Bret said. "If you throw anything, you'll be down on your knees picking it up."

The tablecloth landed soundlessly on the desktop. The jewelry rattled. Hassie shook out the cloth, checked both sides, refolded it, and tucked it in her bag with the necklace and ring.

To her surprise, Bret broke his gun in two and replaced the empty cartridges with fresh rounds. "Six is better than four," he said, his voice almost normal. "Let's go."

6

Bret's hand was gentler on Hassie's arm as he pulled her back out of the hotel, but it tightened once out on the street. "Over there."

He pushed her across the street to the door of the mercantile.

The storekeeper's hair was grayer and middle thicker, but Hassie remembered Mr. Tate. If he remembered her, he gave no sign. He tried to block the entrance to the store with his bulk. "This is a respectable establishment. We don't cater to Sally's girls."

Bret shoved Tate out of the way with a stiff arm. "Good, because Mrs. Petty isn't one of anyone's girls, and you're going to fix things so she doesn't look like one."

As with the Restons, Mrs. Tate was braver than her husband. She stepped from behind the counter to his side, expression belligerent. "You can't force us to sell you anything."

"You can sell it or watch me take it. I want her outfitted for the trail. No dresses or women's things, trousers. Boy's clothes ought to fit. From the skin out, two of everything. After that a decent coat, oilskins, blanket, hat, boots, toothbrush, tooth powder, soap, washcloth, towel..."

Hassie listened to the growing list with as much amazement as the storekeepers. The stubborn look on Mrs. Tate's face disappeared, and she exchanged a look with her husband. They probably didn't sell that much merchandise in a week—or a month.

Bret pointed at the curtains hanging over the doorway to the back of the store. "Take her back there and get her out of that dress. Get her face washed and her hair decent. Charge for the soap and water if you want."

Hassie didn't wait to see what anyone else would do. She hurried through the curtains to the back. Piles of crates and merchandise left little empty space, but a washstand sat against one wall, and the pitcher contained enough water for face washing.

The soap was a gray, gritty lump, and she didn't care. She bent over and scrubbed. And scrubbed.

In spite of her best efforts, when she used the towel by the stand to dry her face, she added red stains to the gray and black already there. She folded the red to the inside and put the towel back where she found it.

Mrs. Tate pushed through the curtains, her arms piled high with clothing. "Whatever made that man decide to rescue you from Sally's, he's not sparing a dime. I think this will all fit, and if not, we'll try larger. Or smaller," she added, eying Hassie.

Unable to explain anything to the woman, Hassie undid the garters and pulled off the raggedy black stockings, then worked on getting out of the hated dress. It closed with a line of hooks down the front, making it easy to shed.

"This is beautiful material," Mrs. Tate said wistfully, fingering it.

Free of the thing, Hassie dropped it to the floor and kicked it to a corner.

"Oh, my," Mrs. Tate said, shocked first by Hassie's action and then by her nakedness. "Let's get you into…. Here, no matter what that man said, I brought you female under things." She burrowed in the pile and came up with cotton drawers and vest.

Hassie donned the clothing gratefully and ventured a small smile.

Mrs. Tate gaped at her. "My goodness, that man called you Mrs. Petty, but I never.... You're Julia Grimes' daughter, the one who can't talk, and you married Cyrus Petty. That scar on your throat is.... My goodness, my goodness, I never knew...."

Ignoring the woman's discomfiture, Hassie kept pulling clothing out of the pile. The first pair of trousers she tried on were too large, the second, coarse black wool, fit well enough. She pulled a red shirt from the pile.

"Wait. Wait." Mrs. Tate had regained her composure. "Before you do that.... You aren't any bigger on top than I am, but he said an outfit for the trail, and without a corset, well, I brought this." She held up a length of flannel yard goods. Her voice fell to a whisper, "I was thinking you'd need it for, you know, that time of the month, but you could use a length to...."

She made a gesture, circling her torso, and Hassie nodded, understanding and agreeing with the suggestion to bind her breasts.

"I'll get scissors, and we'll cut a length," Mrs. Tate said, still whispering.

The front door banged open with almost as much force as Bret had used at the hotel. They both jumped at the sound. Boots stomped on the wooden floor. As if by agreement, Hassie and Mrs. Tate parted the curtains enough to peer out and see what was happening.

Marshal Dauber and a younger man with a badge stood in the middle of the store, cradling shotguns in their arms. Sally Nichols, Zachary, and the Restons crowded in behind the lawmen.

Bret leaned against the counter as if he were the storekeeper, the butt of his pistol resting on the surface, pointing at the marshal. As they watched, Bret reached out, pushed on Mr. Tate's shoulder, and said a few inaudible words. The storekeeper dropped down and crouched behind the counter.

"Thank goodness," Mrs. Tate whispered.

"You ladies get behind something solid back there," Bret said, loud enough for them to hear this time.

Hassie didn't move. Neither did Mrs. Tate.

"You're under arrest, Sterling," the marshal said. "You can't go shooting up the hotel and stealing from businessmen in my town. Put down that gun before Jimmy and I blast you into next week."

"Who claims I stole, and what do they claim I stole?"

The silence stretched out for long seconds before Sally Nichols shrilled, "They stole a purple silk dress from me is what. It was made by a Kansas City modiste, and it cost a fortune."

Glued to the scene out front, Hassie didn't move, but Mrs. Tate picked up the purple dress and brought it back to the curtain along with what was left of the stockings. She pushed the clothing through the curtain and held it out at the end of her arm.

Sally Nichols darted forward and grabbed the dress, clutching it to her large chest.

Bret looked like he could stand there all day. The marshal rocked back and forth, as if his feet hurt. Considering his bulk, they probably did.

"You can't just steal a woman out of Sally's," the marshal finally blurted. "Sally paid good money for her."

"Then arrest Sally for buying and the Restons for selling. In case you forgot, we fought a war a few years ago. Buying and selling people is illegal now."

At his words, Sally turned and marched right out of the store, taking Zachary with her. Mr. Reston only endured the tense silence a few more seconds before slinking after Sally and Zachary.

Mrs. Reston stayed, still prepared to fight for her lamps and mahogany desk.

"Does Mrs. Reston realize she's right in the line of fire back there?" Bret said.

Mrs. Reston paled and backed up a step. The deputy looked over his shoulder. "I'll just—I'll escort Mrs. Reston to a safe place," he stammered and hurried out with her.

The marshal ignored them. "I should have known you were a damn Yankee," he said. "Men been buying and selling women since the beginning of time and will be until the end."

"If a woman wants to sell herself that's her business. Mrs. Petty doesn't want to."

"She ain't no virgin."

Bret didn't even answer. The two men stared at each other, the air thick with their anger.

"He's going to win," Mrs. Tate whispered. "Two of them came in here with scatterguns. That deputy already flickered, and your man is going to back the marshal down."

Bret Sterling was not hers, thank Heaven, but Hassie had already reached the same conclusion.

The marshal took a hand off his shotgun and pointed a sausage-like finger at Bret. "You finish up here and get the hell out of town. If I see you again, I'll start shooting, stealing or no stealing."

Bret still said nothing. He stayed still as a statue until after the marshal lumbered out of the store. When Mr. Tate struggled to get his feet under him, Bret finally moved, held out a hand, and helped the older man up.

Hassie closed her eyes, light-headed with relief. Mrs. Tate patted her on the shoulder. "I don't know whether to pity you or envy you, but we'd better hurry because if Mr. Sterling ever looks at me the way he did at the marshal, I'll fall over dead on the spot."

The new clothes felt strange, not only because Hassie had never had store-bought clothing before but because trousers left her legs and bottom feeling almost as exposed as the purple dress. The coat, which hung down past her hips, helped, but everything still felt stiff, new, and strange.

Her hair felt strange too, braided and hanging down her back instead of pinned up, but at least a little water had almost straightened the burned in curls.

She walked out from behind the curtain, half-expecting Bret to send her right back, want it all exchanged for a dress. He didn't. He examined her from head to toe.

"And a bandana," he said. "And a slate. The kind you sell for school children. A slate and a chalk pencil."

While Bret paid, Hassie tied the bandana around her neck, covering her throat. However much he didn't want to see the scar, she didn't want him or anyone else to see it more.

He used the better part of her forty dollars to pay. Hassie pulled her brush and comb out of the carpetbag, waved them around, and set aside the new ones in the pile on the counter. No one remarked on the small savings, and she stuffed the underclothing, flannel cloth, and some of the smaller items in her carpetbag.

"My horses are at the blacksmith's," Bret said. "We'll be back before you close and load this up."

So that's why he was still in town. Hassie's eyes pricked with tears at the thought of what could have happened.

He didn't hold her arm or shove her along as they left the mercantile, and she walked through town beside him, eyes on the ground. When she first realized who had caught her in the street, joy and relief had stabbed through her more sharply than the pain in her side. Shame had chased those feelings, worry that he would think she had gone to Miss Sally's on her own once he was gone.

She needn't have worried. He had understood from the start, and his anger had never been at her. Still, she had never seen a man so angry, never imagined anyone could be like that, like a fire so hot anything nearby would turn to ash. No wonder "mad" was another word for anger.

The clothes and all the other things meant he was going to take her with him, but what else did he intend? Another glance at his set jaw and expressionless face squelched any hope of an explanation.

Her life had just taken a sharp turn on a different path. She didn't know where it was headed this time, but if the past was any indication, nothing was about to get better.

BRET KNEW HE should be ashamed, losing control like that. Should be, but wasn't particularly, and if he had it to do over, he'd only shoot another lamp or two.

The last time he'd gone off like that was before the war. His arguments with Will and Albert back then had been vicious, sometimes violent, but they'd never done more than bloodied each other's noses.

Today he hadn't even done that much. He'd managed not to shoot the Reston woman, or the gorilla who chased Mrs. Petty through the middle of the town, or the marshal whose big belly was one of the most tempting targets a man ever resisted. Hell, all considered, someone should pin a medal on Breton J. Sterling.

Now that it was all over, today's problem was exactly the same as yesterday's—what to do with Mrs. Petty. Seeing a preacher or anyone else in this rotten town was out of the question, which was why he'd outfitted her for the trail.

He'd just have to drag her along for a while, at least until he had a chance to visit the Chapmans. Eligible women were scarce in that part of the country. Gabe and Belle could be talked into keeping Mrs. Petty for a while, helping her find a decent husband, and they'd know who could be trusted.

The livery came into sight, and Bret steered Mrs. Petty in that direction. He could put her on the cavalry horse for now, but that would just mean buying something else later. The big bay's tendency to snap at one end and kick at the other didn't recommend him as a lady's horse anyway.

Close to the stables, Mrs. Petty left his side suddenly. Bret had a hand out, reaching to grab her and haul her back, when he realized she was headed for a pen where the toast-colored nag she'd ridden to town stood by itself. She slid through the rails and hugged the miserable thing around the neck.

The dog followed, making a perfect reunion of underfed canine, equine, and human flotsam. Bret rubbed a hand over his face, refusing to watch, and went looking for the livery stable owner.

"We made a mistake yesterday," Bret said when he found the man. "Mrs. Petty needs her horse back."

"Can't do that. I got a man coming for her. Should be here any time."

Bret's hands went to his hips. "You can't tell me you found someone who wants that nag already."

The livery owner shrugged. "He keeps hounds. You know."

"I know Mrs. Petty is fond of that damned horse, and I want it back. There isn't enough meat on it to feed a dog for a week anyway. The hound man can take his hounds and go hunting."

"I can't do that."

"Did you get those four gallons of whiskey?"

The man licked his lips, his eyes looking everywhere except at Bret. "I sent my boy for it. He found it."

"Good stuff?"

"Yeah, it is. Old Cyrus always brewed the best."

"Would you rather let Mrs. Petty have her horse back or pay her for the whiskey?"

"Now look, mister, you said I could have those jugs. I wouldn't have taken that nag unless...." The man's voice tapered off. "All right, doggone it, you can have her back."

"Good. You can make your money selling me a decent saddle and bridle for her."

The blacksmith had finished with Jasper and was working on Packie when Bret and Hassie arrived. The man took one look at what they were leading and all but leapt out from under Packie's hind leg.

"No," he said, shaking his head. "I don't care how much you pay. I'm not shoeing that, not today and not tomorrow either."

"Of course not," Bret said, "I wouldn't ask it of you."

The man relaxed visibly, picked up Packie's leg again and finished nailing and clinching the last shoe.

When he was done, Bret said, "Just trim the mare up a little. We're headed for Fort Leavenworth, and I'll get her shod there, but I don't want those flares breaking off before then."

The smith picked up his tools. "I heard there was shooting in town."

"There was. Nothing serious. Nobody hurt."

"I heard it was you."

"It was."

"Are you going to shoot me if I don't trim that horse?"

"Don't make me decide."

The smith walked over to the mare and threw his tools down by her front feet. "All right, but you have to promise me one thing. There's another smith on the east side of town. If you ever get back this way, take your business there."

"It's a deal."

7

Bret must have spent her forty dollars at least twice over. On top of everything else, the smithy had transformed Brownie's big platter feet into mere dinner plates.

They rode back to the mercantile, Bret ahead, leading both the packhorse and the cavalry horse. Hassie trailed behind, trying to make Brownie move faster and keep up, scanning each side of the street for signs of the marshal or his deputy. If the marshal shot Bret, it would be her fault. Everything that had happened today was her fault.

The pile of clothing and equipment waiting on the counter at the store looked bigger than ever. Bret packed most of it in the panniers on the packhorse. Some, including the slate, went into her new saddlebags, and he tied her carpetbag behind her saddle too.

Hassie mouthed a thank you at Mrs. Tate as they left, remembering what the woman had said about pity and envy. Envy? Never. Pity? Hassie fervently hoped not, yet she had feared what Rufus would demand in return for leaving her a mere ten dollars. If Bret wanted a husband's rights in return for all he had bought, what would she do?

Fighting him might make him smile at last—or laugh. His strength dwarfed hers. But could she force herself to simply yield? She could run, and with the help of darkness even get away. After that there were only three possibilities.

She could walk back to Werver and hope she could avoid the Restons, the marshal, Sally Nichols, and Zachary and get help from Reverend Lyons or perhaps the Tates. She could walk home and hope to find a way to avoid starvation. She could walk to the next town and hope the people there were more charitably inclined than those in Werver, for she no longer had a penny to her name and would need charity.

Hope, hope, hope. Her empty stomach churned.

Up ahead, Bret stopped again. Hassie studied his back and the half-profile she could see when he turned his head slightly, waiting for her to catch up. What he would do to a woman would be different than what a sickly, elderly husband had done—the few times Cyrus had abandoned his whiskey long enough to do anything. What had been uncomfortable, unpleasant, and humiliating with Cyrus would be painful, frightening, and humiliating with a man as coldly indifferent and strong as Bret Sterling.

The sun hung low in the western sky by the time they left Werver; the air cooled. Hassie buttoned her new dark gray wool coat all the way up and settled deep in the saddle.

She found a rhythm. Her left leg bumped the horse as one foreleg stepped and her right leg bumped as the other foreleg stepped. Brownie did quicken a little, but not enough. They fell farther and farther behind—even though Hassie was sure Bret was holding the other horses back.

He reined up, waited until she was close, and let his horses start again. If he lost patience and turned that temper on her.... She redoubled her efforts to hurry Brownie.

Gentle hills rolled into the distance as far as the eye could see. This early in the year the groves of oak, hickory, and maple were still bare-branched skeletons, but under the brittle brown and yellow stalks of last year's grass, new growth sprouted green. To the west a soft pink slowly stained puffy white clouds.

Hassie stopped fretting. Her unhappy stomach settled enough to growl a little, but very little compared to what had become familiar in the last year. The fresh, cold air on her face contrasted pleasantly with the snug warmth of the rest of her inside layers of cotton, flannel, and wool.

The rhythmic clop of the horses' hooves soothed away the day's troubles, and her spirits rose. So far, Bret Sterling had only made her life better. She didn't want to contemplate where she'd be right now if he hadn't decided to come back to Werver to have his horses shod.

After years confined first by Mama's marriage to Ned Grimes and then by her own to Cyrus, she was following a man unlike any she had known or imagined to places she had never been. And after all, he hadn't shot anything today except lamps.

Bret stopped his horses for what must be the twentieth time. Before Brownie plodded alongside, he pulled his rifle from the saddle scabbard. Accustomed to gunfire, his horses barely twitched when he fired. Brownie threw her head, snorted, and danced sideways but had no energy for more.

"If your dog was worth his salt, he'd fetch that rabbit, and I wouldn't have to," Bret said.

Hassie looked around anxiously. Yellow Dog had disappeared again, which was a good thing. If he got hold of that rabbit, he'd run off with it, not fetch it.

Half a mile on, Bret turned off the road, wove through trees until they came to a small clearing, and stopped there. After tying Brownie beside Bret's horses, Hassie reached for the cinch.

"Loosen it a little, but leave it on," he said.

She loosened the cinch, fighting dismay. The horses had all drunk from the smithy's trough, but even Bret's well fed horses needed to eat. The saddles and packs needed to come off. The horses needed to graze.

Bret didn't seem to think so. He gathered dead branches and arranged them ready for a fire. She hurried to help.

"That's enough," he said when she brought an armload of dry branches. "We only need a small fire for cooking. Fire is nothing but a beacon trouble can home in on."

Before long he had the fire burning, the rabbit roasting on a makeshift spit, corn meal mush frying in a pan, and coffee boiling in the pot. Golden light from the setting sun gilded the little clearing. Hassie resolved to try to convince him to picket the horses after they ate.

Glad she'd abandoned her fears and worries, she sat near the fire, experimenting to find a way to sit in trousers that didn't seem wicked. Folding both legs to one side was the best and still felt vaguely indecent. Not as indecent as the purple dress, though, and a whole lot warmer.

She closed her eyes, enjoying the scents of roasting meat and coffee, hard put to feel anything but content.

"You don't have to worry that I'll leave you somewhere like that again," Bret said abruptly as he turned the spit. "I know better than to take anyone at face value, and I won't do it again."

Hassie couldn't believe her ears. He couldn't think anything that happened was his fault. He had fixed it; she had caused it. She was the one who had seized on the idea of working for the Restons. She was the one....

Remembering the slate and chalk pencil, she jumped up, ran, and brought them back to the fire.

Sitting back down close enough to pass the slate to Bret but not too close, she wrote, *"My fault, my idea."*

"Was it? Would you have had that idea without the performance they put on in the hall this morning?"

It had never occurred to her. Now that it did, she realized he was right. The Restons had done it on purpose. Even so.... *"I took the bait."*

"So did I, and I've dealt with enough weasels like those two to know better. We both were saved by a loose horse shoe."

Both? He hadn't needed saving. He would never have known what happened unless he came back to Werver some day. She stared at the hard lines of his face, a strange warmth spreading through her.

He would have come back. He had planned to come back. The next time chasing outlaws brought him this way, he planned to stop and see how she was doing, and if leaving her to starve *might* bother him, finding her in a brothel *might* do the same.

How foolish to worry he would hurt her. A laugh escaped. She didn't even try to choke it back.

He lifted one brow slightly. "Maybe your voice is shot, but that's a nice sound."

She sobered and hid her confusion behind her coffee cup. From the time of the accident that stole her voice, no one had ever described any sound she made as nice.

"I have friends homesteading in Kansas. As soon as I finish a little business here, we'll head that way. You can stay with them until you find a good man."

Her fingers twitched on the pencil, but he wouldn't want to hear—*read*—the truth. She didn't want to marry another man like Cyrus. To Bret Sterling that might seem better than working as a maid in a hotel, but not to her.

They ate in silence. Yellow Dog joined them and stared at the remainder of the rabbit as if he could levitate it to his mouth by an act of will. He probably thought he succeeded. Bret gave the dog what remained of the carcass.

Emboldened by his charity to the dog, Hassie wrote on the slate again. *"Why are you going to Fort L?"*

Bret poured the last of the coffee into his cup, and for a moment she thought he wasn't going to answer. "I don't know how much Rufus stole," he said finally, "but his saddlebags were in the barn, and there's almost six thousand dollars in them. The army's willing to pay me the five hundred they had on his head as a finder's fee. I figure to hand it over to the colonel there personally, see if they'll fork over a little extra for the horse."

Six thousand dollars! Such a vast sum barely seemed real. No wonder Bret was nursemaiding those saddlebags. And Rufus, the lying, thieving murderer, had said he'd give her ten dollars and acted put upon at that.

Bret threw the last of his coffee on the fire. "Leavenworth is days away. Right now, we need to move on while we can still see well enough to get through the woods."

"We're going to ride all night?"

"Just a mile or so. It's safer not to bed down close to where we had a fire and cooked."

"You think the marshal will come after us?"

"No, but that fellow who chased you may feel up to it."

The thought of Zachary behind a tree with a gun made Hassie eager to leave the fire behind. She emptied the coffee pot and scrubbed out the frying pan as best she could while Bret smothered the fire. They packed up and rode into the gathering dusk.

The forest gave way to open grassland before another mile passed. Bret stopped amid the last of the trees. She tied Brownie beside the other horses and rubbed her down with handfuls of dry grass as Bret did the same for his saddle horse. Finished, and thinking to help, she moved toward the cavalry horse only to feel strong hands on her shoulders.

"You do Packie," Bret said, turning her toward the packhorse.

The feel of his hands stayed with her as she rubbed down the packhorse. Her mind went over every touch, from his palm cupping her elbow to guide her yesterday, to the relentless hold of his arm imprisoning her against his side and chest today.

Every time he had touched her, he had a purpose. Why did he push her away from the cavalry horse? Moving from the left side of the packhorse to the right, even in the fading light, she saw Bret twist away as the big bay lashed out at him with a hind leg. Hassie gave the placid animal under her hands a pat and went back over the place on Packie's back that made him stretch his neck with pleasure.

When they finished the rubdowns, Bret hobbled the horses and turned them loose to graze. Relieved of anxiety over the horses, Hassie's worry over sleeping arrangements and what she was going to do about them returned. Even if Bret wouldn't hurt her intentionally, what if he didn't think sharing a bed would be hurting her? After all she had been married.

She fidgeted with her coat buttons as Bret carried his bedroll and saddle blankets to a sheltered spot just inside the tree line. "Watch."

He walked over an area almost six by eight feet. "When there's enough light, you can check by looking, but one way or another, check for holes. You don't want to sleep on a hole with a snake in it."

Something light fluttered over the ground. "Ground sheet."

Saddle blankets thumped down next. "Mattress."

A dark blanket he didn't bother to explain topped the bed. "If you want a pillow, figure out what to use. Leave your clothes on, loosen anything tight. Boots off. Shake them out in the morning before you put them on."

He sat down on the blankets and pulled a boot off. "This is mine. You make your own."

Hassie ran back to where the saddles and packs lay, her heart light. The only decision left for her tonight was how close to Bret Sterling to make her bed.

8

Bret lay on his back, staring at the night sky, and listened to Mrs. Petty obediently stomping through the grass, following his instruction to check for holes.

This early in the season as cold as it had been, it wasn't strictly necessary, but tracking down the thief rumored to be hiding in a small town in Nebraska and dragging him to where Wells Fargo could check him out and approve paying the reward could take two or three weeks.

Cloth whispered as she shook it out, rustled as she did—whatever. Was she loosening anything? Those trousers didn't exactly fit tight. Without the galluses, they'd be down around her knees in two strides. Tight or not, no one with decent vision would see her from behind and believe for a minute she was anything except female. The coat helped for now. Except when she walked.

Keeping her in one piece in parts of the country where white women were rare was going to be one long repeat of today. From a distance she might pass for a boy or young man if she stayed on the horse. Hair under hat, hands in gloves. Dirt on face, purple eyes closed.

Bluish gray, damn it. The way they looked tonight was just the setting sun and the fire.

Seeing her naked breasts exposed in the gap between her chest and the front of the too large whore's dress hadn't aroused lust in any way. The small, firm breasts had moved with her heaving chest. Her nipples had been flushed almost red after her frantic run and peaked not from arousal but from cold.

The sight had been sad somehow and only made him angrier. Only made him more aware how vulnerable women were. No one should be able to do that to a woman who smiled and hummed, happy to be doing menial labor, thinking she was safe.

Today wasn't the first time someone had done something very ugly to Mrs. Petty. The scar on her slender neck was a shiny gray rope. If the wound had gone deep enough to ruin her voice, the wonder was she lived. Bret had seen slashed throats, knew how fast blood fountained out.

And it bothered her. She hid the scar under high collars that reached to the bottom of her chin, and she didn't make a sound unless really provoked.

He'd spent the war worrying over his own women, his mother, sisters, and Mary, because of that vulnerability. And his worry had been wasted. They all survived the war just fine, but hardships that Mrs. Petty wouldn't recognize as hard had left them bitter, and Albert, strong, laughing, opinionated Albert, had been the one to die.

No, the naked breasts weren't responsible for heat of a kind he barely remembered from before the war spreading through his belly, leaving him hard and throbbing. Her laugh had done that. A woman with a ruined voice shouldn't have a whispery, silvery laugh that crawled up a man's spine with delicate little female claws and roused things long dead and better left that way.

Not that he'd hadn't had a few women since the war. But that was like a trip to the bushes, relief not pleasure. Or maybe it was like picking a scab.

What would she do if he got up and joined her in her blankets? Not that he would, but toying with the notion was an entertaining way to wait for sleep. He imagined her hoarse, almost soundless gasp of horror, pictured her running across the prairie by the light of the stars, boots in hand maybe, the dog circling and barking, the hobbled horses spooking and hopping into the next county.

By the time his unfettered imagination had added one last herd of buffalo east of the Missouri stampeding through the town of Werver and flattening both the hotel and brothel, the last of the anger and impatience of the day dissolved along with the unexpected lust.

Resentment still prickled over having walked into the responsibility of keeping Mrs. Petty safe until he could offload the problem on Gabe and Belle, but even that dulled. The sounds of the night soothed. He fell asleep.

The nightmare came as it always did, starting with scenes from the war as he had lived them. Men and horses screamed. Bret slipped in greasy mud, fell across bodies. The roar of cannon bludgeoned his ears. Scents of blood and death roiled his stomach. A man in Confederate gray rose from behind a stone wall. Bret centered his sights, started to squeeze the trigger....

Something cold and wet pressed in his ear, something warm and wet slid across his cheek. Bret jolted awake panting and flailing, scrambled to his feet in time to see a four-legged shadow disappear in the trees. He sank back down, shaking, used his sleeve to dry his ear and wipe dog saliva from his cheek.

The dog had awakened him before he pulled the trigger on a man whose face he knew as well as his own. Even knowing how the nightmare would end, because he'd dreamed it countless times before, waking before killing Albert in the dream was better than waking after.

More of a gift was waking before another figure rose from behind enemy lines and died with blood spreading across her chest and an accusation on her face. Albert had really died, although not by a brother's hand, and Mary still lived, but after the dream Bret always needed the rest of the night, sometimes part of the next day, to put a dream that seemed so real behind him.

"Do that sooner next time," he said softly, aiming his voice toward the trees. "Do that sooner, and you can have your own rabbits."

SCENTS OF BACON and coffee woke Hassie the next morning. She opened her eyes to a gray world damp with dew and shivered. The sun wasn't up yet, but Bret was.

"Shake out those boots," he said when she reached for them.

She shook her boots, went far enough into the trees to be sure she was out of his sight before attending to personal matters. Wiping her hands on particularly damp bits of grass, she wondered how she could pull her weight in a camp like this. Evidently he wasn't going to let her cook. He didn't want more firewood than he gathered himself.

After bundling her bed away, she returned to the fire with the slate, ready to volunteer to get the horses. Brownie would come to her. Catching the others might be a different story.

"Here," Bret said. "Make sure nothing burns while I get the horses. Bacon crisp. Don't lift the lid on the other pan."

So he thought she was a dummy of a different kind, the kind who would lift the lid on his pan biscuits. And probably a slug-a-bed to boot. She turned the bacon strips, amazed at the number of them. He really didn't stint on food. Even in Ned Grimes' house, this much bacon would feed four.

He brought the horses in two at a time, and fed each one a little something, using the saddle blankets for feeders. Oats. He was feeding them oats, and he just gave Brownie twice as much as the others.

Hassie looked at the pan crowded with bacon again, looked at Yellow Dog, salivating on the far side of the fire, and told him, "I think things have changed for the better for us this time."

Bret returned to the fire and took the fork from her. "If all that hand-waving means you burned yourself, I have some ointment in the packs."

She fetched the slate from her saddlebags. *"No burns. Sign language."*

"The dog understands sign language."

"More than anyone else since Mama died."

"So you spell things out with your fingers."

"Only sometimes. Mostly words, phrases, more."

"Huh. Doesn't seem too likely."

Hassie used one of her gloves for a potholder, grabbed the coffee pot from the fire, and gave it an inviting little heft.

"No, my cup is still...."

She smiled at him. His gray eyes were still cold, his lean cheeks and strong chin under dark stubble more menacing than yesterday. If he smiled he'd be handsome. Maybe he was a little handsome even without the smile. He didn't seem so intimidating this morning.

"All right," he said after a moment. "I take your point."

They ate in amiable silence. Two of the fat biscuits wrapped around a disgraceful amount of bacon left Hassie comfortably full. Bret ate twice as much, and as she had suspected, that still left two biscuits and several strips of bacon for Yellow Dog.

Bret gestured with his cup toward the horses. "You have a name for the horse?"

"Brownie."

He said nothing, drank more coffee.

Hassie ignored her twitching fingers. She was not going to defend the way Cyrus named things, and his name for the horse was better than most even though Brownie was not really brown, more of a grayish tan with a lighter mane and tail, a coloring common on plow horses. Draft horses in her ancestry had probably contributed both to Brownie's coloring and appearance. And her sweet nature.

"I know you're fond of her," Bret said after a while, "but even fattened up, a horse that old may not be able to handle days on the trail."

"Brownie is not old. 6."

"Twenty-six maybe."

"6."

Bret went over to Brownie, slid his hand in the side of her mouth and pulled out her tongue, examining her teeth as she fought his hold with her mouth wide.

When he came back to the fire, he said, "I'm no expert on teeth, but you could have made a lot of money betting me on that one. I'll give you six. Was she born with her lips hanging loose like that?"

Hassie didn't answer. She didn't think he expected her to.

"What about him?" Bret said, pointing with the cup again.

"Yellow Dog."

Bret's head jerked around toward her. Maybe he was just as intimidating today as yesterday and the day before after all.

"Who the hell named him that?"

"My husband."

"Whatever you call him, I'm not riding around with a dog named as a coward, especially when he's not. He looks like an artillery sergeant I once knew. I'm calling him Gunner."

Yellow Dog had given up on more food and was sniffing around near the horses. He had a long pointy muzzle, hound ears, and a wiry, tan coat a few shades darker than Brownie's. At best, he'd weigh sixty pounds and right now wouldn't reach forty. Hassie tried to imagine any man looking like that and failed. The thought made her laugh.

Bret got up so suddenly Hassie searched the trees for trouble.

"You clean up here, and I'll saddle the horses," he said as he strode away.

Hassie cleaned up as best she could in the dry camp and smothered the fire. Why would a man like Bret Sterling stomp off like that over the dog's name?

9

Bret had changed his estimate of how long it would take to reach Fort Leavenworth from five days to eight and wasn't far wrong. Late the seventh day, his small cavalcade topped a rise, and there before them was the wide river, snaking away to the northwest and southeast as far as the eye could see.

After sitting a while admiring the view, or in Bret's case, enjoying the look of wonder on Mrs. Petty's face, he turned back and set up their supper fire a prudent mile away from the river. Bandits preying on travelers would be thick on the ground here.

Bret had been avoiding Mrs. Petty as much as possible under the circumstances for days. They ate meals in silence. Each did a share of routine camp chores. She read from her Bible until the light faded. He memorized descriptions on wanted posters.

It was better that way. He didn't want to get to know her, didn't want to know more of her history. Gabe and Belle could deal with all that.

Still, before they approached the ferry, he needed to give her some serious instruction. Not only was she too damned cheerful, too eager to help, she was too friendly. At least twice he'd caught her waving at people they passed on the trail. He'd ignored it at the time, but she had to stop.

Once he had potatoes frying and quail roasting, he broached the subject, "Before we get to the ferry tomorrow, Mrs. Petty, we need to talk."

The chalk pencil scritched on the slate, and she held it up. *"Hassie."*

He'd almost forgotten seeing her given name on the bill of sale. How did a woman whose face all but had "Irish" written on it end up with a name like that? He pushed it aside. One more thing he didn't want to know. "Mrs. Petty. Before we get to the ferry tomorrow, we need to talk about how you should act."

Her face fell, her eyes dropped from his to the fire. In a minute she'd be clutching at her stomach the way she did when she was upset.

He ignored the urge to say something reassuring. "No one who gets a good look is going to take you for a boy or a man, even dressed like you are. So you need to do your best not to give anyone a reason to look. Put your hair up under your hat tomorrow, wear your coat and gloves, a little dirt on your face wouldn't hurt, and pull your hat down."

Her chest wasn't the problem. Bret eyed that area speculatively. The breasts he'd seen bare were small, but they were definitely female breasts. A man would need a magnifying glass to find anything female under her shirt now. She must be tying everything down flat.

Her rump and walk were a different story. She was not a properly curvy woman, nothing like Mary, but that rump had a distinct heart shape loose-fitting trousers didn't disguise. She'd be too warm, but the heavy coat would hide things that needed to be hidden.

Nothing could disguise or hide the female way she moved. Keeping her on the horse so she could never take a single step on her own was the only chance there. He continued with her orders for the morning.

"Don't laugh. Keep quiet. If you can keep the horses between you and anyone else on the ferry, do it, except stay away from the cavalry horse." He turned the potatoes and remembered another thing. "And stay as close to me as you can."

She nodded, already looking anxious. *"Brownie and Yel...."* The last three letters disappeared as she rubbed them out with the side of her hand. *"...Gunner have never been on a ferry."*

"Have you?"

She shook her head. *"Train and stagecoach when Mama and I came west."*

West from where? He didn't need to know. Didn't want to know. "I'll give you a rope in the morning. You get it on the dog before he disappears after breakfast and keep hold of him. That way he won't miss the boat. Your horse will be fine."

Her horse wouldn't be fine on its best day, but at least it was better. The mare's speed had increased from that of a turtle to that of an ox, an old slow ox.

Mrs. Petty was doing better too. The dark circles under her eyes seemed gone for good, and her skin no longer had the pallor of sickness. He'd guess her age at mid-twenties now. She hadn't pressed a hand over her stomach for days, and there was nothing wrong with her appetite.

Gunner's spine had disappeared, and you had to look hard to see his ribs under the scruffy, wiry coat. With the help of a little jerky, the dog was responding to his name. He still growled at Bret regularly but no longer sounded serious.

The nightmare hadn't come again yet, but Bret had kept his promise about rabbits. Of course if the dog didn't wake him next time the dream came, it better get to hunting for itself.

The worried look stayed on Mrs. Petty's face, and she didn't eat as much as usual. When they remounted and moved into the dusk, away from the fire, he caught her with her hand over her stomach. He should have waited until after breakfast tomorrow to talk to her.

Then again, he wouldn't have to lie awake fighting the effects of her laughter tonight.

HASSIE'S FIRST GLIMPSE of the Missouri River unsettled her even before Bret told her what she had to do the next day. From bank to bank the water must be a mile wide, or at least half a mile. Knowing the Missouri was a major river had not prepared her for anything so daunting.

Brownie was never going to get on a ferry, and neither was Yellow Dog, who still didn't seem like a Gunner to her. Brownie would balk, and Bret would lose his temper and leave the poor horse on this side. Yellow Dog would growl and throw himself around like a mad dog at the end of the rope, and if Bret didn't shoot him, someone else would.

Squirming and turning in her blankets, Hassie fretted half the night away before falling into a troubled sleep.

The next morning getting a rope on Yellow Dog—Gunner—proved easy. He was too busy gulping down the breakfast Hassie had been unable to eat to pay any attention until it was too late.

The river disappeared behind trees and thick brush as they descended to its level. Twists in the trail to the ferry continued to hide the water until they were almost on the bank. The scent of wet mud and vegetation hung heavy in the air long before the trail ended in a large clearing and the water came into view.

They didn't travel the trail alone. A group of rough-looking men rode ahead, two more followed close behind. Hassie tugged her hat lower, understanding why Bret didn't want anyone to know about her.

She pushed Brownie as close to Bret's horse as she dared. Keeping Yellow Dog on one side of Brownie and not letting him tangle the rope was hard enough without getting so close to Bret the dog could interfere with the other horses.

A wide platform of heavy logs protruded into the river. Solid though the landing appeared, Brownie balked before getting anywhere near it. Would all these men be able to ride their horses across the landing and a less solid gangplank onto some little....

"Here she comes," a man near the front of the line shouted.

A flat-bottomed vessel with a cabin the size of a house in the middle steamed toward them. Steamed. White clouds billowed from a stack. Hassie's visions of the ferry as a raft propelled by men with oars disappeared.

Mouth dry, heart racing, Hassie fought Brownie's attempt to whirl and run when a whistle blew. Giving up the effort for the moment, Brownie watched the ferry loom larger and larger. She threw her head high and swiveled her big furry ears so far forward they almost touched. Yellow Dog panted and whined.

Bret turned in his saddle, took in her struggle at a glance, and wheeled all three of his horses in spite of the strangers hemming them in. He dismounted and took hold of Brownie.

"Get off."

Hassie got off, thankful to reach solid ground in the usual way instead of flying through the air off a panicked horse.

"Hold him." Bret handed her Jasper's reins, leaving her holding Jasper and the other two, whose lead ropes were wound around the saddle horn. Bret led Brownie and Yellow Dog into the brush beside the trail and tied them there.

The ferry docked. The gangplank crashed down. Men shouted, cursed, and laughed.

A rider on a flashy pinto shoved his way through those waiting their turn. When he came abreast of the cavalry horse, it lashed out, narrowly missing his knee. The man cursed and shook a fist at Hassie. Startled, she looked up into angry dark eyes for an instant before remembering, dropping her gaze, and moving behind Jasper's head.

Bret returned and pushed Hassie toward Jasper. "Get on."

Get on his horse and leave Brownie and Yellow Dog tied in the woods? No. She tried to shake Bret off.

"Stop moving around and get on the horse," Bret hissed. "I'll come back for them."

Unsure if she believed him, sure he would toss her up on the horse if she didn't mount voluntarily, Hassie crawled up on Jasper. Her feet dangled far above Bret's long stirrups. She grabbed the saddle horn in a death grip, barely remembering to keep hold of the reins. Bret had the leads of both other horses. He swung up on the cavalry horse, and led the way across the landing, over the gangplank, and onto the ferry.

The flood of men and horses boarding slowed to a trickle. Bret found a place by the rail, tied the horses, and shoved Hassie between Jasper and Packie.

"Stay here," he ordered as he rummaged through his saddlebags. "Don't move around. If anyone gets too close, push him over the rail. If you can't do that, push him into the horse," he said, jerking his chin toward the cavalry horse.

He hurried toward the gangplank, his spare shirt hanging from one hand, his long legs carrying him quickly past the last stragglers coming the other way. Once off the gangplank, he broke into a run.

Men moved into position, ready to pull the gangplank up. Hassie stared at the empty end of the trail. What was she going to do?

Bret had already paid their fare. If the ferry left without him, could she get the three horses off on the other side by herself and wait for him? He never let her near the cavalry horse.

She forgot to stay still, bounced nervously on her toes. There. Bret came into sight, leading Brownie with his shirt tied over her eyes. He held Yellow Dog's rope so close to the dog's neck when Yellow Dog pulled back, Bret pulled up, and the dog's front feet paddled air.

On they came. Although his clothes were similar to the men on the ferry, and like them his lower face was obscured by beard, Bret looked—better—as if he really should be wearing an officer's uniform, clean and crisp.

All over the ferry men watched, yelled, and whistled. Brownie first balked then jumped onto the dock, pulling against Bret one moment, crashing into him the next. Yellow Dog whirled and lunged, a growling, snapping demon.

Shoulders square, gait purposeful and rhythmic as if the antics of neither horse nor dog affected him, Bret strode onto the gangplank, his face giving no hint handling both animals was difficult, and no one came forward to help.

Unable to bear it, Hassie ran out from between the horses, across the deck to the gangplank, and met Bret halfway. She reached for Brownie's reins.

"Leave the horse to me and take the dog," Bret ordered coldly.

The dog was almost too much for her. Hassie wrapped the rope around her gloved hands, used all her strength and weight, and managed to drag the struggling dog across the deck to the horses. She hung on while Bret tied Brownie between Jasper and Packie, and handed Yellow Dog's rope to him with relief.

Now that no one was forcing Yellow Dog to go where he didn't want to, he stopped leaping and snapping and contented himself with murderous growls. Bret tied the dog beside the horses with no slack left for jumping overboard.

"I'm sorry," Hassie mouthed.

Bret's glare made her stomach hurt.

Half a dozen men crowded around, muttering and gesturing. "See, I told you," one said. "It's a woman, a white woman."

The man who had ridden the pinto shoved through the others the same way he had shoved to the head of the line on his horse. "It's a white woman, all right. Looked me right in the eyes, bold as brass."

Bret stepped between Hassie and the men. "She's mine. Find your own."

"Oh, come on," the pinto man said. "No reason to be greedy. How much you want for sharing a little?"

Bret moved so fast Hassie was never sure how he took hold of the pinto man. The man flew over the ferry rail the way

Hassie had feared flying off Brownie. He landed with a loud splash in the muddy water of the Missouri River.

By the time anyone who witnessed what happened tore disbelieving eyes from the yelling, floundering man, Bret had his coat open and a hand on his gun. "Anyone else?"

A couple of the men shook their heads. Most shuffled off without word or gesture.

Icy gray eyes pinned Hassie against Packie. "You looked him in the eyes."

"It was an accident."

"Just wave your hands around. I'll understand you better. And next time I tell you in plain English to stay somewhere, you stay there."

Hassie closed her troublesome eyes and nodded. At least he wasn't shouting. He never shouted at anyone in Werver either. He probably never shouted.

He was angry, though. Angry at her, and she didn't want him to be. She wanted him to find her helpful and not mind having her with him. She wanted him to forget about taking her to his friends and let her stay with him.

How angry could he be really? He had just stroked Jasper's nose. Angry men didn't pet horses, but then most men didn't pet horses no matter what mood they were in. He had recovered from that awful, terrifying anger in Werver before they were even out of town. She relaxed a little, remembering.

She also remembered the way pinto man flew through the air and into the water, the loud splash, the way water sprayed higher than the ferry deck. She hid her face against Packie, bit her lip, and smiled. She hoped pinto man could swim.

BRET LEANED AGAINST the rail, watching the west bank of the Missouri come closer and closer, and reconsidered his plans. Taking Mrs. Petty into Nebraska and trying to track down the bounty there with her along would be courting trouble.

She admitted giving the jackass on the pinto horse a good look at those big purple eyes, but the jackass wasn't the only one who recognized her as female. The minute she ran out like that, rough clothes and a dirty face were useless.

Taking her straight to Gabe and Belle would save a lot of trouble. It would also cost time and money. At this rate he'd be lucky to make half as much this year as last. The farm was looking as good as it had before the war, producing again, but the family still needed what he sent home.

Getting rid of the cavalry horse would make things more manageable. With the bad-tempered bay gone, all that would be left to make a hash out of his life and business were Mrs. Petty and her scrawny entourage. That should be easier. He'd decide about Nebraska after seeing how things went at the fort.

Getting them all off the ferry proved a lot easier than getting them on. Gunner had settled down, spent the entire trip across the river studying the brown water flowing by as if the fish underneath were visible. Once everyone else disembarked, Bret untied the dog and let him run ashore on his own.

Bret urged Mrs. Petty up on Jasper again, ignoring her pale face and white knuckles as she seized the saddle horn.

Her excuse for a horse had settled down. Old Brownie probably didn't have enough energy to raise another fuss, but Bret left the blindfold on just in case and led them all back to solid ground.

"You're lucky that fellow didn't drown," said one of the ferry men as they passed where he was tethering the pinto horse to a hitch rail.

Bret tipped his hat. That was him. Lucky.

Leavenworth covered more ground than any of the other western forts Bret had seen, but it had been laid out in the same pattern. Long rows of buildings hemmed each side of a large central parade ground.

Ready to repeat his instructions to Mrs. Petty, Bret glanced back at her and abandoned the idea. Her head was swiveling around as she took it all in from the flagpole, to a cannon below it, to a troop of buffalo soldiers marching in formation.

Bret held out through several attempts to pawn him off on lesser beings and finally was admitted to the office of Colonel Grayson, Fort Leavenworth's commanding officer. Mrs. Petty stayed close and behaved perfectly, eyes downcast, hands in coat pockets. The colonel never glanced at her and didn't invite them to sit, which was fine with Bret. He didn't intend to spend much time here.

"I'm not sure I understand why you needed to see me," Grayson said, his thin face tight with impatience. "We agreed on five hundred dollars. You've held that much back, and our business is concluded, although I have to wonder what happened to the rest of the money. If you hadn't killed Petty we could have found out what he did with it."

"If I didn't kill him, he would have killed me, and you'd wouldn't be getting a penny back, much less finding anything out," Bret said pleasantly. "It seems Mr. Petty wasn't eager to come back here and hang."

Grayson made a sound of amusement, his thin lips curling. "Mr. Petty was never in danger of hanging. The troopers who saw him run from the paymaster's office were from the Tenth Cavalry. No one would hang a white man on their testimony."

Bret held on to his temper with an effort. "Maybe Mr. Petty worried about evidence that would verify testimony from a Tenth Cavalry trooper."

Bret dropped Rufus Petty's saddlebags on the colonel's desk with a thump, knocking a few papers this way and that. "What I need now is either the worth of the horse Petty was riding or a proper bill of sale so I can sell it and the U.S. Army saddle on it without worrying about anyone wanting to hang *me* for a horse thief. A hundred dollars ought to do it."

"And that gives you more than the ten percent you originally wanted."

"It does. If you were a western man you wouldn't ignore the value of a good horse."

The colonel opened one bag, took out a small sheaf of bills, and counted out fifty dollars. "Take it or take the horse. As far as I'm concerned, the first wire I sent you is all the bill of sale you need."

Bret scooped up the money and tipped his hat.

Pleased with the transaction, Bret couldn't help sharing with Mrs. Petty. "I might not get hung for a horse thief for selling that horse," he said, "but I would get shot for a swindler by anyone who paid fifty dollars for him."

She gestured toward the men still doing drills on the parade ground and held up both hands, all ten fingers extended.

Bret nodded. "They're an all-Negro regiment. Good Indian fighters from what I hear, and if they're lucky they'll get sent west to do just that soon. Serving under Grayson must be a trial."

He untied Jasper and Packie and waited till she was mounted before swinging up himself. "What do you say we check out the establishments catering to civilians around here."

She didn't say anything, but she didn't have to. Unless she was frightened, Mrs. Petty was a pretty agreeable female.

10

Cassie had never been so happy. Staying in towns meant a hotel room to herself, baths, restaurant meals, and sending clothes to a laundry. Even though tracking down one man like Rufus brought more money than most people earned in a year, she marveled at Bret's generosity.

Out on the trail, the days in the saddle were long but hardly ever boring. Wildflowers bloomed on hills that rolled away to the horizon. Birds sang. Prairie dogs stood like tiny sentinels over their towns and whistled warnings as she and Bret rode by. Now and then antelope appeared in the distance, tan and white specks that bounded away long before the horses got close.

The only small blight on the intoxicating luxury of traveling with Bret was that he didn't talk to her. Sometimes she suspected him of deliberately avoiding her, but much as she wished things were different, she was used to the way he was acting. Mama's second husband and his family had never been willing to talk to her and neither had her own husband. They talked *at* her, gave orders.

Of course Bret didn't need to give her orders any more. They had arrived at a satisfactory division of chores and rode northwest into buffalo country with few words between them, spoken or written.

Things changed the first day Hassie ran. She couldn't help herself. Morning chores were done. Bret had breakfast on the fire, and he never let her help with cooking.

Fresh, cool morning air, bright sun, and level ground all around the camp provoked a burst of exuberance. She took off, whirling and pirouetting at first with arms outstretched, laughing as Gunner whirled too, barking encouragement. Then she ran.

When the stitch in her side stopped her, she picked wildflowers to weave in Brownie's mane until she caught her breath and could take off again. By the time her wild joy calmed, breakfast was ready.

Bret said nothing until they were almost finished eating. "The women I know would say running like that isn't ladylike," he said finally.

She fetched the slate and pencil and left the flowers by her saddle. *"Ladies don't wear trousers and ride astride."*

"That's my fault."

"Ladies have soft voices and can sing."

"That's not your fault either." He hesitated then asked, "What happened to your throat?"

Hassie studied his face. Was he really interested? The whole story would be a lot to write out, and no one cared how it happened. They just despised the effect.

"It is my fault. We went to the park. I climbed a tree when Mama said not to, and I fell. The man who took care of the park used a wire to tie a branch up." She shrugged.

"If falling into a wire didn't take your head off, I'd expect you to bleed to death from a wound like that."

"It didn't cut straight in. More...." She used one hand to show him the angle. *"A doctor was in the park. He saved me, but then he was sorry."*

Bret's mouth thinned. "He thought you'd be better off dead?"

"Breathing was hard."

In fact the effort to breathe after it happened had been terrifying. She had stayed unmoving in bed or in a chair day after day, unable to think of anything else except her next breath, whether she could draw it, whether it would be enough.

"He said there would be more scarring inside than outside. My throat would be too narrow inside, so any illness, and I wouldn't be able to breathe, and I would die."

"But you didn't."

"Mama said it would never get better unless I made it better. She made me walk, and when I could walk and breathe, she made me go faster. Until I could run."

"So running fixed your breathing."

Hassie smiled at the memory. *"Mama thought so. I think scars shrink, and when little girls grow, so do their throats."*

"How old were you?"

She held up eight fingers.

"So you could already talk and sing and shout, and you lost all that."

"I can whistle."

"Let's hear."

As soon as he said that, her mouth went dry. She only managed a thready warble.

"That's not much better than your voice. The next town we come to we better see about a tin whistle."

Trying to decide if this sharing of history went both ways, Hassie nodded absently, then wrote, *"Is your home in Kansas near your friends?"*

"No, my family has a farm in Eastern Missouri. I go home every winter."

"You have a wife there, children?"

His face closed. "No." He rose and started toward the horses. "We better get going."

She gave the scraps left over from breakfast to Gunner, smothered the fire, and cleaned up. If he was willing to have a conversation of sorts once, he would be again. The thought of another conversation where he talked to her and even listened made her want to run some more.

Mrs. Petty had no right to be so damned happy. Joyful. Sometimes Bret wanted to tell her about things he'd seen and done, crush the smiling and eagerness and softness right out of her, make her properly somber and realistic. Yet what could anyone say or do to a woman like that to change her?

Her father must have died early on. A childish accident stole her voice. The mother's second husband only tolerated the young girl Mrs. Petty had been. She should have had a line of suitors, but because of her voice she had to marry an old drunk when she was shoved out of the nest.

The drunk left her to starve. Bret Sterling killed the only man who was even close to kin right in front of her, took her from home, and left her with people who tried to force her into prostitution.

And he was going to leave her with more strangers soon.

She had no right to run with her arms outstretched as if embracing the morning, to weave flowers in that excuse for a horse's mane. Or to hum in the evening as she groomed the horse. Or to smile at him as if he should share all these delights. Or to laugh.

Gunner sat beside Packie as Bret positioned the pack saddle, loaded up, and lashed everything in place. The dog looked as pleased with life as his owner.

"You have nothing to smile about either," Bret muttered. "You're a liar and a cheat."

Twice in the last weeks, a cold nose and warm tongue had awakened Bret. He had no memory of the nightmare starting either time. Still, every two weeks was about how often the dream had haunted him since the first battle he'd been in.

Bret finished with the packhorse and tossed the dog a piece of jerky before saddling Jasper.

Days before they came to the little settlement rumored to be a haven for outlaws, Bret turned off the trail. The rolling hills of open prairie provided no cover for miles in any direction, and he didn't want to stumble on the town unexpectedly.

When they came to a secluded spot near a small lake, he left Mrs. Petty there and scouted ahead until he located the town. Even with his spyglass, finding a place in the nearby hills where he could observe anyone moving between the few buildings of the town took half the day.

Satisfied, he slid back down the hill to where he'd left Jasper. Mrs. Petty and the horses could stay in this hollow behind the hill while he kept watch. Pulling a thief out of a nest of thieves would take a little planning, but he'd done it a time or two before in the last six years.

AT FIRST HASSIE was glad to move closer to where Bret had set up his observation post. As each hour of waiting passed more slowly than the one before, the necessity of staying in the small hollow between the hills began to chafe.

She read for a while, groomed each horse and gave it some grazing time on a lead rope, made Yel—Gunner a necklace of grass and flowers. The sun had barely moved from the eastern to western sky when she finished all those things and looked around for something else to alleviate the boredom.

Her searching eyes lit on the panniers. Bret had amazing things squirreled away in there, and she hadn't seen everything yet. Taking inventory would keep her busy for a while.

The first curious thing she unearthed was a tin box, a shallow rectangle. She turned it over, gave it a little shake.

Whatever Bret kept in there was none of her business. Photographs of his family maybe. Or letters. Temptation proved too much. She wouldn't read any letters. Would just take a peek at photographs.

The box didn't contain photographs or letters. It contained wanted posters. Sheet after sheet of descriptions of men and their crimes. Some of the posters had penciled notes in the margins or on the reverse side, Bret's notes, written in exactly the neat, strong hand she would expect.

The poster on top, Moses Jensen, was the man Bret hoped to find in this ugly little town. Jensen had been one of five men who robbed a Missouri-Pacific train, and the only one of the five identified. The Missouri-Pacific Railroad Company was willing to pay three hundred dollars to see Mr. Jensen brought to justice.

Her restless boredom evaporated. Hassie sat and read about one criminal after another. Most were thieves. Some, like Rufus, had through intent or happenstance killed during a robbery. They had stolen from stage companies, railroads, and businesses. They had killed in order to steal, in order to get away, and from the descriptions, out of pure meanness.

By the time she finished reading about each man, the light was almost gone. She wiped the black smudges of ink from her hands on tufts of grass, but what Hassie really wanted to scrub was her mind. Fascinating as the descriptions were, so much evil was overwhelming.

Bret didn't come down from the hill until it was too dark to see words on her slate. Confessing to going through the box would have to wait until tomorrow.

"Not a sign of him," Bret said. "Either he's not there, or I didn't start watching early enough. We'll stay here tonight, and I'll start at first light tomorrow."

The thought of sleeping so close to men like the ones on the posters made Hassie shiver. Gunner would growl if strangers approached, but sometimes his growl wasn't very loud.

"I'm going to keep watch," Bret said as if he sensed her uneasiness. "You get some sleep."

She didn't need the slate to tell him how she felt about that. She pointed to herself, to her eyes.

"All right," he said. "I'll wake you in a few hours, and you can take second shift."

But he didn't wake her.

BY THE SMALL hours of the night, Bret's eyes grated in the sockets every time he blinked or moved. He'd gone without sleep a lot longer during the war, but fear kept a man on his toes better than the thought of dragging one more thief to jail, collecting one more reward.

He should let Mrs. Petty keep watch for at least a few hours, but that idea grated worse than his eyes. He'd rest after sunset today, and he'd worry about what Mrs. Petty would think of his plan for Jensen's transportation once he had to tell her.

She was still asleep when he crawled up the hill an hour before dawn. No one moved below until well after sunrise. After that men moved from one building to another now and then. Hotel or rooming house to saloon probably.

Staying awake with the sun warm on his back and shoulders became more and more difficult as the hours passed. The spyglass drooped in his hands, his eyes closed.

Bret startled awake as a lithe female form crawled up beside him. She had her message all written out and ready.

"You sleep. I'll watch."

"You don't know what to watch for."

She flipped the slate over and showed him her second message. *"Short man about 30, black hair, bushy sideburns and big mustache, pockmarked, blue eyes, silver on hatband and belt, fancy boots."*

Bret glared at her. "Did that nose of yours get turned up on the end from sticking it where it doesn't belong?"

The chalk pencil came out. She rubbed out some words, wrote others. *"I'm sorry. I was bored."*

Anyone could watch better than a sleeping man, and much as he hated to admit it, Bret knew she was right. "You have to stay down in this tall grass."

She nodded.

"What are you going to do if a snake shows up?"

"Run."

Too tired to argue, Bret gave up and slid down the hill. He'd sleep a couple of hours and chase her back down again.

His couple hours had passed twice when Mrs. Petty shook him awake, her face alight with excitement. He didn't have to read the words she'd written to know she'd seen Jensen, except the words on the slate said, *"I saw them. I saw them both!"*

"You saw Jensen and another man?"

She dropped the slate, ran to the packs, and brought the box of posters back. Her fingers flew through the papers until she reached one near the bottom and held it out. Ollie Hammerill, thief and murderer, had killed a Western Union operator and made off with less than the five hundred dollars he was now worth.

"You're sure?"

Her head bobbed. Her fingers traced a line from the corner of her left eye to her jaw. The line the poster described as a knife scar on Hammerill's face.

Bret stared at the poster, considering the changes taking custody of two men at once would mean. Mrs. Petty's excitement faded.

"You don't believe me."

"Yes, I do, and I may be able to get two of them out of there without much more trouble than one, but transportation is a problem."

Her brows furrowed.

"One man I could put on your horse, and you could double up with me from here to the nearest town. Two of them means taking two horses."

"Good. Brownie is not carrying bad men. They can walk."

That was about the reaction he'd expected out of her, and it didn't matter now anyway. He wasn't passing up a second even larger reward, which meant he'd have to take not only the men but horses.

He quizzed her about what she'd seen. The spot on the prairie below hardly qualified as a town. A few ramshackle buildings clustered on either side of the road. Mrs. Petty had seen a wagon drive in from the north and stop by the saloon. Half a dozen men had come outside, talked to the wagon driver, and helped roll a few barrels inside.

The wagon still stood in the road when Bret went to look. It was still there when night fell.

Bret moved their camp back to the lake and cooked a decent meal. In the pre-dawn darkness, he brought the horses in among the trees, saddled them all, and loaded the packhorse.

He didn't have to wake Mrs. Petty to tell her what he was going to do, what she needed to do. He felt rather than heard or saw her coming close, sheltering from the morning breeze beside him in the lee of Jasper's bulk.

"Don't worry," he said. "I've done this too often to count, and I'll be back before you know it, but you need to be ready to move out fast then."

Her hand rested on his cheek, fingers soft by his temple, palm warm even through the growth of several days' beard. Her body pressed close. She hugged him and was gone.

The cool wind blew in vain as he rode toward the town. The memory of her touch warmed him every step of the way.

11

Cassie took each of the horses in turn to the water and waited patiently until sure each one had quenched its thirst. She checked saddles, bridles, and canteens. An extra trip to the bushes assured her own bladder was empty and she was ready to leave at a moment's notice.

After that she paced. And paced.

If only they were still camped near the town, she could climb the hill and watch. She shook her head ruefully. Probably a good part of the reason they weren't still camped near the town was to keep her from doing just that.

He'd be back soon, back with those men trussed up and helpless. Except how would he truss them? Did he have rope? Enough rope, the right kind of rope? She couldn't remember.

Her hands were on the packs, ready to finish the inventory she had started the day before, when she brought herself up short. Opening the packs and spreading their contents around now would be a very bad idea.

She resumed pacing. Gunner whined where he was tied. Tied with rope that Bret probably forgot he used for the dog. Rope Bret needed right now and didn't have.

The eastern sky still showed traces of the pink of sunrise when the horses shifted, ears pricking. Packie gave a low whicker of greeting. More suspicious than the horses, Gunner growled.

Hassie's knees trembled with relief. Bret was all right. The two men on the strange horses wore heavy metal handcuffs, not ropes. Only their angry, sullen presence kept her from running to Bret.

He dismounted and led Jasper to the water. Hassie fumbled with the slate and pencil. *"How did you get them?"*

His eyes gleamed for a moment as if he might laugh. "Waited by the privy. It doesn't make for a sweet-smelling wait, but it makes for catching a man when he's not in a position to argue."

Hassie did laugh, and Bret's expression changed. "You mount up. We need to get going fast."

"Their friends will follow us?"

"Men like this don't have friends, but I had to take the first two horses I could catch and throw the first saddles I came to on them. They may come for the horses, and right now I'm a horse thief. Mount up and stay behind me. I'll get the dog."

Jensen and Hammerill both tried to hold their horses back until Bret threatened to tie their cuffed hands to their saddles and drive the horses. The pace he forced them to set was relentless, and neither man showed signs of paying attention to Hassie or recognizing they rode with a woman until the first time they stopped to give the horses a breather.

"That's a woman," Jensen said. "I can't believe it, the bounty hunter has a woman in trousers with him."

Hammerill ran hot eyes over her the way Marshal Dauber had. "Damned if you ain't right, and a nice little package she is." His gaze shifted to Bret. "You're a dead man, bounty hunter, but maybe I'll let you live long enough to watch what I do to your woman. I'm going to...."

His words were so vile, so beyond her knowledge or experience, Hassie didn't react. Bret cut off the stream of filth by stuffing his bandana in Hammerill's mouth and tying the man's own neckerchief over that.

After taking a long drink from his own canteen, Bret screwed the cap back on and eyed Jensen, "How about you?

It's going to be a long, dry ride, you want to make it with a mouthful of cloth to chew on or are you going to keep quiet?"

Jensen licked his lips and swallowed hard but didn't say a word.

"Nice to know one of you is smart," Bret said. "Now get going."

The angry, brooding presence of the strange men frightened Hassie, but so did the way Bret treated them. He had reverted to the icy-eyed stranger who had killed Rufus, all traces of the man who shot an extra rabbit or quail for Gunner every day gone.

When they stopped a few hours later, Bret let both men have a drink. Hammerill gulped greedily first and started with more invective right after. Bret jammed the bandana back in his mouth.

This time Hassie understood some of what the murderer said. She shuddered, no longer bothered by how Bret shut the man up.

They pushed steadily through the day, stopping near a creek an hour before dark. Horses, humans, and dog all drooped with exhaustion.

Bret adjusted the handcuffs on the outlaws so each one sat with his back against a tree, his arms behind him and around the tree. After hobbling Jasper, Packie, and Brownie, Bret turned them loose to graze and got busy with a hot meal.

No fresh meat tonight. Hassie didn't care. At least Bret looked halfway approachable again.

"*Do we have to stay awake and watch them?*" she asked, not sure she could manage to wake up and watch anything even after several hours of sleep.

"No, we need to get some sleep. Gunner can watch them."

Gunner was tired enough to be stretched out, head on paws, but he was only a few feet from Jensen and Hammerill and looked more than ready to watch them—or take a few bites out of them.

"*Their horses don't eat?*"

"Later. I don't have hobbles for them all. Better we keep two saddled, just in case."

She didn't want to think about just in case, watched with dull eyes as Bret let Jensen and Hammerill eat and drink one at a time and took them out of sight behind bushes.

On the way back to the trees, Hammerill lunged at Bret, giving Gunner an excuse to sink his teeth in the man's calf. Hassie flinched at the sound of Bret's pistol against the man's skull, but the dog bite bothered Hammerill more.

"I'm bleeding and my leg hurts like a son of a bitch. You have to do something to stop the bleeding. Dirty damn dog. What if I get rabies?"

"It will save you hanging," Bret said. "Better yet, keep acting like a jackass, and I'll forget that poster doesn't say dead or alive."

The man kept moaning and complaining, but Hassie was too tired to care. She made her bed so that Bret was between her and the prisoners. And close. Never before had she positioned her bed so that she could touch Bret by reaching out an arm. He didn't remark on it, and she fell asleep almost instantly, comforted by his closeness.

Three more days of the same kind of travel cured Hassie of any illusions that Bret earned his money easily. She rose stiff and aching in the morning and fell asleep at night stiff, aching, and exhausted. Brownie and Gunner, who had gained weight in the last weeks and rounded out a little, looked gaunt again. For that matter so did the other horses and the men.

Reaching a town with a stone jail house and a real jail cell with iron bars left her giddy with relief. Not caring that night was still hours away, she crawled into bed in a hotel room Bret didn't bother inspecting and sank into a dreamless sleep.

WITH MRS. PETTY safe at the hotel, Bret forced his tired mind to focus on the details he needed to take care of before giving in and sleeping. He sent telegrams to the Missouri-Pacific and to Western Union, informing them Jensen and Hammerill were in custody and asking for instructions.

He led the two extra horses he could all too easily be accused of stealing more than a mile from town and turned them loose, relieved to be out from under that shadow. With nothing left to take care of until he heard back from the railroad and telegraph company, he headed for the hotel. All that kept him upright was the knowledge he'd soon be in a real bed, not limited to the edgy, aware-of-danger half-sleep of the past days but able to let go and fall right off the end of the world.

The hotel owner didn't agree.

"What do you mean you don't have a room," Bret said incredulously. "You rented me a room a couple of hours ago, and I told you I'd need another."

"Yes, sir, but you didn't pay yet, and another gentleman arrived after that, and he did pay. He paid for the last available room. This is a small establishment."

There were no lamps to shoot on these walls, and angering the town marshal here would mean losing use of his jail to store Jensen and Hammerill while getting desperately needed rest. Neither one had committed crimes in this town.

Bret thought of making camp outside town, thought of a pile of hay or straw at the livery where a smith was banging away at his anvil, thought of the room one flight of stairs away he'd escorted Mrs. Petty to not so long ago.

"I assume you haven't turned Mrs. Petty out because someone came along and paid more?" Bret said.

"It's not a matter of more," the hotel man said unctuously. "It's a matter...."

"Spare me." Bret cut him off and slapped bills on the desk. After pocketing his change, he said, "Give me a key to Mrs. Petty's room."

The man's mouth pursed into a prim, disapproving circle. "When you rented the room, you said...."

"I don't care what I said. We both know you have another key. Hand it over before I come over the top of the desk and take it."

For the first time the man looked nervous. He handed over the key.

Bret almost knocked on the door to her room, but after two hours Mrs. Petty should be so sound asleep nothing but loud shouting or water in the face would rouse her. For more than a day now she had been shaky on her legs, the huge dark circles under her eyes like bruises in her pale face.

The key turned in the lock with barely a sound. The door eased open with only the slightest squeak.

Her boots and outer clothing were in a heap on the floor beside the bed. Her hair was still in its unraveling braid, and Mrs. Petty slept curled on her side, oblivious to his presence and probably to cries of fire or gunshots in the hallway should they occur.

He eased the door shut and locked it, pulled his own boots off right there by the door, and padded to the window to close the curtains and shut out the last of the afternoon sun. In the dim light left in the room, he stood beside the bed for a moment, watching her sleep.

The one dark brow in view arched gracefully over the delicate skin of her eyelid. Her skin still looked unnaturally white, but the shadows under her eyes were already smaller, or maybe he just wished it so. Her lips twitched, nice lips really.

Yawning, knowing he couldn't stay awake another minute even if the woman in the bed was Mary, Bret moved to the other side and stretched out next to Mrs. Petty. Mrs. Cyrus Petty, widow. His responsibility until he could get her to Gabe and Belle. His burden for another couple of weeks or so.

Of course a woman who pointed out an extra, unexpected five hundred dollar reward wasn't much of a burden. Not really five hundred, though. He'd split it with her, give her something to start her new life.

Mrs. Hassie Ahearne Petty, respectable widow, would probably fall out of the bed with shock if she knew he was beside her. Although she sure bedded down close to him on the trail these last days. She'd used him for comfort the way little girls used rag dolls.

Bret fell asleep considering whether he'd need to open the curtains in the morning before sneaking out of the room. Would Mrs. Petty notice a detail like that, or would she remain ignorant of the fact they'd shared a bed so long as he got out of here while she still slept?

The first light of dawn leaking into the room around the closed curtains woke Bret. Or maybe it was his own intense state of arousal. Mrs. Petty's breath fanned softly across his cheek. One breast pushed against his arm. If she had climbed half on top of her elderly husband like this, Cyrus Petty had been a lucky man.

Her hand on Bret's belly burned right through the clothing and sheet separating them. The leg she had hitched over one of his played havoc with every nerve in his body. His breath rasped so loudly in his own ears, her sound sleep was a miracle. Hell, his heart was banging against his ribs so hard it ought to wake everyone in the place.

Bret moved her arm away, eased his shoulder out from under her head, his leg from under hers, and slid off the side of the bed. She sighed, her arm reaching out as if to find him again, then drawing back and curling under her chin when it found only bedclothes.

Bret soft-stepped to the door and leaned against it until his erection subsided and his breathing returned to some semblance of normal. Finally, he pulled on his boots and slipped from the room.

The sooner he got rid of Mrs. Petty, the better for both of them.

12

With the prisoners mounted on horses he purchased and had legitimate bills of sale for, Bret stopped driving them all so hard. Even so, Hassie couldn't really enjoy the freedom of being out on the trail until they left Hammerill in jail in the town where he'd robbed the Western Union office and killed the telegraph operator.

Traveling with Jensen a few more days in order to hand him over to Missouri-Pacific detectives wasn't such a strain, but being free of both men would have had Hassie whirling and running with joy except for the knowledge of their next stop—the end of her grand adventure. The end of the intoxicating freedom of traveling with a man who avoided her as much as possible, but who didn't sneer or belittle and treat her like a servant. The end of admiring the way he sat his horse as he rode ahead of her, his easy walk as he moved around their campsites, the way the hard lines of his face relaxed when he cooked.

Perhaps because she had slept so close to Bret during the nights when Hammerill had still been with them, she couldn't shake a feeling of an intimacy they had never shared.

In truth, he had only ever touched her arm occasionally, rather forcefully in Werver, but still only her arm. So how could some part of her be sure she knew his scent, the texture of his skin and hair, the rhythm of his breathing?

She had taken liberties she shouldn't have when fear for him had filled her mind, touching his cheek, hugging him. Now her mind took further liberties, and her imagination ran wild.

Soon they would reach his friends' homestead. He would leave her there, and it would all be over. His friends would look at her and wonder how a sterling man had ever come to bother with a petty woman, and they would find a man willing to marry her, a man like Cyrus. Not exactly like Cyrus, but like him in that he'd have a weakness which would make him settle for a wife like her.

Hassie tried to hide her feelings. Any future was more future than she had the day Bret first appeared in her life. She had no right to wish for more, no right to want more. She worked hard at each campsite, smiled brightly at Bret whenever he looked her way, but she stopped running, stopped dancing with the wind and sun.

They reached Gabe and Belle Chapman's homestead late in the afternoon of the day spring became summer, no matter what the calendar said. The horses slogged along, their necks dark with sweat. Hassie slumped in the saddle. No rivulets of perspiration ran between her bound breasts, but the binding was soaked as was the waistband of her trousers.

After seeing other homesteads with houses built from bricks of prairie sod, Hassie expected the Chapmans' house and outbuildings to be the same, and they were. The surprise was the size. Nestled in a sea of wheat still green and half height, the Chapmans' house wasn't a one-room minimum shelter, but two, even three rooms.

The children in the yard shouted and pointed. A brown and white collie barked and ran to meet Gunner. A tall woman appeared in the open doorway, one hand raised to shade her eyes from the sun, the other tucking loose strands of brown hair behind her ear. She waved and walked into the yard, gathering the two children to her as she came.

Bret reined up a few feet away. "It's good to see you, Belle. Can you stand visitors for a few days?"

"You know you're always welcome here, Bret. Get down and come on in. Gabe probably saw you ride up and will be here before you know it."

The woman's tone didn't match her words. Not that she was unfriendly, but she didn't smile, and no one could call her greeting warm. Her dark eyes flicked over Hassie, then back to Bret as he dismounted.

"This is Mrs. Cyrus Petty," he said, "recently widowed and needing help I hope you and Gabe will be willing to provide."

Belle Chapman looked at Hassie again, this time studying her. "Mrs. Petty."

Hassie nodded and stayed where she was, wondering what would happen if she turned Brownie around and rode away.

"We'll put the horses up and be back in a few minutes," Bret said. "Maybe by that time Gabe will be here, and I'll explain about Mrs. Petty."

Belle nodded and turned back to the house, taking her young son and daughter with her.

This was one of his good friends, the friends he wanted to leave her with? If she could think of words to write, Hassie would have pulled the slate from her saddlebags, but the only words she could think of were "Let's go," and she couldn't write those.

Bret led Jasper and Packie to a corral beside the barn, and Brownie followed with no signal from Hassie. When her horse stopped beside the others, Hassie finally dismounted, hoping Gabe Chapman would share his wife's attitude and the two of them would refuse Bret's request to help the widowed bit of baggage he'd brought them.

If they refused, maybe Bret would let her keep following him. Maybe they would ride west through Kansas to Colorado or even Wyoming. Maybe they would ride back to Missouri and south to Arkansas or Indian Territory. Didn't a lot of bad men hide in Indian Territory?

She had the saddle off Brownie when a man bellowed as he walked around the barn. "Captain Breton J. Sterling. It's about time you got back this way. How the hell are you, you son of a gun?"

The two men came together in that way men had that was almost but not quite hugging, more back pounding. Gabe Chapman, for that's who the man must be, was an inch or two shorter than Bret, barrel-chested and thick through the neck and shoulders. The strands of hair Hassie could see sticking out around his hat were red, a color that fit with his ruddy, freckled complexion.

Finished pounding on Bret, Gabe grinned at Hassie, curiosity all over his wide face. "Well, now, who's this? Tell me you've finally done something sensible."

All signs of Bret's enthusiastic greeting for his friend vanished. "This is Mrs. Cyrus Petty," he said stiffly. "Her last living kin, if only by marriage, was a foolish thief and murderer."

"Foolish meaning dead, I suppose." Bright blue eyes assessed Hassie. "If Bret killed your husband for filthy lucre, I'm surprised you're willing to travel with him, handsome, charming devil that he is."

Charming? That was a word that had never occurred to Hassie in regard to Bret Sterling. She finally had seen a trace of a smile a few times, but charming required more than that, and right now he had a typical very uncharming glower on his face.

"Her husband died without any help from me. It was one of his sons who made the mistake of pulling on me, and the two of them left Mrs. Petty in a bad way. I'm hoping you and Belle can find her a decent husband. If men are writing back East and marrying women they've never met, there ought to be a few around who'd rather have a pretty widow they can meet in person."

Pretty? He thought she was pretty? No one could think that when she was covered with days of trail dust, smelling of her own sweat and Brownie's, and dressed like a man. For a moment the compliment distracted Hassie from the fact Bret was pushing her off on his friends, wanting her to find a husband and stop being a burden to any of them.

"We'll have to see how Belle feels about that," Gabe said. "Let's get these horses put up and go see her. Say what you want about living in a soddy, it will be cooler inside than out here in the sun."

It was cooler inside, and Hassie had guessed right. Three rooms. She was also right about Belle Chapman's attitude.

They no more than all sat around the kitchen table when Belle said, "I hope that male dog out there isn't going to be getting pups on Collie."

Hassie wondered at people who named their collie Collie but decided someone whose own dog had been named Yellow Dog until recently had no call to wonder.

Gabe smiled at his wife as if he understood her feelings, sympathized, and expected her to get over them anyway. "It's only been a month since the last time we had to tie her in the barn. They're just playing."

Belle shrugged, fussed over the children, and shooed them back outside. She thumped four glasses down on the table, dipped water into them, and sat, still vibrating disapproval. "You said you'd explain once Gabe was here. He's here."

Bret told them about Rufus. And Werver. To Hassie's relief, he left out the purple dress and her frantic flight from the brothel. In fact he left out the brothel entirely. As he talked, Belle visibly relaxed, most of her hostility disappearing.

Hassie stared down at her hands, heat flushing across her cheeks. Belle Chapman must have thought Bret arrived for a visit in the company of the kind of woman respectable wives didn't acknowledge existed.

By the time Hassie was paying attention to the conversation again, most of Bret's explanation was over.

"She can't talk?" Belle said incredulously.

Bret, bless him, didn't correct Belle with a description of Hassie's ruined voice, which would inevitably lead to demands for a demonstration.

"She writes," Bret said. "Slate and pencil. She does fine, and no one can accuse her of nagging."

"When we make a list of her virtues, I'll put that as number one," Belle said, the barb back in her tone. "And what do you think of all this?" she said to Hassie.

Hassie lifted one shoulder slightly and forced a smile.

Belle pointed a finger at Bret. "Go get that slate and pencil."

"Yes, ma'am."

Bret and Gabe disappeared as fast as two big men could. Five-year-old Sarah, who didn't want to relinquish them to an adult, delivered the slate and chalk pencil.

"You have your own," her mother said, "and you've never been that fond of them. Scoot back outside now and keep an eye on your brother."

Belle put the slate in front of Hassie. "Now, let's talk. When did your husband die?"

"The night before Bret came. I lost track. Maybe 6 weeks ago."

Belle blew out a big breath. "And you're not ready to remarry."

Hassie just shook her head, glad for once she wasn't expected to say anything because even if her voice worked as well as Belle's, right now it would tremble.

"You won't be the first woman who had to do what she had to do," Belle said. "I'm sorry, but Bret's right, and that's the truth of it."

Hassie kept her head down, blinked rapidly to disperse extra moisture. *"I know."*

"You don't have any fanciful illusions about Bret, do you?" Belle said sharply.

Hassie shook her head again, maybe too fast, or maybe too vigorously, because Belle called her on it.

"Of course you do. You wouldn't be the first woman to waste time and emotion on Bret Sterling, and you better chase ideas like that right out of your head. If Bret ever marries, it will have to be someone that family of his approves of, and they only approve of people as grand as they are, not that that's how they put it. The only thing a Sterling man would do with an Irish girl like you or the daughter of a small farmer like me is ruin her. One of my sisters found that out the hard way."

At the other woman's words, a wave of indignation ran through Hassie. *"I don't believe that. Bret is honorable."*

Belle made a face. "Oh, yes, he's honorable. He's the best of the lot of them, I'll give you that. His brother William is the one who gave my sister false hopes, but then he went and...." Belle stopped as if realizing she needed to censor herself. "Never mind any of that. We need to concentrate on you and your problems."

Her own problems were exactly what Hassie didn't want to think about, much less concentrate on. *"How do you know Bret and his family when you live here, and they live in Missouri. Did you live there once? Did you have to leave after the war?"*

For a moment it seemed Belle wouldn't answer, but finally she said, "Gabe and I grew up on small farms bordering the Sterling place. We didn't *have* to leave after the war, but we had no reason to stay in a place that's a nest of Southern sympathizers. If Bret had any sense he'd leave too, but his loyalty to that family is beyond reason or explanation. Now enough of that. Do you have any decent female clothes out there in those packs?"

Hassie shook her head.

Belle made a disapproving sound. "Then what we need to talk about is getting you dressed proper and introduced to some of the bachelors and widowers around here."

After not experiencing so much as a twinge for weeks, Hassie had all but forgotten the many ways her stomach could hurt. Now a familiar cramping sensation warned of misery to come. She spread a hand over her middle, knowing it wouldn't do any good and unable not to do it anyway.

Oblivious, Belle said, "I can probably talk Gabe into a trip to town tomorrow or the next day, and Bret can just pay for a decent outfit, but right now I could use some help getting supper ready. We'll need to stretch what I planned. A few more potatoes should do it."

Hassie nodded, more than willing to help. Keeping busy and not thinking about introductions to marital prospects might quiet her stomach.

In spite of what Belle thought, Hassie didn't have fanciful illusions about Bret Sterling. She knew he regarded her as an unwanted burden.

In spite of that she wished she could stay with him. She'd been a little help by recognizing Ollie Hammerill, hadn't she?

She wanted more long days in the saddle, plain food over a campfire, luxurious stays in hotels with restaurant meals, and even frightening encounters with ferries and outlaws.

No matter where he went or what he did, her days following Bret Sterling had been the best in her life, and she wanted more of them. Which meant Belle was right. It was all a fanciful illusion.

13

After giving Gabe's young daughter, Sarah, the slate and chalk pencil to deliver to Mrs. Petty, Bret followed Gabe through the fields to where his friend was working on fence repair. Again.

"It seems like the last time I stopped by, you were fixing fence," Bret said.

"It chronic. The horses spend half their time pushing on any weak spots, trying to get into the crops. Last time they succeeded, it was in the middle of the night, and I almost lost a couple of them. Belle and I had to walk them for hours before their guts straightened out."

"Someday someone will come up with better fence than post and rail."

"Yeah, or an animal smarter than a horse."

Bret grunted, putting his back into tamping a fence post. "Maybe you want dumber, not smart enough to escape."

"Speaking of dumb...."

"She's not dumb," Bret said, aggravated. "She fell across a wire when she was little more than Sarah's age. It almost took her head off and ruined her voice. She and her mother learned some kind of sign language, but her mother's gone now. A husband could learn it."

"And she writes."

"She does. We need to cross any illiterates off the list."

"List?" Gabe stopped with a fence post in his arms. "You can't seriously think there's going to be enough men interested in a mute Irish papist to need a list."

"If she's a papist, she's not much of one. She hasn't crossed herself once, and she reads her Bible every chance she gets. Catholics don't do that, do they?"

"Fine," Gabe said, upending the fence post in one of the holes he'd already dug. "So she's a mute Irish widow, past the first blush of youth and childless in spite of how many years of marriage?"

"You sound like a poet. When exactly does the first blush of youth end? She can't be more than twenty-five or six." Bret stopped tamping, chucked more dirt in the hole, and started pounding again. "Seven maybe."

"Then the blush has faded." Gabe returned from shooing off curious horses before they could take advantage of the gap in the fence and returned to the subject of Mrs. Petty. "I'm still not clear why you think you owe Mrs. Petty anything. Her husband died. His son tried to kill you, and you killed him. She owns that farm back there now. Why not leave her to it?"

"If you saw the place, you'd know. It's only maybe forty acres to start with, and the fields look like the last time they were planted was before the war. The only livestock on the place was that excuse for a horse, and hard as it may be to believe, Old Brownie looks ten times better right now than she did then. I guess the husband scratched out a halfway decent living selling moonshine until his sons didn't come back from the war and he started drinking everything he brewed himself."

Gabe stopped fitting rails in place, a frown on his broad face. "You said you found the son who robbed the army right there."

"The sons didn't die in the war. They just never came home. Having seen the place, I can't blame them. Rufus ran home for the first time in years with almost six thousand stolen dollars and who knows how long he was planning on hiding there. Or what he would have done for Mrs. Petty. Maybe he would have given her enough to get by until she could marry again. For all I know he would have plowed and planted this year or started up the still again. If nothing else, as long as he was there, he'd have seen she had enough to eat. There was hardly any food in the place, but I could smell fried meat in the kitchen. He'd been hunting."

"He was a thief and a murderer. More likely he would have used and abused her. Killed her maybe. Definitely left her worse off than she was."

"Maybe." Bret finished tamping the last post, threw the iron bar aside, and grabbed the other end of a rail. "The fact is I killed him and left her with nothing. Even if I gave her some of the money, she'd have nothing before long. And then I left her in that damned hotel."

Bret told Gabe the sordid details about the events in Werver he'd left out earlier with Belle listening and the children around.

Gabe whistled. "You hear stories of things like that, but I always figured any woman whoring was doing it because she decided to, even if what decided her was the need to eat. At least any white woman."

"Obviously not, and who'd ever know? It's not like she could yell for help."

"Even so, she shouldn't be your problem. We better keep quiet about the whorehouse, though. Just the fact she's been riding around alone with you will raise some eyebrows. With luck we can help you offload her on somebody desperate for a woman, although I'm telling you there isn't going to be any list. How long was she married and no children to show for it?"

"From what I heard in Werver, since the end of the war. The husband was an old man and busy pickling his liver, so you can't blame her for the lack of children. She'll do fine with a healthy man."

"You should have been born a gypsy. You could travel the country selling crowbait like that horse of hers as bloodstock. Now you're going to tell me she can't talk but sings like a bird, and she's not an ordinary bogtrotter but descended from Irish kings."

Bret considered swinging the fence rail at Gabe's skull and decided against it. The two of them had fought each other to a bloody standstill often enough over the years. No use getting an early start this time. "I'll tell you she's a hard worker, agreeable, and cheerful. The only thing clean and halfway kept up on the Petty place was the house, and she managed that while caring for a dying man."

"She's not bad looking, I'll give you that. Not your kind of beauty, but pretty enough."

Bret thought of the way Mrs. Petty looked when she smiled, the real one, not that too bright forced smile. And her laugh. Come to think of it, he hadn't seen or heard much of either the last few days. She must be worried about meeting strangers.

"How many eligible women are there around here? How many men looking for wives?"

"A few women. A lot more men," Gabe conceded.

"I hear all the time about men answering advertisements in newspapers and writing to agencies that have catalogs of women and paying to get them out here without knowing a thing about them."

"They exchange letters and photographs. They probably know as much about the catalog women as you do about Mrs. Petty. You've been hauling her around the country with you for almost two months and you don't use her given name?"

"Her husband's hardly cold in the grave. No harm keeping things a little formal." Bret hoped Gabe would take the hint and leave the subject alone, but leaving things alone was never Gabe's way.

"So you've really been riding around for weeks with the widow, and you never...." He rocked one hand suggestively.

Bret gave Gabe a glare that would shut most men up. "Of course not. She's a widow left in a bad situation, not some painted woman." Bret ran a forearm over his face, not to wipe away sweat but to hide a smile at the memory of Mrs. Petty flying down the street toward him in the purple dress, her face definitely painted.

"And you, of course, have to remain faithful to your one true love, even though she drove a knife in your back as hard as she could and twisted."

"Gabe...."

"All right, all right, if Belle sees me with another black eye because I dared to speak the truth to you, she'll throw you and the widow out before supper."

The two of them worked in silence for a while before Gabe spoke again. "Letters we get from Belle's family and mine say you've got the farm back in better shape than it was before the war."

"I don't know about better. They built the house back a little bigger, but then Will has two children already. Vicky's married and gone but Caroline's still there and will be for a few more years. According to her she has absolutely no smallest chance of ever, ever finding a husband. Ever." Bret imitated his younger sister's dramatic tones.

"Maybe she ought to try an advertisement in a St. Louis paper."

"Over Mother's dead body." Bret paused a moment. "And mine."

"How is Will?" Gabe asked, his voice carefully neutral. "And Mary."

"Same as ever," Bret said, debating whether to tell Gabe about the loose horse shoes. After a moment, he did.

Gabe whistled. "He always envied you and Albert. Something about being the middle brother galled him. Sounds like that's turned into something worse. He could have got you killed doing that."

"He probably didn't think of it that way."

"Stop making excuses for him. He spent his war in the cavalry. He knew damn well what could happen."

"It didn't."

"It's easy to hate somebody you've wronged."

"He didn't wrong me, and he doesn't hate me. It's just brotherly—competition."

"Cain slew Abel because of brotherly competition."

Bret gave Gabe another change-the-subject glare.

Gabe shrugged. "The last letter from Belle's sister said your father is buying race horses and hired some horse trainer from Kentucky to take care of them."

Bret only just managed not to show a reaction to the news. Race horses? He carried rails to the last open gap in the fence and let them fall with a clatter.

"How long are you going to keep supporting them all?"

"The farm is producing again," Bret said shortly. "They're not relying on me entirely any more."

Race horses? Bret wasn't sure he believed it, didn't want to believe it. If it was true, this would be his last year tracking men for the bounties on their heads.

He and Gabe finished the fence work in silence and walked to the house as the first orange of sunset tinted the western sky.

FOOLISHLY, BRET HAD imagined once Mrs. Petty was with Gabe and Belle, word would go out on some grapevine, and prospective suitors would begin visiting in an orderly and eager manner. They'd drive to the homestead in their Sunday best, take Mrs. Petty for a walk or ride, and she would return smiling.

Belle disabused him of that idea the first evening over supper. In an area thinly populated with far flung homesteads, the only way to start news on the grapevine was to go to town. Everyone showed up there sooner or later for supplies, church services, and to catch up on news and socialize.

For socializing and courting, the best opportunities were at the barn dance held on the last Saturday of every month, and the last Saturday was only a few days away. Bret almost groaned.

Mrs. Petty didn't make a sound, of course, but the way she held her left arm clamped to her side made him sure her hand was spread over her stomach. She probably didn't know how to dance, probably had never been to one.

"Hassie and I will go visit the Browns tomorrow," Belle said. "If they'll keep Sarah and Gabriel for us and milk the cow while we're gone, we can go to town Saturday and get Hassie decent female clothing. Then we can all go to the dance and introduce Hassie around a little, stay over, and attend church in the morning. There may be a few who come to town for services who weren't at the dance."

Hassie? They hadn't even been here a day, and already Belle was tossing around Mrs. Petty's given name as if they were old friends?

"And you're paying," Belle said to Bret as she passed the bread. "A decent dress and shoes and some other necessaries won't be that much."

"I don't have to pay," Bret said. "Mrs. Petty pointed out a five hundred dollar bounty I'd have missed on my own. I figure she's entitled to half, and after we settle up, she should have about two hundred of her own."

Bret enjoyed the astonished looks on all their faces, particularly Mrs. Petty's, although a small twinge of guilt pinched at him. He should have told her about the money before this.

"So she has a dowry," Gabe said, amused.

"It's not a dowry. A dowry goes to the husband. This is her money."

"When she marries, whatever she has is his."

"Like he...." Just in time Bret remembered Sarah and Gabriel and managed to choke off the curse. "It's hers, and it's staying hers. She can sew it inside some unmentionable something no man would mess with."

Gabe shook his head, but Belle didn't find it amusing. "That's ridiculous. Any decent wife would give it to her husband, and I'm sure Hassie intends to be a good wife."

A good wife with no voice and only one arm and hand because the other one was spread tight across her belly as if she needed to hold her innards in place. Bret shoved a big chunk of potato in his mouth to keep from saying anything more on the subject.

14

Belle doubled Sarah and Gabriel up in one bed and made up the other in the room the children shared for Hassie. Bret was to sleep in the barn. Hassie wondered if he really would or if he would make a bed as they always did on the trail somewhere outside under the stars.

She lay quietly in the too-short bed and wished she had the courage to throw off her nightgown, get dressed in the clothes Belle found so offensive, go find him, and make her own bed somewhere close. More, she wished she had the courage to saddle Brownie and ride away into the night.

Two hundred and fifty dollars. Did she really deserve that much? Anything? Once she repaid Bret every penny he had spent on her, she would surely still have a lot, not two hundred dollars, but a lot.

She imagined saddling up and leaving on her own. Imagined coming to a town, approaching strangers, and wanted to weep. Even before what had happened in Werver, she would never have had the nerve to do such a thing. The thought made her shrink in her skin.

No, she would do what they all wanted and expected, what Bret wanted, and marry the first man who asked. After that she'd sink back into the shadow life, doing what she was told, never even trying to communicate with someone who wasn't interested in her thoughts and opinions anyway. A perfect dummy.

After her miserable night, Hassie's spirits rose over breakfast when she realized Bret wasn't going to ride off and leave her right away. The conversation at breakfast made it clear he visited Gabe and Belle for a few days at least once a year, and he was going to stay and visit now. Hassie's relief was so enormous she managed to smile at Belle and eat an entire flapjack.

Helping with chores and the children kept Hassie's hands busy through the day, and Belle's constant chatter about plans for Hassie and every widower and bachelor for a hundred miles in every direction was easy to ignore.

According to Belle they were all the same. Perfect for a woman who needed a husband. Any husband. The only time Hassie gave Belle her full attention was when the woman told stories about growing up in Missouri next to the Sterling farm.

"Bret and his brothers used to sneak away and visit us all the time. By us I mean my family and Gabe's. We all used to help each other out, work together, play together, squabble, make up. Albert and William liked to visit well enough, and that's how my sister got notions she'd have been better off never to have about William. William and Albert were like all that family. They didn't believe in getting their hands dirty, and they did believe they were better than us. They were raised that way. Bret never rubbed it in, though, and hard work never scared him. I always had a notion he got a few whippings over going home dirty and sweaty, but he never admitted it."

By the time the two of them started preparing supper, Hassie knew in detail how stuck up Bret's family was and how his mother believed she was descended from English aristocrats and named her children to reflect her supposed heritage.

"Bret figures he got off easy," Belle said. "She didn't latch onto royalty until after him. He's the oldest, you know. His brothers are William and Albert. Only William now. Albert died in the war. His sisters are Victoria and Caroline."

Hassie tried to picture it. A man and his three sons and a farm of thousands of acres. If only one son was willing to work, how had they farmed? As Belle kept chatting, a coldness spread through Hassie. She knew how men who didn't believe in getting their hands dirty farmed.

"Bret was always the odd man out in that family. Why they were surprised at what he did when the war came is beyond me. Bret was never shy saying how he felt about secession or about slavery. I figure he spent so much time with us to get away and not have to even see what was going on at home, but that family acted like a viper cropped up at the supper table and they couldn't figure out where he came from."

Hassie almost cut her finger instead of the carrot on the cutting board. She thought about going to get her slate, but she didn't need to ask questions. Belle kept right on going.

"Gabe was the same, but then so was his family. Gabe was all ready to join up right there in Missouri the day we heard the war had started, but Bret said he was going far enough east so's he'd never find himself looking at anybody he knew over his sights, and off they went all the way to Ohio. They fought the whole war side by side and never got near Missouri the whole time. But facts don't matter to that family of his. They act like Bret killed Albert himself when the truth is Albert died of dysentery right there in Missouri."

By the time supper was on the table, Belle was through with the shortcomings of the Sterlings and every other bushwhacker, Southern-sympathizer, and Confederate veteran in Missouri and had returned to Hassie's problem.

Gabe joined his wife in speculating about the men in the area in need of a wife. Bret was almost as quiet as Hassie. When Belle mentioned it, Bret shrugged.

"I'm not used to this work any more, Belle. Tired is all."

"Well, we'll all get to rest Saturday and Sunday. It's been a long time since Gabe and I went to town and did more than pick up supplies and head right home." Belle reached a hand toward Gabe. He enveloped her hand in his massive paw for a moment and winked at her.

Hassie stared in wonder. She never would have reached out to Cyrus like that, even when they were alone, and she had never seen Mama do that with Ned Grimes. Had Mama and Papa ever had moments like that? Her father had died when Hassie was six. Her memories were all of a man ravaged by consumption, but she wanted to believe her mother had once shared moments like that with her father.

"We'll all have a grand time," Belle said. "For us there's visiting with folks we don't see often, a dance, and Sunday services, and for Hassie a new dress and maybe meeting the right man." She sipped from her glass of milk and regarded Bret thoughtfully. "And if you stay here to get some rest, you can save Milo Brown having to ride over to milk the cow."

"No, thanks," Bret said. "I'd rather dance than milk a cow, so Mr. Brown is out of luck."

Hassie swallowed the three peas in her mouth and smiled brightly at them all. At least he'd be there. If one of the men Belle wanted her to meet turned out to be like Pinto Man—or like Zachary—Bret would make him go away.

Hassie eyed the small town of Hixton without any of the enthusiasm new places usually evoked. The town was as new as many of the homesteads it served. Buildings clustered around a rutted crossroads on the flat prairie, most built with lumber hauled from the north and a few from sod. An open-sided tent on the outskirts of town served as a saloon.

A room in the town's only hotel would be a considerable expense for Gabe and Belle, and Hassie suspected Bret paid for all their rooms. Since Belle didn't wait for the men to finish registering before tugging Hassie toward the stairs, Hassie couldn't confirm her suspicion.

Washed and ready for the ordeal of shopping, Hassie gave a long, considering look at her slate. She really didn't want to walk around town carrying the thing. She dropped it and the chalk pencil in the middle of the bed and went to meet the others.

Under different circumstances, a new dress would be a good thing. Right now it was just part of finding an unwanted husband, and the thought made Hassie tired. Something mustard-colored with gray buttons would suit her mood.

Belle was excited enough for the both of them and chattered happily as they all walked from the hotel to the store. "Now they won't have many ready-made dresses, but I brought my sewing basket, and we can take up a hem or do a nip and tuck before the dance, and you'll be the real belle at the ball."

Making sure the dress had a high collar that hid her scar was Hassie's only concern, and the sewing basket would take care of that.

"If we're lucky, they'll have something lavender," Belle said. "Not old lady purple, but a summery lavender that will set off your eyes. You have the most extraordinary eyes. I've heard talk about violet eyes, but I never thought to see them."

Bret stopped dead on the wooden walk. "Her eyes aren't purple, and she doesn't want a purple dress."

"Of course her eyes aren't purple. They're violet, and I just said we don't want a purple dress. Lavender. That's pale...."

"Purple. Her eyes are bluish-gray, and she doesn't want a pale, medium, or dark purple dress. Let her buy what she wants."

Speechless for once, Belle stared at him with her mouth ajar. A ghost of the feeling she'd had when Pinto Man flew over the ferry rail rose in Hassie. She ignored the hard, tight look on Bret's face and gave him a genuine smile, took Belle's arm, and started down the walk toward the general store again.

Once inside, Hassie and Belle both studiously ignored the single lavender dress in the store. Hassie held a conservative dress in soft blue up, considering.

"That would be perfect," Belle said. "Perfect for church, not the dance."

"Then buy it for church," Bret said from the other side of a table covered with men's clothing. "Two dresses won't break the bank."

It might break her bank, Hassie thought, and he hadn't handed over a penny directly to her yet. Then again if some husband she didn't want was going to get all her money anyway.... Her hand reached for a cool, minty green dress with twice as much skirt as any of the others.

"That needs a hoop under it—or several petticoats," Belle said disapprovingly.

"We don't have hoops, but we have lots of petticoats," the storekeeper said, pointing.

Hassie bought the blue dress, the green dress, and three petticoats. Back at the hotel, decked out in her new finery, she whirled around her room. The skirt of the green dress swirled around in an almost embarrassing feminine way. The new corset emphasized her bosom.

An hour's work added a stand-up lace collar that covered the scar. Trying the dress on again, Hassie had an urge to rip out everything she'd done. A lower collar would be more comfortable, and sight of the scar might scare off some of the men Belle was determined to introduce.

What would Bret say? He'd seen the scar. Would he say cover that ugly thing up or tell her to be comfortable and not worry about it?

Stop that, she scolded herself. He wants rid of you. No matter what you do, no matter what you look like, he wants rid of you. Stop worrying about what he thinks.

Hassie slumped on the bed, all her pleasure in the new dresses gone. Soon a knock would sound on the door, and it would be time, time to go to the dance like a piglet to market.

BY THE LIGHT of a dozen or more lanterns, bits of hay and straw shone on the hard-packed dirt of the barn floor. None of the crowd gathered for the dance gave any sign of noticing, much less caring. The women were dressed in everything from calico to silk, and Hassie abandoned visions of the imaginary mustard and gray dress, glad to fit in after all.

She half-expected all those other women to flock toward Bret. He looked beyond fine in a dark gray suit, maroon vest, and white shirt, his boots polished to a high gloss, but he disappeared into a shadowy corner mere moments after they arrived. Belle's firm grip on Hassie's arm kept her from following him.

Belle guided Hassie around the room, repeating introductions over and over. "This is Mrs. Cyrus Petty from Missouri. Mrs. Petty is a widow staying with Gabe and me. An accident some years ago damaged her throat to where she doesn't speak, but we've had wonderful conversations with her writing out her thoughts for me."

Heat rose up the back of Hassie's neck and spread to her ears and face as Belle went on to describe how helpful the Widow Petty was with the children, cooking, and laundry. *This little piglet is pink and chubby and eats anything you have to give it.*

Hassie forgot the names of the people Belle introduced her to a second after hearing them. She lost track of which of the men who approached were bachelors and which were widowers. She smiled and nodded at each one who asked her to dance and held the smile through awkward silence or nervous babbling.

The exception was Ehren Kulp. While other men danced with her once, Mr. Kulp returned a second time, then a third, delighting Belle if not Hassie.

"You have a conquest in Mr. Kulp," Belle whispered. "He really likes you."

So far as Hassie could tell, Mr. Kulp would like any female he could acquire as a stepmother for his five children. During their three dances, in his ponderous, heavily accented voice, he told her all about them and about the wife who had died trying to give him a sixth child.

Memories of how Ned Grimes' motherless children had greeted Mama rose in Hassie's mind unbidden. Mama had been able to use a strict, no-nonsense voice to at least curb the worst of their hateful plots, and the first year had still been awful. Five little Kulps would be daunting. More than that. Dreadful.

Avoiding Mr. Kulp's watery blue eyes, Hassie concentrated on the unfamiliar feel of the corset tight on her ribs, petticoats swirling airily around her legs.

After the third dance, Mr. Kulp kept her hand in his too long. "May I call on you next week at the Chapmans'?"

Hassie bobbed her head, forced a smile, and blinked away unwanted extra moisture in her eyes as he guided her back to Belle's side. She turned away as soon as she politely could.

Mr. Kulp was much younger than Cyrus, probably not much past forty. He didn't reek of liquor but of something sweetly unpleasant he must have rubbed in his thinning blond hair. If they married, he wouldn't grab at her the way he had tonight. A man who could touch anything he wanted any time he wanted didn't have to grab at a dance.

She had no excuse to be fighting tears and an insane urge to lift the hem of the green dress and run into the night. Run until she dropped from exhaustion and then run some more. She had already accepted someone like Mr. Kulp was her future. At least now she had memories of the globes on fancy lamps shattering as gunshots cracked, Mr. Reston squealing from under the hotel desk, Pinto Man flying over the ferry rail into the Missouri River.

And Bret Sterling. She would always have memories of Bret Sterling.

BRET LEANED AGAINST the wall in a dark corner of the barn and watched Mrs. Petty. In many ways she didn't resemble the often scruffy-looking woman who had followed him across hundreds of miles of Missouri, Nebraska, and Kansas in the last weeks.

Pinned high in that magical way women managed, her hair gleamed like polished ebony whenever lamplight played over her. In spite of the high collar she had added to the dress to hide her scar, the sleek arrangement emphasized the elegant length of her neck. The green dress clung to modest but definite female curves. Her breasts had reappeared.

The swirling skirt and petticoats hid the one thing the rough trail clothes never could—that distinctive heart-shaped rump.

He needn't have worried about her ability to dance. She danced just fine, moving with more grace than any other woman out there.

Bret controlled the urge to yank her away from the man now dancing with her for a third time by speculating as to whether the dress and imagination or trousers and an eyeful were more provocative.

He forced his balled fists open. She needed to meet eligible men. He'd brought her to Gabe and Belle for this. He wanted this for her.

Except he didn't. He wanted better for her. She had already danced with at least half a dozen potential suitors, and she had smiled at them all with that too bright smile he didn't want to recognize but did.

He had tried hard not to get to know her. When had he come to know the difference between her real smile and the way she was smiling now? And what it meant. He knew what that forced smile meant.

Gabe had been wrong. There were enough men for a list. Too Old, Too Short, Too Fat, Never Stopped Talking, Barely Said a Word, and Squint Eye. The list already sported a thick black line right through Too Old. She'd already had one of those.

Barely Said a Word had a tentative black line. Maybe he was shy and would get over it if he got to know her. If not, the last thing Mrs. Petty needed was a man who didn't talk any more than she did.

And if Too Fat kept monopolizing her and letting his hands wander while he did it, he was going to get crossed off more than an imaginary list.

Gabe joined Bret in the corner. "You're glowering like an overprotective father."

"What do you know about that fellow who seems so keen?"

"Ehren Kulp? His homestead is about an hour north of ours. He was here before we were, so he's proved up. Widower, several kids. Good farmer, doing well so far as I've ever heard."

Bret grunted. "Hands all over the place."

"Looks like he's pretty taken with her." Gabe examined Bret with narrowed eyes. "You know if he's really interested, we'll check him out, visit his place, talk to anyone who knows him. I'd say you should stick around a while longer and see for yourself, but with you hanging over her shoulder and that look on your face, the devil himself wouldn't have the courage to come courting."

Bret watched the green dress swirl. "She deserves better."

"And I deserve less than I have, and you deserve more than you have. How many people get what they deserve, the outlaws you haul in to prison or to a hangman's rope?"

Bret shook his head, trying to ignore the feeling of sadness. Mrs. Petty deserved better than she had ever had or was ever going to have, and Gabe was right that what she deserved didn't figure in the reckoning.

He watched her until the musicians packed their fiddles away, and he escorted her back to the hotel in silence. Afterward he slipped out to the nearest saloon by himself. A few drinks didn't chase the bleakness out of his head, but then they never did.

Sunday morning was a quiet affair, with everyone still a little tired after staying at the dance until almost midnight. Bret appreciated the blue dress Mrs. Petty wore to church services. Nothing swirled.

On the wagon ride back to the farm, Belle's chatter made it clear she considered Hassie as good as married to Ehren

Kulp. Belle went so far as to speculate whether she should save Hassie's shirts and trousers for Gabriel to wear someday or use the material for smaller garments now.

The false smile disappeared from Mrs. Petty's face as Belle talked. Good. Her face muscles must ache from holding that expression by now.

He'd leave in the morning, Bret decided. Leave Mrs. Petty to her imperfect but inevitable fate and leave her in Belle's determined, well-meaning hands.

15

When faced with the choice of marrying Cyrus or being left penniless and alone on the streets of Werver, a thick fog had descended over Hassie, letting her go through the necessary motions while feeling nothing. She wished that fog would return.

Instead she sat through the church service Sunday morning with images of the rest of her life sharp as knives in her mind. First she saw the angry faces of five Kulp children, all resentful of their mute stepmother. Then she saw Ehren Kulp's face as it would be over her, flushed, watery eyes protruding with effort as he grunted....

She swallowed hard, fighting nausea, and glanced around. Such thoughts in church had to be a terrible sin, and everyone else was concentrating on the sermon, something about forgiveness.

Next to her, Bret shifted on the hard wooden seat. Cool gray eyes met hers, which was better than icy, but even so.... She dropped her gaze and studied her gloved hands against the blue dress. The dress brought to mind Bret's reaction to the idea of a lavender—light purple—dress and banished thoughts of the Kulps, at least for a while.

How could he know it would be a long time, if ever, before she would willingly wear a dress in any shade of purple and not know how she felt about all the rest of his plan for her? Probably he did know. He just didn't care.

Why should he care how hard she tried to be a help to him on the trail and in camps when she slowed him down and embarrassed him? After weeks of enough food, Brownie could keep up better now, but when men looked at Brownie and grinned, the look on Bret's face would freeze water if he stared in the trough.

He didn't like it when someone assumed she was his wife, and he didn't like it when they assumed she was something other than his wife. Even though he once said she had a nice laugh, he had changed his mind. He disliked the sound of her laughter so much he walked away every time she forgot and laughed. He wanted rid of her, her horse, and her dog.

And who could blame him? Ned Grimes had complained constantly about how much money it cost him to support an extra female, and Ned hadn't spent as much on her in all the years she'd lived with his family as Bret had spent in less than two months.

No matter what he said about giving her half that reward money, the money should be all his. Because he felt bad for her, he would give her some undeserved amount, ride away, and never look back. Why should he? He'd done all he could, more than anyone else she'd known would.

She caught him looking at her again and forced a smile. Smiling at a man in church was probably sinful too. The woman in the pew in front of Hassie wore a hat covered in tiny flowers. They swayed with every tiniest motion of her head. Hassie counted flowers, concentrating intently.

The wagon ride back to the farm provided no opportunity for private thoughts, whether melancholy or mutinous. Belle sat in the back of the wagon with Hassie, determined to share every tidbit she had gleaned about every one of the men who had showed so much as a sliver of interest at the dance. Hassie smiled, nodded in all the expected places, and didn't listen to a word.

Bret and Gabe's conversation about people they knew in Missouri and men they'd served with in the war was far more interesting. Even when the wagon creaked over a rough patch of the road and Hassie couldn't catch their words, the low hum of masculine voices soothed her troubled mind.

Gabe stopped at the Browns' farm for the children, and after that no one heard anything but Gabriel and Sarah's excited stories about everything they'd seen and done at the Browns'. Hassie leaned back and listened to their happy babbling. Her new life would have good moments. Maybe she would even be blessed with a child of her own. Her mind skittered away from who would be the father of such a child and how that would happen.

When they finally reached the farm, Hassie climbed out of the wagon with relief. She tucked her old clothes out of sight under the small bed. Sooner or later Belle would get her hands on those clothes and turn them into something else. Later would be better.

After trading her new town shoes for boots and the small, ribbon-trimmed bit of fluff for her wide-brimmed slouch hat, Hassie approached Belle with the slate.

"I would like to go for a walk," she wrote. *"I will be back in time to help with supper."*

Belle waved her off. "You go ahead and don't worry about anything except getting back in time to eat. I know you have a lot to think about."

Pangs of guilt didn't override the need to be alone. Hassie held her gait to a walk until she was past the first field of knee-high wheat. Then she ran, wishing for hills and trees, places to hide. Past the fence that separated pasture from cultivated fields, she spied a slight dip in the land and slowed. The slight hollow wasn't much of a hiding place, but it would have to do.

The slate made a seat of sorts to protect the blue dress from grass stains and dirt. She sat with her knees drawn up, arms around them. A cricket chirped nearby. The scent of warm earth hung in the air. Wispy clouds drifted across a milky blue sky.

Even Gunner had deserted her. What would happen to him when she married? If Ehren Kulp and those other men wanted a dog, they would already have one.

If Gunner stayed here, the next time Collie had a season, Gabe would shoot him, or Belle would wring his neck. Gabe would sell Brownie and give her the money. Give her husband the money.

Footsteps whispered through the grass behind her. She didn't need to turn to know who it was.

"Here. Sit on this, and you can talk to me," Bret said, dropping down beside her.

She couldn't talk, and if she could, wouldn't want to talk to him, but after a moment she took the bandana he held out, spread it on the ground, and shifted her bottom onto it and off the slate. The pencil was in the grass somewhere. If she changed her mind about talking to him, she'd search for it.

"You don't have to marry him, you know," Bret said. "If you don't like him, turn him away. There will be others."

She shrugged.

Plucking the chalk pencil out of a tuft of grass, Bret held it out. "Tell me what you want. Talk to me, Hassie."

She grabbed the pencil. *"HASSIE?"*

"I figure if Belle and Gabe can use your given name as if they've known you for years, I might as well too."

And he'd be leaving soon, not needing to be formal and keep her at arm's length. She dropped the slate and pencil, rose, and walked away.

The man who had avoided her more often than not for the last six weeks followed. When she stopped, he held out the slate and pencil.

"Tell me what you want. If you want to go back to the Petty farm, I'll take you. You'll have the two hundred I owe you. If that's what you want, you can get by for a year or so on that, find someone you really want to marry."

She took the slate finally. *"You owe me nothing. I owe you. It doesn't matter. I will marry him."*

"Half the Hammerill money is fair, and so is subtracting fifty dollars for expenses. Two hundred is a good round number."

Hassie finally dared look at him. He didn't look angry or cold but determined.

"We both know you don't want to marry him, and Belle's glad for your company. Wait. Someone better will come along. Someone you like."

She shrugged again.

He rapped his knuckles on the slate, almost knocking it out of her grip. "Talk to me."

"They're all the same. I will marry him."

"All the same? You know better than that. The one that yapped at you non-stop isn't the same as the one who could hardly look you in the eye and say a word. The old gray-hair isn't the same as the short fellow who's still wet behind the ears, and none of them is the same as Kulp with his half a dozen children."

"5."

Bret's brows furrowed. He stared at the single number on the slate as if he had never learned to count. She added, "only" in front of it and "children" after it.

They stood in silence so brittle Hassie thought any sound, even so slight as the cricket starting up again, would shatter it, and he would leave. Or ask again.

Her fingers twitched with the desire to answer his question, but why admit she wanted something impossible? At least this way she was only wretched, not humiliated too.

"Do you really want to work in some menial position?" he asked finally. "If you'd rather do that, maybe we could find you something like at the hotel, but something safe with decent people."

Her fingers twitched again. A position would be better than marrying, but after what had happened in Werver, she couldn't face trying that again. She shook her head.

The silence weighed on her, more pressing than continued questions. Finally she wrote, *"I want to go with you."*

He barely glanced at the words. Cold gray eyes bored into hers. "That's too bad because you're not going to."

"I know."

"Why the devil would you think such a thing? You know what it was like with Hammerill and Jensen. It was brutal, dangerous, and it can be worse."

She touched the words already on the slate. *"I know."*

"Come winter, I go home to family. That leaves you exactly where you are now, except without Belle and Gabe to help you. Is that what you want?"

She didn't try to answer, turned her back on him, and started back toward the house. She should get back and help with supper. She climbed through the fence into the wheat fields. And she ran, ran as if Zachary chased her again. Ran as if she could escape false hope and foolish dreams.

BRET TOOK A few steps as if to go after Hassie then stopped and watched her duck through the fence rails, take off running on the other side. Soon she was just a small blur of color racing down the lane beside the field, and then—gone.

What could he do with her, shake her until she showed some sense? Even if she didn't want to marry again so soon, how could she say she wanted to go back on the trail?

Hell, moving constantly hunting men wasn't what *he* wanted. His life was supposed to be Mary, family and children, friends and neighbors, the farm. Not dust, dirt, and danger. Not men like Rufus Petty and Ollie Hammerill.

After days on the trail with Hammerill and Jensen, Hassie had been half-dead when they reached the first town, so exhausted she never knew she had a man in bed with her that night.

Things would only get worse from now until fall brought relief. Soon the summer heat would suck moisture out of every tissue. Insects would torture man and beast alike.

Trying to talk to her would be a waste of breath and time. The woman was so lacking in sense she didn't want to marry again, but she *hummed* doing menial labor in a hotel, although at least she didn't claim to want more of that.

He'd done all he could. Belle was enthused about the marriage effort. Let her take it from here. Come first light tomorrow, he'd saddle up, pack up, and get back to business.

Supper was a quiet affair. The children were tired and cranky, the adults just tired. No one looked surprised when Bret said he'd be leaving in the morning. No one argued. Bret excused himself as soon as he could and headed out into the night.

He bedded down on bare ground far from the house or barn. A good night's rest would make an early start in the morning easier. Except neither his body or mind planned to cooperate. He considered getting up and walking the fields, but instead lay quiet, staring at clouds silvery with reflected light from the moon and stars, and mentally arguing with Hassie Petty.

An argument with a woman who couldn't argue back should be easy to win, but that was part of the problem. She'd probably never won an argument in her life. Never been able to make one.

The dog. She'd stopped him from shooting the dog the first day he'd laid eyes on any of them, and she'd been right about that. Even so....

He didn't know whether her father had died before or after she lost her voice, but obviously he'd left her and her mother with no support. The Grimes fellow had wanted the mother enough to take Hassie too but had shoved her off on Petty as soon as the mother died. Cyrus Petty, old and drunk. Rufus Petty, mean and criminal.

Then along came Bret Sterling, who didn't bother to ask her what she wanted, just ordered her off that farm, left her at the hotel, dressed her in men's clothing, and dragged her off after a bounty or two and then here to Gabe and Belle. And to a husband, whether she wanted another one or not.

Bret turned restlessly on the unyielding ground. A shadow loomed over him, blocking out the sky. A cold nose bumped his neck.

"I'm not even asleep much less dreaming, so you can quit your fooling," Bret said, sitting up and grabbing Gunner by the neck.

He expected a growl but got a whine as the dog sat then eased down at the edge of the blankets.

"Collie turn you out?"

Bret settled back down, fingers of one hand still woven in Gunner's wiry coat. Talking to a dog, especially talking to a dog as if expecting an answer, had to be a very bad sign. Then again, who was around to hear?

"She wants to go back out on the trail with me. She doesn't have to marry Kulp. She could wait and find someone better, but no, it's Kulp and misery or us and misery. And when I say 'us' I mean it. If I have to rope you and drag you off tomorrow, you're coming. You're not welcome here."

Bret stretched a little, finally feeling sleep coming on. "Not only that, you owe me. This business tonight proves you've been lying for weeks about waking me when the dream starts, so you owe me at least four dozen rabbits."

The dog sighed and rolled over. Bret fell asleep, his last thought of Hassie running with her arms out and the real smile on her face. She wasn't wearing trail clothes but the green dress. The skirt swirled. Bare legs flashed.

16

Bret was leaving this morning. Flipping, burning, and roiling, Hassie's stomach reflected her state of mind. She left the privy knowing she couldn't eat breakfast and unsure if she could help Belle prepare it.

Head down, lost in the darkness of her own unhappiness, she was unaware of Bret's presence until his hand closed around her upper arm and he pulled her around the side of the house.

"Why do you want to come with me?"

Her heart leapt, started banging away double time. Why would he ask such a thing? The slate was in the house, and she didn't want to go get it. "To be free."

He glared at her. "You know what I think? I think there's nothing wrong with your voice. You just speak Greek on purpose to drive me crazy."

"I'm sorry." This time she only mouthed it.

"No, you're not. You're pleased with yourself because you win. You can come, but only if we get a few things straight first."

She could go with him? If he didn't still have a hard hold on her arm, she might have fallen, the wave of relief that flooded through her was so strong. A thrumming, buzzing joy followed.

"You know you can't come back here in the fall and pick up where you left off. People make assumptions about a man and woman traveling together. Kulp will make assumptions."

Good. She didn't want to so much as see Ehren Kulp or any of those other men ever again.

"That means we'll have to find something else for you come fall, something that may not be as good. I'm still heading home to Missouri come first snow, and I can't take you there."

She knew that. Belle had been clear about what the Sterlings were like. Like Mama's family, they'd slam the door in her face.

"You have to do what I tell you, no matter what. If I say stay put, you stay put. No more running out on gangplanks because you think I need help."

She bobbed her head frantically, afraid a single nod wouldn't do.

"You're going to stop that fake smile business. I'm not some ogre who needs appeasing."

Her breath caught. He looked very much like an ogre who needed appeasing at the moment. Without thought, she started to force a smile, caught herself, and pressed her lips together.

"That's better. The same goes for running around trying to do things that are too much for you. Anything heavier than your saddle, I'll do the lifting. You can curry and groom to your heart's content."

She gave another small nod, waited.

"You're going to have to learn a few things to take care of yourself."

She had no idea what that meant and didn't care. She bobbed her head again.

"All right, I'll explain to Gabe and Belle and apologize over breakfast. You don't need to help with that."

He let go of her arm. She waited for more orders, but he just muttered, "Go on, get."

Unable to contain herself, she spun in place, hugged him, and ran inside.

Gabe and Belle didn't take the news well.

"You can't be serious," Belle said after Bret announced he was taking Hassie with him. "Do you think if she rides all over the country with you for another five, six months, you can bring her back here and the men who are interested now will feel the same?"

"No," Bret said. "I know she can't come back here. She knows it. We'll find something else come fall."

"Something else?" Belle's voice rose shrill. "What else? Where do you think you can just leave a woman when you're through with her?"

"Belle. I think the children are finished with their breakfasts." In contrast to his wife, Gabe spoke in soft, low tones, and with visible effort Belle got hold of herself.

She rose, wiped the children's hands and faces, and shooed them outside. Without another word, she began clearing the table. Hassie gathered her own empty plate and Bret's only to be shooed like the children.

"You need to pack," Belle said. "I'll do this."

Unsure, Hassie glanced at Bret.

"She's right," he said. "You get your things. I'll saddle up." He headed for the door, hesitated there. "There's room in the packs for a dress and whatever you need with it. Packie can stand that much more."

As soon as the door closed behind the men, Belle stopped fussing with the dishes and followed Hassie into the children's bedroom. "I can't believe you're doing this. How can you trade a secure future for—nothing?"

Hassie didn't try to answer. All she wanted to do was get out of the blue dress and into shirt and trousers, pack everything she'd brought here, and race outside so Bret wouldn't have to wait a minute for her.

He had already apologized for the time and effort his friends had wasted because of her, and whether anyone else had noticed or not, Hassie had seen him slip a gold coin into the sugar bowl.

"Do you understand what you're risking?" Belle asked.

Digging under the clothing she'd thrown on the bed, Hassie found the slate and pencil. She owed her own apologies. Belle had been kind. *"I do know. I'm sorry, but I have to do this. I <u>want</u> to do this."*

"Why? Maybe he's handsome, but you have to see what else he is. Doing the right thing in the war cost him too much. There's a hardness, an anger. There's nothing for you down this road but a broken heart. He won't go against that family, and they'd never accept you."

Hassie pulled off her chemise and bound her breasts, ignoring Belle's astonished gaze. Once decently covered, she pulled the pins from her hair, gave it a quick brush, and reached back to braid.

"Here, let me." Belle took the brush, sectioned Hassie's hair and fashioned a plait with swift efficiency. "There's something else I should tell you. Gabe and I, we knew from the time we were little that it would be the two of us. We just always knew, and it was like that for Bret and another girl. By the time I knew either of them, it was like that. He always loved her. He proposed as soon as he came of age."

Hassie stayed still, her head bent. Belle did not need to tell her this. Hassie had no fanciful illusions about Bret Sterling.

Belle had finished the braid but stayed behind Hassie as if she couldn't say what she wanted to face to face. "Her family, his family, they're Southerners, all of them. They came from Virginia originally. When Bret went for the Union, she broke the engagement and married...." Belle's voice broke, and Hassie heard her swallow. "She married somebody else as fast as she could, and it didn't make any difference to him. He still loves her, and if he ever marries, there will be three in the marriage bed."

Hassie remembered all too well how high passions had run before and during the war. Even so, all wars end. How could any girl turn her back on a man she loved over which side he chose? That girl could not have really loved Bret, and she must be stupid.

Not that it mattered. What would happen when Bret married was of no concern. Making him so impatient he left without her was. Fighting the urge to hurry, Hassie turned and hugged Belle.

"I enjoyed having you here," the other woman whispered. "I didn't mean what I said before. You can come back here. We can find something for you."

Grabbing the slate, Hassie all but scribbled, *"You know he will leave me in a safe place. I will write to you. Thank you for everything."*

Another hug and she was free. Free and running.

GABE HELPED BRET catch up the horses, brush off days of dust, and load Packie.

Finally, Gabe said, "What changed your mind?"

Bret checked the balance of the load on the packhorse again. Hassie's clothing wouldn't weigh enough to throw things off. "Did you ever wonder how I came to see how wrong slavery was when from the day I was born people who considered it the natural order of things spoon fed me their ideas?"

"I always hoped it was exposure to Chapmans."

"By the time I met you, I'd already made up my mind. One day I looked at the field hands out there working in the sun, and I wondered what it would be like to be one of them. After that I spent entire days spying on them, imagining it."

Gabe groaned. "You and your imagination. I still haven't forgiven you for the time you convinced me your horse could talk."

"Forgive me now. I've been visited with a dog that sees inside my head."

Gabe looked over to where Gunner and Collie lay side by side watching the proceedings.

"You can change your mind again and leave Hassie here, but the dog has to go."

"Don't worry. One way or another, he's coming with me."

"So you're telling me this time you imagined yourself into the skin of a female, a widowed, mute female. You didn't by any chance find out what it's like to be on the other side of...." Gabe rocked his hand suggestively.

Bret finished with the packhorse and started saddling Brownie. "No one would ever guess from your conversation you're a respectable husband and father. She said she wants to come with me. At first I figured she must be crazy, and then I started imagining what her life has been like, why she'd want such a thing."

"Maybe because she sees you as a better prospect than Ehren Kulp."

Bret shook his head. "There's no sign of that, and she's still half afraid of me."

"Why the hell would she be afraid of you? You helped her."

"I killed Rufus about thirty seconds after she first laid eyes on me, and she was standing no more than ten feet away."

"Oh."

"I lost my temper in Werver over that brothel business."

"Really lost it?"

"Really."

"Then I'm surprised she's not still hiding under a table."

"I dragged her out of town with me and didn't give her a chance to hide. So if she wants a few months of something different than what she's had, it won't hurt me to let her have it. She's not bad company."

Gabe put away currycomb and brush. "She's a fascinating conversationalist all right."

"Not your kind of woman," Bret said agreeably, remembering how he'd climbed trees and crossed creeks as a boy to get away from Belle's constant chatter. He tied off the latigo on Brownie, let the stirrup fall back in place, and smoothed saddle blankets on Jasper's back.

"Once Belle calms down she'll change her mind, you know," Gabe said. "If you can't figure out what else to do when you're done with her, bring her back, and we'll do what we can."

Bret shot Gabe a hard look. "It's not a matter of being done with her."

Gabe grinned. "You're the only man I know I'd believe that from, but damned if I don't believe it." The grin slowly faded. "Maybe while you're imagining, you should try imagining a life of your own. You can't keep this up forever."

Reaching under the horse for the cinch, Bret avoided Gabe's eyes. "I have been imagining that. I've been keeping a little for myself every year, you know. If you're right about race horses, maybe I'll be using it soon."

"I hope so. You keep this up much longer, and you won't be good for anything else."

The front door to the house opened, and Hassie appeared. She stopped a moment where the children were building forts in the dirt and put down everything in her arms. Her hands moved, fluttered, and waved, and the children imitated the motions. She hugged each one, picked up her things and continued on, almost running.

"I guess I'd better get back inside and rescue that double eagle you left in the sugar bowl before Sarah finds it and lays claim or Gabriel eats it," Gabe said. "You take care of yourself." His hand rested heavy on Bret's shoulder for a moment, and then he was gone, striding toward the house, nodding at Hassie and saying a few words as he passed her.

Hassie's arms were full. She'd brought the green dress. Good. He stored her things in the space left in one pannier, considered the balance of the load one last time, and decided he had it right.

"Check your cinch before you get on," he ordered, watching her dutifully check not just the cinch but her bedroll and saddlebags. Her breasts had disappeared again. Probably just as well.

By the time Bret finished with the packhorse, Hassie was mounted. She smiled the real smile at him, her face alight with eagerness, and Bret let himself enjoy the sight.

He swung up into his saddle and led the way down the farm lane. As they approached the town road, he turned and looked back. Hassie actually had Old Brownie keeping up. Gunner trotted alongside as if he'd never had ambitions of a romantic interlude.

Bret straightened in the saddle, a cynical smile curling his lips. Any owlhoot who saw them coming would probably just give up.

17

Cassie followed Bret west so filled with giddy joy she had trouble staying on Brownie. The urge to jump down, run, and spin filled her. The morning air was at its sweetest. The sky its bluest. The grass its greenest.

The rising heat of the day couldn't wilt her high spirits. When the sun beat down from straight overhead and Bret stopped and dismounted near a small stream, Hassie chomped her way through one of the sandwiches Belle had packed, several slices of dried apple, and two cookies.

She expected Bret to mount up and start out immediately after they ate. Instead he drew his pistol. Not the rifle he used for rabbits, or the shotgun he used for birds, but the pistol.

"This is as good a place as any for your first lesson," he said. "We'll start with this."

First lesson? Hassie looked from the gun in his hands to Bret's face. This morning he'd said something about learning to take care of herself. He couldn't have meant learning to shoot things. She didn't like guns. She didn't want to learn to shoot things.

"Have you ever shot a gun before? Pistol, rifle, shotgun?"

Her mouth went dry. Shooting things was what he meant. She needed to get the slate, tell him she didn't want any part of his guns.

And if she did that, he'd take her back to Belle and Gabe.

When he beckoned, she walked on stiff legs to stand beside him, half-listened as he showed her how to make the revolver break in two, how to eject the cartridges, how to put them back. She almost dropped the thing when he handed it to her. It weighed more than an iron.

If she didn't do this, he'd take her back.

She set her jaw, went through all the motions, lifted the gun the way he directed, and practiced pulling back the hammer and squeezing the trigger with the gun empty.

"Good," he said. "Now load it, aim at that little hump of ground over there, and squeeze the trigger."

Everything about it was terrible. The gun jumped in her hands like a live thing. The sound assaulted her ears. Fire spurted from the end of the barrel. The stench of gunpowder filled the air.

"Try it again."

She flinched as she pulled the trigger, but this time was better because she couldn't see the blast of fire through her closed eyelids.

Bret was patient through a dozen shots. "You'll get better with practice." He holstered the reloaded revolver, pulled up his right pant leg, and brought out another gun.

Hassie gaped at him.

"It's for emergencies," he said, "and since it's a smaller caliber, you may do better with it."

The smaller gun was only marginally less awful. Another dozen wavering, blind shots, and Bret took it back, shoved it in the holster in the top of his boot, and walked to Jasper.

Hassie watched him pull the rifle from its scabbard. No. He couldn't be serious. He could not want her to learn to shoot that too. She thought again of refusing, of how close they still were to Chapmans'. She took the rifle with trembling hands.

By the time Bret was satisfied, her hands had progressed from trembling to shaking. The shotgun was the worst of all. Bret claimed if she held it tight to her shoulder, what he called recoil wouldn't hurt, but he was wrong. Her shoulder hurt as if someone had hit her. She'd have a bruise there soon. Her wrists ached. Her jaw and teeth ached, and he was already talking about more practice tomorrow.

Hassie mounted Brownie, all giddiness gone. Had he done this on purpose, hoping she'd refuse and he could take her back to Belle and Gabe? If so, he was going to be disappointed. She would hate every minute of it, but if she had to, she would point the guns where he said to and pull the triggers.

Except for the guns, traveling with Bret was everything Hassie expected. In spite of her promise to obey Bret absolutely, all she saw was the freedom of it. No Ned Grimes complaining about her very existence, none of his sons trying to corner her in the barn to grope and steal a kiss. No husband so drunk he forgot a wife couldn't live on whiskey, so sick he needed constant nursing until exhaustion turned the world gray.

They traveled from one small town to another, zigzagging west across the state. In every town, every encounter on the trail, Bret fished for information. He talked to men in mercantiles, feed stores, and cafes, at blacksmiths and gunsmiths.

If a town had any safe place where Hassie could stay alone, he left her and spent a few hours in each saloon. For a man so reserved, he could be friendly when he wanted to—or needed to.

This was how he had found out about Rufus, she realized. Someone had noticed a man riding a horse with a US brand and received a dollar or two for the information. Or maybe the informant had just let it slip in conversation and never known.

Thieves and murderers, men who sold guns and whiskey to Indians, and deserters who had done something so egregious the army was willing to pay to get them back for court martial. Men like that were Bret's business, and before long he picked up the trail of a man who had robbed a general store, not a robbery that would usually have resulted in a reward, except this store included a post office, and the thief had robbed it too.

They caught up with the thief no more than fifty miles from the scene of his crime, broke and trying to peddle stamps from one end of a small town to another.

He tried to run when he realized who Bret was, stamps fluttering down around him.

Hassie was almost sorry when Bret turned the stamp thief over to the nearest U.S. Marshal. At least with a prisoner along, Bret didn't make her practice with his guns.

Better yet, as he went back to searching for another trail, he showed signs of accepting every blind shot she made was a waste of ammunition. Daily practice slipped to every two or three days, then once a week.

He still had every intention of enabling her to take care of herself, though. He proved it when he led her into a bank in Wichita on the way to pick up the horses and leave town.

"You need to sign this with your full name," he said, putting it down on the counter next to a pen and ink bottle.

A letter to Belle and Gabe? No, it was a letter to a bank in Missouri, and it directed the bank to take two hundred dollars from Bret's account and put it in a separate one in her name.

"They'll need a sample of your signature to set up your account," he said.

She didn't have the slate, but there were papers in slots under the counter. She reached for one and wrote on the back. *"Even if I should have half that reward, you know you have spent most of it on me by now."*

"You had forty dollars to start with."

"Not after you bought Brownie back."

"I didn't exactly buy her back."

"You bought a saddle and bridle."

His eyes bored into her. She wiped a clammy hand on her trousers, fighting the urge to just do what he wanted.

"We'll settle up at the end of the year."

"You say that, but you don't keep track."

He shrugged. "You keep track if you want to. If something happens to me, you need to be able to get that money. You don't have to go to the bank where the account is, you know. You can write a draft and take it to a bank wherever you are. It will take a while, but they'll give you the money. Here I'll show you." He pulled one of the papers from its slot.

Her clammy hands turned to ice. *"Nothing will happen to you."*

"Probably not. I've been doing this since the war, and I'm still here, but just in case. Sign it." He tapped his finger on the paper.

She signed the letter, and she didn't argue when he gave her a gold double eagle and told her to keep it handy.

As they rode out of town, she fingered the coin in her pocket, watching the material of Bret's shirt pull taut over his shoulders and the play of muscles along the length of his back when he bent forward to slap some pest off Jasper's neck. His profile was clear in the bright summer sunlight when he glanced over at Packie. Harsh, strong.

She huffed out a short breath, caught her bottom lip between her teeth. Imagining anything happening to him was like imagining the prairie opening up before them, swallowing them and the horses with a great crushing roar. What he did was dangerous. Yet somehow it never *seemed* dangerous because faced with Bret's icy eyes men like Zachary and Marshal Dauber faded away. Maybe she made her bed close to Bret's when he had a prisoner in custody, but that was caution, not fear.

She took her hand out of her pocket. He had been through four bloody years of war. He had been hunting men for six years since then, and he was fine. Nothing was going to happen to him.

18

Surprises came along now and then, but for the most part Hassie found Bret's way of hunting men followed a comforting pattern. Search for a trail, follow it, take a man prisoner, transport him to wherever necessary to collect the reward.

In a small town in Central Kansas, one of the surprises ran up to Bret on the street. "Is it true?" the girl gasped. "Is it true you're a bounty hunter?"

Bret nodded warily.

Petite and pretty in a washed out blonde sort of way, the girl never glanced at Hassie. "Then you go after Johnny Rankin. He talked about Colorado all the time. He was always talking about his friends in Fort Collins, Colorado!"

She held out a small square of paper until Bret took it, whirled, and ran away faster than she'd come. Bret unfolded the paper carefully. The poster had been opened and folded so often it was worn through along some of the creases. Hassie moved close, reading at the same time as Bret, enjoying the closeness as much as satisfying her curiosity.

Another thief. A three hundred dollar thief who had stolen thousands in jewels from the daughter of a man wealthy enough and angry enough to post a reward. At six feet and a hundred and sixty pounds, Rankin would be as tall as Bret. Would he be noticeably thinner?

Reading her thoughts again, Bret said, "If whoever put this out is right, he's on the scrawny side. Army put me at one eighty when I was younger than this."

Twenty-five, curly blond hair, blue eyes, thin.

"Strange to have a girl run up and hand him over like that," Bret said. "From the look of her dress, she never owned jewelry worth stealing, and the address on this poster is a town north of here."

Hassie agreed about both the jewelry and the dress, which had looked like a twin of the one Hassie had been wearing the day she first saw Bret. *"A different girl, and Hell hath no fury,"* she wrote.

Bret folded the poster and pocketed it. "I expect you're right. I better wire and make sure he's still on the loose before we start a wild goose chase. Fort Collins is a ways."

In fact Fort Collins lay far enough west to invoke another surprise. Two days later when they reached a town with a depot, Bret bought tickets on the Kansas Pacific Railway.

Brownie didn't load into a stock car on the train any better than she had onto the ferry. This time Hassie did stay put while Bret blindfolded the horse and other men shoved, shouted, and beat Brownie's rump with their hats until she scrambled up the ramp and into the car.

Gunner was easier. Bret ignored the dog's attempt at escape, picked him up, and carried him into the stock car. Hassie wished she could ride with them rather than in a passenger car where people would stare at her in her trousers, but Bret didn't have to carry her onto the train or tie her in place. His hand on her arm was enough.

BRET HALF-EXPECTED HASSIE to come running when he and the railroad men forced her reluctant horse into the stock car. The eyes he had to concede were something beyond bluish gray glimmered under a film of extra tears when he finally finished with the dog and joined her beside the tracks. He wanted to run his thumbs along her lower lashes and catch the tears. Instead he took her by the elbow and guided her toward a passenger car.

The car was battered, dirty, and hot. Hassie ought to save her wide-eyed, smiling wonder for her first sight of the luxury of a private car. Someday he'd show her one, find a way to get her a ride on one.

Bret caught that line of thought up short, closed his eyes, and pulled down his hat. At least the modern miracle of the steam engine would get them to Colorado fast.

What could Johnny Rankin have done to that girl to make her so determined to see him caught and sent to prison? Probably he squired her around for a while and then left her.

Bret shoved his hat back, straightened in the seat, and stared out the window as if what he saw was interesting, not a monotonous view of flat prairie all the way to the horizon. Modern miracle or not, if he couldn't control his own thoughts better than this, it was going to be one hell of a long ride to Colorado.

A day later, Bret left Hassie behind a locked hotel room door and began the search for Rankin. Fort Collins was no city, but it was big enough locating Rankin would have been hard if the man made any effort to hide. Young and brash, Rankin wasn't that smart.

Bret found the jewel thief bragging about his exploits at a faro table in a saloon. The only problem would be if Bret fell asleep at the bar waiting for Rankin to leave the table and walk out where he could be taken into custody without a sympathetic audience.

The dealer finally shut down the game as the first traces of dawn lightened the sky outside. Rankin stumbled into the street, half-drunk and fully pleased with his winnings and the attention of the woman steering him along the sidewalk. Bret moved in and slipped handcuffs on Rankin before he or his lady friend knew what was happening.

Getting Rankin away from the snarling, spitting woman was a challenge. When she kicked him in the shin, Bret stopped treating her like a lady, dumped her in a water trough, and dragged his prisoner away while she was still standing there, dripping and screeching.

Rankin protested in a slurred drawl. "You're makin' a mistake. You've got no call to arrest me. I never broke a law in my life except maybe spittin' on a sidewalk here and there."

"That's strange because there's a Kansas warrant out for you for robbery. So I'm taking you back, and you can argue what you did or didn't do back there."

"Kansas! Why I've hardly spent time there. I passed through, of course, on the way here. I have friends here who invited me to stay with them. Good friends."

Rankin was sobering up fast, and the last words carried less wronged indignation and more threat. Bret ignored it all. He'd been threatened by men who were better at it. Keeping one hand on Rankin and one on his gun, Bret guided his prisoner down the street to the town marshal's office.

Chairs sat on the walk there. Bret shoved Rankin into one and sank down beside him. No use waking anyone up this early. The marshal would show up soon and for a few dollars would store Rankin in a cell. Bret needed sleep, a bath, food. Tomorrow would be soon enough to start south to Denver and a train east.

When he arrived back at the jail the next day, Bret realized he was going to earn every penny of his three hundred dollars in aggravation. Two men about Rankin's age sat drinking coffee with the marshal—and Rankin. A washed up, clean-shaven Rankin whose suit showed no signs of drunken revelry.

"Is this a jail or a hotel for wanted men?" Bret asked, fighting to keep his voice level.

"It's hard to believe Johnny here is wanted except by every woman west of the Mississippi," the marshal said with a grin.

"It's all a misunderstanding," one of the others said belligerently. "Johnny explained it to us."

"He can explain it again to the court back in Kansas," Bret said. "I get paid whether they believe him or not."

The smaller of Rankin's friends jumped to his feet. "You're not taking Johnny anywhere, bounty hunter. Girls like him. It's nobody's business but his what some female gave him for his—services."

Bret stiff-armed the man in the chest, thumping him right back down into the chair he'd just left. The marshal restrained the fellow with hands on his shoulders. Before any of the others could react, Bret yanked Rankin up and cuffed him.

"Get in my way, and you'll get hurt," he said when the second friend took a few steps toward him. Bret shoved Rankin out the door, hoping the marshal could keep the others from doing anything stupid.

Out on the sidewalk, Bret paused a moment to be sure no one was charging after him and recognized worse trouble out here than inside.

Hassie sat on Brownie staring at Rankin, her lips slightly parted, expression arrested. Bret glanced at Rankin again, this time taking in the blond curls, clear blue eyes, tailored black suit, and friendly smile. Something hot and ugly stabbed right through Bret. His hands curled to fists.

Just one or two smashing blows and all those boyish good looks would disappear until long after they reached Kansas. Sure and then she'd probably weep over the damned thief and insist on holding a handkerchief to his bloody nose.

The extra horse Bret had bought that morning stood patiently at the hitch rail. He pushed Rankin toward it. "Get on."

Oh, yes, he was going to earn every penny of this reward at least twice over.

SHE COULDN'T STOP looking at him. Hassie had never seen such a handsome man, would never have believed such a boyish, almost angelic face could also be masculine. And he was friendly, polite, and his attitude toward her didn't change when he found out about her voice.

By the time they were on the train again, Hassie was more than half-angry at Bret. He was treating Johnny Rankin like a dangerous outlaw. Johnny had explained how the girl in Kansas befriended him and gave him a little of the jewelry she never wore anyway. She wanted him to sell it and use it for a good start in Colorado. He had sold it. His friends were holding the money for him, and he would pay that girl back if she'd changed her mind.

Bret didn't have to sit there with that disbelieving, cynical expression on his face. Whether it was a misunderstanding or whether Johnny really was lying, it wasn't as if he was a murderer, or even a stagecoach robber. He was a nice young man who had made a mistake.

They unloaded the horses and Gunner at the same Kansas depot where they'd started this trip, having traveled hundreds of miles in so short a time Hassie still had trouble believing it. Bret showed no interest in stopping in the town for so much as a meal, and he drove Johnny Rankin ahead of him the same way he did every prisoner. Johnny managed to throw Hassie one wistful glance over his shoulder.

For the first time, resentment over always bringing up the rear spread through Hassie. Brownie wasn't that slow any more. If Bret didn't work so hard at keeping his distance, he wouldn't mind her riding beside him. He'd talk to her now and then. If he weren't so set in his ways and hard-minded, he'd let her ride beside Johnny, who wouldn't mind talking to her.

When they stopped midday, her expectation proved true. Johnny did talk to her in that honey-smooth drawl. He was from Alabama, he said, laughing. He told her stories of places he'd been, and he didn't just chatter on either. She had to write her own words large on the slate for him to read over the distance Bret had set between them, but he nodded at her comments and questions, paid attention to them.

That night when they bedded down, Hassie didn't make her bed close to Bret. There was no need, and she didn't want to.

By the end of the second day traveling on horseback again, Bret had given serious consideration to shaking Hassie until whatever sense she had rattled back out of wherever she had misplaced it. He rejected the idea, but imagining it gave him considerable satisfaction. Of course, he could just order her to stay away from Rankin, but he could also imagine the resentment that would cause, and if she started holding her stomach again....

In Rankin's case, the solution Bret toyed with was shooting the lying, womanizing bastard right between the eyes and leaving him for the buzzards. That thought brought even more satisfaction until he went on to imagine Hassie cutting a lock of golden hair and putting it in that locket she wore around her neck, sobbing, wearing a black bandana around her arm in mourning until it rotted off in tatters.

Maybe Rankin was just taking advantage of what might be his last chance to charm a woman senseless before a spell in prison, but Bret doubted it. That sugar-tongued devil was bound to be working at getting Hassie to help him escape—either knowingly or by doing something she wouldn't recognize as dangerous until too late. Rankin only had another two days to subvert her.

No escape scheme of the pretty boy's was going to work, but if he succeeded in enlisting Hassie in the effort, things would change with Hassie. If Bret couldn't trust her, he'd have to take her back to Gabe and Belle or find somewhere else for her, and he didn't want to.

Sometime in the last weeks his original urge to crush the wide-eyed eagerness and softness out of her and make her acknowledge life's grim realities and unfairness had changed. The joy with which she approached the most simple things had wormed its way inside him and lightened the darkness.

Bret had no intention of letting a useless scoundrel like Johnny Rankin ruin the first summer since the war that didn't seem like one long, miserable slog. He decided to talk to Hassie first. If that didn't work, he really would tie her on that useless horse, shoot Rankin, and leave him where he fell. She'd get over it eventually.

AMONG THE RIDICULOUS things Bret did was keep Johnny away from the supper fire as if he might grab burning buffalo chips in his bare handcuffed hands and attack with them. With no trees to chain him to, Bret hauled a saddle over, and chained Johnny to that.

Upset by the unfairness of it all, Hassie kept Johnny company until supper was ready. After all Bret never wanted her help with supper anyway. Tonight, as Bret finished locking him to the saddle, Johnny joked about it.

"I guess I'm going to have to escape slowly," he said with a grin. "Very slowly."

Bret straightened, looming over Johnny and Hassie both. "You try to escape, and you'll find out if the ladies still love you with no front teeth and a crooked nose."

Hassie closed her eyes. Bret really had no call to be so mean about everything.

"I need to talk to you, Mrs. Petty," he said, crooking a finger. "Let's go over by the horses."

Uh oh. He was going to yell at her for being too friendly with a prisoner. He was going to give orders, and she'd promised to always do what he said. Her stomach clenched in a way it hadn't for weeks as she followed him.

Bret didn't have Johnny's angelic good looks. His gray eyes were flecked with black and somber, not a dancing, clear blue. His mouth was a firm line, not curled up at the corners with humor, and his features were harsh, not boyish. Her heart pounded too fast. For some reason she felt like crying.

He leaned against Jasper's rump and hooked his thumbs in his belt, his words like nothing she expected.

"When I got home from the war, everything was in ruins. Union soldiers tore things up because my family were Southern sympathizers with sons fighting for the Confederacy. Bushwhackers stole livestock and burned the house because of me—the son in the Union Army. So I headed west thinking about trying mining, finding some way to come up with enough to rebuild. And I didn't get too far before I overheard some talk about a fellow with a price on his head the folks in that area were helping hide out. That's what started me in this business."

The horse shifted, and Bret straightened. "I had good luck with a couple more men, and then I picked up a fellow wanted for robbery, a little robbery of a local stage line, nobody hurt. He was friendly, educated, interesting to talk to, and I had to take him quite a ways to get back to where he was wanted. I liked him, and I even had some sympathy for someone getting back from the war, no home, no job, no money. So I started letting him loose when we stopped so he could eat easier, things like that."

Bret stopped talking and tugged at his shirt, pulled it out of his trousers and his undershirt with it. Hassie stared at the exposed expanse of rib cage—and at the long scar between two ribs. Not a thick rope of scar like the one on her throat, but a thin, straight line.

"I still don't know where he got the knife. He left me to finish dying, took the horses and everything I had. Once I was up and around again, I couldn't pick up his trail. Never did."

Hassie wished she had brought the slate with her, wished she could ask how he'd survived. He seemed to guess her thoughts as he often did.

"I crawled for two days and was just lucky to cross the trail of some families moving west." He tucked his shirt back in. "Maybe Rankin is as innocent as the day he was born. He won't go straight to prison, you know. He can tell his side of the story to a judge and jury. But it will be better if he never gets near a knife."

He left her there among the horses and went back to the fire. Hassie threw her arms around Brownie, hugging the warm neck, breathing in the comforting, familiar horsey scent. She had thought he would be angry and give orders.

Telling her the story and not giving orders was worse. The burden of deciding what to do was on her now.

She thought back to the beginning, the hotel and brothel, the way he insisted half the bounty for Hammerill was hers, her joy when he let her leave Belle and Gabe's with him. She didn't believe Johnny Rankin was bad or dangerous, but she owed Bret and owed him more than gratitude. Respect for his experience had to be part of it. If anyone hurt him.... She shivered in spite of the heat of the summer day.

Her face was wet. She let go of Brownie and rubbed the tears away. Why couldn't he just once smile at her the way Johnny did? Because it would be foolish that's why. In spite of herself she was developing fanciful illusions, and he probably knew it.

Her slate and pencil were still back by Johnny. She went back to pick them up, unsure what to say or do.

"I bet he raked you over the coals and gave you your marching orders, didn't he?" Johnny said sympathetically.

"No orders," Hassie wrote, still unsure what to do. *"He only told me a story."*

"A story about the big, bad wolf, and how that wolf looks just like me, I bet."

Hassie shook her head. *"He is a good man. I'm sorry."*

She meant to write more, paused to consider her words, and caught a look on Johnny's face for an instant before he hid it.

The look was one she'd seen on many faces. Faces of men who called her "dummy" with a sneer, and this time there had been a trace of malice in with the scorn.

Backing away, she underlined the words already written. *"I'm sorry."*

"You're sorry all right. Sorry and stupid. I could have...."

Hassie didn't listen to the rest of it. She turned and walked away, hurried to help Bret carry what he needed to prepare supper to the fire.

Bret was right. Let Johnny Rankin try his charm on a judge and a jury. She hoped they would see through him faster than she had.

19

Two weeks after leaving Rankin to his fate, Hassie woke with a start, frightened for the instant it took to realize the shadow over her in the night was Bret.

"It's just me," he said softly. "It's starting to rain."

A tiny drop spattered on her cheek, so small it dried before another hit her chin. Bret had her slicker, spread it over her. "Go back to sleep." For a moment his hand curved around her shoulder, then he was gone.

The drops fell faster, wetting her face. She felt around for her hat, propped it so it protected her head, and pulled the slicker high. Going back to sleep could wait. For a while she wanted to stay awake, think about how he'd risen in the chilly night, brought both their slickers from where they were tied on their saddles, and covered her.

He could have just given her a shake and handed her the rolled up slicker to spread out herself, or waked her and told her to go get her slicker, or left her to wake on her own when she got wet enough. He didn't have to touch her shoulder that way, making her feel warm, cared for, and safe. The rain pattered down steadily now, the sound against her hat and slicker a soporific rhythm.

Breakfast would be on the damp side, she thought sleepily. Maybe even just crackers and dried fruit if it was so wet starting a fire would be more trouble than hot coffee was worth. The string of summer days marred by nothing but an occasional quick thunderstorm couldn't last forever, but the rain would probably stop by morning.

If she had her way, she'd give the army deserter who had led them back to Colorado a pardon—because the mountains here were the best place she'd ever been. She loved the crisp air, often scented with pine resin, loved the mountain vistas, the late summer days so much cooler than out on the plains, and the even cooler nights.

Since a pardon wasn't possible, she hoped Bret had to keep combing mining towns looking for the deserter for a long time. A little rain was nice. One cold breakfast wouldn't hurt, and when the skies cleared, they would be so blue it would seem holy and touch something deep in her heart.

Hassie fell asleep smiling.

Waking to a steady downpour in a dreary gray morning so cold her breath fogged destroyed Hassie's ideas about the quick return of blue skies. Merely turning her head brought cold water sluicing off her hat down her neck. Before she could pull on the boots Bret had, bless him, tucked under a corner of her slicker, everything she had on was damp. By the time she wrapped up in the slicker, damp had progressed to soggy.

The last town Bret had searched was a day's ride behind them, the one they'd been heading to half a day ahead. Half a day on a dry trail over firm ground.

"Nothing for it but to saddle up and keep going," Bret said philosophically as he dug their winter coats out of the packs.

Hassie nodded glumly. By the time she got the coat on under her slicker, it was damp too.

The rain sometimes slowed to a drizzle, sometimes came down in sheets, but never stopped. By noon, or what she guessed was noon since the sun never showed, Hassie was shivering.

The horses struggled in greasy mud that stuck to their hooves and was probably sucking off shoes. If anyone else had traveled this way recently, their tracks had long ago been washed away.

A tantalizing hint of wood smoke hung in the air once, giving thoughts of shelter in some generous soul's cabin or barn. Bret caught it too, for he stopped and studied the pine forest on each side of the road, but after a minute he shook his head and pushed on.

Hassie understood. She couldn't pinpoint the direction the smoke came from either. Finding the source in the heavy forest and rain would be impossible.

By the time they reached the town of Silver Creek, her teeth chattered. She had hours ago withdrawn her thoughts of pardoning the army deserter for anything and moved on to reconsidering her feelings for Colorado, the mountains, and everything west of Missouri.

Bret reined up in front of a building with a hotel sign and dismounted. Gunner crawled under a bench along the front of the building, looking as miserable as Hassie felt. She lifted her head a quarter inch up from her collar and peered through the rain at Bret in surprise. He always went to a stable first, always took care of the horses first.

He reached up to help her off the horse without explanation, and she used his help gratefully. Cold and stiff as she was, getting down on her own might mean taking a header into the mud.

Built of rough lumber, painfully plain, and as dark as the day, the hotel had only warmth to recommend it. An iron stove radiated heat in the middle of the small lobby, and Hassie couldn't get to it fast enough.

The two men playing checkers at a table on the other side of the stove glanced up and went back to their game. One thing about her dripping slicker, it reached to the floor and hid her unconventional, unfemale clothing.

She pulled off her sodden gloves, shoved them in a pocket, and held her cold, red hands out to the stove.

Dripping every step of the way, Bret squelched his way to the desk at the back of the room. Hassie tried not to look at the puddle forming at her own feet. The unfinished bare wood floor was probably a wise choice in these parts if it rained like this often. For the first time Hassie considered the mountains in winter—snow, wind, bitter cold. She sidled a little closer to the stove and leaned in.

Click, click, click, one of the checker men jumped his red disc over every remaining black checker on the board and swept them all away.

"Ha! That's three in a row for me. You set up again and reconsider your strategy while I take care of these folks." He rose and ambled to the desk, a short, gray-haired man who pushed a lot of stomach ahead of him.

He was the proprietor and a chatty, nosy sort. Hassie smiled, half-asleep on her feet as she listened to Mr. Phineas Vance commiserate with Bret about the weather and work at prying more information out of Bret than his name.

"We need two rooms," Bret said after finally admitting the direction they'd come from and that they'd been on the trail since first light.

"Sorry, this weather has driven a lot of folks off the trail. I've only got one room left."

"Fine. Mrs. Petty will have that, and I suppose you can manage a hot bath for her."

The changed tone of Mr. Vance's next words woke Hassie right up. She'd heard that tone before, knew what was coming, and knew Bret was in no mood to be politic about it.

"You said your name is Sterling," Vance said.

"It is. Mrs. Petty is a widow traveling with me."

"This is a respectable hotel. I don't rent to women in trade."

"Good. Mrs. Petty is a respectable widow, and you're renting to her." The low fury in Bret's voice was as much of a threat as waving a gun. So far it had never gotten to that, but hotels were usually happy to rent two rooms after a token protest.

Phineas Vance showed no sign of being intimidated. His checker-playing friend rose and moved stealthily toward the rifles hanging on the back wall.

Hassie made an inarticulate sound of fear, and Bret looked back. All he said was, "Don't," and the checker player froze in place.

Bret moved to where he had both men in sight. Vance braced his arms on the desk and leaned forward. "Threaten me, beat me, shoot me. If you want the room, you can have it, but your woman can't stay here."

"She isn't my woman," Bret said through his teeth.

"By your own words, she isn't your wife either."

"Is there another place in town to get a room?"

"There's a rooming house at the other end of the street. Four men to a bed."

Vance straightened and took a step back as he said it, as well he might. Hassie half-expected Bret to go over the desk and grab the man by the throat.

"I mean a safe place for a woman, and you know it, you self-righteous prig."

"There's a big white house at the end of First Street where women live. Maybe they'll rent her a room."

The checker player giggled. Hassie couldn't see Bret's eyes turn to ice but knew they did. Vance and his friend both flinched as Bret's hand snaked under his slicker, but the hand came out with a gold coin, not a gun. Bret slapped the coin down on the desk. "As of right now that room is mine. You hold it. You come up with a hot bath by the time I get back here. Where's the nearest preacher?"

The two men stared at him with twin expressions of amazement, their mouths half open. As seconds ticked by, Hassie realized hers was open too, closed it, and started for Bret. He met her halfway, one hand closing around her upper arm in a familiar, steely grip.

"Where!"

The checker player pointed. "Third Street. Turn right on Third. First house after the church."

Bret marched her past the hunched, dripping horses and along the walk in the direction the checker player had pointed.

"No!" Hassie pulled back against him. He couldn't pretend not to understand that word.

He stopped and pulled her into the shelter of a doorway. "We're going to be stuck here for days. If the rain stopped right now, it would still be another day before the mud dried up, and it's not going to stop. So there's not a thing we can do except satisfy that narrow-minded, self-righteous little pis—prig."

Even if she had the slate, by the time she wrote one word, it would be too wet to write a second. She mimed sleeping with both hands folded beside her bent head, then pointed at the horses.

"No, you're not sleeping in the stables. The only way you'd be safe is if I slept there too, and I'm not sleeping in a cold hay loft when there's a warm, dry room with a bed in that hotel. It's not like we'll really be married. We'll say some words, get a piece of paper to show Vance, and we'll both be warm and dry tonight. We'll bundle."

She wanted to argue, make him see how insane this was, but had no way to do it. As if he understood, he looked at the sign on the door behind them. Assayer.

"That will work," he muttered, as he opened the door and led the way inside. "We need paper and a pencil," he said to the man who looked up from his desk when they walked in.

The assayer handed over the paper and pencil willingly enough then stood at the counter, curious and not trying to hide it. Bret sent him back to the desk with a look.

Hassie and Bret both bent over the paper on the counter, heads close together.

"We cannot marry for a hotel room," Hassie wrote. In small letters because she suspected she might need every bit of the paper and both sides.

"I told you. It won't be real, just some words."

His voice was a lovely low rumble, all signs of temper gone. Hassie had to remind herself to pay attention to the meaning, not the sound.

"Those words are vows before God."

"God will know we don't mean them."

"How will He know that?"

"Omniscient. Don't you ever listen in church?"

"It's not right."

"Not letting us have that room isn't right. No decent man would turn any woman out in this weather. You want to set up camp on the mountain?"

She didn't have to answer that. The very thought started her shivering again. *"You will want to marry for real some day."*

"More likely you will, and a few white lies in this town won't make any difference. The whole place will disappear when the silver runs out."

"I cannot lie to God."

He rubbed a hand over his face, and she wanted to take the words back. He was as cold and tired as she was. More probably. He'd been up in the night taking care of things, taking care of her. What would it hurt to do what he wanted?

"Things were easier when you were afraid of me."

She laughed, not much of a laugh but a laugh.

He straightened and half-turned as if to leave, and she thought he'd changed his mind, but after a moment he leaned down again. "All right. Don't think of it as lying. We'll be married on paper for the rest of the season. I'm so tired of raised eyebrows and snide remarks I'm going to shoot someone over the way they act about you soon, and this will save me the bullet. Come fall I'll do whatever's necessary to get it annulled. You know it's not a real marriage until we do more than bundle."

Hassie stared blindly down at the paper, feeling heat rush across her face.

"Yep, you know." His knuckles brushed her cheek. "What do you say? Let's make the next couple of months easier."

She nodded, crumpled the paper, and put it in a pocket. At least he had asked, talked her into it. Cyrus had just taken her to church, and the preacher had said the words without requiring any sign of a yes, no, or maybe from her.

She was going to get married in trousers and a dripping slicker with days of trail dirt and mud on her. She was going to be Mrs. Breton J. Sterling for a couple of months. On paper.

At least he asked.

20

Cassie crowded close to Bret on the stoop of the first house past the church, convinced Bret's knock would summon a huge man with a long white beard who would point an accusing finger at them and spout Scripture, starting with the Third Commandment and probably giving the Ninth at least a mention.

To her surprise, a thin young man opened the door and regarded them nervously until Bret explained their purpose.

"Oh, yes, a marriage. That's good news. I was afraid it would be a funeral. Cave-ins, all this mud, you know. Do you mind waiting in the church? My wife is trying to cope with children who have been cooped up inside all day." He no more than finished the words than an unhappy wail sounded from deeper in the house, joined almost immediately by another.

"The church is unlocked," he said. "I always leave it unlocked. I'll get Mr. and Mrs. Zane from next door. They've done this before."

The preacher, who had still not mentioned his own name, was still babbling away as he draped an oilskin over his shoulders and started for the next house along the way.

The church was another plain building, benches instead of pews, everything made from raw lumber, including the cross at the front. Bret lit two of the lamps along the wall. His breath puffed white in the cold air as he did it, but at least when he finished, the soft yellow glow of the lamps gave an illusion of warmth.

Hassie sank down on one of the benches. Bret sat beside her.

"There were times in the war when I was wetter, colder, and tireder," he said, "but not many, and I was younger then."

He wasn't exactly ancient now. Hassie flashed all her fingers at him three times and gave him a questioning look.

"Thirty-one last month," he said. "How about you?"

Birthdays hadn't mattered for so long she had to consider before flashing ten fingers twice then six more.

He nodded, leaned forward with his forearms on his thighs and said no more until voices sounded outside, the door opened, and three figures shrouded from head to toe in rain gear approached.

Everyone was cheerful, sympathetic about Hassie's voice.

"A good, strong head bob will do fine," the preacher declared. "Now do you have a ring?"

"No," Bret said.

Hassie nodded yes, pulled the chain with Mama's locket and wedding ring out from around her neck, and felt for the catch so she could take the ring off the chain.

"You're not using your old wedding ring," Bret said.

She tapped the locket, but for once he showed no sign of understanding.

"No. I'll buy you one of your own tomorrow if you want one, but you're not wearing that."

The preacher and his neighbors lost their cheerful expressions. Hassie fingered the ring sadly. Using it for a lie would be wrong anyway. She tucked the chain back under her shirt and smiled brightly at everyone.

The ceremony took no time at all. Bret folded the piece of paper they needed into an inner pocket and brought smiles back to everyone's faces with gifts of a few dollars.

Taking Bret's offered arm on the way back to the hotel, Hassie leaned in, needing the support. Her fatigue had reached the point she staggered a little now and then.

Nothing else moved in the town. The only sounds were of water pouring off roofs and pattering against their slickers. Their boots thunked wetly on the sodden boards of the sidewalk.

For bad weather on a wedding day to matter, the marriage would have to be real, Hassie assured herself. Besides, she didn't believe in superstition and portents. The sun had been shining when Cyrus married her.

BRET SLAPPED THE marriage certificate on the hotel desk under Phineas Vance's nose. Nailing it to the man's forehead would be better, but this would have to do.

"Is Mrs. Sterling's bath ready?"

"You really...?" The little man picked up the certificate and held it long enough to read every word twice before glancing over at his checker-playing friend as if hoping for help. Letting the paper flutter to the desk, he sighed in defeat.

"No, I didn't draw a bath, but it's a matter of minutes. We have a boiler, you see. Hot water on tap."

"Fine. The room better be clean, and the bed better have clean sheets on it."

Vance straightened, the same stubborn look as earlier appearing. "Of course the room is clean. If it doesn't meet your satisfaction...."

"Don't," Bret said softly.

Finally showing a modicum of sense, Vance didn't.

A few minutes later, Bret was finally able to return to the horses where they stood tied in front of the hotel, heads low, backs hunched, and angled as much as possible to keep their tails to the wind. He untied all three animals and eyed his saddle with disfavor. Wet as he was, settling his ass on leather the rain was running off in rivulets held no appeal. Neither did leading the horses through ankle-deep muck in the street.

Blowing out a heartfelt sigh, or maybe a groan, he mounted and reined Jasper toward the livery stable.

By now Hassie ought to be up to her chin in hot water. The lock on the door of the first-floor room where they kept the tub wouldn't have been enough for him to leave Hassie alone there, although it was hard to imagine Vance the moralizer bothering a woman.

Still, there was the checker-playing friend to consider, so better safe than sorry. Making sure those two saw and heard Bret give Hassie his revolver took care of any potential problems. They didn't have to know Hassie would dive through the window naked and start running before she'd pick up the gun voluntarily.

Picturing her doing just that restored a little good humor, and picturing her in the tin tub, steam rising, skin turning pink, almost warmed him in spite of the cold rain in his face. It might even heat some parts if they weren't encased in cold, damp cloth and resting against a cold, wet saddle.

He shouldn't have gotten touchy with her over the ring, but how could she expect him to put Cyrus Petty's ring back on her finger, even if they were playacting at marrying? And if this rain kept up for days, which seemed more likely than not, how was he going to sleep in the same bed with her when he wasn't exhausted and keep his hands off her? Sleep on the damned floor probably.

The days wouldn't be much better. Hours in a small room with her except for meals. He could spend most of it in a saloon, but coming back to her with a few drinks in him would be a bad idea. Considering the drunkard of a husband, a very bad idea.

He rode right to the door of the livery. After taking care of the horses, he would get back to the hotel and clean up, and they still needed to eat. Tonight would be no problem. The only problem tonight would be not falling asleep in the bath and drowning.

Their hotel room was like the lobby downstairs, plain, rough, and new. The bed, a wood chair, the washstand, a battered bureau, and a small coal stove barely fit in the small space.

The luxury of the stove was the reason her hair was almost dry. Mr. Vance charged extra to use the stove, of course, but things like that never bothered Bret.

Hassie gave her hair one last stroke with the brush and stared at the bed. Bret would be back soon. He looked almost as exhausted as she felt. His muttered excuse about a last look around was just that, an excuse to leave her alone to get ready for bed. If only she could decide how to do that.

Would sleeping in her clothes make him think she didn't trust him to keep his hands to himself? Would putting on her nightgown seem like an invitation? And what was she going to do if he decided married was married?

If she had learned anything from Ned Grimes' boys it was that men were more than willing to couple with any woman, willing or unwilling, and didn't think it had anything to do with love or marriage. Belle's warnings about Bret had burned their way into Hassie's mind, but sometimes when he did things like cover her against the rain in the night and touch her shoulder the way he did, she just wanted to burrow in against him and forget about warnings and consequences.

Tired of her own indecision, too physically exhausted to stay upright, Hassie took off her boots, suspenders, and bandana and got into bed. At least she'd left the binding off her breasts after her bath. On the trail, loosening the knots often proved too difficult and she left it.

She lay quiet, wishing sleep would come. If she were sound asleep when he returned, he'd put out the lamp, get into bed beside her, and fall asleep the second his head hit the pillow. If he would just get back here, she could stop worrying and wondering.

Bundling. She'd heard of that. It required a board down the middle of the bed, which was ridiculous. She smiled at the thought of him dragging some big long board up the stairs. Wet board. Her smile disappeared, and she shivered.

Footsteps in the hall. The sound of the key turning and door opening. She kept her eyes closed, determined to pretend to be asleep. Boots sounded on the bare floorboards, so did clicking, clicking, the scent of—wet dog. Hassie's eyes flew open, and she sat up.

Bedraggled and still wet, Gunner didn't waste a glance on her and curled up so close to the stove his hair would probably singe.

Bret sat on the chair to pull off his boots. "The checker boys had a few drinks with the last games, and when Vance started locking up, he found a window half-open and a big puddle underneath. Somehow Gunner slipped through the door right when old Vance was getting a mop. I figure what he doesn't know won't hurt him."

And how exactly had Bret opened a window without anyone noticing? Not only that.... Hassie made a wing of one arm and imitated Gunner lifting his leg.

"No, he and I had to go over the rules his first time in a hotel. He's fine."

His first time. Maybe tomorrow she'd ask.

Bret dropped a bedroll, the blanket stuffed plump with who knew what onto the bed. Not a board but a barrier of sorts. He blew out the light, moved around in the dark for a few minutes, and then the mattress sank under his weight.

"If I get—rude in my sleep, just pinch me hard."

Hassie rolled so her back was to him, not sure if she felt more like laughing or crying. The thought of pinching him held no appeal, but she wished she had the nerve to smack him a few times with that bedroll.

She woke once in the night to the sound of rain lashing hard on the windows. Her head was pillowed on the bedroll, her nose against Bret's shoulder, her hand on his arm. For long seconds she barely breathed. He should pinch her. She should ease away back to her own side of the bed.

He smelled good, clean shirt, soap, warm musky male, and he was sound asleep. If she drew away, she'd probably smell Gunner again, and after all Bret himself had said what someone didn't know wouldn't hurt him. She nestled in a little more comfortably, a little closer, and went back to sleep.

BRET WOKE FROM an erotic dream of Hassie running across the prairie covered by nothing but her hair, which didn't cover much because it flowed out behind her like a molten black river.

Small wonder his body was vibrating, throbbing, screaming with desire. Hassie's reaction to a man beside her in bed hadn't changed since the first time he'd tried it. The covers were down around her waist, and most of her upper body was over the bedroll.

Her head rested warm and heavy on his shoulder and chest. The palm of her one hand spread across the other side of his chest, centered over a nipple and burning a deeper brand with every breath. Her breasts were back. He knew that for certain because one pressed against his side.

The pounding of his heart ought to wake her. Or the way his every breath rocked her. Rocked. He gritted his teeth and tried to find a way to ease her back enough to slide out from under. The hand he intended for her ribs cupped her breast instead, obeying instinct, not logic.

She'd filled out since that time he'd gotten such a good look at the front of her. The breast was still small, but not too small, a good size really, firm yet soft. The nipple pushed up against his palm with no effort on his part. She made a soft sound in her throat he had no trouble interpreting.

His treacherous hand left her breast and picked up a lock of hair. Silky, and as black as in the dream.

Another weight pressed against his ankle. Gunner's head. The dog stood there staring hopefully, tail waving slowly back and forth. Smothering a groan, Bret lifted Hassie enough to move her from his chest to the bedroll and pillow, sat up, and rested his head in his hands until he had some semblance of control.

"I should have shot you when I had the chance," he muttered at Gunner as he pulled on his boots.

Vance was nowhere to be seen in the lobby, the front door still locked. Bret raised the same window he'd opened last night, lifted Gunner through, climbed out after him, and closed it behind them. If Vance found it open again, he might sit up tonight with a shotgun.

The rain had eased to a heavy mist, fog obscuring everything more than a few feet away. Bret followed Gunner into the forest south of town, joined the dog in watering a tree, and leaned against another, waiting for the dog to finish any more serious business.

The mist thickened and turned back into drizzle. If anyone were taking bets, Bret's money would be on at least two more days of rain. Figure a day after that before traveling on the steep roads wouldn't risk the horses' legs in the mud.

For the next three days or more, he'd better find some way to control himself around Hassie Ahearne Petty Sterling. His wife. If Gabe knew about this, he'd roll with laughter, and the mud wouldn't stop him.

As he waited, Bret speculated how his family would react if they knew he'd just married the widow of an impoverished, drunken moonshiner, much less the Irish widow of such a blot on humanity. He'd betrayed them and everything they believed in once because his conscience left him no choice. Would they consider a marriage like this another betrayal or just one more typical disappointment from a disappointing son?

And Mary.... He yanked his collar higher, hunched his shoulders. He didn't want to think about Mary.

None of it mattered anyway. A few words didn't make it a marriage. He'd find Hassie a safe place for the winter, take her back to Gabe and Belle if he had to. She could marry for real, marry someone the war hadn't carved hollow, left with regret he could never overcome, obligations he could never meet.

He should have just lied to people like Vance from the beginning, named her as his wife and avoided the indignation of the righteous. After all, Vance wasn't the first one with an attitude. He was just the first one so eager to be a martyr to his principles he couldn't be intimidated.

Lying to a little man like that wouldn't have been much of a sin. Not like lying to God, and where did she come up with notions like that?

So why hadn't he taken the easy way from the beginning? Bret tipped his head back, closed his eyes, and let the rain stream cold over his face. Because for as long as he could remember thinking of any woman but Mary in the context of wife was impossible. Why he could do it now eluded him.

He could have found some other place to spend the night. The preacher would have let them stay in the church—dry but not warm—and not good enough. She'd had so little in her life and still ran at the sun with her arms open and smiled more often than not, even if the smile wasn't always real. She hummed doing menial work, picked wildflowers and wrapped them around the neck of that sorry dog who had better get his ass back here soon if he wanted breakfast.

She deserved what little he could give her. More.

His lust didn't signify. He'd react that way to any female with most of her teeth who didn't outweigh him. The thought of Belle, chattering away, popped into his mind. After that came the image of his sister Vicky's friend who whined like an out of tune fiddle every time she opened her mouth.

So, not quite any female, but a high percentage.

He'd just be careful around her for the next few days, spend the days in the barbershop, around the stove at the general store, and anywhere else men gathered and gossiped. Nights in the saloons. He wouldn't have to drink much.

She'd be bored in the hotel room alone, though. What good was warm and dry if she was going out of her mind with boredom? And what difference would it make if he indulged his curiosity about where she came from and her life in Missouri a little? He could spend some time with her. Just enough to....

A whine brought Bret out of his reverie. Gunner sat a few feet away, canine misery all over his bedraggled face. As soon as he had Bret's attention, he raised one paw and whined again.

"You are the worst liar I ever met. You're the one kept me waiting, and you're sleeping under that bench tonight. I don't care how cold it gets."

The dog wagged a wet tail, unimpressed by the threat. Bret followed him back to the hotel and Hassie for-a-few-months Sterling.

21

Cassie expected Bret to abandon her in the hotel room with her Bible and the newspaper they'd bought after breakfast as her only companions. Instead he led her on a leisurely tour of the few shops in the town.

"I don't see a jewelry shop," he said. "I'll buy you a ring as soon as we get some place that has one."

"Please don't do that. I don't want a ring."

"You wanted one enough to offer up Petty's yesterday."

They were in the town's general store and so were a lot of other people. At least the nosy ones could only overhear Bret's half of their conversation. *"The ring was Mama's. I shouldn't have done that. You were right. Please don't buy a ring."*

"I'm surprised Grimes let you have the ring. He sounds more like the sort to keep it and sell it or give it to the next wife."

She had to write and erase and write again to explain, but she wanted him to know. *"Mama never let him see the ring. It was hers from Papa. The locket was from her other life. She gave them to me to keep when she was sick, and I never let anyone see them until Mrs. Reston took them."*

Bret toyed with a bottle of patent medicine, not looking at her. "I'm sorry I fussed at you then. If I knew that, I would have used it."

"No. You were right. It's better not to have a ring for what we're doing, and Mama's ring...." She stopped there and shrugged, not wanting to put into words that the ring was too precious to be used for a lie.

He put down the bottle with a sharp click. "Then suppose we get you another dress. The one you've got on is all wrinkles, and there's no way to get it pressed with you in it."

She didn't need another dress either, but if buying one would make him forget about the ring, she was more than willing. He bought her the only likely dress in the store, a pretty pink cotton, and a pink hat that matched well but wouldn't survive a week in the packs.

They didn't return to the hotel until after lunch at the same restaurant where they'd had breakfast. Hassie expected, having done his duty by her, Bret would now disappear until supper time. She had stripped off her slicker first thing on returning to the room and draped it over the washstand to dry. Bret still wore his as he stood staring out the window.

Hassie put her new dress away and stirred the fire in the stove, waiting for Bret to take his leave. When he finally moved, it was to take off his slicker. He spread it over the chair and sat on the bed.

"How did you learn those signs you use? Did you and your mother make them up?"

She didn't care if only rain and boredom made him interested. She grabbed the slate and sat beside him, writing, erasing, writing more. *"After I was hurt, Mama was sure I could talk again if I tried hard enough, but it never got better, and my throat gets sore if I talk much. So when Mama read in the paper about a school for deaf children in Connecticut where they teach sign language, she wrote to the school, and they sent pamphlets with pictures."*

"Your mother sounds like a force of nature."

Hassie nodded. That was a good description of Mama all right.

"Did she immigrate from Ireland, or was she born here?"

"Mama's family was in Philadelphia before the Revolution. Papa was from Ireland."

He hid any surprise well. The only sign she saw was a slight jerk of his head. "So how did they ever meet, much less marry?"

"Mama's family were...." She hesitated, pencil poised. She couldn't very well say, "rich snobs like your family," but she did want to be honest. "...wealthy. They had a big house in the city and another in the country, and Papa worked at the country house."

"So they ran off together, and her family disowned her."

She nodded, rolling the pencil back and forth between her fingers.

"How did the daughter of an Irishman and an upper crust Philadelphian get a name like Hassie?"

"Mama wanted Cordelia, and Papa wanted Maeve. They compromised on a plain American name." Very plain. Hassie wouldn't mind being Maeve, but she wouldn't have liked Cordelia.

"Did her family help the two of you after your father died?"

For a moment, Hassie continued playing with the pencil, deciding whether to tell him about that awful day, what to tell him. He would sympathize with Mama's family, and when he did that, it would kill most of her fanciful illusions, and that would be a good thing.

"After Papa died, Mama and I both put on our best dresses. She took me to meet her family. A man came to the door dressed in a very fine suit. I thought he was my grandfather, but Mama called him by his given name, and then I knew, no, he was a servant. He looked sad and called her Miss Julia, but he said we couldn't come in. Mama pushed past him. He caught me and held me by the door. I heard shouting. Mama came back and we left. She wrote an advertisement for the newspaper after that. Three men answered, and she wrote back. Mr. Grimes was the only one who said she could bring me."

There. Now he knew. She waited for him to say something that showed he understood her mother's family or as if being related to them made her marginally more acceptable than being only the daughter of poor Irish immigrants.

"Do you think she regretted what she did? Did she ever say?"

"Before she died, she said the only thing she would change was Mr. Grimes."

Bret laughed, looking as surprised at himself as she was, and doing nothing to squelch her fanciful illusions. "Mr. Grimes sounds as if he could be improved in many ways. Did he learn the signs you wave around at the dog and horses?"

"No. Mr. Grimes had no interest. His sons were curious but never learned."

Gunner and Brownie understood as much as any of the Grimes family ever did, which was nothing. The sad truth was she signed just for practice, just to remember, even though it would never matter again.

"What about your husband?"

She shook her head, wanting to change the subject, wishing she hadn't noticed Bret still considered Cyrus her husband in spite of what they had done yesterday.

"So you wrote things for him, managed the way we do."

"No, Cyrus couldn't read."

If she asked about the Sterling family, would he tell her? Belle didn't like the Sterlings, so maybe some of the things she said weren't true. Hassie stared at her own last words on the slate. Now would be a perfect time to ask. Maybe he would tell her. More likely he'd walk out the way he did when *she* laughed.

Right now he studied her intently with an expression she hadn't seen before. "How many of those signs for letters of the alphabet could I learn between now and supper time?"

Hassie's heart leapt then steadied. The two times the Grimes boys said they wanted to learn, they never got past D and forgot that by the next day.

"6."

"Huh. Gunner could learn six in that much time. The checker boys downstairs could learn six."

Hassie moved his slicker over by hers, sat in the chair so she could face him and started, her hands trembling as she formed the A. Bret didn't just watch her the way Mama and the Grimes boys had. He imitated her, showing her what her own signs looked like from his perspective.

Watching him calmed her. His hands were so elegant, tanned, strong. His fingers were agile, mesmerizing.

By supper time Bret could not only recognize the signs up to J reliably, he could flash them at her. By the time they both were yawning and ready for bed, he was halfway through the alphabet.

Before they could turn in, they had to get Gunner, of course. This time Hassie slipped the dog up the stairs while Bret flattered Mr. Vance into demonstrating how the hotel's hot water supply worked.

All in all the only disappointment of the day came when Bret arranged blankets on the floor instead of using them for a bundling barrier. "Bed's too small," was all he said.

The bed wasn't any smaller than the night before, but it was colder.

BY THE END of the next day, Bret had mastered the alphabet. Hassie couldn't believe it. She and Mama hadn't learned so fast. Of course she and Mama hadn't had long, rain-filled days with nothing else to do.

Some of the miners and other people in town nodded to them now, spoke a greeting. The owner of the only restaurant Bret was willing to take her to wasn't so friendly even though they were eating there three times a day. The restaurant provided no choice of fare. Everyone ate what the owner chose to cook and that was that.

"Venison stew tonight," the owner said as he smacked two cups on the table and poured coffee, slopping it all over.

Bret signed at her as the man stomped off.

"C-l-u-m-s-y a-n-d r-u-d-e."

The meaning of the words hardly registered as the wonder of what he'd just done hit her. She reached out and touched the back of his hand, pulled back, met his eyes.

His cynical smile didn't change the gleam of knowledge in his eyes. He knew full well what he'd done.

They had a private language. The intimacy of it took her breath away.

Her eyes puddled.

"D-o-n-t d-o n-o-t." He frowned. "Is there an apostrophe?"

She forgot herself and laughed, and at least here in the restaurant it didn't make him get up and leave. In fact one side of his mouth curled past the smile in a grin.

"If there isn't, I'm going to use this," he said, hooking his right index finger through the air.

Outside the rain drizzled down. Inside Hassie felt the sun breaking out from behind black clouds, a door long locked swinging open.

He made everything better. She couldn't bear the thought of being left somewhere when winter came and never seeing him again. Wherever he left her for the winter, there had to be a way to persuade him to come back for her in the spring.

Asking him now would be too dangerous. What if he said no?

THE RAIN STOPPED during the next night. They'd have to see how fast the mud dried Bret told her, but one more day ought to be enough. Hassie almost wished the mud would stay too deep and treacherous for another day or two. Staying in one place held a new allure after the months of constant travel.

The late summer sun beat down as if frost had not threatened just the day before. The hard-packed clay in front of the livery stable had dried out enough to be firm. Hassie wiped the last traces of saddle soap off Brownie's saddle and bridle. Bret had already finished with Jasper and Packie's gear, but she didn't care if she was slower. She liked rubbing the soap in circles, turning leather that had dried stiff after the soaking rain supple again.

"Not too much now," Bret cautioned, handing her the can of neat's-foot oil. "Just a thin coat."

She nodded and poured a little oil on her rag.

"I'll be back in a minute," he said. "I'm going to check the horses and make sure no shoes are loose—or gone."

He headed back behind the stable where the horses were penned. Hassie hummed as she spread a thin coat of oil along each rein of the bridle.

The stable owner and a red-haired man appeared in the doorway. She smiled and nodded but kept working.

"So that's the bounty hunter's whore," the redhead said.

Hassie's hand only hesitated for a second before she continued oiling the bridle as if she hadn't heard. Long ago she'd learned how many people believed if she couldn't speak, she couldn't hear. After what they'd said, it would be better if these men never found out they were wrong. If either of them came near her, she was going to use the tin whistle that hung on a cord around her neck along with Mama's locket on the chain.

"They're married now. Phineas is right proud of himself for that. He thinks he saved her soul."

"Phineas is an idiot. Marrying don't change what she is, and she'll be back at it when he's done with her."

A match scratched. Hassie didn't look up as the scent of tobacco drifted in the air. She kept humming, kept working.

"Well, I wouldn't mess with her," the stable man said. "Sterling's not one I'd want to cross, and he's not done with her yet if he just married her. I hope no one says anything about Doosey where he can hear."

"Sshh. Are you sure she can't hear us?"

"She's a dummy. Can't speak a word either. I heard they were waving their hands around in the restaurant, like talking with signs. I guess she writes things too. Don't know how you teach a dummy that."

"You better be right. Anyone who gives Doosey away in this town had better pack his bags and run. Run fast enough to stay ahead of Ma Doosey's shotgun."

The two men were still laughing when Bret reappeared. Hassie's fingers flew. "D-o n-o-t t-a-l-k. I a-m d-e-a-f."

The men disappeared into the barn.

"What's going on?" Bret asked, his voice too low for anyone but her to hear.

She shook her head, wishing she had the slate, but she had left it at the hotel, not wanting to get soap and oil on it. Bret took the rag from her, spread the oil over the rest of the saddle with rapid, sure strokes as she bounced on her toes, eager now to be finished and get back to the hotel.

When Bret pulled the saddle off the fence and took it inside to the tack room, she followed with the bridle, hung it on a peg, and dug the tin box out of their packs. He gave a soft whistle but said nothing, and they hurried back to the hotel room.

Side by side on the bed, they each sorted through half the posters until they found the two for Robert Doosey. Thirty-five years old, approximately five feet eight inches tall and one hundred seventy-five pounds. Brown hair and eyes, full beard. He had stolen shipments of silver the High Country Mining Company was sending east not once but twice. No one had been hurt either time, but the mining company was willing to pay five hundred dollars to see him behind bars.

A Denver railroad company also wanted Mr. Doosey locked up, or maybe hung. He and three other men had robbed a train, dynamited the safe in the express car, and killed a guard. If Robert Doosey wasn't the one who lit the fuse, the company didn't care. One thousand dollars.

"So it sounded like he's somewhere in this town?" Bret said.

Hassie wrote out what she'd heard as exactly as she could and added, *"Why would everyone in town want to protect a man like that?"*

"Mining's a rough business, and the companies treat the miners like dirt. If Doosey's hitting the mining company where it hurts, they probably think he's some kind of Robin Hood. Maybe they don't know about the train robbery. Maybe they like the mother or really are afraid of her and her shotgun. Fifteen hundred dollars, and all we have to do is figure out where he is."

"What about the deserter?"

"That's two hundred. He can wait." Bret put the two posters side by side on the bed. "We'll split fifty-fifty. If you don't think that's fair, too bad."

"Less expenses. Real expenses."

"Fine, but you have to do the bookkeeping."

She had already started a list of expenses. That was also in the tin box. She waved it at him. He pulled it out of her hand. "You can't be serious. The dress is a gift, not an expense." Before long he had crossed out half a dozen of her entries. "And this one right here, you can cut that in half." He crossed out her number and wrote in another.

The entry was for the hotel room in the first town they had reached after capturing Hammerill and Jensen. *"No, I remember how much you paid."*

"Maybe so, but we shared that room, so only half."

"No, we never...." She stopped writing. Was it about that time she had come to know his scent, the texture of his skin and hair and the sound of his heart and thought it was all a hallucination born of fatigue and the aftermath of fear? *And desire,* her mind whispered. That treacherous thought only heightened her embarrassment.

"You were exhausted. I was exhausted. When I got back from dealing with the horses, they didn't have another room.

You never noticed, so no harm done. After all, here we are again."

They were married now, even if only half-married or however one would describe it. *"That was very sneaky."*

"Yeah, it was, but it was worth it. I really needed a few hours sleep in a bed right then."

There wasn't one trace of remorse on his face, but there were hints of amusement. And it *was* funny that she never noticed a six-foot man in bed with her. Although she had noticed—in a way.

Bret jogged her with an elbow. "You're not going to hold a grudge, are you?"

"That bed wasn't too small?"

His eyes widened for just an instant. "You really were easier to get along with when you were afraid of me."

She tried to stifle a laugh and ended up letting out a strangled giggle. No, she wasn't going to hold a grudge, and from the look on his face, if she didn't change the subject, Bret would. *"How will you find Doosey?"*

"By finding someone who knows where he is who will take a bribe. There's always someone. I guess I'm spending most of tonight in saloons, and we're not leaving in the morning after all."

Mining couldn't be any rougher of a business than bounty hunting. Finding where Doosey was hiding wasn't all Bret had to do. He also had to get the man into custody. Robin Hood or not, Hassie had no sympathy for Robert Doosey. All she cared about was that Bret didn't get hurt.

22

Bret headed for the town's saloons that night still thinking about Hassie Petty—Hassie Sterling. No matter what he said about things being easier when she was afraid of him, Bret hadn't seen her as anything but one more burden back then. When she had set herself to appeasing him with the false smile and attempts to do more than her share of work on the trail, she had annoyed him.

A woman who could argue a little, tease a little was much better company. Give her enough time, and she might even be able to fire a gun with her eyes open. A sharp stab of regret followed that thought. They didn't have much more time. Another two months for sure. Three maybe but not likely.

He took more than a little chaffing in the Silver Creek saloons.

"The honeymoon must be over!"

"You must be here to buy us a round to celebrate that wedding!"

Under other circumstances, Bret would have shut them up with a glare, or a fist, but this time he bought rounds in one saloon after another, stayed amiable until they tired of it.

Through it all he kept his eyes open for a certain kind of man, the desperate drunk or gambler, the weasel who spilled secrets because knowing them made him feel important.

Too bad he couldn't go straight at it and ask about Robert Doosey, but that was often the way of it. He bought drinks, told a tale or two about tips he had picked up here and there in the past and hinted how it had paid off for both him and the tipster.

No one bit, and long before he called it a night in the last saloon, Bret could feel the whiskey. Nursing drinks and slopping as much as he could on the tables and floor had saved him from getting really drunk, but he was still half-soaked.

The hotel was locked when he returned. Old Phineas ran the place like a boarding school for wayward children. At least the sanctimonious son of a gun was long abed.

Bret had to use his knife a little to get his favorite window open from the outside, but he and Gunner made it over the sill with only a thump or two. The dog didn't wait for him but bounded up the stairs, which was good. Finding the right room was easier with a dog at the door.

Fumbling the key out of his pocket and into the lock was harder. He considered knocking, pounding until Hassie woke up and let him in, except he had the key on this side of the door. If the dog would get out of the way, he could kick the door in. The key turned before he finished debating the wisdom of that.

She'd left the lamp burning low again, and he could see her, awake, sitting up in the bed wide-eyed. Wide-some-damned-shade-of-purple-eyed. And she didn't have her clothes on. Not that she was naked, no luck there. Some white thing, a woman's night thing. Because she thought he was going to sleep on the floor.

Except he wasn't. The floor was hard, the bed was soft, and he was tired. And married. Married enough to sleep in the bed. Right beside her in that white thing.

He made it almost to the bed, tripped over the dog, and fell across the mattress and Hassie's legs. He'd move in a minute. Right after he rested his eyes a little. The last thing he felt was a tug at one boot.

Sun blazing through the windows woke Bret in the morning. He should have appreciated the rain and gray days more. His head pounded, his mouth was dry and foul, and some instinct told him not to move unless he wanted his stomach to heave. Hassie wasn't snuggled up against him but sitting in the chair watching him, impossibly clean and fresh and sober in the new pink dress. He groaned and threw an arm over his eyes.

His boots were off. So was his hat. He wasn't crosswise on the bed the way he had fallen last night but properly oriented, head on the pillow. Other than that he was as he'd come in from the cold last night, coat and all.

"I suppose you're used to dealing with drunks." He didn't even look, sure she nodded. "Do you know how many saloons there are in this town?"

This time he rolled his arm enough to see her hold up one hand, all five fingers spread. "If you count that shack on the north end of town, and I did, six. I spent time and money in every blasted one and didn't find out a thing. I also had to drink in every blasted one. I didn't realize I was full as a tick until I fell on the bed. I didn't hurt you, did I?"

Hassie came and sat on the edge of the bed with the slate. *"I'm fine."*

He stayed quiet a while, debating what to do about both his queasy stomach and full bladder with her in the room.

"What time is it now?" Stupid question. Neither of them carried a watch.

"I think close to noon."

"Did you get Gunner out all right?"

The chalk pencil twitched in her fingers a little, and her eyes fell, but she nodded.

He closed his eyes and hid behind his arm again. "Do you think you could wait in the hall for a few minutes?"

No feeling of assent came from her, and she didn't move. He let his arm flop down. "Hassie?"

"I could turn my back."

"And I could stagger out to the privy, but I probably wouldn't make it."

A loud knock sounded on the door. Hassie didn't move.

"Mr. Sterling! I know you're in there, and no matter what shape you're in, I want to talk to you. I've waited long enough." From his angry voice, one would expect Phineas Vance to be seven feet tall.

Bret reached out, plucked the chalk pencil from Hassie's loose grasp, and set the slate on his stomach. "Let him in."

She moved at half speed to the door, unlocked it, and stood so that she was behind it when Vance charged in.

"Do you know what your wife did this morning?" Vance sputtered.

Bret heartily wished for a strong enough stomach to take Vance by the collar and launch him out through the window, but since he didn't have that, said, "No, sir, I don't. She and I were just about to discuss it."

"She strutted right through my lobby first thing this morning with that dog. I know you were out until morning or as good as. The whole town knows what you were up to last night, and she had that mangy cur right here in this room. The beast growled at me, growled at me right here in my own hotel, and when I tried to fend it off with a broom, your wife attacked me."

From behind his arm, Bret tried to imagine Hassie strutting and attacking. Couldn't. "I don't believe you."

Vance's voice rose to a screech. Bret shuddered.

"You don't believe me! You, you fornicating sinner, I want you out of my hotel right now."

"I want my head to stop pounding and my stomach to settle," Bret said, "but that's not going to happen for a while yet either. Go away."

"That dog is a menace."

"You shouldn't have threatened my wife."

"I didn't threaten her. I threatened it."

"He probably didn't like that either, and he's only a dog. How's he supposed to figure out who's being threatened?"

"If he sets foot in this hotel again, I'll shoot him."

"If you shoot him, I'll shoot you."

"You would shoot a man over a dog?" Vance sounded incredulous.

"Mr. Vance," Bret said patiently, "right now I'd shoot you over a dust mote. In fact the only thing stopping me from shooting you for the pleasure of it is the fact I'd rather throw you through the window, and I'm not up to it. Why don't you count your blessings and get out of here?"

Bret came out from behind his arm, fighting another wave of nausea. Vance wasn't ready to give up until he saw Hassie hurrying to the bed with the wash basin. The door slammed and Bret's stomach heaved at the same time.

"Go away," he muttered when he could talk.

She smoothed his hair back from his forehead and brought a damp cloth from the washstand instead.

When he was finally cleaned up and feeling halfway human, he said, "I suppose you're starving by now."

She shrugged.

"You could strut through the town, attack someone at the restaurant, and bring food back here."

"I did not attack him. I took the broom away."

"I figured it was something like that. Too bad you really didn't give him a couple of smacks with it while you were at it. You couldn't find a way to sneak the dog out?"

"There was no time. He needed to...." Her hand hovered over the slate then waved in the air.

"I sympathize with the immediacy of his needs."

She laughed. For some reason, getting away from the sound didn't seem the only way to handle the effect it had on him. Probably because he was still too shaky to flee.

He sat on the bed with his head in his hands. "I can't go back again tonight, you know. It's not just that I don't want to poison myself. The whole town knows why we came here, who I was after and why. Now that the weather's cleared, if we don't head out in the direction they pointed us, they'll start wondering why. Since just knowing I'm in town has them worrying about Doosey, they'll warn him, and he'll burrow in deeper. Or run."

"No one you saw last night would help?"

"There were a couple of drunks who would probably sell out in time, but we don't have time, not in this town."

"I can be deaf again. Maybe the general store would be good, and I could get you medicine."

He lifted his head and studied her. With the raven hair pinned up and the golden glow the sun had brought to her pale face, she looked too good to be strutting around the town unaccompanied. Of course his company wouldn't be much use to her right now. Still, he didn't like the thought of her out in a rough, unfriendly town by herself. He didn't like his own not liking it even more.

Before he untangled his feelings about the whole thing, she fished a few dollars out of his saddlebags and was gone. He moved the chair to the window, sank into it, and watched her cross the street below, the dog at her heels. At least that was something, although you couldn't count on Gunner. He took notions and wandered off half the time.

The window didn't let Bret see all the way to the store. He counted the hammering in his head, wishing he did have a watch. Five minutes. He'd count to three hundred and go after her. How long could it take to buy some worthless cure-all?

A knock sounded on the door, and Vance entered without waiting for permission. "Are you feeling well enough to be reasonable now?"

"No."

"This hotel is my property, and I want you gone. As of right now, you're trespassing."

Bret tore his gaze from the window and got to his feet. His head was bad, but his stomach had settled. "We'll be gone in the morning, first light, and I'll pay double for tonight. Good enough?"

Vance's mouth pursed, and he crossed his arms. "No dog."

Bret almost smiled. With the rain ended and the weather warming, Gunner could stand a night out. Or not. "It's a deal."

As soon as the door closed behind Vance, Bret turned back to the window. Still no sign of Hassie. How long could that conversation have taken? Too long. He was down the stairs, across the lobby, and out the door when he saw her coming. Not strutting. She looked demure really in the new dress and hat, but the men she passed turned their heads.

He sagged against a porch post and waited for her to reach him.

"Are you well enough to be up?"

"A little headache. I'm fine." Sweat broke out on his forehead and down his spine as he said it.

"I have headache powder and other medicine."

"Good. Let's get upstairs, and you can tell me about it."

HASSIE WISHED SHE had something positive to report to Bret, but she didn't. The people in the store had certainly kept an eye on her, but that could be because they had already judged her as lacking in moral character and thought she would steal. The chances their whispers concerned Robert Doosey and his hiding place had to be much smaller than that they were whispering about her.

She watched Bret swallow the headache powder mixed in the last of the water in the wash pitcher. *"I will get more water."*

"Oh, no, you won't." Bret caught her by the arm and pulled her back from the door. "You stay away from Vance. We're evicted, but I talked him into letting us stay until morning. No dog."

That wasn't much of an eviction. Bret had already said staying in town any longer would be counterproductive, and from the hard glint in his eyes, Gunner didn't have much to worry about. Hassie had a vision of the three of them strutting out through the lobby in the morning and Mr. Vance turning apoplectic.

Over their very late lunch, Hassie persuaded Bret to let her try again at the stables. After all, the stable owner and his friend were the ones who talked about Robert Doosey in front of her before.

Bret brought each of their horses from the corral behind the barn and tied them near where they had worked on the saddles the day before. He cleaned the mud off Jasper and Packie in record time and disappeared with Packie.

Hassie worked slowly over Brownie, currying, brushing. The stable man was on his own today, though. She caught glimpses of him now and then, raking the dirt floor of the barn, moving horses, but no one came to engage him in conversation.

By the time Bret came back, her new pink dress needed washing in spite of the duster she wore over it, and she was ready to give up.

Bret had another idea. "I'm going to put Brownie away too, but I'll tell him Jasper needs topping off and ask him about trails out of town. Maybe he'll give some sign that he doesn't want me going in one particular direction. You watch him too, see if we see the same thing."

"You're going to search the mountains?"

"You bet I am. There are a good three hours of light left today, and we'll ride out in the morning, swing around, and start in again if we have to."

The pine-covered slopes stretched in every direction around them, and when they'd traveled to this place, every vista showed more of the same. Suddenly Hassie wished she'd never told him about Robert Doosey, but she clutched the slate and pencil to her side and followed him into the barn.

"Guess if you're scraping mud off them horses you and the missus are ready to leave," the man said, friendly-like.

Remembering the way he'd talked about her the day before, Hassie didn't feel friendly. She worked at keeping her face expressionless. After all, she was deaf and couldn't hear him.

"First thing in the morning," Bret said. "Right now, I'm going to take my gelding out, run him a little. Keeping him slow enough for my wife's horse is always a challenge, and after four days' rest, it will be worse than usual. Got some Thoroughbred in him you know."

The stable man laughed in agreement. "I know. Your packhorse shows more breeding than that nag of hers. Now that you're married, you ought to get her something decent. I've got a couple I could sell you."

Bret shook his head ruefully. "Sorry, wish I could, but the Cheyenne killed her whole family. My wife was visiting neighbors, or she'd be dead too. Or worse. That horse is all she has left, and I can't bring myself to make her trade it off."

Hassie forgot she was supposed to be watching the stable man and stared at Bret open mouthed. If he kept telling such whoppers, he'd have a reward on *his* head soon.

The stable man gave Hassie a contemplative look. "It's amazing what a man will do for a woman."

"It is." Bret pulled Hassie close, his arm warm around her shoulders. "But they're worth it, aren't they?"

Busy rolling a cigarette, the man didn't answer. Hassie watched him strike a match and light it and suppressed a shudder thinking of the loft above them filled with hay. Thank goodness Bret had moved their horses out of the barn and into a corral as soon as the rain stopped.

"We saw some pretty country on the way here from the east, and we're headed south when we leave," Bret said casually. "What will I find if I ride west? Are there passes over the Divide?"

"Nothing you'll get to riding for an hour or two, but it will give your horse a workout. Angle a little toward the southwest and you'll come on some decent open ground where you can let him run."

Hassie tried not to stare, to look bored as if she couldn't hear a word and didn't know what they were talking about.

"What about to the north?" Bret said.

The stable man threw his half-smoked cigarette on the ground and crushed it under his boot. "Nah, you don't want to go that way. Country's so rough you could break a leg on that good horse, and you could even run into a Ute or two. I got to get back to work. We'll settle up in the morning."

Bret dropped his arm from her shoulders and carried his saddle out to Jasper. "I'll walk you back to the hotel."

Hassie didn't bother to ask. He was going to search to the north.

BRET RODE OUT of Silver Creek on the trail leading west and swung to the north as soon as he was out of sight. The country was rough all right. Still, there had been a trail leading out of town to the north. Once he reached that, the going would be easier.

The pines were still close around him, blocking his vision in all directions when he heard the muffled sound of a horse running. Bret reined up, waited until the sound faded, and pushed on in the direction the sound had first come from. He hit the trail in minutes. The heavy layer of pine needles masked most of the tracks of the horse that had just passed, but here and there a hoof print showed.

Bret followed slowly, studying the ground to the left and right as he went. Even so, he almost missed the faint signs of the rider ahead turning off. Another half mile, and he smelled smoke. He tied Jasper well off the trail and continued on foot.

The cabin sat in a small clearing, two horses in a small corral out back, one tied in front. The lather on the tied horse was visible even from Bret's position, bellied down in grass at the edge of the forest more than a hundred feet away. He waited as the clouds overhead turned orange with the beginning of another spectacular mountain sunset, calculating how much daylight was left, how dangerous the trail back to town would be in the dark.

Finally three people emerged from the cabin. Two men and a woman. Neither of the men was the stable man as Bret had expected, but as one raised his hat and settled it more firmly on his head, red hair shone like fire. The heavyset woman was hatless, her hair iron gray. She carried a long gun tucked against her side as if it were part of her. Mrs. Doosey and her shotgun could definitely prove to be a problem.

The redhead mounted his tired horse and headed back toward the trail. The other two stood outside a while, arguing from the look of it.

"Run, you son of a gun, run," Bret urged under his breath.

It took what had to be another half hour, but Doosey came back out carrying saddlebags and a bedroll, his mother trailing after him with the shotgun. Bret slithered back among the trees and jogged back to Jasper.

A man who killed and stole wasn't going to ride out of here the hard way. He'd come right down the trail, and he'd be as easy to net as a fish.

The look on Robert Doosey's face when Bret stepped into the trail ahead of him, rifle pointed at his chest, was pure surprise. The guard killed in the train robbery probably had the same look on his face when he died.

"You try to run, and I'll shoot the horse," Bret said. "I'd rather shoot you, but you're worth a lot more. Get down."

Robert Doosey claimed he was innocent, claimed his name was Dave Young, and cursed a blue streak as Bret handcuffed him, searched him, and shoved him back on his horse. They barely made it back to the main trail by the time the pitch black of the mountain night closed in around them. Bret didn't like killers at his back, but he made an exception this time, tied Doosey's hands to the saddle and led his horse.

"I suppose you're taking me to Silver Creek," Doosey said.

"You suppose wrong."

"What do you mean. Silver Creek's the only town anywheres near. You got to take me there."

"I don't, and I'm not."

When Doosey found out what Bret intended, he squawked even louder. "You can't do that. You can't leave a man tied in these mountains. There's Injuns. There's bears and cougars."

Bret gagged him and left both man and horse tied to trees. Phineas Vance would be pleased. Bret and Hassie would be gone before morning.

23

Bret pushed out of Silver Creek to the headquarters of the High Country Mining Company with the same relentless drive he had used months ago with Hammerill and Jensen. Hassie knew this time he wasn't worried the horse Robert Doosey rode was stolen but that some of the outlaw's friends from Silver Creek—or even his mother—might ride to the rescue.

Reaching the headquarters of the High Country Mining Company was a relief, and the partners who owned the company paid the reward in cash without a quibble. The railroad wasn't so obliging, but Hassie welcomed the prospect of a few days' rest.

Telegrams buzzed back and forth. The railroad agreed to pay the reward into the account at Bret's bank in Missouri once their own representative identified Doosey. Bret and Hassie settled in to wait.

For the first time Hassie looked around a hotel, a restaurant with decent food, and a town with halfway decent shops and services and gave a wistful thought to trading it all for permanence and the comfort of familiarity. Adventure was good, but maybe a person only needed so much adventure in her life.

She did not, for instance, ever need the adventure of meeting Indians. Bret's instructions on what she should do if they saw Indians appalled her.

"You kick your feet out of the stirrups and let me pull you off your horse and behind me on Jasper. Their ponies are smaller and never see grain. He can outrun them, and they may not even give chase. They may be satisfied with what they find in the packs."

"But what about Brownie? What about Packie?"

"They can be Indian ponies."

"The Indians will eat them!"

"Whoever told you that doesn't know what he's talking about. The more horses an Indian has, the bigger man he is in his village. Brownie will be pulling teepees, not chasing buffalo, but nobody's going to eat her."

Hassie didn't think Bret would lie to her, but he might decide not to tell her something bad if he thought it would ensure she did what he wanted. Whether Indians ate horses or not, worrying about what could happen left her twitchy for days.

Staying in one place with a kitchen of her own where she could cook what she wanted, never sleep on hard ground, and never worry about thieves, murderers, or Indians sounded good until it occurred to her she would have those things soon, have them but not Bret. And she'd rather sleep on rocks every night for the rest of her life than say goodbye to Bret.

The hotel a few doors down from the mining company office was not full. She had her own room again, and it no longer seemed a luxury. It seemed lonely. She had to ask Bret about next year soon, before he made plans about where to leave her. The nights were already cold here in Colorado. The snow would come soon. Next month maybe. Soon.

Bret's knock sounded on the door, and Hassie put away her unhappy thoughts. She wasn't hungry, but he would be, and she liked sitting catty-cornered from him at a table in the restaurant. He knew more signs now, ones for the everyday things they did, but he still spelled at her in restaurants, and it still lifted her heart every time.

"B-e-e-f s-t-e-w? C-h-I-c-k-e-n? H-a-m?"

"S-o-u-p."

"That's all?"

She watched without envy as Bret's full plate of ham, fried potatoes, and green beans was delivered along with Gunner's tin plate piled high with scraps. Her soup looked suspiciously like the beef stew with a lot of water added. At least it was hot.

A heavy, dark-haired man approached their table. "Are you Bret Sterling?"

"I am."

"Sorry to interrupt your meal." The man went on to introduce himself. He was from the railroad, tasked with identifying Robert Doosey and authorizing the reward if satisfied. At Bret's invitation, the man pulled up a chair and ordered coffee and beef stew.

Hassie pushed her half-finished soup away and caught Bret's eye. "I will feed Gunner," she signed.

He hesitated a moment, then nodded. "Be careful."

She took the admonition less as a caution about her own safety than about not letting Gunner out of the shed at the back of the livery where he was confined. The mayor of this little town owned a spaniel bitch that was in her season, and Gunner's vigorous attempts to meet a new lady love had earned him a temporary prison. The mayor must wield a heavy hand in this town because Hassie hadn't glimpsed a male dog on the streets since they'd been here.

Getting to the shed meant walking through the livery barn or around the side through a maze of corrals. The sound of male laughter from the barn made her choose the maze this time. She bent to place the plate on the ground in order to unbar the door and catch Gunner before he could escape, dropped the plate, and whirled as jeering words came from behind.

"Woo hoo. Look at that ass. There's nothing dumb about that, is there, Walt?"

Three grinning boys stood in a semi-circle around her, trapping her against the shed. They must be the ones she'd heard in the barn. Almost men, taller than she was, but spotty and baby-faced. Their youth didn't make her less afraid. She knew how much stronger they would be. The Grimes boys had delighted in their superior strength.

To run she would have to break through them. Gunner whined and jumped against the shed door, locked in a place he had been trying to escape for days to no avail.

She smiled at the boys, nodded, and gestured toward the plate, hoping frightening her would satisfy them and they wouldn't coalesce into a wolf pack—a wolf cub pack—and work up to more. She raised a hand to her neck as if in surprise—or fear.

"Ah, look at that. She's going to be agreeable." The boy in the center reached for her breast.

Her fingers closed around the cord, and she pulled out the whistle, fumbled for it.

"Get that away from her."

Ducking her head, Hassie twisted to the side and managed two long blasts before one of them ripped the whistle away, seized her by the wrist, and yanked her off balance. He spun her around until she was staggering and dizzy.

Gunner exploded, roaring, barking, throwing himself against the door so hard it shook.

The boys hooted and laughed.

Panic flooded through her. She had to get away, had to run.

As soon as Hassie left, misgivings flooded Bret. Hovering over her as if she were a child had to be wrong, but there weren't many women in this town, and there were a lot of rough men.

The railroad representative was in no hurry. He wanted to explain company policy and procedure in boring detail, and

Bret didn't care. The man had already identified Doosey and promised to authorize payment. It was done.

Done, and Hassie was alone in the green dress with the skirt that didn't swirl so much any more but still gave a man ideas about what was underneath. To hell with it. If nothing else, Gunner might be more interested in his love life than food, push past her and get away, or knock her down.

"I'm sorry," he said, "but I shouldn't have let my wife go off alone like that. I'll talk to you later."

"Letting them run around loose on their own is a mistake," the railroad man said, chuckling at his own wit.

Bret didn't waste time wondering what the man's wife must be like.

A heavily loaded wagon creaked by on the street, almost obscuring another sound, thin and high. Bret sprinted toward the livery. A dog barked, no ordinary sound. He ran faster.

Horses shied and jumped as he sped through the barn. Bret reached the boys surrounding Hassie as the one spinning her by the arm let go and she fell.

A kick in the ass drove that one head first into the shed. Bret grabbed a second by the back of his shirt and lifted him straight up, squirming and choking. The third ran.

Hassie climbed slowly to her feet, one hand against the shed as if she needed the support. Bret almost let go of his prisoner but kept the boy suspended from a straight arm and dragged him over to Hassie instead.

"Are you all right?" He cupped her chin with his free hand and examined her face.

She nodded.

"Sure?"

She took her hand away from the shed and stood straight. "Yes."

The boy on the ground struggled up, ready to rabbit like his friend. Bret twisted a hand in the back of his shirt too, and banged their heads together.

"Let's go."

The boys whined, professing harmless intentions. Too bad Gunner had quieted down and Bret had to listen to them. He ignored the excuses, apologies, and complaints about how much his merciless grip hurt and marched them down the street to the town marshal's office. Hassie opened the door and stood aside. Bret shoved them inside.

The place was empty. Bret shut both boys up by backhanding the one that had put hands on Hassie hard enough to knock him down again. Hassie's hand on his arm barely stopped Bret from using his fist on the other one. He locked the now quiet pair in the cell next to Robert Doosey's, took the key back to the office, and dropped it on the desk.

Pulling Hassie into his arms, he said, "You wouldn't lie to me about being all right, would you?"

"No."

She fit against him as if designed especially to fit there, her hair silky against his cheek. The back of her green dress was dirty from her fall, and the high lace collar she used to cover the scar was ripped. He fingered the torn cloth, felt the softness of her skin against the backs of his fingers, and the red tide of anger rose again.

The office door opened. The harrumph of a clearing throat sounded, and Bret reluctantly let Hassie go.

The marshal took his time positioning his hat on a shelf behind the desk before nodding a greeting.

"Mr. Sterling. Miz Sterling. What's this I hear about you walking Mr. Quentin's boy and one of his friends down the street like you think someone's going to pay you for them."

Quentin was one of the partners in the mining company, the one who had counted out five hundred dollars and handed it to Bret just two days ago. And Bret didn't care.

He did care that the sound of the marshal's voice started the boys yelling from the cell, repeating the same craven excuses they'd blathered on the way here. Bret reached the door between the office and cells in two strides and slammed it shut.

"Those *boys* attacked my wife. I want them locked up. There was a third one who ran, and I bet you know who he is. Find him and throw him in the cell with them."

The marshal sat on a corner of his desk, sharp blue eyes moving over Hassie from head to toe. Bret's jaw muscles bunched. He took a step toward the lawman, who had the sense to leave off staring at Hassie before Bret threw him in the same cell with the boys, badge or not.

"Now calm down," the marshal said. "Whatever happened, the lady don't look hurt."

"She's bruised and scared. Do you only protect women in this town from attacks that leave open wounds?"

"Now, you know that's not the case, but I know those boys, and I know they didn't mean any real harm. You heard them. They were just teasing. You can't tell me you never teased a girl when you were that age."

"Believe it or not, I made it from grass to hay without ever attacking a woman."

"There's no call to make things sound like a crime instead of high spirits. I know you have to take extra good care of a wife like Miz Sterling, but I don't believe those boys did more than a little mischief, and you're not going to convince anyone else in this town it was more than that either."

Bret lowered his voice to a harsh growl. "Then let me convince you of this. Either you keep those high-spirited mischief-makers locked up until my wife and I are long gone from this town, or I won't be responsible for what happens to them. Maybe I'll just tease them a little. Maybe I'll beat them senseless, and maybe my spirits will run so high I'll make them disappear."

"Now, you don't want to be making threats...."

Placing one hand on Hassie's back, Bret ignored the marshal and guided her out of the office, slamming the door behind him so hard the windows rattled.

Hassie touched his cheek and mouthed. "I'm fine."

"I never should have let you go there alone. I should have fed them to Gunner instead of bringing them here."

She smiled and gave his cheek a pat. His anger drained away at her touch.

"You have a very bad t-e-m-p-e-r."

"Believe it or not, there was a time I was known as easy-going."

Her eyebrows rose in disbelief. "Gunner still needs food."

"He does. Let's go see if his plate's still there or if something ran off with it."

At least now that all the payments for Robert Doosey were resolved, they'd be leaving in the morning. Hassie didn't want Bret to end up with a price on his own head for murdering boys like the ones who had attacked her, and he had been in a towering rage, every bit as impressive as what he'd been like back in Werver.

He'd frightened her then. Today her wild relief at the sight of him was unadulterated. When he held her, the comfort erased every bad feeling. If only the marshal had waited another ten minutes—or an hour—before showing up, she could have stayed in Bret's arms that much longer.

The pleasure of pressing against the warm wall of his chest, feeling his arms around her, and drawing in his scent with every breath was unlike anything she'd known before. Except waking up in bed with him, cuddled in close.

Back at the hotel, she changed to her pink dress and began repairing the collar on the green. When Bret's knock sounded on the door, she answered eagerly, hoping they were going to take Gunner for a walk before supper. Bret had other ideas.

"Here, I bought you a present, and I'd better not see it on your of list of expenses."

A gun. Hassie regarded the small revolver, snug in its own holster, unhappily.

"It's called a pocket revolver because of its size, and it's a small caliber like my boot gun."

He must have recognized the blank look his words inspired. "That means even though it's small, it won't have as much kick as my .44," he said, patting the gun at his hip. He threw a box of ammunition on the bed. "We can practice a little later."

"I do not want a g-u-n."

"The whistle didn't work very well. You need it."

In her opinion the whistle had worked fine. Bret had heard it, hadn't he? She picked up the slate, not wanting to deal with the limits of his sign vocabulary right then. *"I will never shoot a person."*

His mouth tightened, expression impatient. "Do you think those boys were teasing?"

"No."

"Do you think they wouldn't have hurt you?"

"No, but I could not shoot them."

"Most of the time you wouldn't have to shoot anyone. Showing it would be enough, and you don't know what you might do if things get desperate. Humor me and carry it. Strap it to your leg, put it in a pocket. Just carry it."

She nodded reluctantly, took the gun, and put it beside the box of ammunition.

Bret sat on the bed. "Suppose right now we practice something else. Show me how you would tell me about my temper if I knew the right signs. For that matter, show me g-u-n."

His forearms rested on his thighs, and he flexed his fingers as if getting ready to play an instrument. How could anyone not love him?

The thought froze Hassie in place until he looked up at her, questioning. She wanted to touch his face again, burrow in against his shoulder.

Her hands moved slowly, demonstrating the signs. Her mind raced full speed, considering her new discovery. She had just skipped right over fanciful illusions and landed in heartbreak territory.

They practiced signing until mid-afternoon and took Gunner for a long walk afterward. Happy to be out of the shed under any conditions, he fought the rope less than usual. Or maybe he was getting used to it.

Still unenthused over her new present, Hassie shut her eyes and pulled the trigger on the small revolver until Bret sighed and gave up. She put the nasty little thing back in its holster hoping never to take it out again.

Since the railroad man had authorized payment of the Doosey reward, they could leave in the morning. The trail of the army deserter they had followed to Silver Creek was too cold to try to pick up now, but Bret would find something else in the next town or the next. There wouldn't be any more trouble with those boys in that short time, and Gunner could soon be free.

Come supper time, Hassie dug into her roast chicken with enthusiasm and was considering apple pie when Bret pushed her chair several feet across the board floor with a boot on the bottom rail. "Get over by the wall and stay there," he said.

Too stunned to move, she sat and watched as James Quentin, a big, well-padded man enlarged by anger, swaggered up to their table, followed by his less impressive, smirking son. The two of them loomed over Bret as he sat at the table, and Bret shrank before them, sinking deeper in the chair.

"Hassie!"

She scrambled up and retreated to the wall.

Quentin leaned over, hands on the table. "Who do you think you are, manhandling my son and his friend, making false accusations, and trying to tell the marshal how to do his job."

"Your son and his friends assaulted my wife."

"We didn't do anything of the kind," the son said. "We heard she was a dummy and wanted to see if we could make her squeak a little. We were just funnin'."

"You heard my boy. I want an apology to him and to me. Now." Quentin brushed back his coat, rested his hand on the butt of the pistol at his waist. His son grinned and did the same.

Bret erupted from the chair so fast, neither of the Quentins had time to draw the pistols under their hands. The muzzle of the big American revolver stopped inches from Quentin's forehead, the smaller boot gun smacked the son, jerking his head back, and leaving a round red mark between his eyes.

"I'm guessing the reason that whining piece of snot you sired has no respect for women is you didn't teach him any. If you want him in one piece tomorrow, you take him back to that cell, lock him in, and be glad that locks me out."

Quentin and his son had gone white, the spots on the son's face stood out like blood drops on snow. He backed away and ran.

"You'll be sorry about this," his father managed before turning and walking out with more dignity.

Bret returned Hassie's chair to its position and beckoned to her. "How about some pie?"

All around them people who had gone quiet began talking again in subdued tones.

Hassie sat and watched Bret scrunch down again to put the boot gun back in place, then spelled a word they should never have to practice, her brows raised to make it a question. "Ambush?"

"Wouldn't put it past him. We'll leave before first light."

Hassie managed not to sigh. Considering how many towns they'd been in, having to leave two in the dark wasn't really that bad. So long as they weren't starting a habit.

24

A strange contentment filled Bret as he finished a last cup of coffee. When he'd reined up beside the small creek gurgling nearby, he'd only intended a short break for a noon meal. At least six hours of good light for travel remained in the day.

Six blazing, enervating hours. After chilly nights and cool days heralding autumn, summer had returned to this part of Colorado with a vengeance. Today the horses had settled into an enduring plod within an hour of setting out. By the time they stopped here, Gunner had been lost behind them for an hour. When he caught up, tongue beet red and hanging halfway to the ground, he ignored their food and plunged straight into the creek.

Gunner's solution to the unnatural weather was too good not to imitate. Besides, Bret enjoyed the way Hassie hid behind bushes to bathe and kept her underclothing on too. Modesty times two.

Afterward she always pulled on one of her dresses and spread her wet undergarments on bushes to dry. Nothing could induce him to tell her the way the sun turned the green dress into a translucent cloud around her. Yes, indeed, that green dress was his favorite.

They sat now in the shade of the cottonwoods along the creek. Her nipples, still peaked after the cold bath, showed perfectly through the thin cloth. Bret's blood hummed through his veins with a pleasant tingle at the sight.

Intent on making Gunner a necklace of odoriferous weeds mixed with wildflowers, Hassie had a small vertical furrow between her brows. The tip of her tongue showed pink between her lips as she concentrated.

Bret shifted a little, moved a leg to block her sight of his lower body in case she looked up. Between what he could see now and what he anticipated seeing shortly, his condition was moving beyond pleasant to obvious.

As her hair dried, one inky tendril after another drifted on the air, lighter than the damp mass loose down her back. The memory of the silky feel of her hair in his fingers and under his cheek aroused him further.

Four year of war, six since then. For ten years, guilt always tainted the simple pleasure of watching a woman, left him sleepless and wrung out if things went further. His mind knew he didn't owe another man's wife fidelity because he loved her, but his heart had never accepted it and punished him for every lapse.

He searched his feelings now, probed the old wounds and found the pain but no guilt. Old feelings for Mary cast no cloud over new and different feelings for Hassie.

He wanted the laughter. He wanted the feeling of partnership that rose from sitting side by side sorting through wanted posters or sneaking Gunner into a hotel room. He wanted to keep her safe and make sure she never had to experience anyone like the Restons or Quentins again.

When she held up the finished circle of the necklace and smiled at him, Bret smiled back. Flowers on that scruffy mongrel were ridiculous, but that was something else he wasn't going to tell her. She claimed the weeds discouraged pests, and he had to admit Gunner had stayed miraculously flea-free all season.

She arranged the bushy wreath around Gunner's neck, rose, and moved into the sunlight. Her body had filled out nicely these last months, but her figure was still lithe, not voluptuous. High, firm breasts, slim waist, and of course the heart-shaped rump nothing disguised.

Long legs moved gracefully under the skirt, legs he wanted wrapped around his, wrapped around his waist. Because he wanted that too, wanted her under him, on top of him, beside him, against walls....

The scorching sun might stop her running but not the way she gloried in moving freely over the prairie. Arms outstretched as if to catch the very air, she whirled, bent, and tried to entice Gunner to give up the shade. The dog resisted. Bret came to his feet as if pulled by invisible strings.

When Bret rose to his feet, Hassie dropped her arms, expecting him to beckon, wanting her to change back to trail clothes and saddle Brownie. They could cover many more miles before sunset.

If the look on his face didn't warn her he had something else in mind, his purposeful stride did. She backed away, still bent at the waist from her futile attempt to lure Gunner out of the shade. Something flickered in Bret's eyes, something as different as his expression. Her breath caught. She spun, ran, dodged when she heard him close behind her.

The tap on her shoulder was distinct, but only a tap. She looked over her shoulder and saw him standing still, bent over, hands on thighs, a challenge on his face now. Laughing, she went after him. Gunner finally gave up the shade and joined the game, barking and getting in the way.

Bret was quick. She only caught him because of Gunner's interference, and by then they were both out of breath, gasping in the hot air.

"Now that you've caught me, what are you going to do with me?" he said.

He was still clean shaven from a visit to the barber shop before they'd left one more small town this morning, no beard blurring the lines of his face. His gray eyes were locked on hers and anything but cold. She wanted to place her palms flat on his heaving chest, kiss him, and taste the salt.

Keeping her hands curled in her skirt, she reached up and gave him a chaste peck on the jaw.

"I have a better idea." He pulled her close. The heat from the day and their game changed to something deeper. Her arms slid around his neck, her fingers combed through his hair.

She anticipated the kiss, expected hard pressure on her mouth and an invading tongue. Instead his lips brushed hers as lightly as butterfly wings before settling more firmly. Her arms tightened. So did his.

Her body molded to his, chest to chest, belly to belly. Her quickened breath matched the rhythm of his. His mouth caressed hers, played against hers. His teeth tugged gently on her bottom lip, and she opened for him, not invaded at all but joined. His tongue teased until she tried to imitate. From the sound he made deep in his throat, she succeeded.

He left her mouth to kiss her eyelids, her temples. The hard length of his arousal pressed against her stomach, distinct through his clothes and hers. She rested her forehead on his shoulder and trembled. He would lay her down here in the shade, and she would welcome him eagerly. His body would be as different from what she had known or imagined as his kiss.

That's not what he did. Bret straightened and cupped her face in his hands, his eyes hooded, his features softened. "What do you say we make this a real marriage?"

His voice pulled her out of the desire-induced trance. Her mind reengaged at least enough to make her hesitate.

"Hassie?"

She had to pull away enough to use her hands. "I need to think."

"You need...."

Whatever she expected it wasn't the short, hard bark of laughter he gave or the way he shook his head. "God knows that's fair. I thought about it enough. You think while I cool off in the creek again."

She couldn't think. Not yet. The surprise of it left her mind blank, and her body was still shaky with the sensations the Kiss had aroused. Or was it the Kisses.

When Bret returned, hair still dripping and turning his blue shirt dark at the neck and shoulders, she took her turn in the creek again. She sank down, dress and all, letting the cold water erase the effects of running in the hot sun and wanting a man more than she had thought possible. The water ran over her skin like a whisper of what could be and didn't cool the internal heat, but intensified it, made her want to catch Bret all over again and do things differently this time.

Lingering wouldn't help anything. He wanted to couple with her and wanted a yes answer, and she wanted that too. Even if she wouldn't really like it when it happened, she would like being held and touched and touching. And more kisses like that. She'd definitely like more kisses like the Kiss.

Yet somewhere in the back of her mind Belle's warnings had embedded themselves like tiny poisonous thorns. At least Bret wasn't claiming an attack of sudden undying love. Hassie was glad of that. She didn't want him to lie, and he was fond of her. Learning signs had been a way to pass boring hours stuck together in a hotel room, but he could have headed for a saloon. He didn't have to make the effort no one else ever had, and he didn't have to keep at it.

In Werver his fury had been mostly because the Restons had lied to him and what they did was wrong and left him burdened with her again, but his anger at the Quentin boy and his friends had been different. He'd been angry then that she was hurt and frightened and could have been hurt worse.

Still, marrying could mean a child. She hadn't conceived in almost six years of marriage to Cyrus, but Cyrus had never had much interest in her that way. She could count on her fingers the number of times he had coupled with her in the first year, and the last years there had been nothing other than an occasional groping hand in the night. Bret was young and healthy. It would be different.

She shivered and left the water, dried off, and dressed in her trail clothes again. The green dress could dry held in her hand as she rode.

The horses still grazed some distance away, hobbled and unsaddled. Bret waited for her where they'd sat in the shade earlier. She pulled the slate from her saddlebags and went to join him.

"What will happen if I say no?"

One side of his mouth lifted in the familiar cynical smile. "You mean will I leave you standing in the street in some town without a penny or beat you into submission?"

Neither possibility had crossed her mind, and she didn't take them seriously now. *"No, I mean...."* She hesitated then finished the question that had cost her sleep and worried at her for months. *"...will you come get me next spring? Will you let me come with you again next year?"*

He looked so surprised she could tell he'd never considered it before.

"I don't know," he said finally. "When I started doing this, I never meant it to last this long. I wanted to quit last year, but my father talked me out of it. Gabe said some things that—if what he said is true, this will be the last year. If Gabe's wrong and I have to come back out again, yes. You may have to stave off some seduction attempts, but if you want to risk it, sure."

"Where will you take me for the winter?"

"I don't know. You don't want to go back to Gabe and Belle's, do you?"

She shook her head.

"The closest town to the Sterling farm is a decent size. You could stay at the boarding house there, or maybe we could even find a house to rent." He looked away, his voice falling. "You know I can't take you home the way things are."

"Belle told me about your family. They would never accept someone like me. I know you can't take me to your home."

"They wouldn't accept any woman I brought home if I wasn't married to her, and if we are married, they'll expect us to share a bed."

"Even married, they would not accept me."

He lifted his hat and ran his fingers through his damp hair, avoiding her eyes for a moment longer before looking directly at her. "Belle exaggerates, although I suppose I'm lucky when I got back from the war they didn't slam the door in my face the way your mother's family did to her. The fact is as long as they're letting me in, they'll let my wife in with me."

Letting her in would not be the same thing as accepting her. Hassie didn't point that out. *"The war has been over for more than six years."*

"For some people it will never be over," he said grimly.

They sat quietly for a few moments.

"That's it?" he said finally. "You're not going to ask me what if you say yes?"

She shook her head and got to her feet. What he'd already said had changed all her assumptions. Now she had a lot more to think about.

BROWNIE COULD KEEP up well enough that Hassie sometimes rode beside Bret these days when crossing open land or on wide trails, but she followed him now, studying his back. His very nice back. He didn't go to the lengths she did to stay hidden when bathing in a creek, so she had seen that back uncovered, the dip along his spine, the muscles on either side.

For that matter, being uncomfortably honest with herself, she'd seen all of him one time or another and wouldn't mind better, longer looks. No, what he wanted wasn't the problem because she wanted that too.

The problem was the way life never seemed to work out the way she expected. In spite of the great lengths she had taken avoiding the Grimes boys' seduction attempts, she had ended up with an enraged Ned Grimes screaming at her, accusing her of trying to seduce his son into marriage.

Marrying an old man famous for miles around for his home-brewed corn whiskey should have meant an unexciting but secure life. Instead it led to frightening moments when his customers caught her alone, semi-starvation, and watching her husband's thieving, murdering son killed before her eyes.

She had taken a position as a maid in a hotel and ended up running for her life, if not literally then as good as.

And of course she had followed an icy-eyed killer into the wilds and ended up gloriously happy and in love with him. Now Bret had agreed to her most cherished hope and said she could go with him as he trailed outlaws again next year. Except he probably wouldn't be doing it next year.

The more she thought about it, the less sure she was it mattered. Sooner or later he would give up bounty hunting. Had she really thought he would just keep doing the same thing year after year while the two of them grew old and gray? She smiled at the thought.

Living in the town near his home would mean seeing him sometimes, knowing about his life, watching when he married someone else because surely he would marry sooner or later and have a family of his own. She couldn't bear the thought.

Saying yes would mean going home with him and living with his family. Thinking about the Sterling family always brought back not just Belle's words but memories of going to see her mother's parents in the big brick house in Philadelphia.

Of all her memories of her life in the city, the one Hassie would most like to have dim with time was the one of the visit to her grandparents. She'd like to forget that even more than the day she fell on the wire, because the memory included Mama's pain and hurt more.

She remembered the man in the black suit answering the door and the look on his face, the way he had held her in the hall by the shoulders when Mama rushed by.

Even though no words of the distant shouting had been clear, she still remembered the sound and the fear that made her try to twist away from the man. Tears had run down Mama's face as she hurried back to the hall and took Hassie by the hand.

"Thank you, John," Mama had said as she took Hassie's hand and led her away.

"I'm sorry, Miss Julia," he had replied, tears on his face too. That was the first time Hassie realized men could cry.

And the door had closed behind them, so solid, so permanent.

She brushed tears from under her own eyes now, remembering. Bret's family wouldn't be like her grandparents. They didn't slam the door in his face when he came home from the war. But now they were only angry that he had fought for the Union. He hadn't yet brought home the daughter of an Irish immigrant.

If they started a baby, and if he did leave Missouri and hunt men again next year, she would have to stay alone with those people. If the fact she never conceived with Cyrus meant she couldn't have a baby with Bret either, it would make him unhappy. Had he thought of that? Probably not. According to Mama, when men got randy they stopped thinking.

That's not what he said, though. He said it was right for her to think about his proposal because he had thought about it a lot. He didn't love her, so he must have thought about it more than he would have if he did.

Her hand spread over her stomach, but the gesture was only habit. Her stomach had not burned and writhed for months, and it was fine now, not as good as this morning, but fine.

She gigged Brownie a little and made her jog up beside Jasper. In the end there really was only one answer.

25

When Bret had asked Mary to marry him all those years ago, she had clapped her hands, declared she might faint, said yes at least three times, and allowed a more thorough kiss than ever before. Of course Bret had to admit that hadn't worked out too well in the end, so Hassie's more subdued approach might bode well for the future.

Except subdued was too exciting a word to use to describe her reaction. After another day baking in the sun, she still hadn't said—written, signed—another word on the subject.

Pretending he'd never asked was probably her idea of an easy way to say no. She'd take up her independent life in Missouri with nine hundred and fifty dollars in the bank and wait for some man to come along who had some magical something that made her want to marry him.

What kind of magic she needed was beyond him. If that kiss hadn't affected her the way it had him, she was one hell of an actress, and he still felt vaguely unsettled over it. A kiss was just a kiss, not a life-changing event. So why did he have an uneasy feeling his life had changed back there by the creek?

Worse, if Gabe was wrong about what was going on back in Missouri, Bret might need to spend another year of his life hunting men and doing it with Hassie along torturing him every mile of the way. That's what she wanted. Hands off. Follow around. Torture.

She'd better be getting good at keeping that list of expenses because if that's how it worked out next year, she could use her new fortune to pay her own way. Every penny.

Except maybe meals. Making her pay for her meals would be pretty low. And a nickel here and there for meat scraps for Gunner wasn't worth writing down. Dividing the cost of supplies was too hard-fisted to consider.

Another small Colorado town hove into sight. The last one hadn't had a hotel, and the last three hadn't yielded a scrap of useful information. Bret was ready to head back to Kansas, where the cow towns would be booming this time of year and a few wanted men would be mixing in with the drovers.

This place did have a hotel. Bret had one hand reaching for the front door when Hassie touched his arm.

"Only one room here," she signed.

It took him a moment. "That means yes."

"Yes."

She wasn't jumping up and down, clapping her hands, or declaring she might faint with joy, but she was smiling the real smile.

He opened the door with a flourish. "After you, Mrs. Sterling."

ALONE IN THE hotel room, Hassie sped through her usual nightly routine. Water splashed over the sides of the basin as she hastily scrubbed and rinsed. Her teeth got more careful attention, just in case he repeated the Kiss.

She brushed her hair only enough to be sure it hung down her back without tangles. No hundred strokes tonight. She pulled her nightgown on, folded her trail clothes on the room's only chair with trembling hands, and hurried into bed. The sunset hadn't completely faded, but the light was failing fast.

A hotel employee would light the lamps in the hall soon. Should she light the one beside the bed? The one on the wall by the washstand? Bret carried matches. Still. A wife should make things easier, not more difficult.

She hopped up, fumbled for matches, and lit the bedside lamp, turning the wick low. When footsteps sounded in the hall, she dove back in bed, heart banging in her chest. Whoever it was walked on by, opened and closed a door further from the stairs.

The last of the light outside disappeared. By lamplight the room was shadowy, a little spooky even. Where could Bret be? Had he changed his mind and taken a room of his own?

If so, it was her fault. She should have said yes the day he asked. All her agonizing hadn't changed her answer. She wanted to belong to him, have him belong to her. She wanted him to touch her more, wanted to touch him.

She really wanted more kisses like the Kiss. She touched the tip of her tongue to the bow of her upper lip, remembering.

Instead of worrying about the coming winter, spring, or next year, she should have grabbed hold of what she could have right then.

Her fingers plucked at the edges of the sheet. She ought to get up again, give her hair those hundred strokes, or at least the ninety or so she owed. She ought to put out the lamp. Ought to but couldn't bring herself to.

She heaved a great sigh, flattened out on her back, the light gone from her as surely as from the sky, her mind and body heavy with disappointment.

Footsteps sounded in the hall again. She turned her head toward the door, waited for them to go on by. They didn't. She closed her eyes, held her breath. The key scraped in the lock. The door opened, closed.

"I didn't mean to be so long," Bret said softly. "I hope you didn't fall asleep and forget about me."

She started at the sound of a thump, sucked in a deep breath, and opened her eyes. He had dropped the leather case he used for his spare clothes on the floor near the door and was already halfway to the bed, beside it, looking down at her. "Since your eyes are open, I'll take that as no, you didn't fall asleep."

He put his hat on the table next to the lamp, soft light gleaming along his jaw as he did it. The only barber shop in town had been closed when they rode in, and except when they stayed with Belle and Gabe Chapman, Bret had never shaved himself that she knew of—until tonight. His hair looked damp at the temples.

The scent of bay rum reached her, faint, spicy. The thought he'd done that for her brought a smile. He smiled back, his eyes warm, features softer somehow. Her already quick breath quickened more.

The pile of her clothing plopped to the floor beside the chair. He sat to pull off his boots and stockings, exposing feet that looked long and white in the subdued light. Hassie rubbed one of her own feet with the other, imagined doing the same to his.

He rose and pulled his shirt off, undid his belt, and let his trousers slide down over narrow hips. She licked her lips. He wasn't going to blow out the lamp. Her racing heart pounded harder, her body reacted more and more strongly as his underclothing came off exposing corded arms, broad chest, flat belly. And already rampant male organ.

She swallowed hard, suddenly so hot she wanted to throw the covers off. Before she could move, Bret solved that problem, pulling the covers aside and leaning over her.

"Tell me I can leave the light on. I want to see you."

Hassie nodded, bracing herself for what was coming. It would be better because she loved him, because she was attracted not repulsed, because he smelled of soap and bay rum and not liquor and stale sweat. Even so, with the way her breasts felt right now, squeezing and kneading would be more painful than ever. Wet as she was, any groping between her legs would be more embarrassing.

Younger, stronger, and more vigorous than Cyrus, surely he would invade her and finish quickly. Maybe he would kiss her at least once before he fell asleep.

The mattress moved under his weight. His lips feathered across hers. Her breath caught. A small moan escaped, and she tried to stifle it.

"Don't," he whispered against her lips, "Don't keep anything inside. If you feel like talking that Greek at me, do it."

She laughed, felt him inhale her laughter.

"You have the most beautiful laugh. It runs up and down my spine, shivers over my skin, and makes me want to grab hold of you like a mad man. You have no idea...." His mouth closed over hers again, his tongue tracing her upper lip, lower, along the seam.

He didn't dislike her laugh? Didn't...? His tongue stroked, caressed, teased, and she lost track of the thought, as the world blurred and spun. She floated on the sensations, grew dizzy on them, moaned a small protest when his tongue withdrew, floated again as his mouth moved across her jaw, behind her ear. Soft, warm kisses, gentle, tugging nips. He moved down her neck, didn't react to the scar as he kissed his way past it.

"Let's get this dress off you."

She didn't care what he called her nightgown, was more than willing. Unbuttoned, wriggled. Skin against skin all over. Their legs tangled, his longer, more muscled, rougher. His organ pressed against her thigh, hard, hot.

Warm, calloused hands cupped her breasts, and any thought of not wanting him to knead or touch fled. She wanted anything he would do, could do. His thumb rubbed a nipple, flicked across it, and she wanted that, wanted more of it.

He kissed her again, long, slow. Electricity sizzled under her skin, deep into her belly, down to her core. Through the haze of sensation and emotion, her only clear thoughts were, *Don't stop. Please don't stop.*

His mouth moved down her neck again, his breath hot and moist on her skin. Across her collarbones, to her breast, to a nipple.

She lost control of quiet. "Bret!"

He laughed, a deep rumble in his throat. "I understood that. You said 'more'."

He knew. Without words, he knew. Her fingers tangled in his hair. She gave a tug, trying to move him into position between her legs. She wanted that too, wanted him deep inside. He ignored her, held a nipple with his teeth, teased with his tongue.

Tugging harder on his hair only moved him to the other breast, down the hollow between her ribs, across her belly. One hand curved between her legs. His long fingers explored. Her hands ran down to his back, and she tried again to pull him into place. Into where she wanted him.

"Not yet," he whispered.

His fingers invaded, stroked. Lightening flashed, not outside but in her head, behind her eyes, the shuddering explosion in her body so intense she cried out as red and white sparks scattered through the soft yellow glow of the lamp.

When it was over, she lay quiet, concentrated on breathing, unsure if what had just happened was real. Bret touched his lips to hers lightly.

"Good?"

She nodded, searching for some word that would describe something so far beyond good and not finding it. "Good."

"I understood that too. You said 'more'." This time her laugh sounded shaky in her own ears. More was impossible. Recovering from something so overwhelming would take days. It would take...

He kissed her again, those maddeningly arousing kisses. Her body stirred. He explored her skin, muscle, and bone with his hands and his mouth. He kissed places she was sure no one should want to touch, much less kiss.

The fever rose again, and soft sounds of desire escaped with each breath. She pulled at his shoulders again to bring him over her, and this time he gave what she wanted, settled between her thighs, slid into her hot, wet core, stretching her past what she had known. Her muscles spasmed, and he groaned.

She did it again, deliberately this time.

"Hassie." Her plain name sounded like it belonged to someone else, someone beautiful and desirable and loved.

She locked her legs around his. Her fingers dug into his back. The rhythm of his thrusts resonated through her, drew an involuntary response from her hips and inner muscles. Pleasure radiated into every fiber of her being, increased until it could no longer be contained and burst through her again, like the first time but different because he was *there*, part of her, and because seconds later she knew from the sound he made and way he thrust one last time hard and deep that he shared what she felt.

When he moved again, she resisted, even though his weight was beginning to crush her.

"Like this," he said, rolling to his back and pulling her half on top of him.

They were both sweaty and more in some places, and she didn't care. She kissed his jaw and snuggled in against him.

His fingers fumbled at the nape of her neck with the clasp to the chain of Mama's gold locket. He let the ring slide free and redid the clasp. "Are you sure you don't want a new ring of your own?"

She shook her head and held out her hand. "This one."

He slid the ring in place. She curled her hand tight around it and nestled back down.

"You climbed on top of me like this the time I got in bed with you when you were asleep, you know."

"No, I didn't."

"I understood that too. Yes, you did. I had all my clothes on, and you were mostly under covers but even so I envied Cyrus Petty."

Hassie yawned. Neither signing or writing would work without moving, and moving was beyond her. Tomorrow she would tell him he had wasted his envy. Tonight was perfect just like this.

26

Cassie had known marriage to Bret would be different, but nothing prepared her for how different. He called their coupling making love, which seemed strange in a way when it could be done without love, but at least in their case love ran in one direction and some kind of affection in the other. She liked the term. She loved loving him.

In the town where she had said yes, Bret finally picked up a new trail. A man convicted of selling whiskey and guns to the Utes had escaped on the trip to prison and killed a guard doing it. Colorado wanted the escapee back enough to pay a thousand dollars for him. Bret tracked the convict north through Colorado and into Wyoming.

Hassie's newfound marital delight faded in direct proportion to how far north they went. She didn't want to meet Indians, and the chances of that grew higher with every mile they traveled toward the last hunting grounds of the Sioux and Cheyenne. Bret didn't laugh at her fears either. He made her practice leaving Brownie and getting behind him on Jasper without ever touching the ground.

He also let her stay behind him on Jasper for the rest of the afternoon after she learned to make the switch. Plastered against his back, arms around him, she almost forgave him for forcing her do such a scary thing.

Bret caught the convict in Cheyenne, sitting in a restaurant feeding his face as if he hadn't a care in the world. Some men seemed to think leaving one state or territory and entering another gave them as much protection as crossing into Mexico or Canada. In a way it did; Colorado lawmen wouldn't pursue a lawbreaker into Wyoming. Men like Bret would.

After stashing the prisoner with the town marshal, Hassie basked in the now familiar luxury of a hot bath and happily ruined some of her pristine cleanliness making love with Bret at their hotel afterward. When her stomach growled, they laughed and walked to a different restaurant for supper.

"That other place is probably feeling less than friendly after I hauled one of their customers away at gunpoint," Bret said. "Especially when he hadn't paid yet."

Hassie had waited outside, but she had no doubt Bret had thrown at least two bits on the table before prodding his prisoner outside. She didn't care. This restaurant looked much the same, bare wood walls and tables, menu chalked on a board on the wall.

She was considering the menu hungrily when a familiar voice stole her appetite.

"Well, I'll be goldarned, if it ain't Hassie Ahearne. Mrs. Petty now, I guess."

Without the voice, she never would have recognized Eddy Grimes, the oldest of Ned Grimes' sons. Thin and stooped, long black hair blending into long black beard, he bore no resemblance to the boy and young man she had known. Of course, if she hadn't changed into a dress, he might never have recognized her either, which made her regret the change.

"She's Mrs. Sterling now," Bret said, voice cold.

"Is that right." Never the most sensitive soul, Eddy ignored the warning in Bret's voice and pulled up a chair without being invited. "I almost had to marry her myself once. Pa caught us kissing out in the barn and went half-crazy. He probably would have made me marry her if she wasn't a...."

For the first time Eddy seemed to notice the frosty atmosphere at the table. "Well, you know. He already decided he wanted to sell out and move on to Texas, only no one was buying after the war. So he told old Cyrus Vance he could have our corn crop in the field for whiskey-making if he took her, and darned if Cyrus didn't marry her."

"Your father sold her?" Bret managed to sound both incredulous and murderous at the same time.

Finally showing signs of recognizing Bret's attitude, Eddy shifted nervously. "No, it wasn't like that. Pa was the one paying, not selling. She didn't have to go along with it, did she?"

Bret looked at Hassie. "Do you have anything to say to Mr. Grimes?"

Go away. That was what she wanted to say, but she signed, "Why isn't he in Texas?"

Eddy whistled, causing heads to turn around them. "You understand those signs she does? None of us could ever get the hang of it for trying."

"Texas?"

"Oh, yeah. Well, Texas didn't work out so good for us. Pa got killed by Comanches less than a year after we got there. After that we all headed north again. I been prospecting, found a little silver in Colorado, but a man's never going to get rich off silver. I'm on my way to Montana now. Gold up there." His eyes shone with the fever.

"There are a lot of hostile Sioux between you and Montana."

Eddy shrugged. "There's ways." He pushed back his chair, got to his feet, and grinned at Hassie. "So old Cyrus kicked it, and you did better this time. Good for you. Nice meeting you, Mr. Sterling."

He waved a hand and left, a man Hassie knew to be no more than Bret's age who looked twice that.

"It's hard to believe Comanches killed his father and he's stupid enough to try going through a few thousand Sioux," Bret said, his voice neutral.

"I did not kiss him. He trapped me in the barn and kissed me, and I did not want to marry him."

"I figured that. Did he hurt you?"

"No." She sighed, picked up the slate. *"Before the war, when they were young, he and his brothers were just pests. They tried to kiss and touch all the time, but it was teasing. When they came back from the war, they had changed. I didn't want to believe any of them would hurt me, but they scared me. I tried to avoid them, but sometimes I couldn't."*

"The war changed a lot of us."

She nodded at the truth of that.

"B-e-e-f s-t-e-w? C-h-I-c-k-e-n? H-a-m?"

Hassie laughed, her appetite returning. Under the table she threaded her fingers into his and held on until their food came.

27

Coffee scented the chilly late afternoon air, and biscuits were already baking as Bret dropped pieces of rabbit into the frying pan. At least Gunner wasn't sitting close drooling and pretending imminent starvation. The dog had crunched his way through his own rabbit already and taken off into the brush.

And Hassie. Bret smiled to himself. Hassie was over in the middle of some bushes she had tied the horses around head to tail. Good thing even Jasper, who could be a mite touchy now and then, wasn't a kicker. She was changing her drawers and doing that double modesty thing.

At first he'd thought she'd gone off to deal with the monthly blood flow. It was about that time. She had to know he knew, but she still went to great lengths to hide every sign. Marriage might mean tangled, naked, sweaty bodies, but it didn't mean letting him get a glimpse of menstrual blood.

The one time he'd half-seen her washing rags, she'd all but fallen in the creek trying to hide the things. At least a simple change to clean underclothing wouldn't take as long.

With supper under control, Bret picked up the tin box of posters and started leafing through. Daylight would disappear faster here amid the pines of the foothills than out on the plains, and he wanted to find a particular poster.

"Halloo the fire. Care for some company?"

On his feet before the man finished the greeting, Bret drew his revolver and moved back into the trees. No, he didn't want company. Refusing wasn't an option, but caution was. Hassie knew to stay put until he called her, and she'd be spending a boring evening there in the bushes unless this fellow proved harmless.

Three men moved through the trees. They'd left their horses back out of sight. Bret thumbed back the hammer.

"Now that's not friendly."

The voice was behind him, as was the gun in his back. The man behind took the revolver from Bret's hand.

"Let's go see what you're cooking."

Four of them.

Bret walked out of the trees to the fire. When he stopped, a man came out from behind him, but the gun stayed in his back. Five. He dared a quick look over his shoulder to be sure. Only five in sight. As if that weren't enough.

With luck, they'd steal everything and ride away, but the wolfish look in the close-set eyes of the pock-faced man facing him made that unlikely.

Bret held his hands against the light gray background of his shirt and began spelling. "R-u-n h-I-d-e. R-u-n h-I-d-e." He kept it up until one of them noticed.

"What the hell. You having fits or what? Quit that."

"Just twitchy. I get twitchy with guns pointing at me."

Two of the men helped themselves to the coffee, using the two cups by the fire, not yet asking why there were two. Another one started pawing through the posters.

"Hey, these are wanted posters. I bet I'm in here."

"Let me see that."

Posters fluttered to the ground, a few fell in the fire and flared for a moment before turning to ash.

"Bounty hunter!"

Bret's own heavy revolver smashed into the side of his face. Before his head cleared, a sharp sound split the air, flame spurted from the gun, and his right leg collapsed as if poleaxed. He hit the ground, the leg numb and useless. The pain came later, a wave so intense the world turned black for a moment.

Pock Face's eyes glittered with pleasure. "You're a dead man, bounty hunter, but don't think it's going to be quick and easy. By the time I'm done, you'll beg to die."

The second shot hit Bret's right shoulder. Fighting to stay conscious he curled on his side, fingers scrabbling for the gun in his boot. He prayed Hassie was gone, running through the night and gone.

WHEN SHE FIRST heard the stranger call out, Hassie crouched down amid the bushes. Bret would not want her showing her face around a stranger. She didn't believe every man who saw her immediately planned a criminal attack, but considering what had happened in Werver and with the Quentin boy and his friends, she had no urge to argue the matter.

After a moment, she crawled forward and peeked through Packie's legs. Five men—five—stood around Bret, and something was wrong. The setting sun and the tall trees all around made it hard to see, but Bret was signing, spelling. Three repetitions, and she understood.

She backed away and rose to her feet. Once she was among the trees, evading pursuit would be easy. Night would help her hide.

A gunshot cracked. Forgetting to stay down, she looked over Packie's back, saw Bret on the ground. Without thought, her hand went to the gun Bret insisted she carry. Reason prevailed. She could never hit one of those men, and there were five.

As if from far away, a man's voice said terrible things to Bret. A second shot rang out followed by furious barking and growling.

"Hell and damnation, shoot that dog."

More shots. She had only ever hit any target with one gun. Two strides and Hassie reached Jasper and yanked the shotgun out of the scabbard on the saddle. She ducked under Packie's neck and thumbed back both hammers.

The men had all turned toward the trees, still shooting at Gunner even though he had disappeared. Bret was alive, one arm moving. Hassie raised the shotgun and jammed it tight against her shoulder. She aimed high, afraid more than anything her wild shot would hit Bret. Her eyes squeezed tight shut against her will as she pulled the first trigger. The shotgun boomed.

Hassie opened her eyes as the man who had shot Bret crumpled to the ground. A reddish cloud hung in the air where he had been and slowly dispersed. Three of the remaining men froze. The fourth reached for his gun, and Bret shot him, the little boot gun barking three times.

The man Bret shot fell. None of the others moved. Hassie stood frozen, her finger curled around the second trigger of the shotgun. Gunner charged back out of the trees, circling the three men still on their feet, darting in, snapping, biting at their legs.

Bret called the dog, twice, three times before Gunner backed off, still growling. It also took Bret several tries to make it to a sitting position, but once he did that he pulled his pistol from the hand of the dead man near his legs, kept both guns pointed at the three men standing.

Blood covered half Bret's face. More blood soaked his shirt and trouser leg. Hassie wanted to run to him but couldn't move.

"Hassie. Hassie, sweetheart."

His voice didn't sound right. She managed to turn her head a fraction.

"Let the hammer down easy and go get the handcuffs. Get a set of hobbles too."

Hassie fought through the haze in her mind and finally remembered how to do that. Swiping angrily at the tears running down her face, she went to get the handcuffs and hobbles.

Without Gunner to help, she never would have been able to do it. Bret ordered the men one by one to back up to a tree and put their hands around the trunk. There were only two sets of handcuffs. She used them on the first two and the hobbles on the third.

By the time she was done, the guns were wavering in Bret's hands. He sagged back to the ground when she had finished. "Take Jasper and head for the next town. It's only four, five hours ahead. You can get help there, and you can be back by morning."

She ignored him. The clean cloths she used for her monthly flow would have to do for bandages. Bandaging the leg was easy, but there was something about it....

"It's broken," Bret said. "Better a broken shin than the knee he was aiming for. I think he did better on my shoulder."

The shoulder was harder to bandage too. He was going to lose consciousness soon. His eyes kept losing focus, snapping back, then drifting again.

She brought Jasper close. The Thoroughbred was used to gunfire, but he didn't like the strangers, the blood, and the pacing, growling dog. He fiddle-footed, sidled, wouldn't stand still. Jasper was faster than the other horses. His saddle was the one with stirrups the right length for Bret.

Hassie stopped fighting the nervous horse, took him back to the bushes and tied him. She pulled his saddle off and re-saddled Brownie with it. It was too narrow for Brownie and would bruise her back. Bruises would heal with time. Gunshots needed a doctor.

Brownie stood patiently. Bret came awake enough to argue. "No, I can't.... No way to get on a horse. Go for help."

"I am not leaving you here bleeding," she signed.

"You have to."

No, she didn't. She pulled her pistol out of the holster in her pocket and approached the man held by the hobbles. He sprang to his feet fast when she undid one cuff. She waved the gun at him, at Bret, at the horse.

"Sure, and I bet you're going to let me go as thanks for heaving him on that horse."

She shook her head and imitated the way Bret had pointed his guns at the heads of Quentin and his son. It worked. The man cursed and muttered, but he went over to Bret, got his shoulder under Bret's good arm and lifted him to his feet. Once he had a foot in the stirrup, Bret managed to struggle up a little, get the broken right leg over Brownie's back, and grab hold of the saddle horn.

Hassie saw the outlaw's hand creeping toward the rifle, still in its scabbard on the saddle. She shoved the muzzle of her revolver in his ear. The hand came away.

She gestured toward the tree. He started for it then stopped a few feet away. "I ain't going back there. I don't believe you're going to shoot me in cold blood just standing here."

This close she couldn't miss, could she? She raised the gun higher, and he lunged for it. She shot him in the upper chest. He staggered back and fell, fell close enough she managed to pull his arms around the tree and fasten them there.

"I'll bleed to death if you leave me here like this."

Maybe he would, and she didn't care. Bret's was the only blood she cared about, and Bret looked as if he was going to fall off Brownie any minute. She hurried to him, tied his hands to the saddle horn and his feet in the stirrups.

She had to climb up on Jasper and use him to get on Brownie's back behind Bret, but she managed it. After that all she had to do was keep Bret's sagging weight in the saddle until they reached town.

THE TRAIL WAS narrow and rough, steep in places. Before long, Hassie's arms burned with the strain of keeping Bret's weight balanced in the saddle. At first he seemed to regain consciousness now and then, help her, but as the hours passed, that stopped. He grew heavier. Or her arms grew weaker.

She considered tying her own wrists to the saddle but couldn't see how to do that from where she was and wasn't sure it would keep him from falling. Brownie plodded on through the night, slow but so blessedly steady.

Resting her cheek against Bret's back, Hassie prayed, her tears soaking his shirt. Dark shadows of buildings rose on each side of the road before she realized they had reached the town. How was she going to rouse anyone and find a doctor?

The tinny sound of a piano drifted on the night air, and a speck of light floated in the darkness ahead. A saloon. She urged Brownie on.

Yesterday the thought of walking into a saloon by herself in the middle of the night would have scared her silly. Tonight she made sure Bret was balanced in the saddle as best possible and slid down off Brownie in front of the saloon.

Her knees buckled when she hit the ground, and she staggered her way onto the walk. Pushing through the doors, she stood just inside, unsure how to ask for help. The slate was hours away, forgotten in the saddlebags on the ground behind Brownie's saddle.

One of the men looked up, glanced away then looked back and stared. "Looky there. That's a female in trousers."

Every head turned. Every pair of eyes stared. The piano stopped. She touched her blood-covered wedding ring, gestured outside. No one gave any sign of understanding.

"Look at the blood," someone said. "She must be hurt bad."

Several of the men rose from their tables. One headed toward her. Hassie backed up. He kept coming. She backed out through the door, ran to Brownie and Bret. And Gunner, who was still ready to take on anything that moved.

The man stopped, so did two others who had followed him out.

"Is that dog going to bite if I come see your man?"

Hassie put a hand on Gunner, and he quieted, although inaudible growls still vibrated under her hand.

The first man approached, touched Bret.

"Is he dead?" another one said.

"Nope, but he ain't very alive either. We better get him to Doc's."

Hassie almost sobbed with relief. They were going to help.

28

More men poured out of the saloon, and a small crowd followed Brownie through town to a house on the outskirts. The first man who had come after Hassie pounded on the door of the darkened house until someone answered.

The men untied Bret from the saddle and carried him around to a side door with surprising care. Hassie abandoned Brownie at the gate to the yard, but Gunner was determined to stay with her. He almost made it into the house before one brave soul blocked him with a leg and closed the door in his face.

A middle-aged woman, wrapped round with a woolen robe, face still heavy with sleep, met them with a lamp as the men carried Bret through a small room furnished with only chairs to another where the light reflected from dozens of bottles on shelves all around. The men gave every sign of having done this before as they laid Bret on a long table without instruction.

Hassie held Bret's left hand, touched that side of his face. All the damage was on his right side.

"This is his woman," the first man said as he was leaving. "She don't talk much."

A wish she could thank them flitted through Hassie's mind but vanished in her fear for Bret. His tan looked like paint on his deathly white skin.

A thin, sandy-haired man about the woman's age came into the room, still pulling suspenders up over a rumpled shirt. "What have we here?"

"Beaten, shot. I think this is his wife. According to Jed Yancy and that lot she just walked into the saloon and lured the men into the street where this one was tied on a horse. She hasn't said a word to anyone."

The doctor grunted. "Shock maybe. If you'll get hot water, I'll see what we're dealing with here. After that maybe some hot tea would help the young lady tell us what happened."

The doctor peeled away the bandages and most of Bret's clothing. So much blood, such ugly dark holes torn in flesh.

After a look, the doctor wrapped the leg wound tight again. The woman reappeared with a pitcher of hot water and tried to get Hassie to leave. "Come on out to the kitchen. Let's clean you up and see about that tea. My husband knows what he's doing."

Hassie shook her head, shrugged the woman off. The doctor exchanged a look with his wife.

"I'll bring the tea here," she said.

He nodded. After the woman left, the doctor took Hassie by the shoulders. "You can stay, but you have to stand back. My wife knows what needs to be done, but you can't help. Understand?"

Understanding was one thing, agreeing another. The doctor pulled Hassie's hand away from Bret's and sat her on a chair by the counter under the rows of bottle-filled shelves. Once she gave in and sat, Hassie feared she'd never be able to get up again.

The doctor's wife bustled back in with the cup of tea. Hassie tried to ignore it, but didn't succeed.

The woman curved Hassie's hands around the cup. "You won't do him any good if you pass out and we have to take care of you," she whispered.

Hassie drank the heavily sugared tea.

The doctor's wife lit the lamp that hung over the table. The two of them scrubbed their hands to the elbows, and the doctor bent over Bret's shoulder.

"This is bleeding the worst, and it needs to be stopped," the doctor said, "but the leg is a mess. If you clean up his face, a few stitches will take care of that. Even if there's a zygomatic fracture, the damage there is nothing. Let's hope no one else needs a doctor tonight."

Hassie clutched the teacup so hard the handle broke off with a little pop. She sat it on the counter and twisted her hands together. Neither the doctor nor his wife noticed.

The hours of the night passed slowly. As the doctor wielded terrible probes, scissors, and scalpels, Hassie prayed Bret wouldn't wake up until it was all over.

Then she prayed that he would wake up when it was all over.

BRET WOKE TO total darkness, his heart racing, body and mind both convinced he was in mortal danger. Memories flashed of men and guns, the blast of a shotgun, a man's face dissolving behind a mist of blood. And Hassie. Hassie not running but standing frozen with a shotgun on her shoulder. Hassie.

Pain tore through his right arm when he tried to sit up. He flailed the other arm, and it came down on silky softness.

Hassie's hair. Bret drew in great gasping breaths as his eyes adjusted to the dark enough to distinguish the gray square of a window, a hint of dawn there surely. He made out Hassie's form beside him and calmed.

Wherever they were now must be safe. She slept peacefully beside him. He fingered her hair, wrapped as much as he could get hold of around his hand and held tight. Reassured by the feel of it, he closed his eyes and drifted away from his questions and his pain.

When he woke again, Hassie was still beside him on the bed, sitting up against the headboard, holding his hand. He tried to sit up too.

"Where are we?"

She let go of his hand to sign. "Doctor's. Stay still."

"I don't want to stay still. I want...."

"Sshh." She held a cup of water against his mouth.

"I need to get rid of water, not take more in."

She laughed. "Drink first."

The water was bitter with minerals, but he was too thirsty to care. After they took care of the other needs, he said, "I remember you handcuffing them to the trees, but after that pretty much nothing. What happened after I passed out?"

The slate was on the nearby dresser. She'd been thinking awfully clearly if she remembered to bring that along with his unconscious body. Come to think of it, she was wearing the pink dress, and how the hell could that be?

She wrote, erased, wrote more.

"I rode that horse?" His horror at the thought disappeared somewhere in the brilliance of her smile.

"The sheriff and his deputies went and got the bad men and Jasper and Packie and all our things. Those men are in jail now."

"Gunner?"

She ran a finger over the crown of her head and then over her shoulder.

"Grazes?"

"Doctor gave me salve."

"You were supposed to run and hide."

She hung her head, looking for all the world as if she was ashamed of what she had done. *"I could not leave you."*

His thoughts were disintegrating, swirling away in heavy fog. He managed to ask, "Did you keep your eyes open?" but not to stay awake for the answer.

IN HIS FEW lucid moments, Bret ascribed the cloud that wouldn't lift from his mind to fever. Until the morning he woke halfway clear-headed and thought about how bitter the water here tasted sometimes but not all the time. He'd never had to take laudanum, but he'd heard it described by those who had.

The next time his sweet wife approached with broth, he said, "Is there laudanum in that?"

Her guilty look confirmed his suspicion.

"I'm not drinking another swallow until you swear it doesn't have that stuff in it."

She put the broth down to sign. "The doctor says you need it."

"I don't care what the doctor says."

"You have to drink."

"No, I don't."

She disappeared, and Bret eyed the water pitcher on the bedside table. He was thirsty, and surely the whole pitcher wasn't poisoned. He rolled to his side, ignoring the fire in his leg and shoulder and reached.

"You get yourself flat back down again, or I'll tie you."

So this was the doctor Hassie had elevated to hero status. Bret had vague recollections of a tall, thin man leaning over him, making the pain worse. "Dr. MacGregor, I presume?"

"Yes, the doctor who put you back together and who says you need to take laudanum for at least another week."

"Why?"

The doctor moved into the room and frowned down at Bret as ferociously as a man with a pale, delicately boned face could. "Because the pain will have you doing something stupid soon, and because unless that leg stays absolutely still for at least another three weeks, you're going to be lame for the rest of your life."

"You don't think the next dose could wait until the pain gets bad, and I could have a few moments of clarity now and then? It's addictive, isn't it?"

"It can be."

"I don't want any more."

The doctor sighed and lowered himself to the chair by the bed. "Your wife says you're pigheaded beyond belief."

"That's the word she used, 'pigheaded'?"

"The word she wrote may actually have been stubborn. Her vocabulary is more refined than mine, and she doesn't deal with fools who won't take care of themselves as often as I do." As he spoke the doctor turned back the bed covers and peered at Bret's leg. "It's a bad break, and I had to take out some sizable pieces of bone. If this had happened during the war, that leg would have been lopped off, you know."

"The surgeons didn't have much time for finesse back then."

A slight smile played across the doctor's face. "No, we didn't."

"I admit I'm grateful to wake up with everything still attached. Thank you."

"Thank your wife that you're still alive. By the time you got here you didn't have much more blood to lose."

Bret knew that. He'd known the odds when he told her to leave him and get help.

Flipping the covers back in place, the doctor continued, "If I could cast that leg, I wouldn't be so worried, but with the open wound, I can't. So you have a splint instead, and you have to behave yourself, no acrobatics of the sort you were just trying. Under no circumstances are you to put any weight on that leg. Don't even put your foot on the floor."

The doctor poured a glass of water from the pitcher and handed it to Bret. "Unadulterated, I promise."

After a wary taste verified the doctor's promise, Bret drank it down. "So how bad will this be in the end? Are you telling me if I play dead for weeks, I won't be lame? What about my arm?"

The doctor rubbed his forehead as if deciding what to say. "No, I can't guarantee how well either the arm or the leg will work after they heal. What I can tell you is that in my experience with wounds like these, some people find the pain of using the limb too much and don't try. Muscles atrophy, and they never have full use again. Others are pigheaded—stubborn—and refuse to let pain stop them from doing as they please. A certain percentage of those people regain full use of the limb."

"What percentage?"

"I don't keep records. More than half at a guess, and the rest do better than expected. First you have to heal properly, and then you're talking a year or so before you know for sure."

Bret stared at the ceiling, thinking about it. He had expected a more cut and dried answer.

"Suppose I tell Mrs. Sterling laudanum upon request only," the doctor offered.

"I appreciate that. How's she doing?"

"My wife is ready to adopt her. They're getting along famously."

Good. Someone needed to be getting along famously.

LYING AROUND LIKE a corpse would be easier if his nurse was some big hairy fellow instead of Hassie. After only a single clear-headed day, Bret wanted to pull her down on the bed on top of him every time she came close.

She slept beside him, and he almost wished she still had to wear the borrowed nightgown from the doctor's wife. He had a hazy memory of the oversized gown and the way it had hung in baggy folds, the hem dragging on the floor. The worn cloth of Hassie's own gown molded to her no longer half-starved body.

What he needed, Bret decided, was a male nurse. A big man with his belly hanging over his belt. Maybe one who chewed tobacco, had brown teeth, and spit often.

When the living embodiment of Bret's imaginary perfect nurse knocked on the frame of the bedroom door and walked in, Bret said, "I've changed my mind."

"Pardon?"

Catching sight of the badge on the man's wide chest, Bret said, "Never mind. I thought you were someone else." At least the lawman's cheeks showed no sign of a chaw.

"Sheriff Thomas Fleming," the big man said offering his hand then drawing it back. "Sorry, guess you won't be shaking any hands for a while."

"Not for a while," Bret said agreeably. He glanced at the doorway, surprised Hassie wasn't right there, worried he might be too tired to see the sheriff, or hungry, or thirsty, or anything else.

"I asked Mrs. MacGregor to talk your wife into going to town with her. I wanted to talk to you alone for a few minutes, get your version of what happened out there."

"There are versions?"

"My deputies and I went out there and picked up two bodies, two live men, and one mostly alive, and let's just say there are variations in their recollections, and it seems like Mrs. Sterling didn't see everything."

"No, she was back by the horses when they first showed up. Thank God." Bret described events until the point he lost consciousness, wondering as he did it what the sheriff meant by "one mostly alive." The sheriff was bound to enlighten him any minute now. "The rest you'll have to get from my wife. She can write it out for you."

"She already did that. The thing is...."

The sheriff pulled some papers from inside his vest and handed them to Bret. "Read that."

Hassie's handwriting was far more elegant rendered in ink on paper than with a chalk pencil on the slate, but Bret still would have recognized it from across the room. After a puzzled look at the sheriff, he began reading.

Halfway through he looked up. The sheriff was studiously scraping a spot on his trousers with a fingernail. Bret finished Hassie's statement and dropped the sheets on his chest.

"I never would have noticed," the sheriff said, "but the fellow she shot is a talker, and he's sure she should be in the next cell. Then the other two chimed in backing him up."

"You can't be thinking of arresting her."

"Of course not. Pretty soon folks around here will be taking up a collection in church to give her a medal."

"I didn't know she shot another one of them. It never occurred to me to ask her how she got me on a horse." And until yesterday he'd been too doped up on laudanum to think straight. Bret read the sentences again. "She didn't lie."

"No, she didn't, but it is a mite misleading. At first I just figured you did all the shooting. Most men would, I guess. Doc says you don't strike him as the kind of man who would get ugly with a wife who let it be known she saved his bacon. So why did she do it?"

"I'll thank the doctor for his character reference the next time I see him," Bret said dryly as he picked up Hassie's statement again.

"The dog distracted the bad men, so it was possible to shoot one with the shotgun." Further on: *The man would not go back to the tree and tried to get a gun so it was necessary to shoot him."*

"She doesn't like guns. I can't tell you how much ammunition we've wasted, and she can't pull a trigger and keep her eyes open. She told me once she could never shoot a human. My guess is she'd rather nobody know."

The sheriff shook his head. "I'd give her that if I could then, but it's all over town now. Doc treated the fellow, and he probably didn't say anything, but my deputies had no reason not to talk about it. Neither did I."

Bret shrugged, trying to hide the effects of the throbbing pain in his leg. He hadn't slept much last night and was already debating the wisdom of his new laudanum-free recovery.

"I have something else to show you," the sheriff said, pulling out more papers.

Bret shuffled through the five wanted posters, gave the sheriff an incredulous look, and went through them again. Starting with the twenty-five hundred dollar reward for Pock-Face, the bounties on the five men totaled forty-eight hundred dollars.

"I set out in early April and haven't made that much all year," he said, still hardly believing it.

The sheriff cleared his throat. "Well as to that, my deputies and I did spend an entire day going out there and cleaning up the mess. We figure that should be worth, oh, say, twenty percent."

The man looked slightly embarrassed but determined.

"If you're the sheriff, you're responsible for the whole county. They were in the county, weren't they?"

The sheriff admitted as much with a nod.

"So going to get them was your job."

"It's not our job to clean up your camp, pack up, and bring everything back for you. Mrs. Sterling wouldn't go back with us, you know. Drew us a map of sorts, but we'd never have found it if the horses hadn't caught wind of us and started raising hell."

Hassie stepped into the doorway. Bret waved the posters. "Did you know about this?"

She nodded.

"The sheriff thinks he and his deputies should have twenty percent."

She held up both hands, all fingers extended, then signed.

"Ten, and you get their horses and gear," Bret interpreted.

Dull red stained the sheriff's cheeks. "Ten and the horses. That's good. I'll tell my men."

He hunched over and left hurriedly as if he'd forgotten an important appointment. Hassie followed him out but returned quickly and sat carefully on the edge of the bed.

"That was a short shopping trip," Bret said.

"Nothing to buy."

"Go back again and buy some dresses and hats and things. There's no use having all that newfound wealth if you don't spend it."

She smiled and spelled, "L-a-u-d-a-n-u-m?"

The desire to be free of the drug warred with the desire to be free of the pain. "You wouldn't like to take off all your clothes and climb in here with me instead, would you?"

"Doctor says no."

"You asked him that, did you?"

Her blush was much more attractive than the sheriff's. Bret gritted his teeth against the rising pain and gave in. "All right, but let's try half as much as you've been giving me."

The half dose didn't kill the pain, but it dimmed it enough he was able to sleep.

29

The one prescription from Dr. MacGregor Hassie simply refused to follow was that she should not sleep in the same bed as Bret. Kicking out in her sleep and so much as jostling the broken leg would be dangerous.

In spite of the fear the doctor's dire warnings inspired, Hassie couldn't bring herself to sleep in another room or even on a cot in the same room. She needed to be close enough to Bret to touch him, breathe his scent, and feel the rhythm of his breathing, so she slept on top of the covers wrapped in a blanket and rejected every other suggestion.

The first night Bret took only half a dose of laudanum, she woke in the middle of the night to the sound of his mumbling and feel of his jerky movements. His head rolled from side to side. She reached to touch him and hesitated. Was this a bad dream or pain from not taking enough medicine?

He thrashed, and the doctor's frowning face rose in her mind. Shaking Bret's good shoulder woke him all right. His hand clamped around her wrist so hard it hurt.

"Hassie? Hassie." His grip loosened. His breathing slowed from gasps to merely rapid and finally to normal. He muttered something else too low to catch, then said distinctly, "Thanks, but the dog is better."

She settled beside him again, not sure if he had really fallen back to sleep so quickly or if he was only pretending.

Gunner was better? Tomorrow he was going to tell her what he meant by that.

In the morning she waited until after breakfast before broaching the subject, standing a good distance from the bed and signing slowly, spelling every word that might be in doubt. "Last night you said Gunner is better than I am. How is he better?"

"You must have misunderstood me."

"I did not. You had a bad dream, and I woke you. You said Gunner is better. Very clear."

He wriggled in the bed as if uncomfortable, and she didn't hurry to fluff his pillow, rearrange the bedclothes, or ask what he needed.

"Since the war, I've had the same nightmare every so often."

"How often?"

"Not too often any more, every couple of weeks or so."

"A dog is in your dream?"

"No, no dogs, but Gunner has some sixth sense about it. Since you've been with me—except for the first time when I guess he was just getting his nightmare-chasing legs under him—he wakes me before it gets going. It's like being free of the thing. That's all I meant, he stops it sooner."

"Last night was my first time. Maybe I am getting my nightmare-chasing legs under me."

Bret smiled, which he hadn't been doing much of since being confined to the bed. "Maybe you are. I'd rather wake up to your face than his. And your breath. Definitely your breath."

"So you do not really like Gunner. You are good to him because he helps you."

"It started out like that, but we're friends now, and I'd be crazy not to appreciate him after what happened with Pock Face and his crew. I'd be even crazier not to appreciate you."

Appreciation was nice. Hassie tried not to think how much nicer love would be. She fluffed his pillow, straightened the bedclothes, and sat in the chair by the bed. "What is the nightmare about?"

"The war. I'm in a battle just like it happened and then...." He swallowed hard, his voice falling. "We're charging a stone wall the Rebs are behind. One raises up, and I shoot him. I see the ball hit, see him fall, and it's my brother Albert. After that there are others. People who weren't even in the war. Being free of that dream for months has been a gift."

"I did not wake you in time?"

"You did. Not before it got going but before I shot anyone I know."

"You did not kill your brother."

"No, I didn't. He didn't even die from a rifle shot. He died of camp fever."

"I waited last night because I was not sure it would be good to wake you. Next time I will be quicker. I will be as good as Gunner."

"There are other ways you are much better than Gunner."

His look started a hot flush she felt in the tips of her ears and other sensations lower down. She ignored them all. "No. Doctor says you must not even jostle your leg. Would you like a book to read? The doctor says you can have any of his books."

Bret turned his head away and didn't answer. Hassie went to see if she could help Mrs. MacGregor, wondering if the doctor had prescribed laudanum to keep the patient quiet in more ways than one.

AFTER TWO WEEKS of bedridden confinement, Bret's face had healed, leaving only a thin reddish scar across his cheekbone that would be all but invisible before another year passed.

To his surprise, Hassie was a better barber than many he'd paid over the years. She had kept his beard from growing near the stitches with a feather-light touch even when the swelling and bruising were at their worst.

"I had to shave Cyrus for many months when he was so sick," she explained.

"He could have done without and grown a beard."

"He did not want that."

Of course not. After Cyrus Petty had pickled himself to the point he couldn't get out of bed, lying there with his head in his young wife's lap while she shaved him was probably the highlight of each day.

Bret laid with his head in the same wife's lap as she shaved *him*, and the pleasure of her touch, the scent of shaving soap and Hassie, the scrape of the razor, all added up to the highlight of *his* day.

Every touch, every glance, and watching her as she fussed over him also added up to a fever that never quite subsided. Long stretches of celibacy had always seemed just another one of life's minor miseries, like sleeping on hard ground instead of a soft bed. A few weeks of marriage had transformed Hassie as wife from luxury to necessity.

And his damned leg was depriving him of her in every way, any way. One word he planned to ban from speech, sign, and spelling forever as soon as he got out of this bed was "jostle." If he heard one more time how his leg was going to turn to dust, fall off, or explode if it experienced a single jostle, he was going to get up, run a race on the blasted thing, and cut it off himself.

Or maybe not. Now that two more slivers of bone had worked their way out, the bullet wound was finally healing. His shoulder already looked pretty good, although his arm had no strength, and he couldn't raise it more than ninety degrees out from his side. Pushing to do more changed the chronic dull ache, to a fierce throb.

Bored, cranky, and in no mood for an examination or wound probing, Bret regarded Dr. MacGregor with disfavor when he walked in the room. The sight of crutches half-hidden behind the doctor's back changed that.

"Hallelujah, hand those over."

"Now, before you get excited and do something you'll regret...."

"Don't. Do not say the word that rhymes with hostile. I won't put my foot down. I'll treat the leg like fine crystal. Just let me out of here."

"I do think if you're careful, a chair in the parlor with the leg on a footstool would be safe. You can even have meals at the table, although it will be awkward with an elevated leg."

Hassie hovered behind the doctor, looking about the way she had on the Leavenworth ferry, hand on stomach and all. Bret pushed up from the bed, positioned the crutches under his arms and rose on his good leg. Between the pain that shot through his right shoulder as it took part of his weight and the surprise as Hassie rushed forward, arms outstretched, he almost fell back down on the bed.

"What do you think you're going to do?" he said, half-amused, half-irritated. "Catch me? I'd flatten you like a flapjack, and you wouldn't even pad my fall much."

The doctor cleared his throat. "Catching aside, do be careful."

Bret nodded and took a single step toward the door. The crutches had been made for a smaller man or a woman, forcing him into an awkward hunch. Ignoring his shoulder's complaints, Bret tapped off toward the door, his mood steadily improving.

In the parlor, he sank into a chair gratefully. No one need worry he'd want to travel long distances on crutches, at least not these crutches. Hassie had pillows under his leg almost before he got it on the footstool.

"Would you like a book? I could find a book."

"Let me just sit a minute. Next time you go to town, though, see about some stationery. I'd better write home and tell them what happened. I'll write Gabe too while I'm at it."

Overhearing, Mrs. MacGregor came out of the kitchen, wiping her hands on a towel. "You're welcome to use my stationery if you don't mind lavender, and I have a lap desk that will work perfectly for you there. I always end up at the kitchen table."

Bret exchanged a knowing glance with Hassie at the mention of pale purple paper. "There's no hurry," he said. "And now that I'm up, we'll move to the hotel in the next day or two and you can have a peaceful household."

The doctor's wife and Hassie both folded their hands at their waists and stared at him with matching unhappy faces.

"Oh, there's no need for that," Mrs. MacGregor said after a moment. "It's nice having young people around the house, and you're far from ready to manage in a hotel. Why you'd have to do stairs. How could you get up and down a flight of stairs? And you'd have to walk more than a block to the nearest restaurant, and it's a wretched place. We have another spare room if we need it, you know."

Bret had no illusions anyone enjoyed having him around these days. Hassie was the one Mrs. MacGregor didn't want leaving. The doctor had been right when he said his wife had all but adopted Hassie, and the feeling ran both ways.

"You're probably right," he said, conceding temporary defeat on the subject. "A while longer then. We appreciate all you've done."

"You're going to get a walloping bill for it too," Dr. MacGregor said, "and you're going to entertain me at times like this when business is slow." He pulled up a table and unfolded a red and black board. "If you can't play chess, you can learn, and if you can't play or learn, it will be checkers."

MacGregor saw patients any day and any time they showed up, and he traveled countless miles around the countryside to those who couldn't come to him. Bret wasn't sure he'd bet on the doctor ever having time for a complete game of chess, at least not in one sitting. Still.

"Chess," he said, "but I'll warn you I'm not very good at it. A few games during the war is all."

"That's good enough for me."

As the doctor set out the pieces, Bret wondered if Hassie could play, would play, or would like to learn. Or checkers.

She'd probably stick the tip of her tongue out every time she debated over a move.

A slight tightening in the groin warned him to give up that line of thought before he embarrassed himself. He shifted in the chair and focused on the painted wooden pieces.

For the next several days, being up and about tired Bret enough during the day he slept through the night. After that his body adjusted, and he lay awake until the middle of the night, fighting the urge to toss and turn. He thought of the crippling, life-changing wounds men he'd fought beside suffered during the war with new insight. Surviving their wounds would have been only the beginning for most of them.

Those men lay awake on miserable cots, often under nothing but a tent. They also didn't have the comfort or the temptation of wives sleeping beside them, all silk, satin, and velvet, although the nurses probably drove some of them half-crazy. Eight weeks MacGregor said. Five and a half to go.

Bret lay quiet in bed, waiting for Hassie to finish whatever last-minute chore she'd remembered in the kitchen and join him. He was a grown man, he could just grit his teeth and manage for a few more weeks.

The door clicked open. Hassie slipped through and closed it behind her. The pale blue robe she'd made with Mrs. MacGregor's sewing machine was a pretty thing, but then anything would look good with her hair hanging loose like that down the back of it.

She was ready to blow out the lamp and climb in beside him except for the hair. One hundred brush strokes. He counted along silently with her as he did every night. When this was over, he was going to brush it for her, let the long strands glide over one hand as the other pulled the brush through.

Ninety-nine. One hundred. She didn't come to blow out the lamp as he expected, but crossed the room to the paper-wrapped packages on the bureau. She brought the top one to the bed, opened it, and lifted out folds of pale green wool almost reverently.

"Feel. It is very soft."

He did feel. The wool had a cloud-like texture. At least she'd finally bought herself some nice things. "What is it?"

"Scarf. For your mother. I have one for Caroline too and one for your brother's wife. What is her name?"

Bret hadn't moved, but everything in him went a different kind of still. He ignored her question. "You bought gifts for my mother and sister because...?"

"For Christmas. Dr. MacGregor thinks you will be well enough to travel in time to be home for Christmas. I have silk handkerchiefs for your father and brother to embroider with their initials. Mrs. MacGregor thinks gray silk on the white would be good. Yes?"

She was too excited to wait for him to give an answer even if he had one, which he didn't.

"I was not sure about the children. Dolls and wooden toys take up too much room for the packs, and maybe they have those things? We can find them gifts in Missouri?"

In some stunned part of his mind, Bret registered that she'd only spelled half a dozen words out of all that, and he'd understood it all. Thinking about his steadily improving ability to understand her signing was a way to avoid thinking of what to say to her.

"Sure," he said finally. "We can probably get anything back home they have here."

"I should not have bought these?"

"Of course you should. You like them, and they might not have those exact things or enough of them in the store in Oak Hills."

"You don't like them?"

"I'd like them better if they were for you. Get yourself one."

"They had to order more from Kansas City. Only one left now. Lavender."

Bret relaxed, shoved aside concerns about his family. "Give that one to someone else and keep another for yourself. The green is pretty. I like the blue of your new robe."

She rewrapped the scarf and returned it to the bureau. The robe he liked came off and went over the back of the bedside chair. Bret's breath caught when she undid the small buttons at the neck of the nightgown. His fingers twitched watching her undo one after another of the tiny discs.

With them all undone, she pulled the gown up over her head and tossed it on top of the robe. Her skin gleamed in the lamplight. She was alabaster and ebony.

"I am too shy for the light," she signed, looking like a goddess and anything but shy. His skin rippled as she blew out the lamp, the flame in him leaping higher, not dying. The slippers still on her feet whispered against the floor as she moved to the side of the bed.

No weight dipped the mattress. The bedclothes lifted, peeled from his chest, his stomach, thighs, and landed at the foot of the bed. Her hand left a warm trail across skin already reacting to the chill of the night air as she pushed his borrowed nightshirt up.

Bret had imagined her straddling him like this at least a hundred times just today, couldn't imagine it without her legs against his, bumping his. And right now he didn't care.

She joined him on the bed, not rising up but curling down. Her palm slid across his belly, which was no longer warm but hot, almost as hot as his aching hard cock. Her hand stroked and cupped his testicles as her other hand grasped the base of his shaft.

She kissed the tip, her tongue swirled around, along the underside, and she took him into her mouth, her warm, wet mouth, and sucked. Bret moaned, his fists balling into the sheet beneath him to keep from grabbing her head, as the pleasure waved over him, through him. "Hassie."

More kisses. Her hair on his thigh, her cheek. Her warm, moist breath.

He lost control, his hips bucked. She didn't pull away.

"You need to.... I'm going to...," and the peak shuddered through him with such intensity, he wasn't sure where he'd spilled or what she'd done.

After a moment, she pulled his shirt down, the covers up, and slipped away. Sounds came from the wash basin. Bare feet padded back and stopped by the chair. When she nestled down close to him on top of the covers, wrapped in the damned blanket, she had her nightgown on again. He worked his good arm free and felt both the soft cotton and the rough wool when he pulled her close.

"Unwrap that blanket and let me pay you back."

She shook her head. "Next time."

At least that's what he thought she said, and she wasn't going to move.

Bret fought sleep for a long time, trying to cope with the wonder of it. None of the women he knew and had long admired had Hassie's generosity. When his letter arrived in Missouri, whatever the reaction to his simple statement that he had married a widow named Hassie Ahearne Petty and she would be with him when he made it home, no one would buy his new wife gifts because of Christmas or for any other reason.

Before the war, his father had gifted his mother and sisters with jewelry at Christmas, trinkets for the girls, expensive pieces for his mother. Bret only remembered the gifts going one way, head of household to females.

Thinking about it for the first time, he realized, "I ordered the cook to make your favorite..." didn't count as a gift.

When he had dreamed of marrying Mary, he had expected she would enjoy their coupling in the same passive way she enjoyed his kisses. Any passion would be his. Mary would no more dance with a flower-bedecked dog than she would shoot two killers and force one to lift her unconscious husband onto a horse.

Mary undoubtedly suffered from double modesty too, but in Bret's wildest imaginings he couldn't see her ever throwing it aside to give a husband pleasure and relief he desperately needed the one way possible without *jostling* his wretched, slowly healing leg.

And how exactly had she known how to do that? He had used his mouth on her in the few weeks they'd had to explore, and she had touched his genitals, but he'd never expected so much from a wife. He knew now her experience with Cyrus Petty had been as basic as that of a female animal only a lot less frequent, and while she wouldn't admit it, probably a lot less pleasant.

Mrs. MacGregor didn't look like the sort to be giving instruction on more than how to use the sewing machine, but looks must be deceiving. The doctor's anatomy books wouldn't be forthcoming on the particulars.

Loving Mary had been one of the certainties in his life since he was a boy. If the war hadn't torn through their lives, she would have been his wife, her children his. Their lives would have been part of an orderly, expected world where neighbors got along, luxuries were available for the asking, and their families were looked up to and respected as the largest landowners in the county, who had connections all the way to the Missouri statehouse.

Those feelings still resided in the back of his mind, but they had faded more this summer than in the years since he'd turned his back on that life and ridden off to war. Like an old photograph they had no color, no longer seemed real.

In contrast, this summer stood out vivid in his mind. Bright blue skies, green prairie, and deep red sunsets. Ebony hair, violet eyes, and ivory skin.

His feelings for Mary had been civilized, part of the world they'd lived in. Hassie evoked something very different. A much heftier dose of lust for one thing. Men joked that having a woman cured intense desire. Little did they know.

Having Hassie escalated every feeling. How could a man not want more of a woman who welcomed him eagerly, met him with passion, and gave the way she'd given tonight?

But that wasn't all. If the dog chased nightmares, Hassie chased anger, sorrow, bitterness. What he felt wasn't love as he had once defined it. It was—more?

He fell asleep still trying to untangle the knot of feelings, old and new. Still marveling over the contradictions of Hassie and his own good fortune.

HASSIE WOKE EARLY the next morning to the sight of gray eyes with a speculative gleam in them only inches away.

Bret's voice sounded hoarse and deeper than usual. "Good morning, Mrs. Sterling."

She giggled and burrowed her face into the cocoon of her blanket.

"I hope you're not so embarrassed you won't do it again."

Sitting up with the blanket around her like a cape so her hands were free, she signed, "I like when you do that to me."

"We'll have a contest someday, see who likes it more. Soon."

She laughed again and reached out to caress his stubbly cheek. He kissed her palm, and her body reacted with all too familiar wanting and frustration. The sooner he could move around enough for a contest like that, the better.

"Did MacGregor really say he thought we could be home for Christmas?"

"He did. December tenth will be eight weeks. Your leg will need more time after that to strengthen, but we can still be in Missouri before Christmas."

"Good. We'll leave on the eleventh."

No, they would not. Convincing him to stay here among friends for even the winter would be impossible. He was determined to return to Missouri. There were ways to keep a stubborn man from being foolish, though. Hassie kissed him again and rose to dress and get his shaving gear.

30

After four weeks, Dr. MacGregor stopped predicting dire consequences every time the foot of Bret's broken leg brushed the floor. After six weeks, the doctor had encouraged a little foot tapping and switching from two crutches to one.

On December tenth, eight weeks after the shooting, the doctor took the crutches back, and Hassie gave Bret a sturdy oak cane made by the local carpenter. That was the last of her cooperation. She didn't want to leave Dearfield.

Bret wasn't looking forward to the trip either. The more he used his leg, the more it ached, but he wanted to get home before the weather made it impossible, and he trusted MacGregor was right. The bone had healed. The pain came from muscles that needed to strengthen again. A few more months and the cane would go the way of the crutches.

Impatience to be on the way twisted through Bret as Hassie made excuses to stay first one day and then a second and third. The MacGregors abetted her.

"You could stay here till spring," Dr. MacGregor said, "It would be wiser, and if it makes you feel better, I'll charge you rent and you can start chopping wood for me next week."

Chopping wood would be acceptable, but a few days' travel wasn't? Bret didn't point out the obvious inconsistency there.

"You've done enough, and my family is expecting us," he told the doctor.

To Hassie he said, "Tomorrow. The weather isn't going to hold forever. Anything you haven't bought or packed we can do without. We're leaving right after breakfast tomorrow."

He suppressed a guilty twinge at the unhappy look on her face, but even the MacGregors admitted the weather was unseasonably fine right now, one mild, sunny day after another. They had already delayed starting out for more days than the trip would take. Two days in the saddle, one cold night in between, and they'd be at the train station. Two days after that, home.

Breakfast the next morning was a bleak affair. In between bouts of forced cheerfulness, Mrs. MacGregor dabbed at her eyes with her apron. Dr. MacGregor bolted off mid-meal, his relief at having a bleeding patient to deal with palpable.

Hassie broke down and bawled at the end before following Bret outside to the horses.

"You are limping," she signed, wiping tears from a sad face.

"I am, and we're going anyway. Once I'm in the saddle, I won't be limping, and all I have to do is sit."

Her shoulders slumped. Abandoning further resistance, she mounted Brownie. Waving one last time to Mrs. MacGregor, who had come out to the porch, they rode through Dearfield and headed east.

After the first day of "just sitting" in the saddle, Bret wished he'd brought the crutches along. After the second, his thoughts turned to laudanum. A night in the ugly, primitive hotel near the railroad restored his strength if not his sense of humor.

For the first time Brownie climbed into a railroad car without a fuss and so did Gunner. Bret didn't believe they cooperated because he was in no shape to force them to do anything. He did believe they sensed at the first sign of resistance he'd turn them over to the tender mercies of the railroad men.

Hassie's sunny nature had reestablished itself within a few hours of leaving Dearfield as Bret had known it would. Now she fastened on new worries.

"I should have changed to a dress," she signed as they took a seat in the passenger car.

An elderly woman in a ridiculous hat and bulky black coat stared at them with a shocked, disapproving expression.

"Stop worrying about what people think," Bret said. "I bet a woman who wears a hat like that would have to close her eyes to shoot a gun."

Hassie's lips twitched. Bret pulled off his left glove and her right one, took her hand in his, raised it high enough to be seen and kissed her knuckles. Might as well really outrage that old biddy. Besides Hassie looked like she could use a kiss, and he felt like giving her one.

She settled in against him, head on his shoulder, and Bret stared out the window. This time of year the vastness of the prairie repelled him. At least now he and Hassie were safe from temperatures sinking to killing lows overnight or clear blue mornings turning to the blinding whiteout of a blizzard before noon.

Even if weather stopped the train, it carried enough coal to keep the stove at the end of the car radiating heat for days. The packs still held a couple days' worth of food. Of course Hassie would insist on sharing it with everyone in sight, which would mean no one would get more than a bite.

His imagination roamed. He saw the train passengers, led by the disapproving hat lady, storming the stock car, wanting to eat the horses. Or Gunner. He saw himself on one side of the open doorway with the rifle, Hassie on the other with the shotgun. He fired. And missed. Hassie closed her eyes, fired, and the raging mob disappeared.

He chuckled. Hassie rolled her head to look at him and let go of his hand. "What are you thinking?"

"Just nonsense." In fact he was procrastinating as surely as Hassie had over leaving Dearfield and the MacGregors. He needed to reassure her about his family and tell her about Mary. Now that the train was up to speed and the wheels clacking loud enough no one but Hassie could hear him, he was out of excuses to put it off.

"I know you wanted to go back out on the trail with me next year," he said, "but the last two days put paid to any notion I had the decision is mine to make. There's no way I'm going to be able to spend days in the saddle by spring. I may never be able to draw a gun with any speed again. I'm sorry."

Angling sideways in the seat to give him a clear view of her hands, Hassie signed, "I did not want more bounty hunting. I wanted to be with you."

He kissed her hand again. "You liked it in ways I never did, not the bounties, but the traveling, new places. You get all wide-eyed, and your face lights up."

The hat lady stared at them more bug-eyed than wide-eyed, her mouth pursed into a disapproving little circle. Hassie reached down and pulled the slate out of the bag at her feet. Either she anticipated exceeding his growing ability to understand her signing or she worried the old lady would report someone having a fit to the conductor.

"It was a great adventure, and I enjoyed most of it, but we had enough adventures. Staying in one place with no bad men will be good."

"I'm glad you feel that way. I'm looking forward to being home myself."

She gave him a trace of the false smile and toyed with the chalk pencil, a bad sign. Come to think of it, all the delaying tactics in Dearfield had to have more cause than just affection for the MacGregors.

Reconsidering Hassie's recent behavior, Bret heard Belle Chapman's voice as clearly as if she had boarded the train with them, and Belle never had anything good to say about Sterlings. He'd better set the record straight. "I know Belle told you about my family, but you should take what she said with a grain of salt. She doesn't have much use for us."

"She never said anything bad."

"She said I'm the best of a bad lot."

Bret almost laughed at Hassie's astonished look. "Gabe, Belle, and I have known each other most of our lives. She's said those very words to my face often enough. Her family and Gabe's have small acreages not far from ours."

"They were for Union."

"They were. I told you Gabe and I joined up together and went through the war side by side."

"They left Missouri after the war."

"He comes from a big family. The farm will go to his oldest brother."

"You're the oldest brother, and you won't inherit."

"That was my choice."

"No, you chose to do the right thing. What your father did was his choice."

He shrugged. "Say it any way you want. I knew what would happen, and I did what I did."

"Because you are a good man. Belle also said that. You are honorable."

"I'm glad to hear she admits it, but she should admit my parents deserve credit for that. They raised me."

"You spent much of your time with Gabe's family and Belle's. Maybe those families should get the credit."

"Some maybe, but I'm my father and mother's son, not a Chapman. No matter our differences, they're good people. You'll see when you meet them. You're going to meet my parents, my baby sister Caroline, and my younger brother William, his wife Mary, and their two children."

"Belle told me. Your other sister is married and doesn't live there, and your other brother...." Hassie hesitated, and Bret finished for her.

"Albert died in the war."

Hassie erased her last words and touched the chalk to the surface, then stared at the blank slate, fingers twitching. Which meant she wasn't going to write what she really thought, and she shouldn't be thinking anything so negative she couldn't express it. Damn Belle anyway.

He tried to reassure her and maybe himself. "I admit things have been difficult between us since the war, but my parents aren't like your grandparents. They aren't going to slam the door in our faces or be rude, even if they won't be as friendly as you are."

"Why did you risk your life every year to give them money if they won't accept what you did? If the farm will be your brother's, he should have gone with you and helped or found another way to earn money."

"Someone had to stay home and supervise the rebuilding, get things going again."

"Your father could do that."

"He did. The two of them did. By the end of the war Will had a wife and a baby. I wanted to help, and the best way I could help was to find a way to finance the rebuilding. No one forced me to do it."

"They took money from you. They should let the bad feelings go."

"They can't let it go. It's all mixed up with Albert's death and pride and a lot of other things. Maybe if the South had won and Missouri joined the Confederacy, but not now. They hate every change in their lives, and if it's not all my fault, I'm the only Sterling to blame. After all, if no one fought for the Union, there would be a Confederate States of America."

"I will not give them the money you say is mine, that you put in the account in my name."

"You're right you won't, and since most of this last money is yours, they won't be getting much more this year."

"Most is not mine. It's ours. If you want to put some in my account, it should be 50-50."

"It should be one hundred—naught, but I'm going to give them five hundred of it."

Hassie's fingers twitched again, her conflict obvious. She wanted to argue with him about who should get credit for the reward money, but she didn't want him to give any of it to his family.

Since she was already riled up, now was the time to tell her about Mary. It would distract her from the money, and Hassie needed to know it all before they got to the farm and someone else told her.

Bret tried one last time to think of a way around it. Couldn't.

"There's something else," he said finally. "One of the people you're going to meet.... The thing is...." There was no good way. He had to just say it. "Before the war I was engaged to marry a girl named Mary Lytton. She was—her whole family was strongly pro-Southern. You know how bad things were in Missouri back then. The worse it got, the more Mary and I argued. When I wouldn't promise not to enlist, she broke the engagement."

Her fingers barely moving, Hassie wrote in small tight letters. *"Belle told me. Miss Lytton married someone else while you were away fighting."*

"Quite a source of information, our Belle. Is that all she told you?"

The chalk pencil twirled some more.

"Did she tell you who Mary married?"

Hassie finally looked up, her brows drawn.

"She married my brother Will."

Disbelief flashed across Hassie's face. Bret couldn't interpret the expression that followed.

"You want me to meet her, stay in the same house with her?"

He nodded.

"I don't want to do that."

"It won't be a problem. Except for a polite please pass the salt, we haven't even talked since I left to enlist."

"Belle said you still have feelings for her."

Double damn Belle. "She's family, my sister-in-law. Of course I have feelings, but it's nothing that matters to you."

His usually agreeable wife had turned into a stranger with narrowed eyes and an angry slit of a mouth.

"I will not live there."

"You're letting what Belle said prejudice you. Just give it a chance."

"You can live with your sister-in-law. I have a farm of my own. I will go back to Werver."

"Like hell you will."

Before he could stop her, Hassie slipped from the seat, crossed the aisle, and sat beside the hat lady. Bret glared, a wasted effort, since Hassie kept her back turned and the hat lady sat rigid, eyes straight ahead.

Head bent, Hassie wrote. And wrote. The hat lady flicked her eyes down. Looked again. Said a few words and glared back at Bret. Moments later she was chatting away to Hassie, pausing now and then to read from the slate.

Bret leaned his aching head against the window. He hadn't expected Hassie to like what he said, but he never expected a threat to leave him, even if he knew she didn't mean it. Surely by the time they reached Oak Hills, his sweet, agreeable wife would reappear.

31

The problem with loving a stubborn—no pigheaded—blind, obtuse man was trying to say no and make it stick.

Hassie said goodbye to the hat lady when the train reached Oak Hills and rejoined Bret. By the time he deposited the drafts for the last reward money in her account at the bank, she relented and promised him she would meet his family and stay at the farm long enough to get to know them.

As they approached the farm, she rode with her free hand clamped over her stomach. The old nausea and burning sensations hadn't returned, but something was flipping around in there as if getting ready. Knowing the gleaming white fence that had bordered the road for the last two miles enclosed thousands of acres of Sterling land didn't help and neither did the elaborate gates leading to the farm lane.

The hard lines of Bret's face gave no hint of his feelings. Was he glad to be back? Relieved? A stiff breeze had chased away what little warmth the weak winter sun brought to the day, penetrated through all the layers of Hassie's clothing, and turned her feet and fingers numb. Bret must be just as cold, his shoulder and leg aching. Like a toothache in the bone he described it.

Barns, sheds, and other outbuildings clustered like a small village behind the house. Bret led the way to the largest of the barns, dismounted, and slid open the big door. The musky scent of horses wafted out on the cold air. Eager whinnies greeted them. Brownie and Packie answered.

Hassie dismounted too, pain jolting through her cold feet as they hit the ground. Bret had already dropped Jasper's reins and Packie's lead and moved off down the center aisle in the barn. She left Brownie and followed.

The bay stallion in the first stall made even Jasper seem like a cold-blooded scrub. The mares in the stalls beyond had the same racy look even with their hugely swollen bellies. There would be foals soon, and before the weather warmed.

Hassie had envisioned a farm that produced wheat and corn, maybe hemp, not horses. Before she could question Bret, the door at the other end of the barn opened, and a man appeared leading another gravid mare. Seeing them, he hesitated before continuing on and putting the mare up, then hurried toward them.

"So you're the son they're waiting on." Wizened, gray, and at least a foot shorter than Bret, he peered up and held out a hand. "Sam Olson. Your father hired me for the horses. They're something, aren't they?"

"Something," Bret agreed, shaking the man's hand. "Where are they from?"

"Kentucky. And me with them. They were some of the best back home, and they're *the* best in this state."

When Bret turned to introduce her, Hassie stopped blowing on her fingers and shoved both her hand and the glove she'd pulled off into a pocket.

Sam grinned. "You and the missus better get inside and warm up. I'll take care of your horses. There's no room at the inn here, but they look like they're used to the weather. I'll put them in the south pasture."

"They're used to some care too," Bret said. "Rub them down and give them a couple quarts of oats each before you turn them out, would you? You can pile our gear there by the door, and I'll sort it later. I need a place for the dog too. I want him inside at night."

Sam stared down at Gunner and frowned. Gunner stared up at Sam and growled.

"Your father won't like having a dog like that around."

"You're right," Bret said easily. "But he's going to have to put up with it. I'll find somewhere out of the way for him when I come back out."

Hassie left the barn reluctantly. She'd really rather take care of Brownie herself. In all the stables where they'd left the horses, she and Bret had always at least done the unsaddling and checked out where the horses would go. And the longer she could put off meeting any of the Sterlings the better. Especially Mary.

The setting sun gave the big white front door on the house an orange glow. Bret brought the big brass knocker in the middle down sharply twice, but didn't wait for anyone to answer before ushering her inside an entry hall of shining oak flooring and pale green walls. The scent of furniture polish hung in the air.

A dark-skinned woman in a black dress and white apron appeared through the doorway to their right. "Oh, Mr. Bret. It's good to see you. Just let me take your things, and I'll tell them you're home." She gathered coats, scarves, and hats and disappeared through a doorway with her arms full.

"Don't look like that," Bret said, reading Hassie's mind once again. "I know where she's taking everything. If we need to make a quick escape, I can grab it all up."

Hassie did her best to look as if the thought of a quick escape had never occurred to her.

A squeal sounded from above. "Bret!" The young woman who ran down the stairs threw herself at him, hugging and laughing, kissing his cheek. "Oh, your face is cold."

Bret hugged her back, lifting her right off the floor. "My sister Caroline," he said to Hassie around the laughing girl.

If Caroline held still long enough, Hassie might be able to find a resemblance to Bret other than dark hair, but Caroline kept moving. And talking.

"Oh, and this is your wife." Caroline turned to Hassie. "Bret sent a letter, but he didn't say anything but your name, and look at you. Even in trousers you look pretty. I knew you would. Not that I knew you'd be in trousers, but I knew you'd be pretty." Caroline stepped closer and peered into Hassie's face. "And your eyes. You must get tired of people remarking on them, but I never saw such beautiful eyes. Oh, I'm so happy to meet you."

Caroline startled Hassie by reaching out as if for a handshake and hugging instead.

The entryway filled with people. Smiling and nodding her way through introductions, Hassie tried not to stare at Mary Lytton Sterling, who put the blonde, blue-eyed beauty Hassie had once imagined as Bret's wife to shame with paler hair, more perfect features, and lusher figure.

Hassie hadn't expected Mary to greet Bret with even a subdued version of Caroline's welcome, but she had expected—something. Instead Mary stayed behind the others in the hall, her expression more reserved than the senior Sterlings, her hands on the shoulders of her two children. Hassie's long ago idea that Bret's old love would be haughty in the nicest way changed to just plain haughty.

Before they'd become friends of a sort, the hat lady on the train had made Hassie wish she'd changed her trousers for a dress. Mary and the other Sterling women made her want to run to the barn, throw herself on Brownie, and gallop into the night. What good would changing to a dress do when her newest ones from Colorado would look hopelessly plain?

These women all wore stylish dresses trimmed with ruffles, bows, or lace. Their elaborate polonaises could only drape so smoothly with dress improvers underneath. Not that Hassie wanted to wear a cage around her legs with a lump of horsehair strapped to her rump, but still....

Their age made it easy to distinguish Bret's mother and father. From the reserve on their faces and the distance they kept, Bret could have been a slight acquaintance here at the invitation of some other family member.

William Sterling looked very much the way Bret had in his suit at the dance months ago, except either William had been ill recently or he didn't spend much time outside in the sun. Bret's darker complexion and the little lines around his eyes gave his face more character.

When the introductions and uncomfortable greetings concluded, William gave Bret a pat on the back that looked more like a blow. "You look as good as new."

Bret tapped the cane against his boot. "Almost."

"You need something with a gold handle. You can twirl it and look more devilishly handsome than ever." William's tone was joking, but as he turned to Hassie, she recognized an intent to cause trouble in the curl of his lip.

"Bret almost lured my wife into marrying him before she came to her senses," he said. "They were engaged to marry for almost two years."

Hassie gave him her brightest fake smile. "He is one I do not like already," she signed.

"Neither do I." Bret slipped an arm around her and pulled her close. "I should have put it in my letter," he said, "but since I didn't—Hassie's throat was injured as a child. She can't speak clearly, so she uses sign language. I'm getting pretty good at it, but for the rest of you—she writes."

"She can't...." Mrs. Sterling's hand went to her own throat, her reserved expression changing to one of dismay.

"You two are well matched then," William drawled. "Crippled legs, arms, throats. You better be careful. There's not much left."

Bret ignored his brother. "I'll show Hassie to our room so she can start settling in while I get the rest of our things, including the slate she writes on."

"How bad is her voice?" William said. "I think we should be able to hear and judge for ourselves."

Hassie drew in a deep breath. "No," she said as forcefully as she could.

"You heard the lady." Amusement tinged Bret's voice. He picked up their bags and escorted Hassie up the stairs.

She stopped when they reached the second floor, but Bret urged her on. "Not here. One more floor, first room on the left."

He had both their bags under his right arm so he could use the cane with his left. His leg must be a throbbing, aching mess by now, the shoulder not much better, and the stairs were so dark only a tight hold on the bannister enabled her to keep going. Yet if she tried to take even one of the bags, he'd resist. Pigheaded. She sighed and continued on.

Their corner room was warmed by a chimney from a downstairs fireplace running along one wall. In spite of that, Hassie shivered as Bret lit a lamp by the bed and another on the bureau. By day, with sunlight pouring in through the large windows, the blues and creams of the room would be lovely. Right now, no matter the temperature, the room left Hassie colder than ever.

A light knock sounded at the door. "It's me, Caroline."

Caroline bounced into the room, waving a sheaf of paper in one hand, a pencil in the other. "I brought writing things so we can talk," she said to Hassie. "Since my sister Vicky married and left, I don't have a single female person to talk to. Mother and Mary are always too busy, and they're not interesting anyway."

"Female chatter will have to wait till later," Bret said. "Right now Hassie needs a hot bath to warm her up. Why don't you make yourself useful and see what you can arrange while I bring in the rest of our things."

Caroline pouted. "You can just tell Leda what you need, and she'll do it. She'll be in the kitchen or somewhere downstairs."

Hassie pulled the paper from Caroline's hand, took it and the pencil to the table, and wrote, "Your brother does NOT need to go up and down the stairs more times. His leg is barely healed. Please find someone to carry things for him." She underscored the NOT a second time when she finished.

Caroline read the words, looked at Hassie, looked at Bret. The lamplight emphasized the whiteness around the tight line of his mouth, the flare of his nostrils.

"Oh, I'm so sorry. I never thought. I'm as bad as Will, and I'll get him and make him help." She hugged Hassie, hugged Bret. To Hassie she said, "And I'll come right back and take you for a bath, and I'll make sure your clothes get pressed so you have a dress to put on afterward."

Before Caroline left in a flutter of apologies and promises, Bret pulled the paper from her hand and read Hassie's words.

The door clicked shut, and Bret pulled Hassie into his arms. "Does that concern for my leg mean I'm truly forgiven?"

It wasn't a matter of forgiveness; she'd given up on making him understand. He kissed her and welcome heat flooded from her head to—about her ankles. If the kiss curled her toes, she'd never know because she couldn't feel her feet. "You need to sit with your leg up," she signed.

"As soon as I get the rest of our things up here, I will. Right now I need to get outside before Will uses the excuse to paw through everything we own."

Hassie waved a hand around the room. "So big. I expected many servants."

"They probably let half of them go in order to buy another horse," Bret said, his tone and expression flat.

The way he had looked at the horses with his hands on his hips made it clear he didn't like something about them, but Hassie decided not to probe that subject, at least not now. And if she had to wear mittens the whole time they were here to keep from doing it, she wasn't going to say a word about Mary.

Bret kissed her again and headed for the door, limping heavily.

Hassie caught him before he started down the stairs. "I stored willow bark tea in the coffee pot. Be sure to bring that."

"Yes, ma'am."

She stood there listening until his footsteps faded to nothing.

32

Foolish though it was, Bret would have preferred going back out to the barn himself, taking time to hang saddles, bridles, and other equipment in the tack room and sort through everything in the packs. Lame or not, he could haul all the clothing and other personal items he and Hassie needed to the house with a lazy man's load or two trips.

In years past, seeing Mary again after months away left him disturbed, restless, and dwelling on what might have been. This time relief that Hassie was over her uncharacteristic anger overwhelmed every other emotion.

Right now he'd like to be alone awhile to reflect on how different everything seemed this year. Instead he had Will dogging his steps and grousing about being treated like a porter. Since the war, Bret had avoided his brother as much as possible, and Will's snide performance in the entry hall hadn't recommended him as good company.

In spite of Sam Olson's earlier words, a tie stall across from the tack room housed nothing except a few tools. Bret forked straw under the manger and made a bed for Gunner. It would do for tonight.

Will hunched in his coat, stamped his feet, and complained about the cold and the dog.

"I can't believe you'd even bring an ugly mongrel like that here. You know what Father's going to say when he sees it.

One glance at a chicken and he'll order it shot. He won't try to make Sam shoot it so that means me or you, and who's going to dig a hole in this damned frozen ground? Not me."

Bret gave Gunner a rough caress behind the ears. "You, Father, and Sam all need to get straight on something. I don't care how you feel about the dog. Tomorrow you'll get a good look at my wife's even uglier horse, and I don't care what you think about that either. They're staying here, and you can all keep your mouths shut about them around Hassie."

"So the dog came with the widow. I can't believe you went from Mary to that."

Bret's hand tightened on the pitchfork. "I don't think a ten-year interval during which I didn't live in a monastery qualifies as 'went from', and since I'm sure you didn't mean to insult your wife or mine, I'll put it down to the cold."

"Oh, come on. We all expected you to stop sulking and marry eventually, but we expected at least a decent try at a proper Sterling bride."

After exchanging the pitchfork for his cane, Bret glanced in the tack room. Sam Olson had hung the saddles and bridles on pegs and racks along the wall, bless him. All Bret needed to deal with was the contents of the panniers. He began sorting, stuffing what needed to go to the house in the empty cases he'd brought back out. Clothes. Coffee pot. Definitely the coffee pot.

He poured what was left of the small supply of oats he carried for the horses in the grain bin, stuffed the food that remained in a canvas bag. "Here," he said to Will. "How about you take this in? No use letting mice get into it out here."

Will made no move to take the sack. "So what happened?" he said. "You decided you couldn't do me one better and figured you'd embarrass us all by bringing home some Irish tart in dirty trousers?"

Bret forgot barely healed wounds and drove his right fist into Will's face, pain searing through his shoulder like fire.

Will recovered and charged, only to slam into the wall when Bret sidestepped.

Gunner joined the fight, grabbing a mouthful of coat and yanking Will further off balance. Bret shoved the tip of the cane under Will's chin, pinning him where he'd fallen.

"Let's give it a day or two before we bloody each other up. I think in spite of everything, Mother likes the illusion her sons are civilized. But you watch you mouth around my wife and about my wife or I'll shatter Mother's illusions and your jaw."

"You and the dog and two or three other helpers," Will said as he pushed the cane away and rose. "Your mouth was busy enough on my wife once."

"Oh, for pity's sake," Bret said. "A few kisses, and we were engaged. Find another excuse to act like an ass, why don't you."

Will fingered the tear Gunner had ripped in his coat. "You're a damned traitor. How's that for a reason?"

"Better."

"Carry your own trash inside. I'm not your servant."

Glad to be left alone, Bret tied Gunner in the stall and made two trips from barn to house carrying supplies and gear.

Done at last, he dug the coffee pot out and headed for the kitchen. A cup of willow bark tea right now would be like throwing a thimbleful of water on a raging fire, but it would be better than nothing. After that he'd see if Hassie was still in the bath tub, skin flushed rosy, tendrils of hair curling around her face. Now that she was back to her agreeable self....

"Breton. We need to talk. Come have a drink."

So much for catching Hassie in the bath. Bret nodded at his father. "Yes, sir. Give me a minute to leave this in the kitchen, and I'll be right there."

Tea first. Whiskey after. His leg wouldn't know what hit it.

Bret accepted a glass of whiskey and settled into a chair, smothering a groan. The dark study with its heavy mahogany furniture was a good replica of the one he'd been called to many times as a boy for praise as well as discipline.

His father didn't look that different than he had then either. His stomach protruded over his belt a little, but not much for a man in his late fifties. Silver streaks in his dark hair only lent a more distinguished air. Bret hoped to age as well. His father was still a handsome, vigorous man. And determined to live his life as if the war had never happened or as if it hadn't changed anything.

"I'm glad you're home. We were beginning to wonder."

Admitting they were beginning to worry would be a step too far. Bret took a swallow of whiskey, enjoying the way it burned a path to his stomach.

"It's all come at a bad time," his father said. "I shouldn't have counted unhatched chickens, I suppose, but you've sent more each year than the year before, and I did count on it. You saw the horses." The last was said with pride and a self-satisfied smile.

"I saw the stallion and half a dozen in foal mares. They look like they must have cost every penny I sent and then some."

His father waved his glass, enthusiasm animating his features. "That they did, and I was lucky to get them. Those Kentucky breeders don't want to sell stock that fine, especially one like Augustus Caesar. He won dozens of races before proving himself as a sire, important races, and he's only eight now. A stallion like that would never be available if the owner wasn't desperate."

"So the farm is producing enough to live on again, and you used my money to buy horses."

"Oh, no, with grain prices where they are, the farm would feed us, but that's about all, and you didn't send enough.... What I mean is everything together wouldn't have been enough. I took out a loan."

Bret closed his eyes for a moment. Not only was Gabe right, things were even worse than he'd predicted. "I can't believe the bank would approve a loan to buy horses."

His father waved that concern away. "Charlie knows I'm good for it, and it's a mortgage. Any banker would be happy to hold a mortgage on this property."

No, they wouldn't. Too many land owners had been unable to meet their obligations since the war. No bank would want to foreclose on one more farm. If his father and Charles Inman, President of the Oak Hills Bank, hadn't been close friends for decades, a loan would be a tough proposition.

Bret glanced at Will. Why the hell had he gone along with a gamble like this? Will sat studying his fingernails as if the discussion didn't concern him.

Even in the room's dim lamplight, bruising and swelling showed on the left side of his face. Good. If he mouthed off like that again, Bret would remember to hit with his left and give Will a balanced look.

"How are you planning on making payments on this mortgage if the farm income barely supports you?" Bret asked. "You can't think half a dozen foals from those mares will bring in enough, and they won't be ready to sell until fall."

"Of course not. We won't sell anything for another year. What you send will make the payments."

A twist of anger chased some of Bret's fatigue. The assumption he would be the one paying off a mortgage he hadn't consented to was just too damned casual. The desire to get out of this room, use a bath to warm up, and get back to Hassie almost lifted him out of the chair, but he needed to make his father face reality.

Bracing himself with another swallow of whiskey, Bret said, "I promised to help out until the farm was a going concern again."

"Of course," his father said, "and once the horses...."

"No."

"No?"

"The horses are a pipe dream and a luxury, and you know it. Sell them, pay off the loan, and start living off what the farm brings in."

"Sell them! I'm not selling a one of them, and you can't expect your mother and sister to live the way they did during the war!"

Bret gestured around the room with his glass. "This isn't a barn you're living in. No one's dressed in rags or eating corn meal mush three times a day."

His father's face flushed red. "We need what you send, and you've led us to count on it."

"You don't need it. You're living high off the hog on it. I have another five hundred for you, but that's the last of it."

"Five hun.... That will barely get us through the winter."

"What would you have done if I died? Look at me. Do you see me chasing down killers and thieves in another three, four months?"

"You need to see the doctor here. No sawbones in some whistle stop town in Colorado can be worth his salt."

"MacGregor practiced on thousands of bullet wounds and worse during the war. He managed to save the leg and that was no mean feat."

His father slumped back in his chair. "I can put the bank off for a while, but you can't quit yet. By mid-summer...."

"No," Bret said. "You're not listening. I did what I could. I was glad to help, but I'm not supporting race horses." Or any other wildly lavish spending, but Bret left that unsaid. "I told you last year I'd had enough, and I have a wife now. It's time to settle down, find our own place."

"This is still your home. You don't need your own place."

His father had to know how Will's bruised countenance had come about, and he probably knew why, or at least Will's version of why. "You know that's not a good idea. A few months every year is about as much of each other as we can tolerate."

"It's high time the two of you stopped brawling like boys."

Bret said nothing. He and Will no longer brawled like boys. Somewhere in the last years brotherly jousting between them had turned into real dislike. The damaged clinches on his horse's shoes this spring had forced Bret to face that Will had gone beyond dislike and wanted to do harm.

The three of them sipped whiskey in silence.

"Charlie told me about the private account you have at the bank, you know," his father said at last. "You haven't got enough to buy a place of your own."

"Isn't a bank president supposed to keep information like that confidential?" Bret said, kicking himself for being so careless. He should have anticipated Inman wouldn't see anything wrong with telling his father about the account, or the balance in it to the penny. He should have set up that account elsewhere, and Hassie's account.... Bret tensed, waiting for his father to mention Hassie's relative wealth, but it didn't happen.

"If you think holding out will make me change the will, you're wrong. What you did was a disgrace my grandchildren will have to live down."

Bret wrapped his hand around the cane, ready to end this by leaving the room. Nothing he'd ever said made any difference once his father started down this well worn path. Long ago, Bret had discovered the simple solution of walking away.

"However, I have thought of a solution that would benefit us all."

"Why do I have a feeling it won't benefit me in the slightest?" Will said.

"Because you've yet to accept that anything that benefits the farm, benefits you," their father said.

Bret waited, intrigued by the unexpected turn of conversation.

"We've never really integrated the land across the road," his father said. "It's good land, produces well, but it's always an afterthought. Suppose I sell you that for what you've put aside. The government won't sell you land any cheaper, and nothing as good. You can live here until you get a house built, and that will be better than some dirt house on a homestead, which is all you'd get on your own."

A year ago, Bret would have jumped on the offer. Now he had Hassie's attitude to consider, and her resistance to even staying here for a while made him cautious. The barely suppressed rage on Will's face advised a different kind of caution.

"I appreciate the offer," Bret said, getting to his feet. "Maybe you're right it would benefit us all, but I need to talk to Hassie. I don't think she wants to live here."

"Talk to.... That woman has nothing to do with this family or this farm."

"Marrying me made her my family and part of this family," Bret said.

"I suppose it did," his father conceded, "and I'm glad you finally married, even if I don't understand the attraction, but if you want to get your marriage off on the right foot, you make the decisions and then you tell her."

Bret laughed at the idea, enjoying the startled look on his father's and brother's faces. "Two months ago five killers caught me flatfooted in Colorado, and I told Hassie to run and hide. When they started shooting, she ignored me, blew the head off one with a shotgun, and tied the others to trees. Then I told her to leave me and get help. She ignored that too, got me on a horse and to the nearest town and a doctor. If she'd done what I told her either time, I'd be dead. If she doesn't want to live here, we won't. I'll talk to her, and I'll let you know what we decide."

Bret left the study feeling surprisingly cheerful. Even if the offer of the land was only an attempt to clean out his bank account, it was a generous offer, worth considering. Better yet, throwing off the self-imposed obligation to support his family had diminished every one of his various aches and pains. Or maybe the combination of willow bark tea and whiskey was more potent than he imagined.

Voices sounded in the small parlor down the hall. The way his mother and Mary stopped their low-voiced conversation and regarded him warily when he appeared in the doorway meant he was the subject of that conversation. Or maybe Hassie. Or the two of them.

He stared at Mary and for the first time really saw not the girl he'd once loved but a woman he barely knew. "I thought Hassie might be with you."

"She's upstairs with Caroline," his mother said. "As I understand it, as soon as Hassie's hair dries, Caroline intends to arrange it in a more appropriate way. In the meantime, she is bedeviling your bride with questions."

"Good, because I want to talk to you. I need a favor."

His mother and Mary exchanged a look he couldn't interpret. "Of course," his mother said. "Do you need someone to show you the new bathing room and how the hot water supply works?"

"No, I can find it and figure it out myself. What I need is for you to beg, borrow, buy, or make Christmas presents."

"Christmas presents? We have gifts for the children, of course."

"For everyone. Except no scarves for ladies and no handkerchiefs for menfolk."

Both women frowned at him.

"You'll be going to town again before Christmas, won't you? Or if not, you can send someone and tell them what to buy. I'd do it, but if I disappeared to town she'd figure it out. You see, Hassie has Christmas presents for everyone, and I don't want her to feel awkward."

"Excuse me," Mary said. "I need to be sure the children are cleaned up for their dinner." She brushed by him, a trace of the scent of roses lingering after she hurried away.

"Mother?"

"We are not awash in pin money for presents, Breton."

Bret pulled a few bills from his pocket and laid them on the table beside her. "Is that enough?"

"I suppose you told you father you're quitting."

"Yes, and unlike you, he's surprised."

"The very look of you told me you minimized your wounds in your letter. You almost died, didn't you?"

Bret acknowledged the truth with a slight nod.

"And your father has been very foolish with the horses, hasn't he?"

"I think so, but he can sell some of them and get by. Why did Will go along with it?"

"To put further pressure on you I expect." She studied him, her eyes resting on the cane and his leg before lifting to meet his. "And a year ago it would have worked in spite of your injuries."

Bret wanted to tell her she was wrong but wasn't sure she was. He tipped his head toward the bills on the table and asked again. "Is it enough?"

"It's enough," she said, and swept the money from the table into her pocket.

HASSIE WALKED ALONG the farm lane, her breath huffing white in the cold air, one gloved hand warm in Bret's.

"I'm holding you to a snail's pace," he said.

Smiling up at him, she shook her head a little, unwilling to bare her hands to sign. On her own she could move faster, maybe even run a little, but now that the past days' anger had dissolved and they were at peace again, she preferred strolling at Bret's gimpy pace to striding out alone.

Gunner burst through a clump of bushes at the side of the lane, tail waving, a wide doggy grin on his face. Hassie skipped a little, understanding his exuberance. How could anyone spend every hour of even a gray winter day like this one inside the house?

At the end of the lane, Bret kept going, crossed the road, and led the way alongside fields plowed and waiting for spring. He stopped near an old stone foundation, more evidence of a building that had not survived the war.

Sweeping the cane in a wide arc, he said, "This land wasn't part of the farm originally. A family named Abbott lived here. They were older, their children grown and starting to take over the farm, so I never knew any of them the way I did Belle and Gabe, but they were good neighbors."

Hassie tipped her head, waiting. He'd brought her here for a reason.

"Their house burned one night. I guess old Mr. Abbott used to smoke a last cigar in bed at night. He and his wife didn't make it out of the house, and none of the rest of them wanted to rebuild and stay. They sold the land to my father, packed up, and left. California, I think."

So it wasn't the war but one family's tragedy. Hassie shivered.

"Last night my father offered to sell us this land for what I've got put aside. I told him I'd talk to you and let him know what we decide."

Hassie froze for long seconds before pulling her hand free from his, yanking off her gloves, and shoving them in a pocket. "He knows about our money?"

"No. He knows about *my* money. His good friend who happens to be president of the bank told him I've been saving a little for myself and how much. No one said a word about your account so at a guess Charlie Inman doesn't realize Hassie Petty is now my wife. Next time we're in town, we're going to close both accounts and move that money to a bank my father never heard of."

Hassie focused on the bigger problem. "You want to do this, give your father the money and live here."

Bret looked out over the land as if assessing then turned back to her. "I guess you know I had trouble with the way you reacted to coming here."

She gave a stiff nod, ready to argue, but he went on before she could pull her hands back out of her pockets.

"Last night, after you fell asleep, I spent some time thinking about it. I tried to imagine how I'd feel in your place, how

I'd feel if you wanted me to live somewhere with an old beau of yours, even if he was married to someone else now and there was nothing between you."

"I do not have an old b-e-a-u."

"I know that, so I made one up."

"How could you make a man up?"

"I started with that Kulp fellow."

Once she remembered who he was talking about, a wave of indignation flooded through Hassie. Ehren Kulp was not exactly a male equivalent of beautiful Mary Lytton Sterling.

Bret ignored her expression and continued. "The trouble with that was just thinking about him made me want to get up and head for Kansas and smack him around a little, make sure he knows if he ever sees you again, he'd better keep those grabby hands to himself."

Good. Never seeing the man again would be better. "Who else did you think of?"

"No one. I conjured someone up from scratch. He's a little short on hair and chin and some other things a woman might care about and a little long on teeth, nose, and ears."

"Does he have a name?"

"Percival."

She was not going to let him charm her out of justified anger. She was not. Hassie pressed her lips together to keep from smiling, lost the fight, and laughed.

Bret grinned at her. "The thing is I still want to kill him, which is to say I understand how you feel."

"You want to buy this from your father," Hassie said, making the same kind of sweeping motion Bret had earlier.

"A year ago, I'd never have thought twice. It's a good offer. We'd be paying about what the government sells land for, and the government is fresh out of land this good."

No, it was not a good offer. Instead of trying to squeeze more money out of his son by selling him land, Mr. Sterling ought to change his will, leave this to Bret and the land across the road to Will. Their father should let each of them work the land while he was still alive and playing with his horses. Hassie decided to keep that opinion to herself.

"What is different this year?" she signed instead.

"You are. I know you don't want to live this close to them, and you're probably right. Will would never make an amiable neighbor."

"He feels g-u-I-l-t-y because of what he did to you."

"Mary broke our engagement months before he married her. He has no reason to feel guilty."

Maybe he had no reason, but as little as Hassie knew these people she suspected both Will and Mary had intended to hurt Bret, punish him for following his conscience instead of doing what they wanted him to do.

She changed the subject. "Will your father lose the farm without the money?"

"No, but he'll have to sell some of the horses."

"You want this land. You will be unhappy if you say no."

"If my lovely wife augments my paltry funds with her fortune, we can buy something good enough to make me happy and far enough away to make you happy."

Hassie put one icy hand on each side of his face and touched her lips to his. Heat where they touched and cold everywhere else contrasted in interesting ways. He ended the kiss and rubbed her nose with his. "I'll tell Father what we're going to do right after Christmas. He'll try to change my mind so we might as well have a few quiet days first."

Hassie laced her fingers through his as they started back, hoping Bret wouldn't change his mind with or without importuning from his family and wondering what she would do if he did.

33

Admitting it came hard, but Hassie did have to admit Bret's family was not as terrible as she had imagined. In fact Caroline, accepting, curious, and laughing, already felt like a friend. The girl now carried paper and pencil in a dress pocket all the time.

"For when your slate isn't right to hand," she said.

Since Mrs. Sterling treated everyone from her husband to her grandchildren with the same unfailing politeness and consideration, her reserved manner no longer intimidated Hassie. Mr. Sterling's bluff heartiness did put her off a bit. Was it real, or was he hoping to influence her in favor of accepting the land and handing over Bret's money?

Mary and Will, though? Living here with those two would never be comfortable. This morning, sitting on the other side of the breakfast table, one on each side of their children, they made a perfect picture. Mary helped five-year-old Charlotte, called Lottie by everyone except her grandparents, with her food. Will didn't need to give nine-year-old George much help, but he did keep an eye on the boy and murmur a few words to him occasionally.

The sight didn't loosen the hard knot of dislike Hassie felt in the slightest. Will looked up, saw Bret's attention focused on Mr. Sterling, and raked his eyes over Hassie in a deliberately insulting way that only increased her aversion.

Mary showed no sign of noticing her husband's bad manners, her lovely face set in its usual serene expression. Hassie tried to work up a modicum of guilt over her prejudice against the woman and couldn't. Maybe she could get over the bad feelings if Mary and Will showed any of the small signs of the kind of affection she had observed between Gabe and Belle Chapman or Dr. and Mrs. MacGregor, but so far everything between them had been all Sterling-like reserve and politeness.

Bret turned toward her. "H-a-m? B-a-c-o-n?"

"Ham." Hassie suppressed the urge to show him more than a small sign of affection, wanting to believe what he felt for her was more than fondness, more than he felt for Mary or ever had.

Will had to comment on what Bret had done. "Is that your sign language? That looks different than what your wife does."

"I'm not very good at it yet," Bret said. "She uses words and phrases. I can't do much more than spell."

"You don't have to do it at all. You can talk."

Bret shrugged. "It's how I learned."

"And it gives you a way to talk about us behind our backs with us sitting right here."

"Yes, it does."

"I like your sister," Hassie signed. "You should check for bounty on your brother. Maybe he has worth."

Bret made a sign anyone could recognize with one hand. Zero.

"What did she say?"

"She said she's happy to finally meet my family."

Hassie patted Bret's leg under the table. He put his hand over hers and held it there.

George blurted into the silence that followed. "Father and I are going for the Christmas tree together after breakfast. He's going to show me how to use an ax."

"I want to come too," Lottie said.

"Ladies don't use axes," Will told her, "and it's cold out. If you bundled up enough to stay warm, you'd fall down on your back like a turtle and be stuck until we're done with the tree and can pick you up."

"I won't fall down," Lottie said, the beginnings of a pout showing. "I want to come too."

"You'd better let her go," Caroline said. "Without a feminine eye to help you choose the tree, you'll drag home something flat on one side or with a scrawny top again."

The idea of cutting a tree and bringing it in the house struck Hassie as so fascinating, she barely noted one of those knowing, married looks finally passing between Will and Mary, and there was nothing particularly affectionate about it anyway.

"Lottie and I will both bundle up," Mary said. "We'll choose a perfect tree and stand back while our menfolk handle the ax."

"Christmas tree?" Hassie signed to Bret. "What is a Christmas tree? What do you do with it?"

Caroline hardly waited until Hassie stopped signing. "What's she saying? What's she saying?"

"She's curious about the Christmas tree," Bret told his sister. To Hassie he said, "It's a pine tree we bring in the parlor and hang gewgaws all over."

"Oh, you'll love it," Caroline said. "It makes the house smell so good. Decorating it is fun, and it's so beautiful when we're finished." She threw Bret a quelling look. "Even if some people have no appreciation for gewgaws."

Hassie's hands flew. "I never heard of such a thing. Where did you get such an idea?"

Bret said, "Mother read about it in some magazine that had a story about what Queen Victoria and Albert did...."

"Prince Albert," Mrs. Sterling said.

"Prince Albert. When they married, he introduced her to the custom of bringing a tree into the house at Christmas and decorating it. He was German...."

"A Prince of Saxe-Coburg and Gotha."

"As Mother says." Bret didn't roll his eyes, but Hassie could tell he wanted to. "So as word spread, people who admire the royal family began to adopt the custom."

Abandoning conversation limited to Bret, Hassie changed to writing on her slate. *"When do you decorate it? May I help? What kind of decorations? Do you have to make them? I will help make decorations."*

Caroline laughed, took the slate, and showed it to her mother. "We'll bring down the boxes of decorations from the attic after breakfast if you like, and we'll decorate the tree this evening, and we expect you to help. Doing it by lamplight is best, and when we're done we put out the lamps, light the candles on the tree, and sing Christmas carols."

Whole boxes of decorations? Candles? Hassie took the slate back. *"How big is the tree?"*

"Oh, almost to the ceiling. There has to be room on top for a star—like the Star of Bethlehem, you know."

A tree almost as tall as the ceiling. She couldn't sing carols, but Hassie had every intention of hanging gewgaws.

BRET SANK INTO a chair near the fire and watched his father and Will struggle to get the tree into the parlor and anchored in place. Servants did not deal with Christmas trees and neither, thank God, did men with recently healed broken bones and bullet wounds.

Finished with their manly roles, the two men headed for the sanctum of the study and whiskey. They would grumble and complain but return when summoned to hang decorations on the highest branches the women couldn't reach.

Bret didn't want whiskey and didn't want more pressure about the land from his father. He propped his leg on a footstool, feeling like grumbling himself.

Watching hours of tree decorating and admiring the thing afterward would be a lot easier after an uplifting bout in bed with Hassie, but he accepted that prying her away from the boxes of decorations, much less the tree, would be impossible. Hassie's enthusiasm dwarfed even Lottie's.

Proving him wrong, Hassie tore herself away from the tree long enough to fetch a cup of willow bark tea and a pillow to go between his leg and the footstool. She left him feeling half pleasantly coddled and half like an old man with gout.

His mother supervised Leda as she cleared a table top and set out hot cider and cookies. Caroline, Mary, and the children pulled decorations from their boxes, unwrapped them, and reminisced about past Christmases.

Enthralled by the tree, Hassie paid no attention to the others. She touched the end of one branch after another, a look of awe on her face. Finally, prodded by Caroline, she began tying decorations on the middle branches.

The scent of pine resin filled the room. The women's voices blended into a soothing background sound. Bret's mood lifted as he watched. They made a pretty sight. Even his mother looked relaxed, smiling as she unwrapped a glass ornament and held it to the light. Caroline and Hassie worked side by side, their dark heads close together. Mary helped Lottie, kept an eye on George.

He loved them all in different ways. Surprised by the thought, Bret examined it as he continued to study the women. Did he? He knew Gabe and Belle's children better than his niece and nephew. Sensing their father's hostility, George and Lottie kept their distance. The blood tie brought obligation, but love?

Loving Mary had been a constant in his life for as long as he could remember. Maybe the emotion had lingered without purpose or support because there had been nothing to take its place until now.

Hassie stretched high, her nimble fingers tying a bow on a branch she shouldn't be able to reach. Finished there, she bent to take another decoration from the box at her feet. Lithe, less curvy than Mary or his buxom little sister, she moved with a supple grace they didn't have.

Except for occasions like this, Mary and Caroline directed servants in their work. They didn't do physical labor. No servants had helped Hassie keep the Petty house or care for a dying old man. This summer she'd spent days on horseback, lifted her saddle on and off her mare, carried supplies—and run across the prairie afterward for the joy of it.

Given the chance, other women would develop the physical strength, but how many ever had the inner resilience, the strength of spirit that kept joy alive no matter how oppressive the circumstances? He didn't have it. He'd stolen some from her, and without her, it would fade away.

Hassie laughed, and every other thought flew from his mind as the sound shivered through him. Tonight she wore a dark green dress, a lace collar high at her throat. A vision of another green dress rose in his mind—a lighter shade, the skirt swirling, translucent in the sun. Her crow's-wing black hair shone in sunlight then, gleamed in lamplight now.

The same force that had lured him into a ridiculous game of tag on the prairie pulled Bret out of the chair and toward the tree. Why wait to be summoned and grumble over helping when he could volunteer?

Intent on tying a painted wooden horse in place, Hassie didn't notice him behind her until she backed into him. She turned and tipped her head. "We will always have a Christmas tree in our house."

"We will," Bret said. "And we're going to have mistletoe too."

He kissed her, knowing she wouldn't pull away with dignified reserve. She slid her arms around his neck and kissed him back, her body melting against his.

"What is m-I-s-t-l-e-t-o-e?" she signed when they parted.

Bret laughed. Surprise flashed on his mother's face. Caroline giggled, and Mary hustled the children to the table for cookies.

"I'll show you later," he said.

BRET STEPPED OUT into the cold with Gunner's food hours later than usual. Still entranced with the Christmas tree, Hassie had merely nodded when he mentioned feeding the dog.

Gunner appeared before Bret whistled for him, prompting a twinge of guilt. Until tonight, he had been careful to take Gunner to his bed as soon as Sam Olson finished putting the Thoroughbreds in their stalls. If the dog started hunting on his own in this area, too many people, including Sam and Will, would be happy to shoot him and pretend they mistook him for a coyote.

Tonight, though, Bret had followed the rest of the family from the dinner table to the parlor, unwilling to miss the look of wonder on Hassie's face as his father lit the candles on the Christmas tree one by one and extinguished the lamps. Bret had stayed through the first carols, his arm around Hassie, feeling her humming the songs.

If he hurried, he might get back before they stopped singing, put out the candles, and relit the lamps. Holding Hassie like that in the semi-darkness, his cynical attitude toward the tree and the fuss had dissolved. He wanted to get back, share more of her pleasure with things new to her.

"When we get our own place, there's going to be a bed in the kitchen for you," Bret told Gunner. "Now that she's got the hang of it, she's better about the dream than you are, but you have other talents."

Busy gulping ham laced with vegetables and cornbread, Gunner didn't answer. He did look up long enough to growl at the sound of the barn door opening and closing but went right back to his food. So Hassie had been unable to resist coming along after all.

The woman who walked into the circle of lantern light wasn't Hassie. She lifted her scarf off her hair and let it fall to her shoulders. Blonde hair shone gold.

Surprised, Bret stilled in place. "Mary."

Since breaking their engagement, Mary had never spoken to him except for an occasional polite sentence or two. Once he would have given anything for an opportunity to talk to her privately. Now her seeking him out like this struck him as odd—and made him wary.

"I need to talk to you," she said.

"Talk to me about what?"

"About your decision regarding the Abbott land."

Ah, so that was it. Bret leaned down and picked up Gunner's empty dish, wondering if she had come on her own or if Will had sent her and if either of them really thought she could cajole him into making the decision they wanted, whatever that was.

"Why would you and I need to discuss the Abbott land?"

"Because it's unfair of you to drag out your decision like this. We all know you've already made up your mind."

"Pretty much," he admitted. "I planned to talk to Father day after tomorrow. No use getting involved in business at Christmas."

"You can't let that Irish gypsy influence you to turn down such a good offer. You know you'll never get land like that at a price like that any other way."

Irish gypsy. Even knowing Mary meant it as an insult, the words made Bret smile at the memory they invoked—Hassie running with her arms outstretched, hair streaming behind her.

The smile was a mistake. Mary's reasonable tone took on an edge he remembered from their arguments before the war.

"So you're deliberately torturing Father Sterling and Will, making them wait for a decision when you know what you're going to do."

"No, I'm waiting until after Christmas to make someone unhappy. It looked to me as if Father wants a yes, and Will wants a no. He sees that land as his already."

Her eyes widened. "Will doesn't want you to say no. We *need* that money. How could you possibly think you could quit without warning and not turn all our lives upside down?"

The first signs of temper pricked hot at the back of Bret's neck. "You had warning. I wanted to quit last year. The farm's looking as good or better than before the war, but my father and your husband swore it wasn't producing well enough to keep the lot of you comfortably yet."

"It wasn't. It isn't."

Bret ignored her protest. "So I went back to hunting thieves and murderers, baking in the sun and freezing in rain and mud, sleeping on hard ground, and getting eaten alive by insects. Oh, and getting shot, let's not forget that detail." He tapped the empty dog dish against his bad leg. "And I get home, and what do I find? Race horses. Plumbing to rival the best hotels in Kansas City and Denver."

"Oh, for pity's sake, you can't begrudge us...."

"Yes, I can," he interrupted. "I can begrudge race horses and hot water taps, and I damned well do."

"I don't appreciate your language."

"Well, what the hell do you appreciate?"

"Or your sarcasm. I'd forgotten how unreasonable you can be."

"Strange. I was thinking the same thing."

"You aren't going to do it, are you? You're going to leave us all with nothing and with a mortgage payment due in January."

"I'm going to leave you with a farm in better shape than anything else in the state and a bunch of race horses to sell. If you need more, my wife thinks Will should strap on guns and try bounty hunting next year, or maybe he could pick up a shovel and try mining."

Even furiously angry, Mary controlled her voice and expression. She always had. "So that's what *Hassie* thinks, does she? You tried for years to buy your way back into Father Sterling's good graces, and when you failed, you brought home the mute Irish widow to embarrass us all."

"Now you're parroting Will."

"Because he's right. You never would have married her for any other reason. You're still in love with me and always have been."

Mary looked as beautiful as ever in the lamplight. Also cold, controlled, and not particularly lovable. "I loved the girl you used to be. Why don't you leave and not spoil the memories of her."

She stepped closer, one hand raised as if to touch him, whether gently or with a slap, he never found out. Gunner growled.

Mary let her hand fall. "Will says he's going to shoot that dog."

"If you don't want to be a widow, dissuade him." Tired of it all, Bret gave Gunner a reassuring pat and picked up the lantern. "Come on. I'll walk you back to the house."

"No, thank you. I know the way." She whirled and melted into the darkness, and Bret let her go.

"I thought you didn't growl at females," he said to Gunner.

The dog wagged his tail, no apology on his narrow face.

"You picked a good time to change your policy, but don't do it again."

Gunner curled up in the straw, nose to tail. Bret left him there and headed back to the house and his Irish gypsy.

34

Hassie sifted flour once, sifted again. Leda and the cook were happy to have help in the kitchen, and after gently pointing out that Hassie didn't need to do the work, Mrs. Sterling had left her to it. Which was good. Reading, sewing, walking with Gunner, listening to Caroline's chatter, and letting the girl experiment with more and more elaborate hair arrangements only filled so many hours of the day.

Bret had left with his father and brother before dawn, off hunting turkeys for Christmas dinner. Hassie sincerely hoped turkeys were the only ones who returned to the house worse for wear.

Softened butter went into the bowl, quickly turning creamy under Hassie's attack. It was good that Bret told her how Mary followed him to the barn last night and tried to talk him into agreeing to buy the Abbott land. Bad that it happened. How would Mary like it if Hassie followed Will to some out-of-the-way place for a talk? Not that Hassie had any intention of ever being alone with Will.

Sugar, eggs.

"Slow down, Mrs. Bret," Leda said. "You only have to mix the dough, not subdue it."

Hassie smiled and added the first cup of dry ingredients. According to Bret, Will must have sent Mary to the barn, but then why did Will and his father show no sign of knowing what Bret told Mary? Of course Bret was certain once he told his father no, the family would shift from trying to ferret out an answer to trying to change it, so maybe that's what they were up to right now on that turkey hunt.

The dough stiffened as Hassie folded in more flour, providing a far more satisfactory outlet for her feelings. She'd like to use the wooden spoon on more than dough right now. Bret *said* he and Mary quarreled and he no longer saw much of the girl she'd been in her, that she and Will probably suited, and what did that mean?

The cook set two cookie sheets on the table. "I'll have the last batch of gingerbread out of the oven in a minute, and then I'm ready for yours."

Hassie nodded, added the last of the flour, and worked it through the dough.

"May I speak to you a moment, Hassie?" Mary stood in the doorway, a slight smile on her lovely face.

Bret said Gunner growled at Mary last night. Hassie fought an urge to do the same, her hand fisting around the spoon handle.

The cook pulled gingerbread out of the oven. "You go ahead, Mrs. Bret. I'll finish your cookies. Don't you worry."

"Mother Sterling took the children outside to run off some energy," Mary said. "You and I can have the small parlor to ourselves and get to know each other a little."

Hassie treated Mary to her brightest smile, blew a fine layer of flour off the surface of the slate, and tucked it under her arm. Whatever Mrs. William Sterling wanted to talk about, she must not want the senior Mrs. Sterling involved. Good. Neither did Hassie.

When they were seated, Mary made polite inquiries about Hassie's health. Since Hassie suspected if her health failed completely and she died suddenly, Mary's chief regret would be having to pretend to care, the social niceties did not soften Hassie's attitude.

Finally Mary got to her purpose. "I know your opinion carries great weight with Bret," she said. "As well it should. Will told me what Bret said you did in Colorado. You were unbelievably brave."

Unbelievably. Hassie raised her brows slightly in polite inquiry.

"I wanted to be sure you understand what a great opportunity Father Sterling is offering you and Bret," Mary continued. "Men are often not good at explaining things, and I know Bret is worse than most."

"He is very good at explaining. I understand about the land. It is better for us to live farther away."

"But that's just the kind of thing we need to talk about. You would have your own home across the road and wouldn't even see us except at church and perhaps for Sunday dinner if you wanted to. Moving an hour, even two hours farther away wouldn't make a particle of difference."

Moving two days away would. *"He told you last night we have decided no."*

Mary's eyes widened slightly. So Mary had expected Bret to keep the fact she had followed him to the barn a secret.

"He bears a grudge over what happened years ago," Mary said. "He admitted he's angry over Father Sterling's horses—and the plumbing of all things. He's always been a difficult man, but surely you can keep him from cutting off his nose to spite his face—and your face I might add."

Hassie thought of blazing heat and freezing rain, dust and mud, practicing what to do if surprised by Indians, Bret bleeding on the ground and a man with a gun standing over him. If she had her own gun on her right now, she might shoot a lamp or two.

"He is not difficult. He is a good man." Writing that wasn't enough. Hassie took a deep breath, added, "No," as loudly as she could, and left Mary sitting with her mouth open.

Upstairs in their room, Hassie tossed the slate on the bed and paced restlessly, thinking of all the things she should have told Mary, including to stay away from Bret. After a few minutes she changed to her boots and headed outside. Gunner was tied in the barn today so he couldn't follow the hunters. She would take him for a walk. A long walk.

HASSIE RETURNED TO the bedroom, calmer after her walk with Gunner, only to find Bret sitting on the bed staring at her slate. She had to sit beside him and look to remember the last words she'd written there.

"*He is not difficult. He is a good man.*"

He tilted the slate back and forth. "This looks like you were trying to convince someone. Was it yourself, or someone else?"

Hassie took the slate from him and the chalk from her pocket. "*Mary wants me to convince you to buy the land. They have suffered since the war and are entitled to race horses and hot water. I hope they have to sell the bath tub.*"

Bret laughed, and Hassie smacked him with a pillow.

He ran his fingers along the bottom of the words on the slate, smearing them a little. "Did I tell you she called you an Irish gypsy?"

Hassie shook her head.

"It suits you. An Irish gypsy has to be a woman of magic and mystery, the kind of woman who makes a man forget the past and plan for the future."

"*You wanted a future with her.*"

"I wanted a lot of things when I was twenty-one that I don't want any more."

What he said about magic and forgetting the past was almost as good as admitting love, wasn't it? Why couldn't he lie just a little and say, "I love you, Hassie?" Because he couldn't. He wouldn't lie, and she really didn't want him to. She touched the back of his hand. He turned it palm up and closed his fingers around hers, his thumb stroking her knuckles.

"Come lie with me," he whispered.

She went to him willingly if not eagerly, Belle's warnings and Mary's confident tones still echoing in her head.

They lay quiet in each other's arms. Outside the pale winter sun set and the light faded as night approached.

His heart beat strongly under the palm she spread on his chest. The musky scent of a man who had spent the day tramping over fields and through woods rose around her, tinged ever so slightly with horse, leather, and gun powder.

He was so still, his heart and breathing so regular, he must be asleep. She should get up and cover him against the chill creeping into the room. The thought died when his fingers stroked lightly on the nape of her neck, traced around her ear, across her temple.

His fingers played across her face, and her entire body reacted to his light touch. Her nipples peaked. Heat and moisture rose at her core. Moisture filled her eyes too, and he caught the first tears on his fingertips before she could blink them away.

"Don't," he whispered. "Don't cry."

The tears wouldn't stop at her command, but they did at his kiss. Uncertainties disappeared. Desire rose. She kissed back with abandon, wanting his mouth and tongue and possession. This was hers, only hers.

He undid her dress, slid it off with expertise she refused to consider.

"I haven't decided if this is better or worse than getting you out of those wrappings you used around yourself on the trail," he said, working on the hooks of her corset.

The same. They were both barriers to his hands on her skin and both made her impatient. A soft bed was better, though, especially on a winter night, but she couldn't tell him so without more light, and she didn't want him to stop long enough to light a lamp.

The corset yielded. Her chemise and drawers followed it to the floor, his clothes after that. She sprawled on the bed, naked except for stockings. He sat near her knees, lifted a foot to one shoulder, and undid the garter. Her heart hammered in her ears. Removing stockings could not be doing this to her, but it was. She whimpered.

Finished at last, he kissed her feet, her calves, behind her knees. His slightly bristly cheek contrasted with the feathery kisses as he moved higher on the sensitive skin of her thigh. She parted her legs, expecting what he had done before. He kissed her once there at her core, his tongue swirling, and she shivered with pleasure.

Not what she expected, as different as the stockings, the skimming kisses moved across her stomach, higher. He cupped a breast with one hand, thumb stroking that nipple while his mouth worked on the other.

His heat enveloped her or maybe only merged with hers until the room lost its chill. Sweat prickled along her spine, and the tiny knot of reservation inside her dissolved in the flood of pleasure. She moaned softly, her teeth in her lower lip. *Mine*, she thought. Her hands fisted in his hair. *Mine*.

"I want. I need...."

"Sshh. Sshh."

Whether he'd understood her or not didn't matter. She reached for him, barely touched the velvety skin covering the erect shaft when his hands closed over hers.

"Not this time."

He kissed her palms, each finger, the insides of her wrists. His mouth skimmed her arm to her collarbone. One hand trailed from her breast, across her ribs and stomach to cup her sex. From the heel of his hand to his fingers, his hand rocked, firm, gentle. Her hips responded. One finger pressed deeper, stroked, and electric pleasure jolted through her.

When she recovered, he enclosed her, resting on his forearms over her. "Say 'more'."

"More."

"I understood that."

She wrapped her legs around his, welcoming the thick, hard heat, waiting for the first thrust. Instead his body surged against her as slow and gentle as his mouth and hands. A sound of wonder escaped her.

Like breathing, like wind on the skin, like the beat of her heart. Her inner muscles squeezed and released. The pleasure intensified until she could not contain it, had to release it outward, be released by it. Her soft husk of a cry died away.

He thrust hard half a dozen times and finished, slumping quiet on her until she lost him, and he rolled away. "Here. Get under."

He lifted the bedclothes, and she squirmed underneath, feeling the chill of the room now. His body was better than a fire. She snuggled close.

A man could not make love like that to a woman he felt only fondness for. It felt like love. She felt as if she had just been thoroughly loved, was still wrapped in it.

He moved slightly, his voice as soft in its way as his hands had been. "I think this moment right now is worth every day of the years wandering in the wilderness it took to get here."

Reluctantly, Hassie wriggled away from him and lit the bedside lamp. He lay on his back, one arm over his eyes. How could she talk to him when he did that? His arm rolled a little, eyes gleamed from underneath.

"Is that how you think of it?" she signed.

"I was being poetic, but yes, it got harder every year. I'm glad to be done with it. My only regret is I'll never again see the look of wonder on your face when you see something like the Missouri River for the first time."

"There will be other things to wonder at."

"Without mountains and rivers what will there be?"

She fought the temptation to tell him of the greatest thing they would wonder over.

"There will be Christmas trees."

35

Christmas Day dawned bitter cold with an occasional snowflake swirling through the air. So excited she danced like a snowflake on the wind herself, Hassie accompanied Bret to give Gunner breakfast and let him loose for the day. In Philadelphia, Christmas had always been a special day, even after Papa died.

Although none of them had ever heard of a Christmas tree, they had all exchanged small gifts in the Grimes household. At least when Mama was alive they did.

After the first year with Cyrus, when he had still managed to sober up and make it to church most Sundays, she had never been sure which day was Christmas. This year would make up for the ones she had missed. A tree, turkeys, mountains of baked goods, presents, carols, candles. Hassie had great expectations for the day and evening.

And Bret. Having Bret made everything easier. Better. After his love-making last night, Hassie had actually looked at Mary with pity over dinner.

"Maybe we should stay out here a while," Bret said. "Take Gunner for a walk. Brush the horses up a bit."

She made as if to punch his arm, and he laughed. He knew she wanted to get back inside and give and get presents as much as the children. They walked back arm in arm.

George and Lottie went through their stockings quickly and tore tissue paper off their other gifts with enthusiasm. They thanked Hassie politely for the wooden toys on wheels she gave them and saved their hugs for the rest of the family. In the past the children's coolness toward her had stung. Now she accepted it philosophically. Not wanting Will and Mary in her life meant never being close to their children and was a small price to pay.

Early in the morning, Hassie had peeked inside the paper wrapping on each of the scarves from Colorado. Now she handed the one with the lavender scarf to Mary with a smile. From the look on his face, Bret noticed, knew full well she'd done it on purpose, and found it amusing.

Her single gift from the Sterling family was an obvious attempt to bring her up to their standards, but she had to admit the brown dress, trimmed with black, was very stylish and would probably be becoming, even if she didn't much care for the color.

"There is another part to it," Mrs. Sterling said. "Leda has already left that in your room so you can wear the dress properly this afternoon."

A dress improver, a cage for her legs and cushion to make her bottom stick out. Other women managed to sit in such things. Maybe with a little practice before coming downstairs rigged out like that, she could too. If she didn't fall on her face on the way down the stairs. She thanked them all profusely with gestures and signs Bret interpreted.

Caroline wrapped the soft cloud of her pale blue scarf around her head and left it on. "I'm not part of the dress present," she said. "That's from Mother and Mary."

The surprise on their faces said this was news to Mrs. Sterling and Mary. Caroline grinned, pleased with herself. "This is for you from me," she said, handing over a small package, "and you will be very impressed because you think I'm useless, but I made it myself."

The small reticule was brown with black trim to match the dress, but Caroline had marked the gift as her own by embroidering an exotic red rose on each side. Hassie hugged her, kissed her cheek.

BRET ACCEPTED THE gloves and stockings he'd paid for from his family with quiet thanks, watched Mary unwrap the light purple scarf with amusement. Another woman would "forget" anything for Mary. Hassie didn't have that kind of smallness in her.

Given the color of the dress they gave, which in his opinion would rank behind purple for attractive, he suspected the women in his own family did harbor that kind of smallness.

Not his sisters. If Victoria were here, she'd help Caroline try to compensate for the rest of the family, but Vicky was expecting her second child in the spring and wouldn't be traveling for a while. Not Albert. Albert had been as good-natured and generous as any man ever born. He had none of the discontent and envy that marked Will from childhood.

Even now, when Will had everything he ever coveted, discontent marred his expression more often than not. At least the children's happiness had banished that look for a while this morning. Will was good with his children.

Hassie had her hand on one last wrapped package. Bret pulled a small box out of his pocket, rose, and moved behind her chair.

"Close your eyes."

Instead of closing them, she turned and gave him a wondering look.

"Pretend you're going to shoot me, and close your eyes."

After a mock glare, she closed her eyes. He removed the ivory comb from the box and pressed it where he thought it belonged in her hair. Her eyes flew open immediately. She reached and pulled the thing right back out to examine it, show to Caroline.

"Oh, look at the carving. It's so beautiful, and it will look perfect in hair as dark as yours," Caroline exclaimed.

Taking the comb from Hassie, Caroline skipped to show their mother and Mary. Will waved her off, but she managed to get a grunt of acknowledgment out of their father. Lottie wanted to keep it.

"When your hair is long enough and thick enough to hold a comb like this, you'll have one," Caroline told the little girl and brought the comb back to Hassie. "I'll fix your hair especially for it later," she said.

Later wasn't what Bret had in mind when he talked to Mrs. MacGregor about finding the right present. He wanted to see the ivory against the shining black of Hassie's hair. Was she only going to wear the comb when her hair was fixed especially for it?

Hassie turned the comb over and over, touching and tracing the carved design of flowers and vines. Then she smiled at him and pushed it back where he had first placed it. Caroline was still fussing over a more perfect placement when Hassie jumped up, hugged him, and kissed him. On the mouth. With an intensity that ignored the presence of anyone else in the room.

His father cleared his throat loudly. His mother made vague remarks on the need to put things away. Bret kissed back and forgot about anyone else for long moments.

"Thank you. It is very beautiful," she signed when they finally parted. "I have this for you."

The carving on the leather of the knife scabbard resembled that on the comb so closely he wondered about the MacGregors' part in the purchase.

"Dearfield?"

"Yes. I took your knife to the saddle maker. He measured and made it. He let me pick the pattern to put on. He showed me how to oil it when he was done. Now I know why the MacGregors smiled at each other when they saw it. They knew about the comb too."

"The scabbard I have is falling apart and never looked this good. Thank you."

"I have another present for you, but it's like what Leda left upstairs that goes under the dress, a private thing. Come upstairs with me, and I will tell you."

Tell him? His idea of the best kind of present would be one she'd show him, not tell him. Curious, Bret muttered something at his family and followed Hassie from the room.

As soon as they were out of the parlor, Bret stopped her and imprisoned her against the wall, an arm on each side of her head. "We can take the dress back next week and get something pretty. Anything would be better than that old lady color."

Hassie had a feeling the dress had been made originally for an older woman, that it was one of Mrs. Sterling's made over and there would be no place to take it back to. "It's fine. It's very stylish."

Bret made a disapproving sound and dismissed the subject. You can't mean you're going to tell me about my other present. You're going to show me, right?" He wiggled his eyebrows suggestively. "Does it have to do with laying on of hands and mouth maybe?"

"I will do that too if you like, but the present is because of what we did with hands and mouths and other parts before you were shot. We will have a baby in the summer."

He jerked upright. "You're sure?"

"Dr. MacGregor said."

"He knew, but you didn't tell me?"

Was he angry? Hassie's heart sank. "He said the beginning is not so certain, better to wait a little longer and be sure, and I did not want you to think I told you just to...." Her hands stopped moving.

"Just to what?"

"Make you stay in Colorado."

"You don't have that kind of deviousness in you, but you're right, if you told me, we'd still be there. I can't believe you didn't tell me and let me drag you through the foothills in winter like that."

He wasn't angry. He was concerned. And he was pleased. Considering-it-a-gift pleased.

"I am fine."

"And you're going to stay fine." He looked back toward the parlor. "Can I tell them, or do you want to keep it a secret?"

"You can tell."

"Maybe tomorrow. Or the next day. Just us, for a little while." He kissed her as gently as the day before. "What about the kind of thing I thought was the second present? What did MacGregor say about that?"

"Fine until the end. He said happy mothers make healthy babies."

He kissed her again. She wrapped her arms around his neck, raised one leg....

"Damn it, Bret. I have children in this house. For that matter there are ladies. Take her upstairs where that belongs."

In other circumstances, Will's contemptuous voice would have had the effect of a dousing in cold water. Today Hassie gave a disgraceful giggle.

Bret scooped her up in his arms. "Right. The bedroom. We belong there, and we're going there. Right now."

He had to put her down when they reached the stairs, but that was all right. By that time they were out of sight, and it had been such a grand exit.

36

Gloomy faces at dinner the day after Christmas told Hassie that Bret had gone through with his plan to catch his father alone and turn down the offer of the Abbott land. To her relief, anticipation of an upcoming visit from old friends postponed further attempts to change Bret's mind or influence her.

Hassie expected to like the Durhams, but Caroline was not happy about the visit. "Everyone wants me to marry Carl Durham, and I'm not going to," she said, rolling her eyes. "He's Bret's age, not half as good looking, and twice as arrogant. I can't stand him, but he's a war hero so of course he's perfect."

"Choosing a husband who suits you is very important."

"I guess I can trust you not to talk," Caroline said, laughing at her own words. "I've already chosen who I'm going to marry. He's only two years older than I am, so he wasn't even in the war, but his family was Union, so you can guess the chance of anyone in this family approving. As if that isn't enough, he doesn't live in a big house in the middle of thousands of acres and order servants around. He works for wages and lives in town."

Oh, dear. In that case, how was this young man going to support a wife? *"What does he do?"*

Caroline hesitated, and Hassie could almost see her assessing, deciding how far she could trust her new sister-in-law. "He's a clerk, but it's not as if that's all he'll be forever. He's saving so we'll have a start, and then we're going to marry, and he'll find a better position in Kansas City or St. Louis. I used to talk to him after church, but Will saw us once, and now Mother and Mary all but hold on to me from the pew to the carriage. They're wasting their effort because they aren't going to stop us."

Hassie remembered Johnny Rankin and the girls he had seduced and hurt. *"You need to be careful."*

"We know," Caroline said, uncharacteristically serious. "If anyone sees us together again, I'm not sure what they'll do. Send me back to Virginia probably."

Keeping her family from stopping the romance wasn't what Hassie thought Caroline needed to be careful about. Telling Bret would be breaking a confidence, but would not telling be worse?

After wrestling with the problem, Hassie decided telling Bret could wait until after the Durhams' visit. Maybe Caroline didn't really dislike Carl Durham and just wanted the excitement of a secret beau before settling down.

The Durhams arrived right before lunch the next day. By the time Mr. Sterling finished introducing them all, Hassie was firmly in Caroline's camp. Husband and wife, two sons and a daughter, the whole family were arrogant snobs. So were all the Sterlings except Caroline, of course, but except for Will they managed to hide it behind good manners most of the time.

After the meal, Mr. Durham wanted to hear from Bret about places he'd seen in his years traveling through the western states.

"Let's go to my study," Mr. Sterling said. "We'll be more comfortable there."

"Of course," Mr. Durham agreed. "Carl, why don't you take Caroline for a walk? Perhaps she'd like to show you the new Thoroughbreds."

Hassie almost laughed at the speed with which Caroline invited the sister and younger son to join the outing. She wanted Hassie to come too, but Hassie had seen the Thoroughbreds and begged off. She'd rather visit Brownie and her less prestigious companions.

"Be careful out there with the loose horses," Bret said. "You don't need to be j-o-s-t-l-e-d." Hassie did laugh at the way Bret spelled the hated word.

Not minding some time to herself, she gathered two apples and half a dozen cookies from the kitchen, bundled up, and set out. First, she would give the apples to the horses. Then she and Gunner would each have a cookie, leaving the rest to fortify them on their walk.

Brownie, Packie, and Jasper shared a small pasture south of the barn. At her whistle, Jasper came at a fast trot, Packie behind, and of course Brownie brought up the rear at a slow jog.

Hassie gave half an apple to each horse and the extra half to Brownie. She petted velvety noses and necks covered with thick winter hair and didn't leave until the horses lost interest in a human with no more treats for them.

Still struggling with the heavy wooden bar that secured the gate, Hassie glanced toward the barn at the sound of angry shouting from that direction.

"Stop him!"

"I can't!"

A huge, dark form charged toward her. Letting the bar fall and bounce on the ground, Hassie threw herself to one side. She was almost clear when Augustus Caesar crashed through the opening, and the wild swing of the gate clipped her side, knocking her to her knees. The stallion thundered across the pasture straight for the two peacefully grazing geldings and Brownie.

Jasper tried to run, but he had no chance. The bigger horse smashed into Jasper's side and bowled him over. Wheeling around, still intent on savaging the helpless gelding, Caesar caught sight of Packie and Brownie fleeing along the fence line and changed targets.

Shaky and shaking, Hassie climbed to her feet. Angry men and a screaming female bore down on her. The air reverberated with the pounding of hooves on frozen ground and Gunner's frantic barking as he gave chase. Hands seized Hassie's upper arms and pulled her away from the gate.

"Oh, God, Hassie, I'm so sorry," Caroline said, her voice thick with tears. "That idiot wouldn't listen. I told him not to go near Caesar. He just had to go in the stall, and I don't know what anyone can do now."

The screaming had drawn the men from the house at a run, Bret hobbling close to full speed without the cane.

Caroline babbled an explanation as Bret folded Hassie against his chest for a long moment. "Did he knock you down, run over you, what?"

Once she got her hands free, she told him. "No, the gate bumped me, and I was off balance. I'm fine." She gestured toward the pasture. "He will kill Jasper, our horses."

"No, he won't. You two get behind the barn and stay there."

Hassie let Caroline pull her to the shelter of the barn wall. The men climbed on the fence, waving their arms, their shouts adding to the chaos.

"At least Carl's stupid sister shut up," Caroline muttered.

Bret didn't join the others on the fence rails. The gate had bounced back to its closed position, although it wasn't fastened. He threw it wide and whistled. On his feet again, Jasper ran in terror along the fence line with Packie. The two geldings tore down the side of the pasture toward the gaping escape route as fast as they could run. Bret slammed the gate closed behind them and rammed the bar home.

"Gunner," he yelled, "Gunner, get over here and shut up." Gunner kept running and barking. Bret cursed and shouted again. The dog finally gave up the chase and crawled out of the pasture, head and tail lowered apologetically.

The stallion pursued Brownie relentlessly, his teeth sunk deep in her neck. He tried to mount every time she slowed. The mare ran at her own ponderous pace, kicking, squealing. Bret whistled, whistled again. How could Brownie come with that monster all over her?

Hassie left Caroline and ran to Bret. He glared at her. Hassie pointed. Brownie had turned toward them.

"I'll get a rope on her. You hold her," Bret ordered. "And you stay on this side of the damned fence."

The two horses running straight at the fence loomed like a railroad locomotive bearing down at full speed. Brownie crashed into the rails, still trying to fight the stallion off. Bret ran a rope through the mare's halter and shoved it at Hassie. She grabbed and held.

The stallion squealed in frustration, trying to breed the unwilling mare as she bucked and kicked. Her big feet hit his chest with wicked thuds like a mallet on meat.

Sam Olson ran to Bret. "Here. Here's a stud chain."

Olson showed no inclination to try to get the chain on the stallion himself. Bret vaulted over the fence, fastened the chain on one side of Caesar's halter, and jerked. Caesar snaked his head at Bret, mouth gaping, ears flat, but Bret's hold was too short and too hard for the stallion to sink his teeth in an arm or shoulder.

Bret wrapped the chain over Caesar's nose. Furious, rearing, and striking, Caesar fought futilely before submitting to the inevitable. Once Bret had him under control, Olson led the stallion away.

A chastened Carl Durham and his younger brother caught Jasper and Packie and brought them back to the pasture. Jasper had skin and hair missing on his side and signs of bruising, but no worse injuries. Brownie had scrapes and cuts all over, and the ugly bites on her neck were already swelling.

Bret pulled Hassie into his arms again. "You wouldn't make light to make me feel better, would you? How hard did the gate hit you?"

"I am not making light. Just a bump, and I was off balance, so I went down."

"You go inside. I'll take care of the horses."

Hassie shook her head. Not only did she want to see the horses doctored, calm, and settled, she wanted to stay close to Bret. Behind them, Carl Durham rationalized his own actions. Caroline angrily contradicted him, and Mr. Sterling sent her to the house.

Bret finished treating Jasper's wounds with a blue concoction Olson brought out and dabbed the medicine on Brownie's wounds. Hassie crooned under her breath to the mare, stroked her nose, rubbed behind her ears.

Mr. Sterling sent the younger Durhams back to the house with sympathetic pats on their shoulders. The arrogant idiot who had caused all the trouble might get sympathy, but Brownie didn't and neither did Bret.

Mr. Sterling approached them so angrily Brownie sidled away nervously. Gunner, stiff and growling, stopped the man in his tracks.

"I won't have a scrub like that in foal to Caesar," Mr. Sterling said, his voice tight with anger. "Do you understand me? You get rid of that sorry piece of crowbait before it comes into season and lures Caesar again, and while you're at it, you get rid of this damned dog."

Bret's face turned to an impassive mask. "The only crowbait on this place I'll get rid of is your foul-tempered stallion. If Hassie had still been in the pasture, he could have killed her. Hell, he almost killed her as it is."

"It won't happen again. Sam is careful...."

"Sam wasn't careful! No one was careful."

Will straightened from where he had been leaning on the fence. "Oh, come on. No one got hurt, and Sam will be more careful from now on. You need to get your story straight. Either your wife is the shotgun-toting avenger you boasted about the other day, or taking a little tumble when she's startled is going shatter her like porcelain. It's not as if she's in a deli...."

Will stopped mid-word, staring at her. To her chagrin, Hassie felt heat flushing across her cheeks. So much for Bret telling his family over a pleasant dinner.

"Oh, but she is, isn't she?" Will said. "Congratulations on expanding the Union branch of the Sterling family."

Bret ignored his brother as he so often did and spoke to his father. "I'd better not find so much as a bruise on my wife or I'll shoot that son of a bitch, and it has nothing to do with her condition. You want the mare gone and the dog gone, fine. We'll all be gone come morning."

Mr. Durham cleared his throat. "Perhaps everyone would benefit from some time to reflect and calm down."

"Yes, of course." Flustered, Mr. Sterling seized on the excuse to back out of the confrontation.

"You let me know," Bret snarled, "because banged up as they are, these horses can make it to town in the morning."

Mr. Sterling and his friend retreated to the house. Will hesitated as if he would say more then followed, leaving Bret and Hassie alone with the horses. Finished doctoring Brownie's wounds, Bret gave her a pat on the neck and turned her loose.

"You're sure you're all right?" he asked Hassie again, his face still set in hard lines.

"My d-e-l-I-c-a-t-e condition would not make me lie. What about you? You ran on your leg."

"I did, and it hurts like the devil. Willow bark and whiskey tonight."

"Your father may not want to share whiskey."

"Then I'll steal it. I had lots of practice as a boy."

She smiled, and his face softened. She tried a small kiss on his cheek, and he laughed.

"Do you realize Old Brownie just kicked the stuffing out of a blue-blooded Thoroughbred aristocrat without the sense to recognize a female not in the mood?"

Hassie laughed too. Unlike Brownie, by the time Bret checked her for bruises, she would be in the mood. Bret's approach to romance had considerably more to recommend it than Caesar's.

As to the angry words, she didn't care. Soon she would have her own home and the Sterlings would be a minor irritation she would only have to visit or play hostess to occasionally.

37

In one way Hassie wished she hadn't told Bret about the baby yet, for any chance she had of accompanying him on the search for a place of their own had disappeared with her news. He skipped right over objections to her doing any more traveling on horseback in winter and went straight to forbidding her to even get on a horse.

Hard as she tried, Hassie couldn't work up a single mutinous feeling over Bret's protective behavior, and the thought of staying alone among the Sterlings for a week or two while he searched for their new home no longer upset her. It seemed as if the family had finally accepted their decision about the land. Mr. Sterling consulted with Sam Olson daily as the two agonized over which horses to sell and how.

Will, Mary, and their children avoided Hassie as carefully as she avoided them. Caroline continued as the center of laughter and fun in the house, and Bret calmed Hassie's worries for the girl.

"There's a practical streak under all that fluff," he said. "If she says she's waiting for this clerk of hers to save up enough to give them a start, she'll wait and hold him to it. If he can't reach the mark, she'll find someone who can. Don't worry about her."

News of another grandchild on the way pleased both the elder Sterlings and helped smooth over the ragged feelings between Bret and his father. Mrs. Sterling admitted more than that to Hassie.

"I know you saved Breton's life in Colorado," she said. "Killing a man must have been terrible for you, and I will never, never stop being grateful. Losing him would be just—unbearable."

"You should tell him. He thinks you are so angry with him you would not miss him."

Mrs. Sterling's expression froze, then she sighed. "That's not true. That never was true, and he was as angry as we were. Hearing him laugh again makes me realize how very angry he was. We have you to thank for that too, don't we?"

Hassie mentally compared the icy-eyed man who had killed Rufus to the one who had made love to her that morning. *"A little,"* she wrote. *"He makes me happy too. He made everything better."*

Her reserved mother-in-law patted Hassie's hand. "I'm glad he found you."

The first morning after the New Year that dawned with sunny skies and rising temperatures, Hassie accepted that Bret would be off as soon as he packed, and she was right. He told the family his plans over breakfast.

"That young lawyer in town claims he has contacts and promised to find me a few leads to farms for sale. I figure to ride into town today and see what he has. I can stay overnight there and set out in the morning."

She didn't want him to go, did want a home of their own. As soon as they finished eating, she set herself to helping him pack.

BRET SAW NO reason to trail a packhorse along on this trip. Unlike the open spaces to the west, towns were close here. He planned to take just enough gear for safety. Only a fool took chances with the weather this time of year.

Without Hassie's help he would have been finished and on the way to town in less than an hour. With her help, he finally fastened bulging saddlebags over his bulging bedroll shortly before noon. Still thinking about where in town he could stash the unnecessary gear she had insisted he pack, Bret kissed Hassie goodbye, and led Jasper out of the barn.

His father waved from across the yard and hurried over. "I need you to tie up that dog for the day," he said. "Those men who drove up while you were packing are interested in the horses, and it growled at them already."

He glanced over his shoulder and shifted nervously, before continuing. "And I have a favor to ask. Would you delay leaving one more day? I mentioned how you've traveled through most of the West, and they'd like to talk to you. I want to keep these fellows happy, and I want them to look at the horses at least once more after lunch. Help me keep them here, will you?"

How could he refuse? With his father showing the first signs of facing reality, Bret felt compelled to help as much as he could. With luck, these potential customers wouldn't ask for his opinion of Caesar.

The thought of what happened the last time idiots went to look at the stallion gave Bret a more powerful reason for putting off his trip. Hassie liked to walk around the farm with Gunner, and he didn't want her out there if some fool let Caesar loose.

"All right, I'll take care of the dog and meet you in your study." To Hassie he said, "Wait, why don't you, and we can walk together this afternoon?"

She beamed at him and nodded before disappearing toward the kitchen. Bret went to ruin Gunner's day.

HASSIE TRIED NOT to feel too happy over having Bret stay one more day. If the delay ended up keeping him from her longer in the end because he had to wait out a snowstorm somewhere, she'd be sorry.

For now, though, she enjoyed having him beside her at the table for lunch. The visitors seemed like nice men—Mr. Sterling's age, a bit pompous, and certainly single-minded. Their conversation centered on two topics—horses, and only race horses, and new lands to the west. In fact, while they continued to quiz Bret, they also expressed disappointment that he hadn't actually traveled over every inch of land west of the Mississippi.

"Kansas and Missouri are filled with enough sinners to make a man wealthy if he could catch them all," Bret said unapologetically.

The table wasn't crowded because Will had taken Mary and the children to visit her family. Dinner would be different after they returned. The children did have good manners, but Hassie wondered how the visitors would react to a five-year-old at dinner.

In spite of Mr. Sterling's suggestion they look at the horses again after lunch, the men retired to his study. Resigned to the fact that Bret had never traveled west of the Rocky Mountains or much farther north in Wyoming than Cheyenne, they still wanted to know about every blade of grass he had seen.

An hour passed. Two. Hassie gave up waiting for Bret to walk with her. If those men were going to keep Bret until dinner and beyond, she would go for a long walk. Gunner would be happy to be off his rope and come with her.

At the sight of Will helping Mary down from the buggy in front of the barn, Hassie hesitated then changed directions. Gunner would have to settle for a brief run later. Right now she didn't want to have to be polite to the pair.

Maybe Bret really didn't still have feelings for Mary, but Hassie did still dislike Mary for hurting him all those years ago. As for Will—he could disappear from the face of the earth, and Hassie wouldn't mind a bit.

Frozen weeds and grass crackled under her boots as she walked briskly across the fields. The winter air felt crisp on her face but not so cold as to burn and force her to wrap her scarf high to protect cheeks and nose.

She worked her way through a fringe of trees at the edge of one field and started into the next, daydreaming about the new home Bret would find. Something large enough for more than their one coming child, but not monstrous like the Sterling farmhouse. She didn't want servants. She could....

"So, how is a woman as hot-blooded as you going to manage with Bret gone for a week or two?"

Will. How could she not have seen him? Hassie froze, heart pounding. He wanted to frighten her, and she was frightened. She backed up a step, two, regretting her decision over Gunner, wondering if she had any chance of outrunning Will.

"You and I are in the same boat, you know," Will said, eyes raking over her in a way that made a transparent veil of her many layers of heavy clothing. "We're married to people who have such a grand passion for each other it survived ten years. Do you ever wonder how it was between them? Don't you agree you and I are owed a little—extra?"

Hassie shook her head violently and backed another step.

"Oh, come on. Just a kiss or two." He laughed without any real humor. "Bret got that much out of Mary, if not more, and you can't blame me for wondering what's got my brother acting like a farm animal in front of us all."

He lunged for her. She whirled to run, tried to bolt through the trees and underbrush, but he seized the back of her coat before she got away. He yanked her around.

"Now I'm going to hear what your voice sounds like. I'm going to find out a lot of things about you."

Hassie's low, whispery scream had no volume to carry on the cold air. Will's cursing did as she kicked his knee, drove a fist into his eye, and bit through his glove. His grip loosened. She broke free and ran, this time along the edge of the field, avoiding the trees and brush.

THE VISITORS WERE on the subject of horses again, and Bret joined his father in urging them back to the barn. Bret was ready to heap praise on Caesar's head if it would get him away from these probably decent but boring as hell men.

If they wanted to inspect every inch of Wyoming Territory, including those the Sioux were defending with bloody effectiveness, they needed to saddle up and go do it. Same for Texas and Comanches and New Mexico Territory and Apaches.

Eager to get away, Bret made it outside ahead of the others and broke into a hobbling run at the sound of furious barking from the barn. Gunner lunged against his rope as if intent on breaking his own neck.

Bret untied the rope and let the dog drag him out of the barn, past the visitors without a growl or glance, and toward the vacant fields to the north. The fields Hassie usually started out across on her walks.

Bret let go. Gunner streaked away. After only a few steps in the direction the dog had run, Bret dropped his cane, and limped and hopped at his best speed toward the pasture where his horses stood at the gate hoping for treats.

Jasper hightailed it in the other direction at Bret's frantic approach, Packie right behind. Slowing and forcing a soothing tone, Bret caught Brownie before she followed the others, yanked a lead rope off the fence, and attached it to the mare's halter.

He scrambled onto the wide back and drummed his heels against her sides. She lumbered through the gate, worked herself up to a canter, and reached something approaching a gallop halfway across the first field.

Gunner had disappeared. The mare plunged through the trees at the edge of the field, heedless of Bret's attempts to direct her. He barely managed to duck under low branches, took a smashing blow to his bad leg as she ran through a narrow gap, and had to fight to turn her once through the trees.

Hassie ran along the tree line like a deer fleeing wolves. Gunner had Will down, savaging him in spite of blows to the head and back. Bret pointed Brownie right at the snarling, cursing tangle of man and dog and urged her on with legs, heels, and voice.

At the sound of reinforcements, Gunner let go of Will and dodged. The only thing that saved Will from Brownie's platter-sized hooves was her refusal to run over a man. Unbalanced by the mare's violent shy, Bret let himself fall on top of Will, grabbed him by the collar, and drove a fist into his gut, his face.

Gunner dove back in to help, attacking Will's legs with renewed fury.

"Call off the dog," Will gasped, fending Bret off as best he could. "Call off the damned dog."

Disgusted, heartsick, Bret let up and pulled Gunner off. Hassie had returned. She stood a little distance away, wide eyes huge and dark in her pale face.

Bret limped to her, gathered her against his chest, and held her hard. She trembled against him, her breath still coming in the kind of gasps he'd felt once before when she'd run from a man intent on harm. Bret wanted to hold her forever on the one hand and finish tearing Will to pieces on the other.

"Did he hurt you?"

Even though he knew she couldn't sign when he held her so close, he couldn't let go. Her whispered, "No," had to be enough.

Growling and barking made him look up. Will had staggered to his feet and retreated to the trees. Cautious now that Will had a branch he'd picked up as a club, Gunner circled him slowly.

"If I had a gun on me, I'd shoot that cur!"

If Bret had a gun on him, he'd shoot something too. Since he didn't have a gun, he called Gunner off before Will landed a lucky blow with that branch.

"You know my wife as the Bible says. Turnabout is fair play."

His bad leg wouldn't bear weight. Bret had to watch his loathsome brother limp away.

He rocked Hassie in his arms, kissing her tears away when she looked up. After a while, her breathing steadied, and she pulled away enough to use her hands.

"I did not see him. I came through the trees, and he was there. He caught me and held me, and I was afraid I could not get away. I was afraid I could not run fast enough."

The top button on her coat was gone, the next one hanging by a thread. The high collar of her dress was torn, her hair uncovered and hanging down. The pretty green scarf she would have had over her head and around her throat still hung on branches that had caught it as she fled.

"You did get away, and you did run fast enough."

"Only because Gunner came. I thought he would kill Gunner, and then you came."

"I think Gunner was winning. If you're all right, that's all that matters."

"Your leg is hurt again."

"It got banged up a little coming through the trees. It'll be fine, but I'm not walking back on it for sure."

"We can ride Brownie."

Brownie grazed unperturbed a little distance away. Bret didn't want Hassie riding anything, much less bareback and astride on that barge of a mare.

Hassie still looked pale and shaky. He only had one leg able to bear weight. Sometimes....

Bret hopped over to the mare, caught her up, and lifted Hassie to the broad back, struggling up behind her. At least there was no chance of their mount running away. Bret convinced Brownie to take an easier route back through the trees and let her head back to the barn at her own plodding pace.

Hassie slid down off the horse as soon as Bret dismounted, ran to where he had dropped the cane, and brought it to him before he finished closing the pasture gate behind Brownie's big rump.

"Come on, let's get inside and get you warmed up, and then I'll deal with Will."

"No, I will not go in there again. I want to go to town."

One thing Bret would have sworn his wife would never be was unreasonable. She had come close that time on the train, but generally she was the most agreeable female he'd ever encountered. Which was why he had trouble believing she was serious.

"We'll leave in the morning. It's too late today. It would be dark before we got there."

Her hands moved with jerky emphasis. "I do not care. I will not stay here."

And if the look on her face didn't tell him he'd have to physically force her into the house, the way Gunner stepped between them and growled did.

"Hassie...." His leg was on fire, pain throbbing from his ankle to his hip. Even though Will was the one Bret wanted to kill, her stubborn expression had him holding on to his temper by a thread.

He sucked in a deep breath. "I'll take you around to the back door. If you'll wait in the kitchen and get warm, I'll pack everything up and we'll go to town even if we don't get there until midnight, but you have to go in and warm up. Don't buck me on this, sweetheart. Just—don't."

After a tense moment, she nodded.

Sam Olson hurried out of the barn as they passed. "What happened? Did something happen out there? I couldn't believe you running off bareback on that mare and leaving the gate wide open. I rounded up the other two for you."

"I appreciate that," Bret said. "My father will explain what happened later, but right now I need more help. Will you hitch up the buggy horse, catch up my horses, and saddle them? Packhorse too. Throw anything of ours in the packs and tie all three of them to the back of the buggy. I need to get my wife to town tonight."

Olson looked at Hassie, back at Bret, and then away. "Yes, sir. Glad to help."

Good. Bret's hand, which had tightened on the cane at the questions, loosened a little. He left Hassie in the kitchen with Leda, who took one look at his face and had more sense than to ask any questions. "I'll just make Mrs. Bret some tea," she said and hurried to put the kettle on.

Bret crawled up the stairs. He could take Hassie to town and come back for everything in a day or two, but he didn't want to have to come back and had a feeling he wouldn't be willing to leave her for days. He threw clothing and everything else into their bags any which way. When he ran out of room he started throwing things in the middle of the bed.

A soft tap sounded on the door. He ignored it. Caroline stuck her head in anyway, of course. "What's going on?"

"Hassie and I are leaving. If you want to help, go downstairs and keep her company. She's in the kitchen."

Caroline gave him an unusually sober look. "You look like you're the one who needs help. What are you doing?"

"Packing. I told you, we're leaving."

Caroline dumped everything out of his leather valise and started repacking. "Did you quarrel with Father again?"

"No," he said curtly. "Will attacked Hassie."

"What? Is she all right?"

"She says so, and I think she is. Scared, angry. Won't stay here even until morning."

Caroline finished with his bag, having fit half again as much in it, and started with Hassie's. "I'll help you get everything downstairs, and then I'll talk to her."

"Good. Maybe you'll get somewhere. It's like talking to a stone wall."

"I don't mean I'll try to talk her into staying here. You have no idea.... I wouldn't stay under the same roof as someone who did that to me either. I can't believe.... What's *wrong* with him?"

Too angry to consider his sister's age or gender, Bret said, "He's seems to have some inflated notion of what went on between Mary and me years ago and think he's entitled to the same from my wife, whether she's willing or not."

Caroline gasped. "But you never...."

"No, I never, and he has to know it."

"He's not so bad when you're not here, you know," Caroline said almost wistfully. "Do you think envy can make a person crazy?"

"Evidently so."

"He even envied Albert, said he was the favorite, and Albert was so good." Finished with Hassie's bag, Caroline strapped it shut. "Not that you're not good, but you have no give in you, and you upset people. It would be better if you were like me. I sneak."

Another time she'd make him laugh. This time all she did was take the urge to kill Will down a notch. Bret strapped on his gun belt and picked up the rifle and shotgun. "The only way I'm getting back down the stairs is on my ass, can you manage the bags?"

"If I can't, we'll throw them," she said practically as she tied everything that wouldn't fit in the bags inside a bed sheet. "Down is never a problem, only up."

"Thanks, sis."

"Will you write?"

"You bet, but just in case a letter here would get lost, check with Gabe's family from time to time."

Actually Bret made it down the stairs on one leg, swinging between the stair railings. Caroline did throw the bed sheet bundle down but lugged the cases. Bret had everything stowed in the buggy or on Packie and was on his way to get Hassie when his parents stopped him in the hall.

"What the devil is going on?" his father demanded. "You and William had to pick today of all days to brawl like boys again? Haven't you any sense? Those men would have bought horses, and you've driven them off."

"Talk to Caroline," Bret said. "I'm leaving."

"Leaving? Just like that. Your brother is going to need stitches from that dog. What if it's rabid?"

"If I stay, my brother is going to need a coffin. I'm taking the horse and buggy. I'll get someone in town to bring them back in the next day or so."

Bret started to brush by them, when his mother's hand on his arm stopped him. "Hassie wanted me to talk to you, and I should have listened. Promise I'll have a chance to know this grandchild, all your children."

Bret kissed her cheek. "We'll find a way."

In the kitchen, Caroline pressed a last pin into Hassie's restored hair and wrapped her own pale blue scarf over it. "You can give it back next time you see me," she said.

The two of them hugged and kissed, clung for a moment.

"You had better write," Caroline said fiercely.

Bret gave his sister one last squeeze around the shoulders before shepherding Hassie out the back door and into the buggy. He drove away and didn't look back.

38

Cassie hunched on the buggy seat, feeling dreadful. In some part of her mind she suspected she was being unreasonable. There would be no danger in staying overnight at the Sterling farm with Bret right beside her. But she didn't care.

His leg was bothering him badly. She did care about that. She wished she could fix it, but trying to do anything for it would have to wait until they were settled in town. They had to get away from that place, from Will and Mary, even the elder Sterlings since they not only put up with Will but were going to give him everything because of which side he fought on in a war long over.

Yes. She needed to be away. Right now. Tonight.

Will hadn't hurt her, although she was sure he had intended to. What he had done wasn't as bad as what the Restons at the hotel and Sally Nichols and her minions at the brothel had done. But it *felt* worse.

Bret pulled the carriage robe higher and tucked it tighter around her. She leaned into his warmth, wishing she could ask about his leg, but it was too dark now, and what could he say? "It hurts like hell." And what could she do about it? Nothing.

The night was black and bitter by the time they reached Oak Hills. Bret registered at the hotel, left her in their room, and went to take care of the horses. By the time he returned, she had a fire going in the little pot-bellied stove, and the chill was off the room.

Bret had a bottle of whiskey in the hand he didn't need for the cane and Gunner at his heels. "No laudanum and no willow bark," he said lofting it. "This will have to do."

She pointed at Gunner.

"The livery won't have him, and the clerk here is susceptible to bribes. This place already looks better than home. Used to be home." He sank down on the bed with a groan, pulled the cork on the bottle and took a long swallow. Not his first from the sound of him.

"I'm sorry," she mouthed.

"It's not your fault, and we'd have been gone in the morning anyway. If we stayed, I'd kill him." He took another swig. "It's not true, you know."

She didn't pretend to misunderstand. "It does not matter. I do not like her anyway."

Bret rolled his head toward her. "I noticed. We never got beyond a few kisses, and she wasn't all that enthusiastic about that much. Since she married him only months after deciding she could never marry me, I can't believe she had a passionate affair in between."

Mary having a passionate affair didn't seem likely to Hassie either. "Then why does he believe such a thing?"

"I'm not sure he does. Caroline thinks he's crazy. I think he just needs a reason to be miserable. Some people are born like that. Just like you were born happy." He took another swallow. "You were you know."

No, she wasn't. She had just learned to be happy with what she had because coveting made things worse, not better.

She pulled off Bret's boots and then his trousers. His knee was swollen to twice its normal size and colored an ugly black, blue, and purple with occasional reddish tones.

He lifted his head enough to look and let it fall back on the pillow. "Hate purple. Makes me think of that whore's dress every time, and it's an ugly damned color. Except your eyes, and they're violet. Ask anyone. Violet."

He was asleep by the time the last word was out. Hassie eased the whiskey bottle from his hand, folded the bedclothes over him, picked up the slate, and chirped to Gunner. Surely a clerk who was susceptible to bribes could come up with another blanket and enough hot water for some compresses.

By the third day, Bret's leg had recovered enough he could get around as well as ever with the cane. Hassie seemed to have recovered too. To his relief, she was once again behaving like her good-natured, loving self.

After considerable thought about moving Hassie to a boardinghouse while he investigated available properties, Bret decided the room at the hotel was better. The widow who owned the place had lived in Oak Hills since he was a boy, raised her children here. She was a decent sort and willing to keep an eye on Hassie while he was gone.

"Not that she needs taking care of or anything," he explained. "It's just that people sometimes take advantage, and she can't complain."

"I understand, dear. She'll be fine."

The first sign of trouble came when they returned to the hotel after visiting the lawyer who had made inquiries about farms for sale. Hassie had smiled at the young attorney and seemed perfectly agreeable until they returned to the hotel. That's when she grabbed the list of properties out of Bret's hand and tore it in two.

"No, I do not want to live in Missouri. I want to live somewhere so far away I will never see them again." Once again her hands moved in a jerky way that was worse than shouting.

Bret rescued the halves of the list. "You don't have to see them. None of these places is closer than ten miles. I know the land here. I know the weather and what works and what doesn't. I'm not spending everything we have on dry land in Kansas and killing myself trying to make a living off it."

"There is other land with good water."

"The better the land, the more it costs. Right here in this area I know what to look for, and we can get good land and enough of it. There's livestock and equipment and seed and a lot of other expenses too, you know."

"You are not selling Brownie for a better horse."

Where did that come from? Packie was the only one he was ready to sell, and knowing she'd fuss, he had never mentioned it. "Of course not. Where could I find a better horse?"

She glared at him and crossed her arms under her breasts. Bret decided to stop arguing and pretend she was still the wife he knew—the one who didn't have a bad word to say about the illiterate, drunken first husband who left her to starve, the one who hummed when making beds after taking a menial job, the one who danced with a dog she rigged out with flowers.

Once he found a decent place with a house she could start making her own, she'd come around and be laughing in days. He'd make sure she never saw Will again in her life, but Caroline and Vicky? His parents? She'd come around.

Bret set out on the fourth day after they'd come to town. "If the weather holds, I'll be back in a week. Even with a storm, it shouldn't be more than ten days. I'm not going to buy anything or sign anything until after you see it. I promise."

She didn't look reassured. In fact she looked stubbornly opposed, but she responded to his kiss and clung to him as if a week or ten days was forever.

Determined to keep it to a week, he gigged Jasper and pointed him west.

When Dr. MacGregor had discussed her condition with her, he had advised Hassie on a lot of things—and mentioned in passing that sometimes pregnant women became exceedingly emotional. She didn't think she was exceedingly emotional. Her husband, the man who often understood without words, was refusing to credit her feelings now.

How much more clearly could she tell him that she was unwilling to live in Missouri anywhere near his family? If they stayed here, his father would talk him out of more money and his mother would want her grandchildren to visit at the farm. Where Will and Mary would still be living.

Hassie spent three days considering her plans before putting on the brown Christmas dress, which might be an unattractive color but which was stylish and gave her an air her plainer dresses didn't. She used the last of the money Bret had given her for meals and incidentals to purchase a velvet hat equally as stylish and a black cape that certainly finished things off better than her old winter coat.

Gloves, Caroline's reticule. No lady in town looked better, Hassie thought with satisfaction, twisting and turning before the mirror in the hotel room. Her slate would spoil the impression. She wrote her request with a pen in the hotel lobby, took more paper and a pencil with her, and marched to the bank.

The young man in the teller's cage at the bank read Hassie's note, gawked at her, and ran for help. The help he summoned looked only slightly older, an attractive, dark-haired young man with a kind face and intelligent blue eyes.

"I'm Simon Fenton, head teller and the one in charge when no one else is around," he said with a smile. "Suppose you and I discuss this in private."

Private was a room off the lobby furnished only with two chairs facing a big desk. Walls lined with cabinets and shelves made the small room smaller. Feeling all too much like a supplicant, Hassie perched on the edge of one of the chairs.

Mr. Fenton sat behind the desk and read her note again. "That's a large sum of money, Mrs. Sterling."

She nodded, pulled out her pencil and extra paper. "It's mine. The account is in my name."

"Yes, that's true, but it's unusual for a married lady to come in and make such a withdrawal without her husband along."

"My husband told you the money is mine to do with as I wish. I saw his letter to you. I wish to make a withdrawal."

The young man stared down at the note, avoiding her eyes, then thumped one hand on the desk and muttered something she couldn't hear. "If you'll wait here a moment, I'll get the paperwork. There are forms for you to sign."

When it was over, Hassie walked outside and steadied herself with one hand against the wall of the bank and the other clutched across her roiling stomach, almost unable to believe she'd succeeded. In her reticule she had a bank draft for two thousand dollars and three hundred dollars in cash. Everything else should be easy.

The next morning she dressed in her elegant outfit again, wrote two notes, and left them on the bed in the hotel room. The one for Bret contained only words. The one for Caroline contained words and a hundred dollars.

Carrying everything she could possibly need, she whistled to Gunner, slipped out the hotel's back door, and headed for the livery. If Brownie hadn't changed her mind about getting on trains without a fuss, they would all be gone before anyone noticed.

39

Bret returned to Oak Hills early in the afternoon, eleven days after leaving. No storm had delayed him. Inspecting farms for sale had turned out to be far more time-consuming than he expected.

Cutting off the livery stable owner's attempt at conversation with curt orders for Jasper's care, Bret left the horse there and headed for the hotel, eager to see Hassie again. Mostly eager.

Unless her usual easygoing attitude had reasserted itself in the time he'd been gone, he was going to have an uphill battle convincing Hassie they should buy the best of the three properties available—the one only ten miles from his parents' farm.

First he'd soften her up with a long night of love-making. Then he'd talk her around to his way of looking at it. After all, he wasn't condemning her to a lifetime of misery. Once they moved in, she'd be humming and dancing before the first week passed.

He was halfway across the lobby when the clerk called his name.

"Mr. Sterling, wait."

Not wanting to deal with anything that would delay his reunion, Bret barely turned his head. "I'll talk to you after I see my wife."

"But she's not here. That's what I'm trying to tell you."

Bret pivoted on his good leg. "So where is she? Dining room?" It was an odd time of day for anyone to be eating. "Shopping?"

"No, she's.... Just a moment."

The clerk fled, and Bret's heart accelerated. Hurt? Sick? Why the hell couldn't the man just say?

The hotel owner followed the clerk out to the desk, wringing her hands. "I'm sorry. I'm so sorry, but what could I do? She never said a word. She just disappeared."

"Disappeared?"

The woman flinched at his tone. "Well, not disappeared really. She left these." She pulled two envelopes out of a desk drawer and offered them.

"You said you'd keep an eye on her."

"I did! You didn't expect me to lock her in the room or follow her around when she went out, did you?"

Bret stared at the envelopes, one with his name on it, the other with Caroline's. Ripping open his, he read: *I'm sorry. I love you, but you wouldn't listen, and I will not stay in Missouri.*

"She gave you these?"

"No, she left them in the room."

Bret reversed course back to the livery as fast as he could go. The stable man was still rubbing Jasper down when Bret got there.

"I tried to tell you, but you hurried off too fast. Mrs. Sterling came by here last week, wanted that horse of hers saddled up and the packhorse too. I told her you wanted me to sell the packhorse and the rig, but she wouldn't hear of it. Paid me every penny due and took them away."

"You just let her take those horses out of here?"

"Well they're your horses, aren't they? And she's your wife. Sure I let her have them."

"And she rode away with them."

"Naw, she was dressed up too fine for riding. Looked right smart she did and led them away. I heard she took the train."

Took the train? How the hell could she take a train?

Bret headed for the railroad station, his cane tapping furiously on the wooden walk.

"Sure, I remember," the ticket agent said. "Hard to forget a pretty lady like that who writes instead of talks. Last Thursday maybe, or Wednesday. Bought a ticket to Kansas City and paid for two horses and the dog in a stock car."

"She can't have."

"Well, she did."

"How did she pay for all that?"

"Yankee greenbacks."

Bret bit back a curse. "When's the next train to Kansas City?"

"Tomorrow morning. If it's on schedule, it pulls out at 11:37."

"There has to be something sooner than that."

"Well, there isn't, and by the time you ride a horse to someplace else with something else that leaves earlier, you'll be a day behind, not ahead."

Bret bought a ticket to Kansas City on the morning train, and after a moment's consideration, paid to transport Jasper too.

Pocketing the ticket, he walked back through town at his best speed, reaching the bank minutes before the three o'clock closing time. Each of the young tellers he saw had handled deposits for him in recent years, but he didn't know either.

"I need to speak to the person who handled a withdrawal for my wife last week," Bret said.

"I did that," the taller, older teller said. "Jason, will you lock up? I'll talk to Mr. Sterling."

Bret moved into the small room Simon Fenton indicated, shook the man's hand impatiently, and refused to sit. "Inman isn't here?" he asked, referring to his father's great friend, the bank's owner and president.

"Mr. and Mrs. Inman are visiting family in Alabama," Fenton said. "While they're gone, I'm in charge. Are you here to tell me I shouldn't have let your wife have her money?"

No, and now that it was put like that, Bret couldn't say why he was here except to verify what he already knew had to be true. "No, it's her money. She earned it and can do anything she wants with it, but I thought she might have mentioned what she wanted it for."

At least Fenton didn't ask how a man could not know what his wife wanted such a sum for, but then maybe he knew Hassie had left town. Fenton swiveled to one of the cabinets behind him, riffled through the contents of a lower drawer and pulled out packet of documents. Opening it, he removed several sheets of paper and handed them to Bret.

One in ink, the rest in pencil, not one of them giving a hint what she intended to do with the money. Without thinking, Bret said, "She only took two thousand?"

"Two thousand in a bank draft. Three hundred in cash."

"That's not even half of what was in the account."

"I know." Fenton swallowed visibly, looking very young. "There's something else. I guess if I'm going to lose my position here, I may as well lose it for several transgressions and not just one."

"I've no intention of trying to have you dismissed. I told you it's her money. You did the right thing."

"Thank you. Your father and brother didn't think I did the right thing two days earlier when I refused to let them withdraw from your account. In fact they're very angry. Your father wired Mr. Inman, and I made everyone angrier when I said a wire wouldn't be enough, I needed something with a signature." Fenton pulled an envelope from a pile of papers on the desk. "They were back yesterday, and I had to inform them the necessary instructions from Mr. Inman hadn't arrived yet. This seems to have been lost among other papers."

Bret moved to one of the chairs in front of the desk and sank down. "It's unopened."

"Once I find it and open it, I'm obliged to do what it says."

"What do they want you to do?"

"Take the mortgage payment currently due from your account and transfer the balance to the farm account."

Bret didn't want to believe Will had talked his father into outright theft, but obviously he had.

"What about my wife's account?"

"No one mentioned it. You never directed us to change it to her married name, and we never did."

Caroline's unsuitable young man was a clerk. Bret eyed Fenton thoughtfully. "Do you know my sister?"

Fenton dropped his eyes to the desk and toyed with a pen. "I have that privilege. We attend the same church."

Which explained some things. Even so.... I owe you, Mr. Fenton, Bret thought. I should never have put off moving those accounts, and I owe you.

Reaching a decision, Bret said, "As you've probably guessed, my wife and I are moving, and we'll be banking nearer our new home. Can you do what's necessary to close both our accounts now, or do I need to come back in the morning?"

"Now would be prudent," Fenton said. "I'll get the necessary forms."

Bret ran a hand over his face and sighed. "How much is the mortgage payment?"

Fenton turned back to the cabinet, pulled another package of documents out, and found the right one. "Three hundred fifty-eight dollars and thirty-five cents."

"I'll pay that, follow my wife's example and take three hundred cash, and the balance in a draft."

No flicker of expression indicated whether Fenton thought he was a fool or not, and Bret appreciated the neutrality. "While you do your part, if you'd let me have paper, pen, and ink, I need to write a letter."

Fenton set the requested items out on the desk and left the room. Bret thought a moment, wrote, and turned his letter face down when he finished.

After signing the forms Fenton presented, Bret folded the bank draft and cash in a pocket, turned his letter face up, and pushed it across the desk.

Fenton's color rose as he read. "I'd like to believe I deserve this," he said when he'd finished. "I don't believe I've ever read such a glowing recommendation."

"That's why I put my friend's address at the bottom. If anyone worries you held a gun to my head and wants to verify with me further, Gabe will know where to find me. You shouldn't lose this position for what you did, but if you do, you won't have trouble finding something better. You'll end up owning a bank of your own in a few years."

"A few decades maybe," Fenton said with more realism.

They left the bank together, Bret turning back toward the hotel, Fenton going the other way.

"Take good care of her," Bret muttered as he walked away.

In the hotel room, Bret sank down on the edge of the bed and held his head in his hands. If Fenton was indeed Caroline's secret lover, he wouldn't have much trouble taking better care of her than Bret had managed with Hassie.

In the face of her angry, stubborn declarations that she would not live in Missouri, how had he convinced himself she would? Yes, she was the woman who made light of her trials with Cyrus Petty and hummed while doing a maid's work in a hotel.

She was also the woman who had resisted the hotel owners in Werver so violently she'd left them visibly bruised. She'd gotten away from a brothel enforcer. Preferred following a bounty hunter into the unknown to marrying a safe, if stodgy, homesteader. Blown the head off a killer and hauled her useless husband's carcass to the nearest doctor. For that matter, Will had looked worse for wear by the time Bret got there.

He'd chosen to see only what he wanted to see because he wanted what he wanted, and he damned well deserved the sick fear eating at him now. She took a train to Kansas City by herself with two horses and the dog.

She wasn't going back to the Petty farm as she'd threatened, so what was she thinking? Where *was* she going?

She had enough money to keep her for a long time if no one stole it from her. Or killed her for fun.

Gunner was some protection, but he wasn't invincible. The gun wouldn't help much when she couldn't shoot it with her eyes open. At the thought, he rose and searched the room. Nothing left but his things. At least she'd had the sense to take her gun.

He dropped back on the bed, this time noticing the crackle of stiff paper in his trouser pocket. Hassie's note to him was crumpled. He smoothed it out and read it again. The damning words on it hadn't changed, didn't give any clues. The envelope for Caroline was thicker. Had she written Caroline a real letter, told of plans?

Caroline's note was as short as his: *Add this to your stake. Marry him soon and be happy.* The extra thickness came from the hundred dollars enclosed with the note. Bret stared at it a long time before adding another hundred and folding everything back in the envelope.

In the morning he'd add his name below Hassie's, put it all in a fresh envelope, and address it to Caroline in care of Gabe's parents. Trying to find someone he trusted to hand deliver it would use up some of too many hours before 11:37, and if that failed, he'd gamble on the mail.

Bret finally blew out the lamp and forced himself to lie down. He lay awake for a long time imagining all the things that could happen to a woman traveling alone—robbery, rape, murder. Even without violence some slick talker like Johnny Rankin could take the money and leave her penniless in the middle of nowhere. If she tried to travel on horseback—and she shouldn't even be on horseback in her condition—the weather could kill her. He envisioned her riding through blinding snow, falling, freezing, her body covered by drifts, never to be found.

Worn out by the endless stream of disasters he could conjure up, Bret fell into troubled sleep. And the nightmare came.

The stink of gun powder, blood, and death filled his nostrils. Cannon roared, men and horses screamed. Drenched in sweat, coated with mud and blood, he charged forward as ordered. Men fell ahead of him and to each side.

The Rebel soldier rose behind the stone wall. Bret fired and screamed his own scream as Albert fell. Another figure rose. He fired again, saw the blossom of blood, saw her face. Not Mary, Hassie.

He screamed again, flailed, hit the floor and barely made it to the washbasin before vomiting up everything in his stomach.

"Damned dog," he cursed. "Damned dog, damned fool woman. Damn me." His stomach heaved again. When it stopped, he dressed and waited for dawn.

40

It took the better part of a day, but Bret finally found a ticket agent in Kansas City who remembered Hassie.

"Sure I remember. Poor lady had laryngitis and had to write things out. Bought a ticket to Denver. Might have remembered her anyway, not many ladies travel with two horses and a dog."

Denver. Of course she'd want to get back to Colorado, to Dearfield where she'd made friends, but she couldn't go there by herself, not this time of year, not any time of year. If she found somewhere in Denver to stay, maybe she could eventually find a safe way to Dearfield, but the railroad ended a good two-day ride from the town. The stage line came from the north, and Hassie would never abandon Brownie and Packie to take a stage they couldn't keep up with.

Picturing someone trying to load Gunner into or on top of a stagecoach gave Bret a second of grim amusement.

Freighters. The thought of Hassie alone with some hulking freighter who hadn't been near a woman in years had Bret fingering his gun. She wasn't foolish. The two of them had ridden from Dearfield to the nearest train station in December. She knew how long, lonely, and cold that trip would be. And how dangerous. She wouldn't do it. She wouldn't.

No ticket agent in Denver admitted to remembering Hassie, but one of the yard men remembered Gunner. "The poor lady had to climb in the stock car and tie that dog up herself. Nobody else wanted any part of that mean bugger."

She'd gone on all the way to the end of the line. Bret tried to remember what the town was like. Small, mean, dirty. She couldn't stay there, which meant.... He caught the next train west, feeling sick.

Everyone who had remembered Hassie in Kansas City and Denver remembered a finely dressed woman. The story was different at the railhead. "You got stones if you're after that woman, mister. Arrived looking like a fine lady and left in trousers looking like something you wouldn't want to mess with. Pulled a gun on old Frankie Hamblin when he got smart with her."

"And where is Old Frankie now?" Bret asked, pleased to find someone to vent his spleen on.

His informant's eyes slid to the side. "Caught a ride east a couple of days ago, going to work out of Denver now."

Bret grunted and went to saddle Jasper. The leaden skies and dark clouds over the mountains didn't bode well for an easy ride, and he didn't care. If he didn't stop, he could make Dearfield in a day and a half. If she wasn't there.... He refused to think of that.

DEARFIELD WAS AS Bret remembered, a small town quietly thriving doing business with ranchers to the east and north, miners to the west, and farmers to the south. When the railroad finally reached the town, it would boom.

He resisted the temptation to ride straight to MacGregors' and pound on the door. Jasper was exhausted, the least he could do was get the horse taken care of. Not only that... Brownie and Packie nickered a happy greeting to their old companion from the same corral where they'd spent months while Bret recovered.

The black fear Bret had been fighting since leaving Missouri disappeared. Anger flared for a moment then that dissolved too, leaving him cold, tired, and empty.

"Rub him down, feed him, and put him in with the other two," he told the stable man, ignoring the knowing eyes.

The whole town knew. He could feel all the eyes as he walked toward MacGregors'. Sheriff Fleming emerged from his office and stood leaning against the door frame. Bret raised a hand. The sheriff did the same.

Remembering the attitude of the people of Dearfield toward Hassie, Bret knew he wasn't going to throw her over his shoulder and ride off with her, not that he ever planned to.

Mrs. MacGregor answered the door. "It's about time. What took you so long?"

Bret shrugged, remembering frantic hours wasted in Kansas City and Denver, but unwilling to answer the question.

"She doesn't want to see you."

"Too bad. I'm not going away until she talks to me."

"Suit yourself."

The door closed in his face. He considered kicking it in, decided he didn't have the strength and it probably wasn't a good idea, and sat on the edge of the porch. Gunner came round the corner of the house and growled.

"Don't," Bret said. "Unless you want to pay me back every damned rabbit I ever shot for you, don't."

Gunner gave a suspicious sniff, then a tentative wag. Satisfied at last, he sat on Bret's foot and leaned against his leg.

"At least that makes one part of me that's warm." And one member of the family willing to forgive him, although dogs were all forgiving fools.

He sat, feeling the cold working its way into his bones, wondering how long she'd hold out, how long he could.

The door opened behind him, and she was there, looking both beautiful and implacable, no welcome on her face.

WHEN HASSIE OPENED the door, Gunner, deserter that he was, took the opportunity to slip by her and run for his bed by the stove in the kitchen.

Hassie's heart ached at the sight of Bret, bearded, gaunt. The skin under his eyes looked bruised and made his gray eyes darker, tired, and sad. He rose slowly, using his good leg and the cane, and she fought the urge to throw herself in his arms, go anywhere he wanted, do anything he asked.

She'd known he would come after her and had fled to this place hoping it would help her find the resolve to resist him. People here saw her as a friend. They respected her. Maybe that would give her strength not to give in if Bret kissed her and turned her boneless. She had to keep sight of what she wanted, needed for herself and their child.

The cold already had her shivering. She stepped back and gestured for him to follow. Once close to the fireplace in the parlor, she let him know her position.

"I will not go back."

"I'm not asking you to. I should have paid attention without you scaring me to death traveling across three states by yourself, but I got used to you being agreeable. Caroline says I have no give to me, which is another way to say I'm pigheaded and selfish, and she's right."

Hassie shook her head a little. Pigheaded, yes. Selfish, no, never.

"I was ready to use your good nature as an excuse to have my own way, which is a shameful thing to have to admit, and I'm sorry. If you want to stay here, I'm willing to look for land here. Tell me what you want."

One hand had moved to her stomach. Realizing what she was doing, Hassie made herself stop and sign instead. "Then you will be unhappy. You want to live near them, see them, give them things."

"No, I had a lot of time to think about it. The way things are is as much my fault as theirs. I should have stopped helping them the day the house was finished, but I kept going because it let me avoid the future as much as it did them. We'll all be better off with me far away."

"You will stay here? We will never have to see them?"

"I love you, Hassie. I love you, and I won't lie to you. You don't ever have to see any of them again, but I'd like to. The railroad will be here in another year or two. A visit will only take days. When our children are old enough to make the trip, I'd like them to at least meet their aunts and their grandparents, even my truly foolish father."

She wanted to refuse, remembered Mrs. MacGregor's advice about marriage and compromise. "Not your brother."

"Absolutely not."

"Not Mary."

"No Mary."

"Say it again."

"Say what again?"

"I love you."

"I know you do. I kept your note, so I have it in writing."

"Say it."

"I love you, Hassie."

She gave in and threw herself in his arms.

"I understood that," he whispered, and he kissed her until she was boneless.

Epilog

Summer 1876
South of Dearfield, Colorado

Bret finished reading the latest letter from Caroline, folded it, and put it back in the envelope. "So do we want to visit Denver this winter, or do we tell them to come here for a change?"

"Let's visit Aunt Caroline," four-year-old Julia said, poking at her oatmeal as if she expected to find something interesting in the depths.

Hassie put down the damp rag she was using to clean most of his breakfast from their son's face. Approaching his first birthday, Patrick's enthusiasm for solid food remained minimal.

"Let us visit Caroline," she signed. After one more swipe at Patrick's scrunched up face, she added, "We can get away easier than Simon can from the bank."

"My mother will probably want to visit at the same time then."

"That is fine."

Gunner's visitors-coming bark sounded from the front yard. Julia abandoned her porridge and ran for the front door. "I'll see who it is. I'll see."

Bret jumped up and caught her before she made it to the door. "Suppose we see together."

A quick glance through a front window showed a wagon stopped only a few feet from the porch, a heavy man and his round wife on the seat. Gunner had abandoned guard dog duties and reared up against the side of the wagon. The pretty mahogany and white collie in the bed leaned down to touch noses with him.

"It's the Snarlys," Julia said.

"Sshh." Bret rubbed a hand over his face to hide a smile. "Their name is Narly, and don't you forget it."

Snarly fit the unfriendly farmer better than his true name, and Julia wasn't the only one to use it, but without a reminder she might be the first to use it to Mr. Narly's face.

"We'd better go see what he wants." Bret kept a firm hold of his enthusiastic daughter's hand as they approached the wagon. "Good morning, Mr. Narly. Ma'am."

"Mornin'" At least that's what Bret assumed the man grunted. His wife smiled and nodded.

"What can I do for you this morning?" Bret said, expecting a complaint to do with their common border on the east side of his property.

"The missus says we should give you first choice if you want it. Second choice really. We already picked ours. I told her she's being foolish, but she's set on it. Whole thing's her fault. I'm not blaming you."

Hassie came out of the house carrying Patrick, whose face was shining, but who in Bret's experience would soon need his bottom cleaned. She handed him the wiggling baby, and Bret settled the small form against his shoulder.

"I'm afraid I'm not clear on the problem, Mr. Narly. Would you like to light for a while, have a cup of coffee, and explain?"

"Nope, got to deliver the ones spoken for and talk to some folks the missus is sure will want the others."

Bret felt like scratching his head. "I don't understand...."

"The missus has been wanting a pup from our Meggie for a long time. I admit I put it off, and Meggie's not getting younger, but I wanted a good dog for the sire, you understand?"

All of a sudden, Bret had a feeling he did. A sinking feeling. He and Hassie moved closer to the wagon as one and looked in the bed. Five fat mahogany and white puppies raced to the side and jumped up, tails wagging. Hassie laughed and petted one after the other.

"I want to see. I want to see." Julia tried to climb on the wagon wheel.

Keeping hold of Patrick with one hand, Bret lifted Julia high enough to see with the other.

"Oh, aren't they beautiful!"

Bret closed his eyes for a moment, knowing where this was leading. "You aren't telling me Gunner had anything to do with those."

"He did. Like I said, I'm not blaming you. It was Meggie's time, and the missus saw him in the yard and da— darned if she didn't decide she didn't want to wait any longer for a pup. Didn't admit to me what she done till the old girl was almost bursting with them pups. Lucky thing for Meggie there was only six."

Bret counted again. "Maybe you lost one on the way here? There are only five."

"Aah, there's six." Narly gave a few hard raps with his boot against the floor of the wagon.

A sixth puppy emerged from under the seat, sat, and studied the situation. This one was no mahogany and white butterball. Scruffy yellow hair, coffin-shaped head, suspicious expression. Male. Bret would bet the farm this one was male.

Hassie chirped and hummed. The puppy cocked his head and after a further moment's consideration, strolled over to meet her. She picked him up, and he licked her ear, his tail beginning to wag.

When she put the puppy down, Gunner gave up reminiscing with his old lover and came to investigate. The puppy growled. Gunner swatted him to the ground with a paw. The puppy hopped right back up and growled louder.

"We must take him," Hassie signed. "No one else will want him."

That was as true as any words ever signed or spoken. Julia had the puppy in her lap now, and he had stopped growling. He'd be just like his sire, a menace to half the population and self-appointed defender of the other half.

"You're probably safe for ten years or so," Bret muttered to his son. "We'll take this one, thank you," he said to Narly.

"Missus said you would. I told her she was crazy, I should have drowned that one the first day, but I guess she's right." Narly shook his head and clucked to his horses, and the wagon moved off. Mrs. Narly smiled and waved at them over her shoulder.

"Maybe you should teach that poor woman sign language," Bret said. "She doesn't seem to talk much."

Hassie laughed again and leaned against him. He put an arm around her shoulders and pulled her close. "You know sometimes I look at the front porch of the house and see us sitting there on the porch swing watching children in the yard. More than just these two, I'm afraid."

"How many more?"

"Five. I see five all told."

"That would be nice."

"I'm glad you think so. Then I see us getting older and grayer, and the children getting bigger, and all of a sudden they're full size and sitting on the porch with us and there are other children playing in the yard. I figure those are grandchildren."

"How many?"

"A bunch. The thing is what else I see always seemed impossible. Gunner's already getting his first gray hairs, and I always see a dog running with all those children. A yellow dog."

"You had a vision."

Bret knew he had an overactive imagination, but he'd never had anything he considered a vision. Patrick squirmed on his shoulder, and Bret put him down in the grass long enough to kiss his wife properly.

Her arms tightened around his neck. She pressed against him from knee to chest, and her tongue touched his.

Imagination or vision, the future would be as it would be. He forgot about prospective children and grandchildren. Right now there was only Hassie, and she was telling him everything he needed to know about the present without words.

If you would like to be notified of new releases by Ellen O'Connell and to occasionally receive short works for free before they are published, sign up for her mailing list at her website or blog site:

http://www.oconnellauthor.com

http://oconnellauthor.wordpress.com/

Printed in Great Britain
by Amazon